Behind the
Gold Star

Behind the Gold Star

Rick Stone

Writer's Showcase presented by *Writer's Digest*
San Jose New York Lincoln Shanghai

Behind the Gold Star

Published by Writer's Showcase presented by *Writer's Digest*
an imprint of iUniverse.com, Inc.

For information address:
iUniverse.com, Inc.
620 North 48th Street
Suite 201
Lincoln, NE 68504-3467
www.iuniverse.com

Idea for cover design and author photo by C.A. Stone.

ISBN: 0-595-09166-0

Printed in the United States of America

Acknowledgments

It has been my great privilege to have known many outstanding men and women in the police profession over the last quarter of a century. I am eternally grateful for those officers who truly understand that ours is a calling of a higher order and not just a job. We have laughed together and we have cried together. They have taught me the true value of friendship and courage in the face of adversity. The lessons have not been easy, nor the road without peril. I remain humbled by their praise and recognition, which has been far beyond my worth as an individual. But most of all, I have always been inspired by those extraordinary few who diligently guard the thin blue line between society's good and evil. Though often burdened by others who cannot fathom the concepts of duty, honor and integrity; the men and women who proudly wear the badge toil on with an inherent knowledge of what is right and fair. Always please remember to "Be Careful". My hopes and my prayers will follow you forever.

There is another person in my life who, above all others, deserves a very special acknowledgment.

Thank you, Cindy, for encouraging me to finish what I started so many years ago. Thank you for your patience and the great job you did during the final editing. Thank you for your understanding and loyal support during the long ordeal. But, first and foremost, thank you for giving me my smile back again.

The Author

Prologue

Big Al gazed into the full length mirror and adjusted the double Windsor knot in his wide silk tie. Al liked the red flowery pattern and he made a mental note to order another dozen from that old Italian tailor down on Second Avenue. The pale yellow shirt looked great with his green suit and vest he thought. Green and yellow were his favorite colors. In his younger days, Al's cronies called him "Snorky". Although you would not find it in any dictionary, the word was 1920's "Brooklynese" describing a sharp dresser. Al liked the nickname much better than the "Scarface" moniker that the newspapers insisted on putting in their headlines.

Nervously, Al fingered the slim scars on his plump face. That son of a bitch, Frank Gulichio, had really carved him up. He let his pudgy fingers drift over the scar's raised ridges and smiled when he thought of Gulichio's juicy little sister, Lena.

"Honey, you've got a beautiful ass and I mean that as a compliment. Really," was Al's remark to Lena that suddenly caused Frank to go bananas. The little two bit hoodlum jerked an ivory handled switchblade from his waistband and slashed Al's left cheek to the bone. By the time the other patrons of the Old Harvard Inn had pulled the two apart, Al was screaming for revenge. White flecks of foam frothed from his mouth and mixed with the stream of blood flowing down his face. Al spit the mixture on the saw-dust floor and swore that Frank would pay.

Months later, Al trailed Frank into a dark alley on Coney Island. While the switch-blade artist was going through the pockets of a drunk sailor who had passed out behind Coleman's Pool Hall, Al made good on his promise. Al took a rusty meat cleaver from his battered work jacket and neatly severed Frank's spine between the third and fourth vertebrae. It was crude but very effective. Frank crumpled in the muddy alley and drowned in his own blood.

"Ain't payback hell, Frank?" Al grinned in the darkness. He whistled a tune that sounded vaguely like the Star Spangled Banner and ambled out of the alley in no par-ticular hurry, savoring the moment. The score was settled and Al had been enor-mously pleased with his way of making Frank pay for the scars. He made them all pay.

Al's eleven and a half carat diamond ring flashed on his chubby pinkie finger in the bright light of the chandelier. He paid $50,000 for the ring and delighted in using the huge stone to impress the boys by scratching the expensive mirrors that lined the hotel suite's walls.

"Get dressed baby. We're going out," Al tossed the order over his shoulder as he stood transfixed in front of the mirror. He adjusted the milky white fedora to just the right jaunty angle on his head and smiled again in approval at the sight.

Irene lay completely naked on the tufted sofa. She was Al's latest plaything from a long line of pretty prostitutes that passed through his string of whorehouses all across the south side of Chicago. Al and Irene had spent the afternoon on the floor, and most of the furniture, in his plush suite at the Lexington Hotel.

Unknown to either Al or the whore, Irene had syphilis. She would soon return home to her folk's farm in Missouri, sick and ashamed, and give birth to a little boy who would know no father. Irene would recover neither her health nor her looks. She would die from the disease's tertiary stage in two years with none of the beauty which she showed tonight. In the end, "Big Al" would also fall victim to Irene's affliction.

"Where we goin', honey?" Irene cooed. She was sore and had a strange burning sensation deep inside her vault. The whore was definitely ready for a break. As soon as the big man seemed like he would finally be drained dry, another cold bottle of bootleg beer would stimulate Al's seemingly insatiable sexual appetite. Yep, when it came to women, "Big Al" Capone was a regular Rudolph Fucking Valentino, Irene thought.

"We're going to get you some culture, baby. But you can't go like that," Al leered at her nudity. Her small breasts were perfectly formed and she had a golden thatch of pubic hair to match her mussed up yellow curls. Irene dreamed that she would one day quit work at the "Four Deuces Bar," so named for its address at 2222 South Wabash Avenue, and become a real actress. She had certainly practiced her new profession today; faking enough orgasms all afternoon to win an academy award. If not worthy of an Oscar, Irene's performance at least appeared to keep Al happy.

It did not pay to displease her boss. Those that did found themselves trying to swim across Lake Michigan with a block of cement chained to their ankles. That was if they were lucky. If not, Al was known to beat his enemies to death with a baseball bat. His violent temper was the fabric of legend.

"Drag that cute little ass of yours in there baby and pick out somethin' nice for me to look at. I want to show you off tonight." Al pointed to a walk-in closet in a corner of the ornate room.

Irene rose to her feet and arched her aching back. She spread her arms and stretched her sparse five-feet-two-inch frame.

"What if you don't have my size?" Irene asked with a yawn.

"Baby, I've got your size. Believe me. I've got your size," Al emphasized his pun with a little wiggle to his oversized hips.

He was right. The huge closet was lined, wall-to-wall, with dresses and other ladies garments of every conceivable size and description. The upper shelf held a complete array of women's hats in all shapes and colors. It was a veritable paradise for a call girl earning twenty-seven dollars a week by selling her tits and ass to every hood and penny ante sharpster on the south side of Chicago.

While Irene busied herself in the giant closet that doubled as a dressing room, Al decided that he would tend to a little work. Normally he used this room for his business office but Al was treating himself to an afternoon off from his labors to sample little Miss Irene. She was okay, he thought. A little skinny, but full of enthusiasm.

Al liked enthusiasm. His numerous office buildings were usually filled with junior executives who had enormous enthusiasm for their jobs of helping Al oversee his vast empire. The enthusiasm was clearly motivated by the huge sums of unreported cash that poured into Al's counting rooms each day. He liked to see the college boys jump at his every move. Not bad for a street urchin from Brooklyn who had dropped out of school after the sixth grade.

Actually, Al had not dropped out. He punched his teacher in the gut because the bitch called him a "dumb wop" and the school principal thrashed him with a broad leather belt until the blood stained his trousers. Al vowed revenge when he was expelled. He made sure that both the teacher and the principal were together in the tiny office of the wooden school on West 53rd Street before he tossed his homemade Molotov cocktail through the open door of the office and slammed the locking bolt into place. The resulting gasoline fire engulfed the entire block before its angry flames burned out. He paid them both back…in spades.

After jobs in a munitions factory, a bowling alley and as a book binder; Al found his niche in the rackets. Al's mentor, a hood named Johnny Torio, brought him to Chicago at the tender of age of nineteen to run "Big Jim" Colosimo's night clubs. Big Jim had been the most feared gangster of them all in his day. But his day came to an abrupt end when Al hired an old New York friend, Frankie Yale, to take out Big Jim. Frankie took an old Smith and Wesson .44 caliber breaktop revolver and neatly stitched Jim from his groin to his chin just as the reigning king of crime walked through the lobby of his own nightclub. Now it was Al's time to sit on the throne of Chicago's violent criminal underworld.

"My Jesus mercy," Al used his favorite expression. "Hurry up, baby, I'm getting the urge to come in there and prod you along. "Prod", get it baby? Then we'll really be late," he laughed as he yelled through the closet door.

Al punched a buzzer on his hand-crafted walnut desk and immediately Joey Fusco appeared in the doorway. "Violets", as Joey liked to be called, kept his right hand inside the outside pocket of his pin stripe suit until he saw that his boss was sitting comfortably behind the big desk. Al had his boyish smile in place and the bodyguard knew immediately that everything was okay. Joey looked around for Al's new hooker but he did not see her. Vaguely, he wondered if Al had chopped the little squeeze up into small pieces and swallowed her whole. Joey wouldn't put anything past "Big Al."

"Violets, round up some of the boys and get my car ready. We're steppin' out on the town," Al ordered.

"Sure thing, boss. Anywhere special?" the gunman asked.

Al frowned. "I'll tell ya' later," he growled.

"Sure thing, boss," Violets repeated. "We'll be ready in a jiffy."

It did not pay to tell these mugs too much too quickly, Al mused. He did not stay alive by trusting people. Al believed that three men could keep a secret only if two of them were dead. The number of new graves in Chicago's cemeteries was testament to the value of caution when it came to keeping your own counsel. Over seven hundred men, women and children had fallen victim to the chattering gunfire of Al's mob and the other rival gangs. It was the most violent era in the country's history and it would be a long time before Americans began killing each other like that again.

Al swiveled in his chair and gazed up at the three life sized oil paintings that he had commissioned to add some class to the already posh hotel suite. In the center of the wall was a portrait of "Big Bill" Thompson, Mayor of Chicago. Al owned Thompson; lock, stock, and beer barrel. He also owned half of the officers on the Chicago Police Department. His bribery tab was larger than the payroll for the over four hundred people he actually employed in his various illegal businesses. It was a closely guarded secret that his businesses grossed over a hundred and twenty million dollars in annual sales. That was an awful lot of money and there was plenty of it to go around to lay on the greasy palms of corrupt politicians like Big Bill Thompson.

There were two other portraits on the wall flanking the one of his puppet mayor. George Washington stared down at him from the left and the sad face of Abraham Lincoln seemed to peer off into nothingness toward the right. Al liked the one of Lincoln best of all. It seemed to him that old "Honest Abe" was a friend of the working class just like Al portrayed himself. Why, didn't the one and only Al Capone open up soup kitchens all over Chicago just to feed the guys that were out of work because of the depression? Sure he did. Al smiled at the vision of himself as a protector of the poor and downtrodden. All the mugs on the street thought that he was an okay guy. They waved and cheered when he drove down the street. That was something even 'Ol Abe would have enjoyed, Al figured. Especially if there was some percentage in the action somewhere. Abe was surely a smart guy too.

Al kept a quote from Lincoln mounted in a silver picture frame on his desk. It read, "I do the very best I know how; the very best I can; and I mean to keep doing so until the end. If the end brings me out all right, what is said against me won't amount to anything. If the end brings me out wrong, ten angels swearing I was right would make no difference." It was signed, "A. Lincoln." The little Jewish shop keeper from Cicero, who sold him the parchment, swore that it was an original document.

Al fancied himself in the same boat with the press as Lincoln had been. The papers called Al a gangster and a killer but he was just doing what the public wanted. They wanted beer and broads and Al provided those essentials of life. Well, at a small fee of course. He kept telling the other mobsters that there was enough booze and pussy business for everybody. Why kill each other over it? No matter that it was illegal. A lot of stuff the government and the banks did was illegal the way Al saw things. They had brought down the collapse of Wall Street and now ordinary people were hurting all over the country. Al was a just a businessman. No, better than that, he was a public servant, Al decided. A public servant just like Abraham Lincoln.

"I'm ready, honey. How do I look?" Irene called from the doorway of the combination closet and dressing room.

"My Jesus mercy," Al hissed. "You're a knockout, doll."

Irene chose a full length red silk dress with mink trim on the cuffs and collar. A matching hat, complete with black mesh veil, accented the outfit. She wore no underwear or bra. She would not need either. Al was right. Irene was a knockout.

It was not long before Al, Irene and an entourage of nine body guards took the specially designed freight elevator to the below ground garage underneath the hotel. The guards made sure that the garage was empty before the boss and his girl made the short trip down the elevator. Two giant Buick open top touring cars were positioned around Al's custom limousine. The limo was a specially designed Cadillac which sported armor plate and bullet proof glass. The vehicle was built like a battleship. It weighed over seven tons and cost twenty thousand dollars. In a pinch, the back window could be lowered to let Al toss fragmentation grenades at anyone foolish enough to pursue him in his metal fortress. Everyone agreed that Al had more security than President Coolidge.

Jack McGurn held the limousine's side door open for Al and Irene. McGurn was Al's favorite driver and hit man. Jack would kill without question or mercy. In return for the gunman's loyalty, Al provided him with all the women he could possibly want and all the heroin that Jack so desperately needed to make his angry dreams more peaceful.

"Where to boss?" the gunman asked, his cold blue eyes shifting nervously under a wide brimmed fedora.

"Head over to the Adelphi. You know the place," Al ordered.

The Adelphi Theater was nearby on East Ohio Street. It was one of big Al's favorite night spots. But the Adelphi was certainly not a place that the boys liked to go.

"Sure boss, we'll get you there in no time," Jack promised.

Al winked at McGurn and nodded at Irene as the blonde climbed head first into the rear seat. The crack in her firm ass was clearly outlined beneath the slinky red silk dress.

"Take your time. We're in no hurry," Al flashed his little boy smile again.

McGurn informed the other bodyguards in the lead and trail cars of their destination. Just like the president or other head of state, Jack and his cohorts used the "lead and trail car system" to provide sandwich type protection for their boss.

When the boys heard where their mission was taking them, they all rolled their eyes and groaned perceptibly. It was opera night again.

"Knock that shit off," Jack ordered. "Unless you want me to tell Big Al that you're not happy in your work." The killer took a toothpick out of the hat band of his dark blue fedora and carefully placed it between the gap in his two front teeth. Frosted breath hung in the air and no one said a word.

"I didn't think so," Jack said. "Let's roll."

The three cars pulled out of the garage in single file. In the spacious rear compartment, Al poured himself a glass of champagne from the limousine's built in bar. He did not bother to offer Irene a glass.

"My Jesus mercy. You do look good," Al said. He stared hypnotically at Irene's smooth features. Al absentmindedly fingered the scars on his own cheek and became aroused thinking of Irene's soft thighs. He was facing forward in rear seat. Irene sat across from him and kept her eyes focused downward. Her back was to the driver and the privacy curtain was closed. Al usually left the curtain open so that he could see through the windshield ahead. He quickly gulped his glass of expensive French champagne and poured himself a refill. Al set the bottle in the custom designed silver ice bucket built into the side door and leered at Irene.

"Come over here baby and get a little of this," Al ordered. He slowly and noisily unzipped his pants to direct Irene's attention.

Without saying a word, the prostitute bent to her task like a true professional. Irene knelt on her knees on the thickly carpeted floorboard to orally satisfy the gang leader once again. Al rolled his head back on the padded seat and closed his heavy lidded eyes.

"My Jesus mercy," Al moaned.

Jack McGurn kept his view straight ahead into the Chicago night as the dim street lights slowly flashed by the side windows of the black limousine.

After two extra laps around the South Loop, to give Irene the time she needed to complete her assignment, Al and his entourage arrived at the Adelphi. The manager personally escorted Al and his "guests" to their private box overlooking the stage. Al and Irene sat in the front row of the box. Two bodyguards sat on either side of the couple. Each guard wore a pair of Colt .45 caliber automatic pistols in shoulder holsters under their armpits. Behind the first row stood three more guards whose job included watching the crowd below. Two of the guards carried the favorite weapon of choice during that bloody era, the deadly Thompson sub machine gun or "Tommy" as the doughboys from the world war dubbed the rapid fire monster.

The guards made little effort to conceal their massive firepower under their brown trench coats. The third man was armed with a twelve gauge double barreled shotgun. Its barrel was sawed off to just twelve inches and the shortened wooded stock hung on a leather sling under the guard's coat. His pockets bulged with extra brass cartridges of double ought buck shot. Unlike civilian shotgun shells used for hunting, the brass cartridges were U.S. Army surplus from the "Great War" in France. The metal shotgun rounds were designed to be unaffected by the wet and muddy conditions in the trenches of Flander's fields. They were equally reliable on the bloody streets of Chicago.

Al ignored his guards. He was there as a hard working businessman on a well deserved night out. Most of his guards did not know that Al was legally married to a woman that they had never met. Mrs. May Capone was living quietly at home in their fourteen room mansion on Florida's Palm Island. Al took care of his wife. The $150,000 house was actually in May's name. In fact, everything was in her name. Al did not officially own any assets. Something to do with the federal income tax, his lawyers told him. Whatever, May was happy in Florida with her estate and Al was happy in Chicago with a new girl every night.

"You're gonna love this baby. Opera's the greatest," Al promised.

"Thanks honey. I've never been to an opera before," Irene testified. "What's it about?"

"Well, it's kinda like telling a story by singing it," Al explained. "You know, operas come in all kinds of different languages. I like Italian operas the best, 'cause I was born in Naples. My old man was a barber from the old country and he loved to sing. Too bad he died broke and never got to see a real opera. Not me, though, I made it to the top. Everyone does what I say or else. I get to go to the opera every night if I want, right boys?"

Al shifted a quarter turn in his chair. In unison, seven heavily armed men chanted, "Right, boss."

"See what I mean?" Al leaned over and whispered in Irene's ear. The girl from Missouri only nodded. She was completely out of her league and a million miles from home.

The lights dimmed and the music of Chicago's own "First Metropolitan Opera Company" began. The performance was "Der Ring des Nibelungen" by Wagner. It was in German and Al pretended that he was fluent in the language. He actually could not speak a word of German but he loved the heavy dramatic music and the elaborate costumes of the actors. Al delighted in the crashing cymbals and acted like he was conducting the orchestra during the often wild musical score. He waved his arms, using a huge Cuban cigar as a baton, and grinned like a maniac.

Irene was enthralled even though she had no clue as to what was being said by the actors. She timidly asked Al once to give her some idea of the plot. He mumbled something about Vikings and mythology, whatever that was, and told her to shut the fuck up. The guards were bored stiff and wiled away the time by staring at down at the exposed cleavage of the female opera patrons below; hoping to catch the glimpse of a nipple or two in their low cut evening dresses.

After an hour, the bodyguard on Al's left summoned up enough courage to ask his boss for some directions on when he could tell the boys back at the cars that they might be leaving.

"Shut up Goddamnit," Al snapped. "It's a fucking Kraut opera. It's not over until the fat lady sings!"

The chastised guard was a young guy from Detroit named Eddie "Three Fingers" Garrett. He was new to the Capone mob. Despite his youth, Eddie came highly recommended and had proven his worth in the bombing of a local speakeasy that refused to buy Al's brand of bootleg liquor. Not so amazingly, the six sticks of Dupont dynamite had worked wonders in convincing the owner to buy his supply of booze from the right source. Big Al was even generous enough to lend the hapless owner the money he needed to repair his charred building. At fifteen percent interest, of course. Compounded daily.

Eddie fidgeted in his seat. He was not sure that he liked working for this lunatic. Eddie had important plans of his own. He was thinking about going into politics and maybe become a city councilman or a mayor some day.

The opera dragged on and on, seemingly without end. Eddie fingered the butt of the Colt pistol inside his jacket nervously. He leaned over and gently touched Al on his elbow to ask if he could be excused to go to the bathroom. He did not really need to pee but anything would be better than listening to the wailing of a bunch of Huns. Didn't we just fight a war to kill all of these sausage eating bastards, Eddie thought to himself.

Al angrily jerked away from Eddie's tug and continued to stare with wide eyed amazement at the actors below. The music crashed on. The cataclysmic finale was approaching. The main character, a heavyset woman dressed in a suit of chain mail armor and carrying a spear, was in the throes of reciting her final ballad. The horned Viking helmet on her head vibrated with her powerful voice. It was very exciting to Al and, oddly, he felt himself becoming sexually aroused. This was culture.

Cymbals crashed louder and the carefully controlled theatrical flames leaped from the stage in the colorful final scene. Smoke and fire billowed as the climax neared. Al was transfixed by the image.

"Say, Al," Eddie tugged again at his boss's sleeve, "When does…"

In a flash, Al had shaken the half-size ice pick out of his left sleeve and into his palm. With a savage back hand swipe, Al drove the pointed spike through Eddie's forehead and deep into his brain. The young gangster and would be politician from Detroit fell backwards out of his chair; instantly dead. Eddie's big Colt pistols were useless to the lifeless hands that jerked convulsively at his sides.

Al never killed a man just once. While his other guards watched in stunned horror, Al leapt upon the carcass of Eddie "Three Fingers" Garrett and shifted the tiny weapon to his right hand. He drove the ice pick repeatedly into the dead guard's face. Irene screamed at the top of her lungs. Her frightful wails went unheard over the final crescendo of the opera's climatic scene.

"I told you Goddamnit!" Al yelled at the dead man.

"That it's not over," the pick rose and fell again.

"Until the," the pick rose and fell again.

"Fat lady," the pick rose and fell again.

"Sings!"

xviii   B e h i n d   t h e   G o l d   S t a r

The final word was punctuated by Al leaving the ice pick embedded to its hilt in Eddie's left eye socket.

The killer was almost completely out of breath when he wiped Eddie's blood from his hands by using the mink trim of Irene's red silk dress. Al took one last look at his handiwork and hissed, "My Jesus mercy".

When Irene's syphilis finally killed Al Capone many years later, his favorite expression, "My Jesus Mercy", would be inscribed on the gangster's tombstone. Unfortunately the world would little note Al's perverted use of the gentle phrase.

"It's not over until the fat lady sings", however; would become Al's lasting contribution to the English language. In time, the phrase would rise to cliché status and become the bold pledge of all who harbor the slightest hope that certain destiny will somehow be altered by a surprise ending.

There is great comfort in merely uttering the words:

"It's not over until the fat lady sings."

You just never know how things will turn out.

MONDAY

CHAPTER ONE

When Lieutenant Colonel George Armstrong Custer marched his doomed Seventh Cavalry across the barren Kansas landscape he must have told the local inhabitants, "Don't change anything until I get back."

Since then, nothing much has changed. The people do not like change in Kansas. Although they named streets after Custer, his wife, his horse and his dogs; they really did not seem to notice when he never returned from the Little Big Horn. I figure they are still waiting.

I was not a happy camper at zero five hundred hours. For me, the "zero" indicated exactly how much enthusiasm I enjoyed for the day that lay ahead. Tim David motioned to a foggy field by the side of the highway as our final destination. We had been driving out of Wichita for thirty minutes in the general direction of the North Pole. I swore that I could feel it getting colder with each mile we drove. Billy Wade and Pete Gant were dozing on the vinyl cushions of my back seat. I had accepted the dubious honor of driving since I possessed the newest city owned car and not because I liked to drive. In fact, I hate to drive. I especially hate to drive in Kansas where there is nothing to see but circling buzzards and an occasional Winnebago full of lost tourists wondering on just what part of Jupiter they had landed.

Periodically, Tim would make some simple comment to solicit a verbal response from me. He was simply insuring that my eyelids had not slammed shut while I piloted us through the pre-dawn Kansas prairie. For the most part it had been a very quiet trip; like most of our forced companionships.

As the big Chevy took the exit and turned back left underneath the highway, Billy yawned and stretched in the back seat. With some degree of difficulty he launched into a pathetic kind of chamber of commerce lecture about what a growing community the town of Hesston was becoming, what with their new tractor company and all.

"Who gives a damn, Billy," I growled. "Let's just do our duty and get the hell out of this hole in the wall."

He took the clue like the great detective he never was. Luckily, Billy shut up before my bad attitude caused me to say something else I would probably regret. I often felt bad afterwards when I chastised Billy. He always looked like he was about to cry.

It was a wet and nasty day in October. The ground was soaked with a week's worth of rain that fell in one day. The standard high velocity Kansas wind was temporarily absent. This unusual reprieve from nature allowed an eerie fog to grow up from the sandy ground. I reminded myself that it was only out of some minuscule remaining vestige of loyalty to my boss, whose name was misprinted on the invitation, that I was even awake at this ungodly hour.

In fact, I sincerely doubted if he even knew that the event was being held.

"This is the stupidest thing I've ever done," Pete Gant moaned.

Pete slowly pulled his carefully styled head of golden curls from his chest and peered sleepily through the fogged-up side window. The still darkened Hesston Municipal Golf Course was out there somewhere in the mist.

"Geez, this is stupid," he muttered.

"Oh you'll have fun, Pete, you know you will," I lamely pitched the theory without a whole lot of enthusiasm.

"Fuck this shit. I ain't playing in this kind of weather," he stated flatly.

Obstinate as usual, Pete knew that he most definitely would play. His participation would come after we had either begged him or ignored him. Pete Gant loved to be begged and above all things he simply could not stand to be ignored. He was about as complicated as a lug nut.

The gravel crunched loudly under our tires as we wheeled into the clubhouse parking lot. A limp banner hung between two malnourished trees at the entrance. "Welcome to the First Annual "I beat the City Manager" Employee's Golf Tournament," the dripping sign boldly proclaimed. Its bright red and blue letters were professionally lettered on a white plastic coated canvas background. The garish sign and its happy message seemed hopelessly out of place. Someone had already drawn a line through the "C" in "City Manager" with a big black marking pen. The clever pundit scrawled a "Sh" where the "C" had been crudely canceled out. The change made a much more accurate "Shity" description of our un-beloved leader. Despite my innocence and witnesses to the contrary, I knew that I would be blamed for the crime. Sighing with resignation, I vaguely wondered if "Shity" had one "t" or two.

"Okay, gimme my clubs. I'll play," Pete whined as we all piled out of the warmth of the car's heated interior.

I popped the electric trunk latch with the switch on the dash and Tim handed Pete the only set of expensive "Callaway" golf clubs in the trunk. Just one look at the black and gold custom made leather bag told you that they had to be Pete's. He quietly hefted the bag onto one shoulder of his specially embroidered golf sweater while the rest of us sorted through our off-brand, garage sale sporting equipment. My beginner's set of Wilson's were the last clubs to be dredged out of the trunk. They still had the Wal-Mart price sticker on the cheap nylon bag.

"Would you look at that?" I pointed at Pete's ghostly figure in the dim light.

As three of us sorted through all of our stuff in the still dark parking lot, Pete Gant had drifted away and was already standing on the number one tee. He was methodically hitting balls off into the pre-dawn night with his custom made driver. The distinctive "ping" of the metal wood club was clearly heard above the still arriving cars in the parking lot with each swing. Several more of Pete's golf balls, custom stenciled with his name, flew into oblivion. The rest of us headed for the clubhouse and a cup of hot coffee or just about anything with a lot of caffeine in it.

"That guy is something else," Billy said. "All we have to do is keep Pete in hair spray and other men's wives and the guy is just amazing."

"I hope none of those other wives' husbands are here today," Tim added. "I'm really not looking forward to dodging gunfire at this stage of my career."

Inside the cozy little clubhouse, we all picked up our scorecards and found a little table to rest our sore butts before the scheduled six o'clock start time. As usual the police sat with the police, the firemen with fellow firemen, and the rest of the great unwashed cadre of city employees found some solace in people with whom they felt a kindred spirit. No one sat within speaking distance of our fat finance director, Tad Roadly. Other than the shity, er, city manager, Tad was the most hated man in town.

Curiously, there was no sign of the man for whom the golf tournament was named. City Manager Mel Michaels was conspicuously absent. I wondered just who he would blame if he somehow missed this event that had been planned solely in the interest of boosting his image and improving our flagging morale.

It was certainly possible that the naive young college intern who had thought up this futile gesture had simply forgotten to invite the main man. The intern had probably learned to dislike Mel as much as the rest of us by now. If the intern was a female she had no doubt already been screwed by him one way or another.

"Why are we way out here in the boonies playing golf? We've got a dozen or more of our own city courses in Wichita," Tim asked. It was a great question. The answer was not much of a secret.

"Well, Tim," I ventured, "it seems that the manager sent his trusted, able assistant city manager, Bob Showalter, out to visit with all the pros at the city owned golf courses. Mel wanted to raise their rent and take a bigger cut from the concession

stands and the golf cart rentals. "Bullet Bob" threatened to cancel all of their contracts if they didn't agree to go along.

"Fat Boy" Tad over there," I waved at the sour looking finance director, "backed
him up by citing a little piece of fine print in their lease agreements. As soon as this
here tournament was announced the golf pros got together for a little meeting. They
decided this was the one day in the year that they all had to re-seed their fairways and
replant the greens. The golf pros told the manager that he could play all he wanted
but dodging tractors and shovels all day might add a few strokes to his game."

"Hmmm," was all the response that Billy could muster. We both knew the golf
course managers had won the battle but would lose the war. We had been there before.
I knew we would be there again. Still, I had to smile when I told the story. My estima-
tion of the golf pros went up a great deal in recognition of their futile courage.

Tim looked back at me and returned a wry smile that signified he understood my
thoughts. I had come to this tournament at Tim's urging. He thought it would be a
good political move on my part to smooth some frictions. I had been on the same
police department with Billy and Pete for over six years. At best, we tolerated each
other. They no doubt resented me as their chief because I had been chosen from
outside their own department. For my own part, I thought they were far less qualified than equal level commanders in my former department. Alone, each was very
good at throwing up stumbling blocks for just about every improvement I wanted
to make. Together, the Great Wall of China had nothing on these guys. I depended
on Tim to guide and protect me from these two members of my "loyal" staff. There
was no protection from the constant stress and worry of wondering which one
would lead the inevitable "palace coup" when it came. This worry goes with the job
of every police chief.

Tim, Billy and I moved to the front door just as Pete was coming inside. Pete
grinned and tossed a five dollar bill at the attendant for use of the tee before the tournament. It was against the rules to practice immediately before the game but what the
hell, Pete was a Deputy Police Chief. The young attendant was not going to argue with
a high ranking police official that he readily recognized from television.

"Be with you guys just as soon as I wash up," Pete quipped as he backed out of
his chair.

"Wash up hell," Billy said, "he's just replacing some of the Mary Kay products he
used up out there. I swear I'm gonna buy stock in that company if Pete will promise
to keep his cosmetic habit."

Billy was referring to Pete's obsession for personal cleanliness above and beyond
the call of ordinary hygiene. At every possible opportunity, Pete was primping or

replacing hair spray, lip gloss or some other genetically engineered body additive. I often laughed myself silly watching all the chemicals melt under the hot television camera lights that Pete seemed to love so much. The joke was that turning on a TV camera could draw Pete Gant all the way from across town like a moth to a flame. He always seemed "Johnny on the Spot" with a quip from the lip or a quote from the hip for any news reporter that asked. Sometimes they did not have to ask, I suspected.

As we perpetually waited for the man that would be late to his own funeral someday, Tim slid beside me and spoke in a low voice. "Hey Chief, are you feeling okay?"

I tried to get a hint as to the motivation of his question. I wondered if I looked as old and tired as I felt. "This golf game will be like a vasectomy reversal," I hissed.

"Try to chill out," Tim slowly spoke in his even measured tone that made him such a great advisor. "We'll have some fun even if it kills us."

"Yeah, I haven't had this much fun since I caught my tie in the garbage disposal," I lamented. "What about Harpo and Groucho here?" I asked while nodding towards Billy and the freshly cleansed Pete Gant emerging from the rest room.

"Just humor them and watch your ass. That's what I always do," he offered.

"What are you doing looking at my ass?" I grinned. We were cut-off from further discussion of my butt by the scratchy sounds of a bull horn in the hands of a very cute young woman standing at the back of the room. She had the body of a swimsuit model and the voice of a twelve-year-old.

"The tournament will begin in exactly two minutes," the intern squealed as she tried to explain the intricacies of how to properly begin a golf tournament with a "shotgun start".

I knew the drill. Each four person team started the round on a different hole. They then progressed to the next hole, and so on, until all eighteen are played. "Please drive to your appointed hole to begin now," she ordered.

"I'd like to drive to her appointed hole," Pete leered.

"Relax, Pete. That's the manager's new intern. She's assigned to his office to replace the one that suddenly had to go home to mom when all of her dresses didn't seem to fit anymore. Evidently they didn't teach her much about the birds and bees at Montana University. I don't think the manager would appreciate you lusting after his new squeeze that way," I warned.

"Screw the manager," was all Pete said. It conjured up a downright ugly mental image.

We shuffled to our electric carts and our appointed hole on the number one tee box. Tim drove the cart as I lusted in my heart, Jimmy Carter style, thinking of the manager's sexual exploits. He was at an age when most men were usually thinking more about Social Security benefits than balancing multiple sexual partners.

When we reached the first tee the sun was coming up over the Hesston water tower. The bright orb gave a glow to the faded orange "Seniors 69" graffiti spray painted on the tower's side. The notice proudly upheld a time honored tradition of all American small towns. My guess was that the now aging artist probably still lived in Hesston and ran the Laundromat on Main Street.

"I hit that ball three hundred yards," Billy yelled.

"Bullshit," Pete argued. "Mine went twice as far and I think I killed two ducks at the same time. I hope they're in season." He reached down and picked up one of his specially made tees that was carved in the shape of a naked woman. Pete then strolled triumphantly in front of us and picked up the ball that I had dribbled about fifteen feet with my shot. With great ceremony, he tossed it back to me. It was times like these that I remembered why they called the game "golf". The other four letter words were already taken when the name was chosen.

"Here Chief, try that one again. This time use one of my good luck tees," Pete offered.

"Thanks anyway, Pete, but I could never hit anything with a body like that," I said, referring to the overly endowed carving on Pete's plastic tee. "We can just play your ball."

Since it was a "best ball" tournament, I would be spared the humiliation of having to keep my own score. I really didn't want to compete with Pete and Billy. They had been playing golf together since they were in college at Wichita State. In my case, I had taken up the game last year at the urging of several non-police friends from my church softball team. They thought it would be a good way to relieve stress. What a joke! The only thing it relieved for me was my belief that I could still be a professional athlete. At my rate of improvement I could expect to turn pro on the same day the newspaper headlines read "Jesus Returns", with a sub title that said "And He's Not Happy."

Our game continued on through the next five holes. Tim and I actually contributed with a chip and a putt apiece. Pete drove his shots like a howitzer and Billy was good with his irons when his glasses weren't fogging up. A strip of white adhesive tape held the black plastic frames together over the nose piece of Billy's bifocals. He looked like he could be a candidate for the next "Revenge Of The Nerds Go Golfing" movie. It was commonly believed that there was a picture of Billy in the dictionary under the word "goofy".

As much as Pete Gant was a cosmetic fanatic and model dresser, Billy Wade was the kind of guy whose wife had to dress him. If so, she obviously knew absolutely nothing about the finer points of dressing an adult male. Billy's brown nylon socks, black leather loafers and faded red sweat pants stood as testament to Mrs. Wade's prowess in outfitting her husband. It was just another example of how little control Billy exerted over his own life. Billy's wife pulled poor Billy around by the nose like he was a prize bull. I don't think Deputy Chief Billy Wade, of the mighty Wichita Police Department, dared to pass gas without calling his wife to receive permission.

We grudgingly finished out the last four holes of the front nine. Tim and I never got out of the cart at the tee box. We both let Pete and Billy take their shots driving the ball into the fairway. Only when they managed to get the ball close to the green did we bother to get out with our pitching wedges and putters. On the ninth hole both Billy and Pete put their iron shots on the green near the cup.

"Did you see that great shot?" Gant laughed. "I'm a regular Arnold Trevino today."

"Pete, I think that's Arnold Palmer or Lee Trevino," Tim offered matter of factly.

"I'm better than both of those wimps today," Gant grinned. He started doing a poor imitation of a Mexican hat dance around the flag stick. With a head of fruit, he would have looked just like a blond Carmen Miranda.

"You want to putt it in, Chief?" Billy asked.

Pete broke into an off key rendition of "Wichita Lineman" and I remembered that I had always hated that song. Whatever kind of golfer he was, Pete Gant was no Glen Campbell or Carmen Miranda, for that matter.

"You take it Billy or let Elton John here soft shoe it into the hole," I muttered. No sooner said than done, Billy tapped it into the hole with the back side of his putter. Tim and I headed back to our electric cart in anticipation of enjoying the warmth of the club house before starting the back nine.

Arranging my butt on the cold plastic seats of the golf cart reminded me that I should have worn underwear today.

"Where the hell are we, Tim?" I asked. "And what the hell am I doing in the middle of nowhere?" The wind, to its ever predictable credit, was picking up speed. The temperature was falling faster than Billy's libido around his ugly wife. The icy air perfectly matched my glacial mood.

"You're in Kansas, Toto my boy," Tim said. "The land of Oz and home of the brave. Chill out."

I watched as a flight of doves darted in and out of the scrub pine trees along the fence line. The birds used the tailwind out of the north to push them towards warmer territory in the south. Maybe all the way to Texas, I pondered. For a brief moment I wished I were a dove.

A golf ball ricocheted off the side of the golf cart with a crash and I instinctively looked back at Pete Gant.

"Damnit," I yelled to Tim. "The fool is hitting balls off the green."

With every swing, a big chunk of expensive sod flew off the carefully manicured surface. The grass and dirt followed the flight of a the golf ball for only a few yards before falling to the wet ground with a soft splat.

"C'mon Pete! Knock that shit off," Billy screamed. "They'll put our ass in jail for tearing up the green like that. We're not in Wichita, ya' know."

Gant reluctantly stopped hitting golf balls towards the club house a few hundred yards away. No major damage was done as far as I could tell but it was obvious that even Tim was getting weary of Pete's immaturity.

Pete continued to giggle and try to emulate Glen Campbell in his signature song. For someone who originally professed that he didn't want to play, it sure seemed like Pete was having a hell of a good time.

"He's always like that when things are going good for him," Tim stated.

"Yeah, I know," I replied, "and the first sign that things aren't going completely his way he will fall apart like one of those five cent condoms they pass out at the Health Department clinics."

Pete Gant was the greatest choke artist of all time. In times of crisis you would have better luck getting a decision, or any meaningful assistance, from your pet rock. He much preferred to sit back and passively watch so that he would not have to take any responsibility for whatever the outcome might be in a major issue. That way, Pete could always be the best of armchair quarterbacks to tell you later exactly where you went wrong.

I peered toward the club house as Jim urged the straining electric cart toward the building's warmth and safety from Pete's flying golf balls. A few of his gleaming white spheres littered the ground near the parking area. It was a miracle that no windshields seemed shattered and no car alarms were wailing. What is it that people say about God looking out for drunks and idiots?

The back nine started without much fanfare. The city manager still had not put in an appearance. No one reported seeing "His Shortness", one of the many nicknames that a lot of people called him behind his back. I doubt anyone other than his cute intern cared whether or not Mel Michaels ever showed up at his own golf tournament. In fact, if there had a been a vote, most would have preferred that he be found wrapped around a high voltage power line dangling three inches above the Arkansas River. "Film At Ten", the Channel Twelve news anchorman would no doubt announce. Now that was one newscast I would definitely watch, I told myself.

The decision was made to let Pete and Billy keep up the main part of our team's golfing. I was elected to drive the cart on the back nine to allow Tim the luxury of being a passenger this time around. The "Dancing Trevino Twins", as I had now dubbed Pete and Billy, led the way in their own cart. They were well fortified by two six packs of Budweiser freshly purchased from the concession stand.

As we slowly drove between the remaining holes, Tim filled two cups of hot chocolate from a thermos he brought in his golf bag. The guy was always prepared. We passed the thermos back and forth several times and I began to relax for a moment. I tried to concentrate on the fact that I was alive. The air was clean and healthy. Mainly, I could celebrate the fact that I was not tied to that damn computer back at the office. There, the city manager could heap electronic mail abuse on me without ever talking to me face to face. I comforted myself with the thought that it was a normal work day and here we were being allowed to play golf on the city's time. What a deal. The day before I had finally completed my annual budget submission. It was two weeks ahead of schedule. I knew that the manager would hate all of my proposals. I knew from experience that I should have fun now before he had time to read it and begin making my life more miserable.

As I reached for the thermos again, a day glow yellow golf ball smacked into a squirrel that had ventured into the fairway. The furry creature intended to put just one more nut in the ground, as protection against the fast approaching Kansas winter, before attempting to occupy the same space as one of Billy's high velocity tee shots. One of Newton's "Laws of Physics" said that the ill fated attempt to occupy the same physical space was impossible. I forgot which one and the squirrel did not know about Newton anyway.

"You got him, Billy!" Pete screamed. "Right in his little fuzzy head. Good shootin', Deadeye."

"Yeah, I guess he forgot to duck like those ducks I missed!" Billy howled. Both Pete and Billy rolled on the cold ground in laughter. I failed to see any humor in the joke. The squirrel wasn't laughing either.

No doubt the Budweiser was working wonders. This was particularly effective on Billy who was a notorious two beer drunk. I guessed that his ability to get blasted so quickly was an acquired trait because he needed to get drunk as soon as possible to face his wife after work each day.

She was ugly enough to peel the paint off of an Oklahoma outhouse. To make matters worse, Mrs. Wade looked about twenty years older than Billy and he had already seen forty five candles on his cake. Once, during a formal reception at City Hall, the visiting police chief from Seattle had asked Billy if the elderly woman standing near him was his mother. The woman dressed in the flour sack dress was his wife. I thought there would be a fist fight for sure. Instead, Billy just blinked several times behind his big owl glasses. He tightened his jaw muscles and calmly introduced his wife to the shaken chief as if nothing was wrong with the picture or the sound on his television set.

The squirrel was twirling around on the ground in obvious pain and distress. I stopped the cart and Tim jumped out with a three iron. He was not laughing.

"Crap, you two idiots are pissing me off," Tim breathed through clinched teeth.

Tim David was seriously pissed off and that was very hard to do. He raised his three iron and smacked the dying squirrel with a hatchet chop that would have made Paul Bunyan proud. The animal twitched its tail one last time and quietly died. Tim looked at the smashed squirrel and back at the now panting deputy chiefs who were still giggling and brushing grass from their clothes. Tim hung his head dejectedly and climbed back in the cart. When dealing with people on an intellectual level like Pete and Billy, Tim was as impotent as a referee in professional wrestling match. It did not matter what he said or did.

"Those guys are not wrapped right," I said in trying to diffuse the moment. "We had a guy like them in Dallas who was my partner for awhile. One afternoon we answered a "meet complainant" call to see an old lady who was tenderly cradling her sick cat. The woman said she didn't know what to do about poor "Fluffy". The old lady obviously did not have any money and the cat was probably the only family she had in the whole wide world. My partner told her not to worry and he gently took the cat from her. She had Fluffy wrapped in this old faded yellow bath towel and it got hair and fuzz all over my partner's navy blue uniform. He just looked at her and promised the anxious woman that we would be back. We climbed into our squad car with the mangy cat. He promptly handed me the feline and we made a bee line for Stemmons Freeway with the red lights and siren going all the way. Heck, I thought, this is stupid running code three to the animal hospital for a sick cat. When the speedometer inched over a hundred, my partner slowly rolled down his window. He snatched the cat out of my lap and tossed the animal from the car. Through the rear window, I saw the cat bounce three times and become a hood ornament for an eighteen wheeler about a quarter of a mile behind us. My partner cleared the call on the radio, flipped off the lights and siren, calmly coasted to an exit and asked me where I wanted to get lunch."

"Naw, those guys aren't really like that," Tim argued. "I'm sure the squirrel was just an accident. They're out here trying to have a little fun."

I took the last swig out of my hot chocolate cup and said, "Just keep an eye on them from now on when they are hitting. I don't want to wind up with a yellow ball growing in my forehead like that squirrel."

"Hang on," Tim said. "We'll be heading back to Wichita soon."

"Maybe we can encourage these two clowns to ride home with someone else," I suggested.

In fact, my whole success these last six years had been in finding ways to get around the kinds of problems that Billy and Pete seemed to create or be incapable of solving on their own. I excelled in manipulating circumstances to find the best possible outcome of bad situations. Nothing seemed to come easy in the city of Wichita, Kansas, America, Planet Earth.

By the time the last nine holes were over, we returned to the clubhouse cold, tired, and wet from a new rain that sprang in on the heels of another arctic weather front. Pete had thrown his empty beer cans into the water traps along the course. I had to insist that he not shoot them with his thirty-eight when he decided to sink the evidence.

"Pete, Billy," Tim said, "Alice Faye needs someone to help her pack up things and drive with her back to Wichita. How 'bout it guys?"

Tim was up to his old tricks. I did not know the young intern's name but Tim not only knew her name but he also knew that Pete could not resist being that close to a child in a woman's body. Wherever Pete led, Billy would follow as long as Billy's wife wasn't around to pull his not so imaginary nose ring.

"I'll ride back with the chief and we'll catch you at the party," Tim instructed.

Pete and Billy looked at each other as the parking lot began to clear. They never understood why Tim David would hang out with me. The thought of Tim riding all the way back to Wichita with the chief alone made them even more confused and suspicious. I reveled in their discomfort.

The golf tournament had been designed to be completed by noon. We were all supposed to be back at our desks for an afternoon of work before heading to the next planned Employee Appreciation function that evening. There was as much a chance of that happening as there was for Mel to give me a raise. In other words, zero.

Somewhere above the cold gray clouds the sun was beginning to track west towards Dodge City and the Pacific Ocean. It was certain that the day's weather was not going to improve. Kansas can be the dreariest place on earth. The state has few trees, winds like a hurricane most of the time, and is as flat as Twiggy's chest. In the early days of American expansion, the area was listed on most pioneer's maps as the "Great American Desert." But on the rare sunny and calm days, the sky is the bluest I have ever seen. I had to admit that even Texas could not compete with the crisp, clean air in the summer time. I reminded myself, however; that the only thing between Wichita, Kansas and the Arctic Circle was a barbed wire fence. Even that was blown down most of the time.

I guess I will always love Texas. It is probably only because I was born there. There is some kind of fierce pride and a sense of honor that goes with saying, "I'm a Texan." The state was given birth by a group of rebels who took on and defeated the entire Mexican nation. It began Mexico's slide to become known by the whole world as a political, military and economic disaster. Even today, Texas continues to foster the attitude that it is bigger and better and has more to be independently proud of than any other place on the planet. A Texan knows instinctively that the Texas legislature in Austin would just as soon declare war on Rhode Island as they would Iraq. A fight's, a fight; they would probably say. Let's get it on.

I took my keys out of my golf bag and tossed them to Tim. The big brass slab of metal on my key chain, stamped "Captain's Keys," made the ring easy to throw. My young son had given me that as a present when I was promoted to Captain on the Dallas Police Department. The promotion came on a Halloween. I remembered wondering if the promotion was a trick or treat as we laughed at the coincidence. I continued to carry the key ring as a reminder that the promotion was the pinnacle of my personal and professional career. I always remembered those times as some of our family's happiest. Now, eleven years later, we were all in a different world.

Tim bent to unlock my big white Chevy Caprice. The car had black wall tires, electric door locks, and a myriad of lights, radios, antennas, and other fancy gadgets that come as standard equipment on full sized police cars these days. The vehicle was a constant source of friction between me and the city manager. When I took the job the previous police chief was driving a shiny new Cadillac. That luxury car had been confiscated from a local drug dealer as "Spoils of War" under the federal government's latest anti-drug program. It was one of many "War on Drugs" that had been proclaimed by the president. This was the umpteenth such war declared by every American president since Teddy Roosevelt. The latest twist in the newest "war" was to punish the narcotics traffickers in America by seizing their assets and their toys and convert them for law enforcement use.

The only Cadillac I had ever driven was when my dad let me drive his nine year old version just once when I was eighteen. He relented only because I did not have a ride to meet a college recruiter who had offered me a full athletic scholarship in track. I was so excited that I backed the big car into a fence on the campus parking lot and tore up a fender. My mom fibbed and claimed that she did the damage to save me from my Dad's wrath. I have hated Cadillacs ever since. I also have some strong ethical problems about driving a fancy car taken from a drug dealer. This luxury seemed especially opulent when the basic patrol officer was driving an old beat up Dodge six cylinder with an average of 80,000 miles on the odometer.

I told the city's fleet coordinator that I wanted to be issued a standard police car like the ones being driven by the beat officers. I asked for a plain car with no markings or light bar on the roof.

Cars are very important to police officers. The officers have to ride around in them all day or night and the front seat becomes their only office. They cuss and discuss them endlessly among themselves. The officers compare different departments professionally by analyzing what kind of cars are issued to the patrol officers. There is also a sense of how the police administration feels about its officers by what kind of car is provided to them. I worked hard to junk the puny Dodges and see that the bid specifications budgeted for new cars would fit only the largest version offered by Chevrolet or Ford.

For the police chief to drive something other than the standard issue vehicle sends the wrong message, I thought. The troops applauded the change. I immediately had a common "car" language to talk with officers that I had never met before. The city manager hated the idea. He sent the Public Works Director, Larry Stevens, to encourage me drive the small Ford sub-compact that the Manager had picked out for me before I arrived. I stood my ground. Larry finally confessed that "Mohamar" wanted me to drive the little toy car because he couldn't stand for anyone in city government to drive a car bigger than the mid-size that the City Council provided for his use. I told Larry that "Mo", to use his Mohamar Kadahfi nickname for our dictator manager, would get over it. I was wrong. He never did.

Billy and Pete were walking up the brick path from the parking lot with Alice Faye surrounded on all sides. Tim lapsed into his feeble attempt at a Texas accent, "How'd you like the way I handled them doggies, podner?"

"Not bad, Chemo-sa-bay," I chimed in with a triple syllable name for the Lone Ranger's sidekick. It came out sounding like a Malaysian cancer treatment.

"Man, you have the worst Texas accent for any Texan I have ever heard," Tim protested. "Don't they give you guys no schoolin' down there?"

"Heck Tim, I've lost most of my accent since I've been in Kansas for the last six years. Haven't you noticed?" I answered. "If it wasn't for the fact that I am required by Texas law to make a pilgrimage back to the Alamo at least once each year to keep my Texas citizenship, I would have probably lost it completely."

Tim just stared at me for a moment. He was close to believing my tall tale about the imaginary Texas citizenship law when I grinned and gave him a playful jab in the ribs at his gullibility.

I began to sort through the FM radio channels for the oldies station we both liked. Normally, I did not listen to the regular radio when I was in the city car. I preferred to concentrate on the police frequencies to keep abreast of what was going on in the city. I could never resist the temptation to show up at the scene of a "hot" call like a shooting, barricaded person or robbery alarm. It was one reason that I always, I mean always, carried my pistol. Most other police chiefs considered their job as mainly administrative and left their weapon in their wife's purse or in the desk drawer. I always felt like I was a police officer first and a police chief second. But today some tunes by Johnny Rivers or my all time favorite, Patsy Cline, seemed like a much better method to help us work our way back to Wichita.

Tim passed me a can of Pepsi that he had liberated from Alice Faye's ice chest. He adjusted the steering wheel for his shorter frame as we pulled out of the lot.

"I don't know how you drink that stuff all the time," Tim said. "Give me a glass of iced tea any day."

I laughed and said, "Tim, I didn't even drink coffee until I came up here with you guys. Now you've corrupted me with that nasty brew in the mornings. Give me caffeine with fizz in it rather than squeezed from a bean by some poor dirt farmer in Bolivia. Shoot, Juan Valdez ain't even an American, for heaven's sake!" I pronounced American like any good Texan, as "Ahh-merry-con".

"Besides," I drawled, "if Juan would raise coca leaves for that there Colombian marching powder like any other good south American peasant; all of us "po-leece" gringos would have better job security."

Up ahead, the school crossing lights at the Hesston elementary school were flashing. Tim slowed down and hit the electric button to roll down his driver's side window. A highly polished and crisply uniformed police officer about fifty years of age stood in the middle of the crosswalk. One hand held out a bright red sign that said "STOP". The other open palm gently urged small kids along the white striped path as they made their way across the street. Tim slowly coasted up next to the officer when the rug rats cleared the street. We both smiled innocently at an overweight mom hustling her brood of six kids into a rickety station wagon. A "I Vote Pro Life" bumper sticker was affixed to a dirty rear window. I conservatively guessed that the woman would dress out at about three hundred pounds if she were mistaken for a moose during hunting season.

The letters on the officer's bright gold plated name tag read "Chief O'Shay". His uniform was strictly L.A.P.D. navy blue. He was perfectly attired right down to his military style round police cap set evenly on his head. The cap's bill rested at a regulation two fingers above the bridge of his nose.

"Hey Mike," Tim leaned out of the window slightly. "How's that boy of yours up at K-State?"

The pride of the three member Hesston Police Department looked a little confused. In a moment he recognized Tim and our car. Like any professional police officer, he was somewhat embarrassed to be caught performing the basic duties of a nanny. His pride was especially wounded by being discovered by the real "big city" police. But, hey, that was the job requirement in his town and we respected that. I never allowed anyone to ridicule the smaller towns for their law enforcement officers. In many ways, they were as professional and better motivated than their big city counterparts around the country. I guessed that their pride came not from being a big fish in a small pond but from feeling like they had some ownership in the pond.

Chief O'Shay grinned from ear to ear and waved at me in the front seat. "He's doing great, Tim. How's the best police chief in America today?"

Mike O'Shay believed I could walk on top of the Arkansas River. It was the closest thing to a river we had in Kansas and it sluggishly meandered through the middle of Wichita. I kept trying to tell him that the mud hole was really only about six inches deep and anyone could walk on top of it. Mike was always worried about my mental attitude. It was not unusual for him to call me at the office with a pep talk after he found out that I was going through some tough public battle. The chief watched a lot of television and read three newspapers. He would patiently try to re-build my confidence over the telephone. With over seven hundred members in my own department, Mike and his two officer outfit often seemed bigger supporters of my "Community Policing" philosophy than any of my own troops. I admit that I loved him for it. In return, I went out of my way to give him recognition at the state and even national level for his dedicated efforts in his tiny town.

When one of the regular as clock work Kansas tornadoes touched down and wrecked a Hesston officer's mobile home, Tim and I passed the hat at our squad meetings in Wichita. We raised a couple of hundred dollars to buy the young officer and his family some emergency supplies of food and clothing. The whole town was so appreciative that you would have thought that we had given the hapless family a winning lottery ticket. Their sincere gratitude for our small gesture made me cry and I wished that we could have raised thousands.

We grinned and waved as Tim accelerated past the school zone and up onto Interstate 35. He floored the accelerator pedal and we blasted off for Wichita at about warp factor three.

"Slow down Mr. Spock. Let's not get in any hurry to go back to work," I instructed.

At a more normal sixty-five miles an hour, we charted a course back in time to the "Proud Princess of the Plains." That was the latest hokey motto that the local Visitors and Convention Bureau was using to promote tourism. Wichita was once billed as the

"Air Capital of the World" because of its origin as one of the centers for aviation construction. Boeing, Beech, Learjet, and Cessna had all been big employers in the city at one time. Some companies were still hanging on because they were able to wrangle special political favors for tax abatements or other semi-legal incentives at the taxpayer's expense. Other industries that refused to play the game were leaving. Without political connections there was a oppressive anti-business bureaucracy that city government had either built by design or ineptitude. Now the latest joke was that the "Air Capital" only had airplanes getting "out" of town and none coming in. When the major airlines cut their jet service to Wichita and forced the smaller propeller driven airplanes to service the city's air passengers there was a big hue and cry by the politicians. As usual, nothing really changed. Nothing changed except some money behind the scenes that temporarily stopped the hue and cry.

"Need to pee?" Tim's question broke the silence.

Tim was inquiring of my notoriously small bladder that I purposely used to keep all of our staff meetings to an hour or less. It is a firm belief of mine that meetings which last longer than an hour are a complete waste of time. The necessity for me to take a piss every sixty minutes or so effectively enforced my rule. As soon as I left the meeting room, my staff would be unable to agree on whether or not the sky was blue.

"Uh, no, let's call in and see what's going on," I countered.

Picking up the cellular phone I dialed the office using the one button memory function and waited for Suzie, my secretary, to answer. In the meantime I studied the "Made in Korea" high-tech phone. It was also the product of a confiscation. An unlucky pimp on Wichita's notorious hooker haven of South Broadway Boulevard had been caught selling a different kind of "crack" by our vice officers and contributed his new phone to the war effort.

"Better living through chemistry," I said to no one in particular.

Suzie came on the line. "Chief Starr's office, may I help you?"

"I'm just glad that I've been out of town for over six hours and no one has changed the name on the office stationery. You would tell me if there was a new boss in your life, right Suzie?" I asked.

"Hi Chief, how'd you play?" Suzie politely inquired while ignoring my ever present paranoia.

"Oh, just great," I lied. "You should have seen Tim use his three iron. He was a regular killer with it."

Tim winced at the jab for his mercy murder of the wounded squirrel while I pressed on with Suzie. "Anything going on at the office?"

"Not much," Suzie said. "It's been pretty quiet except for one call from the Manager. He wants to see you in his office at nine in the morning."

"Did he say what the purpose of the meeting is Suzie?" my voice cracked like a little boy on the cheap phone.

My stomach tightened at those rare occasions when the City Manager would deign to speak to me in person. Usually he did any dirty work over the e-mail or behind my back without telling me. In over six years the City Manager had been to my office exactly once. A few years back, one of our local millionaires insisted on coming to my office to thank me for the job our department had done in rescuing his daughter from her overturned Corvette. The Manager was obviously very uncomfortable being forced into that type of positive supporting role on turf other than his own home field. I was gracious. I did not insist on seeing the Manager's identification card to verify that he really was our City Manager. It was the first, last and only time Mel Michaels had visited his police chief's office.

"He didn't say, Chief. He probably just wants to tell you that you're not getting a raise again this year," Suzie stated with a twist of a smile in her voice.

"No, I doubt it. If he ever decided to let me know ahead of time on something like that the manager would just have Bullet Bob tell me," I allowed myself to whine. "Besides Suzie, you know that I always find out by checking my paycheck at the first of the year and seeing that nothing has changed."

After hanging up with Suzie I asked Tim if he knew of anything special going on at City Hall that I should be aware of before my meeting with the manager.

"Maybe he's gonna tell you what a great job you're doing," Tim guessed with no conviction whatsoever.

"Only if his body has been taken over by three headed alien creatures from outer space," I answered.

"Say, uh, speaking of space aliens; remind me to tell you about this new case up in investigations." The car phone rang and interrupted what promised to be another good Tim David story that only he could weave.

It was Suzie reminding me that I had promised "Howlin' Hank", of the "Howlin' Hank and Mickey Show", that I would appear as a guest on their daily television show. Hank had just called and wanted to set a definite date for my appearance.

"Hank also wants to know if you would like to have lunch tomorrow," Suzie advised.

"Call him back and tell Hank that I like to have lunch every day. It's become quite a habit," I quipped.

After I explained the comment to Suzie she suggested that I call him myself tomorrow. Hank was really a nice guy and owned a whole string of radio stations across the

Midwest. Beneath his sometimes corny exterior he was quite the shrewd businessman. He never hesitated to allow me air time on his radio stations or local television show if I needed to take my pitch direct to the public to counter some political move that cropped up on a regular basis. Hank insisted that his radio stations still play the national anthem at straight up midnight every night and he professed a fanatical affection for Patsy Cline music. He was almost too good to be true.

"Howlin' Hank" received the nickname from his radio show audience because of a tendency to howl at the moon during earlier stints as a night time dee jay. He had somehow been convinced to take his talents to a local daytime television talk show with a female co-host named Mickey Blake.

Mickey was about fifteen years past her prime and struggling to find the fountain of youth. She had been a real looker in the days when Gerald Ford was president but gravity was winning the body war and the lines in her face could not be completely filled in with plumber's putty. One of the worst kept secrets about Mickey was a homemade video tape of her and several of her many boyfriends committing just about every type of sex act that humans can conceive. The sizzling tape had become public when one of her lovers contracted herpes from the encounter and decided to extract a little payback for his pain and suffering. Working as a technician at the television station allowed the infected paramour to re-title the video as "Abbot and Costello Meet the Mummy" and insert it into the line-up for a four a.m. showing on Channel Three's "Nite Owl Theater".

By the time some moron on the edge of town called the station and asked them to pump up the power so he could get a better picture on his fuzzy black and white set, at least a thousand copies had been run off by various wide awake viewers who greatly appreciated Mickey's enthusiasm for fun and frivolity that was vividly displayed on the tape. It did not take long for the copies to begin selling for twenty dollars a piece on the street. These original copies begot other copies, that begot other copies, until I do not think that there was a single household in town that did not have its very own version of "Mickey Does Wichita" in living color. The whole incident became so famous that the video tape itself was elevated to a status symbol for the upper crust of Wichitan society. If you did not know from your own observations that the left side of Mickey's cute little butt was decorated by a small tattoo depicting a pair of red lips then you were obviously nobody important. It became a mania. I almost expected to see television commercials late at night advertising the triple X rated video.

"Hey kids! Be the first on your block to see the incredible Mickey Blake suck a bowling ball through a garden hose. That's right, gang, no trailer hitch in town is safe from Mickey's desires. She's gone down on everything except the Titanic, folks. Here's your chance to see and hear for yourself what every man wants and some get. Batteries not included," the announcer would breathlessly scream.

Mickey seemed oblivious to the whole incident. Being interviewed on camera by Mickey, I found myself smiling at her for no reason obvious to the viewing public. Of course, the home audience was also smiling at Mickey for no reason obvious to anyone who had not seen the tape. Some called it the most shocking secret tape since Nixon said, "Let's break into Watergate and steal the shit and kill any son of a bitch that gets in our way", or words to that effect.

Tim stared at the perfectly straight Kansas highway as I fantasized a little longer about Mickey Blake. We passed by "Honest Sal's Stupendous Car Emporium" on North Broadway without slowing. This was where we had bought our first car in Wichita. I spent the entire time there watching my wife do all the talking. She traded in our old Chevy soccer mom car for a shiny new candy apple red Ford sportster. I hated buying cars. I chalked it up to my genetically imprinted inability to deal with people when they had me by the balls and I knew it. Buying a car was always a humiliating experience for me. The Wichita Ford was still going strong years later when we passed it down to our son, Chad.

Chad had won an appointment to the United States Naval Academy in Annapolis by taking advantage of the gifts of intelligence and sensitivity which he inherited from his mom. From me he received a lot of stubbornness, which I guess did not hurt him too much. The Academy rules finally allowed underclassmen to have cars during their third year at Annapolis and our first big purchase in Wichita was given a new home. Chad found that the sporty red Ford, despite its odd purple and brown wheat stalk Kansas license plates, was just the kind of car that a young guy needed when he was turned loose on the world for the first time.

A fit of sneezing brought me back to earth and Kansas in particular. Tim suffered from hay fever and sinus problems all the time it seemed. He was the only man I ever knew who could sneeze and pass gas at the same time.

"Damn," Tim's voice was strained and raspy. "My mouth tastes like elephant dung and my throat feels like a porcupine's ass."

"Well, if you would quit sleeping by the toilet maybe you wouldn't wake up with that kind of circus animal taste in your mouth every morning," I offered.

"How'd you know my wife threw me out of the bedroom?" he coughed.

"Because eventually I knew she would find out about all of those cute little hotel clerks you lust after around the country and make you sleep curled up next to the crapper," was my less than clever response.

Tim definitely did have a wandering eye for anything that squatted to pee. His easy going nature made him seem so harmless to women that they probably did not take him seriously until he bit through the crotch of their panty hose. "Small Island Rules" was the name Tim gave to the pact of secrecy that prevailed when any of us on the command staff went out of town together. In other words, whatever happened without our wives around was not discussed or repeated once we left wherever we had been. I just tried not to know too much. Tim had a great knack for getting all kinds of free goodies from the female clerks at the hotels we stayed in. He also knew all of them on a first name basis and sent them cards and flowers from time to time. Suzie was incensed when these strange women would later call up and ask to talk to "Chief David", knowing that Tim had appropriated my title to further impress the ladies.

At a police convention in Denver, Tim and Pete hustled three female attorneys from Washington into going drinking and dancing with them. When it became known that I knew one of the women from a strictly professional contact in Dallas, I was drawn into the conspiracy. Somehow we finished up driving through a snow storm to one of the women's hotel rooms. I attempted to gently plead with Tim to give me the car keys. I did not want to pull rank and embarrass him. I just wanted to get my tail out of there before the FBI kicked in the door and arrested us all for transporting lewd women for immoral purposes. It used to be a law, I thought.

On that unforgettable evening, Tim quickly convinced his date that he was the police chief of the group. He certainly looked the part far more than either Pete or me. I was pretty sure what was going to happen next. The woman that Pete had gotten stuck with by default was the least attractive of the litter. What was worse, she also became the most drunk of the bunch. Pete's girl puked in his lap while attempting oral sex that she had only actually read about once in a Cosmopolitan magazine. That really hurt Pete's fragile ego. The man who fancied himself the "Hacksaw of the Plains", because he could cut anything he bragged, was now just ready to leave and go back to our own hotel. Married four times to former beauty queens, Pete Gant definitely felt himself a better ladies man than to be left with the ugly duckling of that brood.

Back home, Tim and I would quietly chide Pete about his date that night. We unceremoniously dubbed her "Quazimoto" and referred to the fictitious hump on her back. Tim and I embellished the story with each telling among ourselves until reality became a victim to our chance to raze Pete unmercifully. All within the confines of "Small Island Rules", of course.

"You know, Chief," Tim's voice finally returned to normal. "I really like Kansas. I've always wanted to just retire to some little town here and do something with my hands.

You know, build something that will last. These towns are just full of good people that are honest and hard working and never heard of real crime or politics or any of that crap. In fact, I bet there are plenty of pretty motel clerks in these towns that like country and western music as much as I do."

"Could be Tim, but I bet there are also a lot of motel clerk husbands who have hairy knuckles and tattoos of "Born to Lose" and "Harley Davidson" on their arms. They would beat the stuffing outta you in a small town where you couldn't get on that big silver bird and fly away when the week was over," I grimly prophesied.

Small towns in Kansas still produced about one major scandal a week where somebody did somebody else wrong. The "wrongee" usually blew the legs off the "wronger" with an old rusty twelve gauge in the middle of the local Piggly Wiggly. It was messy, but made great copy in the hometown newspaper. "Clean up on isle four", the gum smacking clerk would announce over the crackling PA system and life would go back to normal, I imagined.

Tim thought about it for a moment and then said, "That's part of what makes it exciting, you know. The thought that you might get caught in the act doing something you shouldn't be doing with someone you shouldn't be doing it with. Would that scare you?"

"Damn right it would scare me. I don't intend to be used for fish cleaning practice by some jealous husband with a glove box full of overdue bills and a carpet knife in a little holster on his belt. It ain't worth it to me and it damn sure ain't no fun if I'm too scared to even find my zipper, much less use what's inside," I lamented.

"But that's all part of being alive, don't you know. Why do you think the manager keeps trying to pork every woman he meets?" Tim asked sincerely.

For a moment I had to admit that Tim had me stumped. "I don't know why the manager does anything that he does. I've thought about why he puts his professional career in jeopardy by lusting after every post pubescent female crossing his path and I honestly don't know," I confessed.

We both fell deep into our own thoughts. I began thinking about the first time that I had met the city manager when he hired me for the chief's job. I was thirty-seven years old and was the up and coming hot dog of the Dallas Police Department's command staff. In only sixteen years I had risen quickly through each one of the civil service ranks to be appointed a Division Commander. Along the way I had won just about every award the department had to offer. Even though I knew nothing about the politics of being a police chief, my over inflated ego inspired me to apply for the job in Dallas when our veteran chief reluctantly retired under pressure after a series of questionable police shootings. When a rookie officer blasted a senile grandmother off of her own front porch, it was the final strain on an otherwise great police chief's career. It didn't seem to matter that granny was randomly firing her own pistol at the house next door where her scrambled brain imagined that Jack the Ripper was raping the neighbor's cat. Since the city could not fire the entire Dallas Police Department, our chief had to go.

No one was more surprised than me when I was named as a finalist for the job. When the offer went to a person from outside the department for the first time in our history, I was not too concerned. As a matter of fact, I was confident that I would still continue my rise through the ranks in what I thought was a great police department.

Our new chief came to us from a thirty officer police department in Alabama. He soon found himself up to his ears in giant alligators trying to manage a department of about three thousand members. He believed that he got the job because of some divine gift for leadership. The truth was that he had known and supported the current Dallas City Manager when that person held a previous political position in another city. Predictably, our new chief accomplished a whole career's worth of managerial mistakes in just his first few months on the job.

He showed up drunk with a female assistant city attorney at a "Led Zeppelin" concert and attempted to force his way past the off duty officers working security for the event. This act was too much for us to take. The time honored tradition of "badging" your way into special events, by showing your ID to the guards, was certainly okay. Hanging out drunk with a homely, skinny female lawyer was also no sin in the eyes of most police officers. She would minimally qualify as a police groupie; also known as a "Hide" or "Hairy Leg" in Dallas Police parlance. No one would be expected to actually marry her or take her home to mama. In this case, the attorney was so unattractive that if you woke up first and found her laying on your arm, you would want to gnaw it off rather than wake her up so you could leave. No, it was the attempt to get the autograph of the lead singer for Led Zeppelin that destroyed our new chief's integrity. I mean, my gosh, Led Zeppelin for heaven's sake! If it had been George Strait or even Dolly Parton then maybe we could have understood his zeal, but Led Zeppelin? Everyone on the department quickly decided that this fool was completely insane and totally without any social redeeming graces whatsoever.

Despite a lot of our senior commanders retiring or taking other jobs after the new chief came to town, I hung on expecting to be rewarded for my work just like always. When it came time to reorganize the command staff, I found that I was slated for the dead end of nowhere. I was repeatedly passed over for promotion in favor of far less qualified and even less senior people on the department. It was my first taste of political retribution. The lesson was very clear. To the victor goes the spoils and the first thing to do is to bury the rivals so they won't come back for round two. I was transferred from a great position in the department, as the Police Academy Director, to the Records Division located in the basement of the old Police and Courts Building. It was about as low as you could go in the organization, both literally and figuratively. My ego could not stand the blow. The City Manager in Wichita sent me a letter inviting me to apply for their police chief's position and I bit hard at the bait.

Surprisingly, the selection process in Wichita was far more difficult than had been the case for the Dallas chief's position. Afterwards, I found that I had scored higher on each one of the evaluations than the other eight finalists. When a competitor for the Wichita job, who was already a police chief in a smaller city in Iowa, withdrew late in the process he told me something important. In retrospect, I should have listened to him instead of ignoring it at the time as sour grapes. He said that he had learned more background information about the city manager and that there was more to life than working for a madman in Kansas.

After the assessment process in Wichita, I returned to my closet size office in the bowels of the Dallas Police Department and waited. And waited. And waited. To kill time in my new mind numbing assignment, I read the secret Kennedy assassination files that are kept locked away in a hidden file cabinet in the Records Division. The only key is kept by the Division Commander on a silver chain worn around his neck. As I long suspected, Lee Harvey Oswald committed the "Crime of the Century" all by himself.

During the next three months, there were many more promotions in the Dallas department. "Affirmative Action" was the new prime directive that seemed to guide all decisions. Lacking the proper heritage or reproductive organs insured that your career was effectively frozen. The new chief obviously had his marching orders from his civilian bosses and we should have understood. Instead, we were bewildered and confused. The chief was moving quickly to change our "good old boy system", as he called it. Those of us who had diligently fought our way through the system by investing thousands of hours of studying for grueling civil service examinations at every step in the promotional process were suddenly expendable. Since most of the highly trained and experienced command staff members thought that our new chief would be unable to pour piss out of a boot unless the instructions were written in large block letters on the sole, it became a nasty situation in a hurry.

One of my fellow veteran commanders, who had also been passed over for promotion, formed the "Dinosaur Club." Membership was for those of us who were considered extinct and obviously going nowhere fast. The new chief began appointing rookie sergeants with only a few years on the department and civilian librarians to deputy chief and assistant chief positions. Unfortunately, their qualifications did not extend past their genetics.

The insult was more than a proud command staff could take. We all started openly wearing our newly minted "Dinosaur Club" lapel pins. They depicted a white tyrannosaurus on a blue background with the universal red circle and slash across it, indicating our mutual extinction. In tiny letters, the slash said "Affirmative Action Victim". We even had a secret sign. When one club member met another club member in the hall, we would take our tie and nonchalantly toss it over our left shoulder like a big dinosaur swinging his lizard like tail. It became more grim than funny as time wore on. We had to do the actual work of our newly appointed superiors who had received no training or experience to do the jobs they had been given. In a way, I felt sorry for them and knew that it was just a matter of time before the whole charade collapsed. I was right.

I finally called Wichita to ask the Personnel Director what was going on with their search for a new police chief there. Her assistant said that he was just about to call me and invite me back up to visit with the City Manager personally about the job. He gave me a date and time and sent me and my wife first class airplane tickets. The assistant made hotel reservations at the Marriott, which was the best that Wichita had to offer in the way of accommodations. When Peggy and I arrived, there was a bottle of wine waiting for us in the room, compliments of City Manager Melvin Michaels. I noted that the last name was misspelled "Michael's." Being a highly trained, highly skilled police detective; it was easy to deduce right away that Mr. Michaels had absolutely no personal involvement in the gesture. For some reason, that did not bother me at the time. It should have.

The next morning I received a telephone call from the Manager's secretary, Maria. She invited me to meet Mr. Michaels in the hotel coffee shop at 9:00 am. Of course, I was only too happy to oblige. Even though I did not drink coffee, I planned on ordering the nasty brew anyway because I figured that all real police chiefs drink coffee.

Thus began a strange dance around the city with my prospective boss going from one coffee shop to another and mainly just driving around in his car. We avoided all other humans as if he was trying to hide from someone. It was like being in a B-grade spy movie. He asked very few specific questions about my management philosophies or policing in general. I kept trying to pin him down on the details of the position. Every time I got close to talking about the job of police chief he would abruptly change the subject. We played this silly game for two full days. An observant waitress from one of our many stops recognized the City Manager and asked my name.

I replied, "Bond, James Bond." I just couldn't resist the temptation.

The manager kept Peggy busy by having a very nice female administrative aide from his office drive her around town. They talked about shopping and houses and schools and that kind of thing, but the middle aged lady was obviously in the dark about anything pertaining to the police chief's job.

After the second day of this run around Peggy asked me bluntly, "Do you have the job?"

I answered truthfully. "I don't have a clue. Do you suppose it's this way for all new chiefs?"

Not having been this far in the game before, we both decided that I would bring this process to a head the next day. We both needed to get back to Dallas to our kids, jobs, dog, and half a dozen other issues that make up life. It all seemed to be so strange. My gut feeling as a veteran police officer was, "There is something seriously wrong with this picture. Get the hell out of Dodge...or Wichita." You learn to trust this sixth sense to keep you alive as a street officer. They say that hind sight is twenty-twenty but I really should have listened to my instincts then too.

Unfortunately, I confess that I had stars in my eyes by then. The closer I got to actually being a police chief, the more I felt like I just had to have that brass ring. If I had been perfectly honest with myself, I would have recognized that I really didn't want the job in Kansas as much as I just wanted to see if I actually could get it. After the rebuff to my ego in Dallas, I needed the conquest. I craved the thrill of victory and not the agony of defeat again. It was kind of like pursuing a woman after the one you really wanted has told you to take a hike. Most of the fun was in the chase, not the capture.

On the morning of the third day I met Mel in the hotel coffee shop as usual. I brought a brown leather City of Dallas notebook with me. It was embossed in gold with the official city seal and was intended to impress him with my big city credentials. Before the manager could lead the conversation away from pertinent issues, I took control.

"Mr. Michaels, I need to know whether you are offering me the job here or not. Either way, I need to get home to Big D and take care of business there," I stated rather boldly. Peggy would have been proud of my audacity as she had already assessed the manager to be some sort of used car salesman type of character.

He seemed rather confused, looked down at the table and mumbled almost inaudibly, "Well, I've got some other candidates I'm talking to."

That was enough for me. I decided right then and there that this guy would have a tough time choosing between mustard or mayonnaise on his burger. Showing my exasperation, I said, "Fine, I'll go on back home and you call me when you finally decide."

"How much salary do you want?" he blurted out.

Lamely, I said "Well, how much did the retired chief make?"

"Sixty thousand," he lied without any show of recognition of his dishonesty. It would not be the last time.

I knew to the penny how much the previous chief had made. The first rule of negotiations is to never ask a question for which you do not already know the answer. I had already spoken to retired chief on the telephone as a part of my research before I applied for the job. It was not any sixty thousand dollars. The job had been advertised at up to ninety thousand plus benefits. I figured that to be the police chief in the fiftieth largest city in America was worth at least seventy thousand. I was making fifty five thousand in Dallas as a Division Commander. When I said that I would take the job for seventy thousand, Mel smiled and looked up from the table cloth. At that moment, I knew that the bastard had me by the scrotum with a down hill pull. Mel knew it too. Mentally, I added city managers to the list of car salesmen and natural blondes who could make a complete fool out of me.

We talked a little more and I wrote down what he said would be the benefits. Insurance, pension, car and a list of other items that Mel mentioned in some detail. After thirty minutes of some real nuts and bolts discussions, he excused himself by saying he was late for a meeting.

"Hey Mel," I used his first name without thinking . "Do I have the job or not?"

"We'll talk later," was all he said as we shook hands and parted company.

Two days later, the Wichita Personnel Director telephoned me and began setting up my return to Kansas. I was quickly introduced at a press conference and given the oath of office before my first stick of Dentine lost its flavor. In truth, I took over the reins of the Wichita Police Department without ever being actually offered the job.

Driving back down the perfectly straight Kansas highway six years later, the whole process seemed surreal. It was hard to explain. Since then, I had seen a lot of other bizarre stuff at the Wichita City Hall that made my little adventure seem sort of normal. Sometimes in a city staff meeting, I almost expected to see the rabbit from "Alice in Wonderland" run out from behind a desk and yell "What time is it? What time is it?"

"You're awfully quiet over there, Chief," Tim broke into my trip down memory lane.

Relaxing a little, I spied the less than impressive Wichita skyline. Squinting, I read the time and temperature numbers on the electronic bank building sign downtown. We quickly passed the Twenty-first Street exit and caught a whiff of the very smelly meat processing plant. In the summertime, a person with nasal diphtheria could sniff the stink at a range of five miles. "Stand By Me" faded out on the oldies radio station and we were treated to the local weather forecast.

"Cold and crappy with a sixty percent chance of more cold and crappy for tomorrow. There is a forty percent chance that it will only be crappy," the bored announcer droned, "but don't bet on it."

We turned right on Central Avenue and drove in silence. City Hall became slowly visible about two miles away in the foggy distance. Most city employees called it the "Leaning Tower of Power", after a near miss tornado had blown down the attached parking garage. The falling walls of the parking structure collapsed the roof of the adjoining building that housed our Police Property and Evidence Section. Over four years later, the city still had not rebuilt either the parking garage or our property storage facility. The insurance money had been paid to the City Manager and promptly disappeared in the electronic financial maze run by Tad Roadly, never to be seen again.

As a result, we were forced to shuffle our storage facility from one temporary run down rented warehouse to another. In the four years since the tornado, we had moved the hundreds of thousands of items in our custody no less that five times. Our current makeshift location was an all time nightmare with the clerks and officers who had to work in the shit hole every day. Previously abandoned by a fly-by-night car painting scam, the Building Inspection Department and the Fire Department had condemned the decrepit structure. It was declared unfit for habitation and in violation of about a hundred different fire codes. Privately, the fire chief warned me. Should the worthless piece of crap ever catch on fire, he would not allow his firemen to go inside to try to save anyone or anything. It would simply be too dangerous to try a rescue and not worth the effort to fight the blaze.

The patched roof leaked when it rained or when there was a heavy dew. The troops told the story that a pigeon pissed on the roof and caused five hundred pounds of aging ceiling tiles to come tumbling down. According to the tale, the falling debris narrowly missed beheading a little old lady who had come to reclaim the stolen and recovered set of plastic pink flamingos that had once graced her front lawn.

The building had absolutely no air conditioning and very little heating. Rats, huge and strangely mutated beyond Darwin's wildest dreams, were seen in the supposedly secure area where narcotics evidence was stored. I could hardly wait for that story to hit the media.

"Yes, ladies and gentlemen, we have identified the culprits who made off with a hundred kilos of cocaine and a ton of marijuana from the police property unit. It was an inside job. The mice ate it," I could announce.

That would be my version of the "dog ate my homework" story that every third grader uses at one time or the other. The inevitable press conference would probably make a "Bloopers and Bleepers" television special and immortalize Wichita for all time. As a part of my job description, according to Mel Michaels, I would be called upon to take the blame for the city not providing us with a proper facility. It was almost funny, but not quite.

We did not slow as we passed City Hall. "Thirteen floors surrounded by reality," as Tim put it.

Tim kept driving west on Central Avenue and we glided by the sprawling "Fox Run Apartments" on the right. It was strange to see such a complex of modern apartments this close to any major city's downtown area. The cookie cutter buildings offered anonymity. Each apartment also had a rather scenic view from the tiny balconies that overlooked the always exciting extra-curricular activities of Riverside Park.

A few more twisted turns through some poorly planned roadways brought us to Wichita's premier garden spot for the green thumb set. Nestled in between one of the city owned golf courses and the ever smelly water treatment plant, lay "Botanica." The site was an elaborate collection of outdoor and indoor gardens, meeting rooms, reflecting pools and quiet walk ways. It was rented to various groups and clubs in the city for special events and functions. Since the operation marginally paid its own way, the City Manager usually ignored its presence. The directors of the facility made sure that the grounds were always available for any city function to our leader free of charge. This fit the cheap bastard's budget for anyone other than himself, we all thought.

The huge adjacent water treatment plant was undergoing some long overdue major repairs and improvements that had been initiated by their outstanding new director, Dale Williams. The manager was pestering Dale about a handful of complaints from the Rose Club at Botanica. It seemed that the giant mounds of sand at the construction site were detracting from the esthetic beauty of their yellow tipped hybrids.

Dale and I, being friends who shared an impish disposition without the brains to match, talked this over. We decided that over a weekend we would get his bulldozer drivers to carve a giant beach art sculpture out of the sand mounds depicting a rather voluptuous naked woman. Giant mammary glands rising thirty feet in the air would be quite a sight, we envisioned. My troops would obviously have to guard the structure to keep the perverts from assaulting "Miss Bathing Beauty Queen of the Arkansas River Valley", but the project would definitely be a worthy contribution to Wichita's cultural scene.

I think Dale would have done it, too. He had balls just big enough to try it. But finally, the city manager came to his senses. Dale had to tell him bluntly that there was no way in Hell to build a one hundred foot tall screen to hide all the construction that was going on at the treatment plant. Pity. The nude and lewd sand woman would have really been something for the tourists to see. It could have really put our humble city on the map.

The Botanica parking lot was jammed. The only open spot was in the handicap space. Tim hesitated and then said, "Naw, I don't think that would be too good."

"Good thinking, Tim," I verified his suspicion that I was basically a straight arrow. We found a spot a half of a block down the street and pulled up on the grass median. I insisted that Tim lock the doors. It was a habit from my Dallas days. Locking your car doors there was the difference between having a vehicle to drive home in or walking to a pay phone to call 911. The Planning and Research Division once estimated that, statistically speaking, every motor vehicle in Dallas had been stolen and recovered at least once.

Once on the sidewalk, I took the lead as required by unwritten protocol. We briskly hurried the last few yards to get out of the brutal wind. Tim began unconsciously humming the last few bars of "Judy's Turn to Cry", another sixties hit that was playing on the radio just before we got out of the car. As we passed under the covered archway into Botanica, I glanced up at the sky. I was hoping to see a hint that the sun might come out or maybe a nuclear flash and mushroom from the bomb storage facility at nearby McConnell Air Force Base. There was no such luck on either count. We walked around the indoor reflecting pool toward the mass of city workers beginning to celebrate "Employee Appreciation Day." It was obvious that the party had begun somewhat earlier than was officially allowed. Naturally, I planned my entrance to be as unobtrusive as possible.

"Everybody up against the wall, it's a raid," I yelled. Half of the people laughed. The other half either thought I was serious or were not quite sure. I thought I noticed some long haired gravel truck drivers from the public works department reaching furtively to unload something out of their jean pockets. I ignored them.

While Tim moved away to talk to some of his non-police friends, I slipped unnoticed into a corner of the big room where the extra food and drinks were stacked. I hopped up on top of about fifteen cases of no-name cola drinks. The soda, no doubt, came from one of our local discount stores at half price or free to the city. Without much enthusiasm, I began observing the party at what I considered to be a safe distance.

There were about fifty people already there who were doing that uncomfortable shake and howdy routine required of all such get togethers. Most of the people in the room were familiar faces. Of course, I knew all of the members of the police department by sight and could recall their full names and most of the information in the personnel files. My memory for the names and faces of the officers under my command, and their families, was one of the things I prided myself on the most. I learned how important that skill was from personal experience.

When I was in Dallas as a young patrolman, I found myself in the "wrong place at the right time" on more than one occasion. This is the real way that fate randomly plucks so-called heroes from the list of ordinary, everyday people. On one terrifying evening, the situation I became embroiled in managed to result in a nomination for the Medal of Valor. When I was notified that the nomination had been approved, I was reminded that the medal was an extremely rare award in our organization. Only twenty-five such medals had been awarded since the inception of the police department in 1880. I later learned that most of the officers who received the medal found it easier to win the little silver disk, suspended from a navy blue ribbon, than to live with it.

I was twenty-six years old and had short hair that was well within departmental regulations. By tradition, the chief of police was required to come to our roll call to personally pin the medal on my chest in front of all of my buddies. The day before this big event was scheduled, the deputy chief of our patrol division called my sergeant into his office and told him to order me to get a haircut.

"But Chief," my sergeant protested, "Rod's hair doesn't seem too long to me."

"Well it does to me, Sergeant, have him get that mop cut by tomorrow and that's that," the grizzled old deputy chief ordered.

My sergeant passed the order down and I dutifully got another haircut although my barber had just performed the same task six days before. He must of thought I was nuts. A week later, I found out that the deputy chief had confused me with another officer named "Jeff" Starr. The other "Starr" was a detective assigned to our divisional Burglary Unit. Jeff probably did need a haircut. I definitely did not. It was not lost on me that I had worked with that deputy chief every day for three years and he did not even know my name. The lesson stuck.

Pete Gant and Billy Wade arrived with Alice Faye in tow. They stood on either side of the little doll and Pete kept leering at her small, but perfectly formed, breasts. Billy desperately wanted to stare also but his squinty eyes kept nervously darting around the room. He was no doubt afraid that his wife would suddenly sneak up behind him and rip off his penis in a vicious surprise attack.

Richard Lopez, the ever serious Hispanic fire chief, was sitting in a chair with his back against the far wall. He was observing the growing crowd with the same lack of intensity that a lion watches the human gawkers outside the zoo fence. Richard was a super nice guy, I thought. He was considered a trouble maker by the City Manager and rigidly unapproachable by his own people in the fire department. Richard's disgusted attitude toward the Manager's chaotic style stemmed from a highly developed sense of logic and common sense. As a result, Richard's devotion to duty was constantly in conflict with some of the insane orders and instructions he received from our boss. I knew the words to that song very well. The Manager could not fire Richard because he was a minority, for one thing, and a respected thirty year veteran of the Wichita Fire Department for another. In thirty years, Richard had also built a fairly comfortable political base in the community. This was an important secret to longevity in appointive posts in city government. It was always unlikely that any city manager would chance a gamble with their own career by causing an open battle over a termination unless they were desperate. It was a slim lifeline for many of us who did not have Richard's other protective layers.

A former Marine, Richard refused to play games. He insisted that the Manager's staff of mental cases deal with him on a professional basis. Not even the most psychotic of Mel's madmen would take him on in public. I knew Richard to be a honest and loyal city employee who struggled underneath his professional demeanor with deep feelings of insecurity. He had real trouble dealing with the conflict boiling in his guts as a result of the constant war between his own honor concept and the compromises that his job required while working for "Mohamar" Michaels. He was sadly angry but had too much class to show it.

When I first came to Wichita, Richard and I were both invited to say a few words of welcome at a local high school celebrating "Hispanic Culture Week." The group was heavily populated with Spanish speaking citizens and probably more than a few illegal aliens. Partly because I wanted to establish a rapport with this segment of my community and partly because I thought Chief Lopez would do the same; I made my short speech in Spanish. My four years of the language in college, and almost two decades practicing it on the streets of Dallas, made the speech a big hit with the crowd even though it was far from grammatically perfect. When I was finished, Richard followed me to the podium. In a low tone and carefully measured English he said, "I wish I could speak Spanish like Chief Starr but, despite my heritage, I never learned the language."

I was shocked at my bigoted assumption that he could speak Spanish because of his race. I apologized profusely to Richard afterwards so that he would not think that I had tried to publicly embarrass him. He studied me carefully and flashed me a smile of forgiveness. We had been friends ever since.

I sat alone atop the drink cases and continued to study the crowd. A man and a woman were standing by the chips and dips nearby. The man was dressed in a shiny business suit and leather tasseled loafers. He was overweight and his jowls dripped down over the knot in his imitation silk tie. The attractive woman was obviously very upset over something.

"Damn," I muttered to myself. What I did not need was to be caught right in the middle of a messy domestic violence argument while attending an official city function.

"It's no big deal, Marla. I'm sure they were just kidding," Porky Pig was saying.

"I don't care who they are. The pricks can't treat me like that," the woman answered.

The more they talked together the angrier the woman got and the louder their voices became. "Don't bring me these parties for your asshole buddies again, Randy. I'm not going to do this shit any more," she ordered.

While I was wondering just what "shit" she was talking about, the two became suddenly aware that I, and a lot of other people, were staring at them. The woman's eyes met mine and I could see that she was crying. Porky turned a harsh glance my way and immediately melted his look when he recognized me.

"Hey Chief, how you doing?" Porky called as he walked toward me with his pudgy hand extended. "Remember me? Randall Anderson, we met at the mayor's swearing in ceremony back in April."

"Sure, Mr. Anderson, how have you been?" I took his hand and immediately regretted the gesture due to the sweaty palms that dissolved in my grip.

"What's the deal with your friend?" I asked. Out of habit, I kept the woman's hands in view just in case she should suddenly pull a forty-four from her crotch and try to blow Porky's ample ass off. It would be quite a sight right here in front of God and everybody, I thought. It happens that way sometimes.

"Oh, you mean Marla? She's just pissed off at some of your guys, but it's nothing." Marla showed us her back and stalked off into the crowd. She quickly disappeared from view.

"Hey Chief, by the way, you are doing a great job!" Randall, alias Porky Pig, patted me on the shoulder with another sweaty paw. Subconsciously, I braced for the inevitable knife in the back.

"That was a great plan you had for dealing with those damned protesters. You're the best police chief this city has ever had, that's for sure. The guy they had before you was a drunk. He ran the department into the ground."

I hate it when people, I instinctively dislike, say things that I agree with. I kept my mouth shut and looked down at the laces on my white and blue Nike shoes.

"I'll tell you what," he said with a rub on my back that made me feel uncomfortable about his sexual orientation. "When you get some free time, I would really like to talk to you about some things."

Porky dug into his shirt pocket and produced a glossy multi-colored business card with his picture printed in the corner of the card. I took the little piece of cardboard and feigned great interest as he turned and waddled in the same general direction as the vanishing Marla.

"Give me a call, okay?" Porky waved and thankfully disappeared into the crowd. The card read "Randall K. Anderson—Entrepreneur." I wondered if "entrepreneur" was French for "obnoxious shithead" and dropped the card between two cases of artificial diet lemonade soda. I decided that I would call him just as soon as I finished discovering a cure for the common cold or won the lottery…whichever highly unlikely event came first.

Our official host, the City Manager, was still nowhere to be seen. Kandi Maldonado, who had a very loosely defined job in city government, was standing near the sliding glass patio door talking to Renee Stark, the Internal Auditor. Kandi's official title was "Inter-Governmental Affairs Officer." The only "inter-governmental affair" she actually did was muff diving between Renee's legs every chance she got. Kandi was easily six feet tall and she towered over the rather smallish Renee as they stood side by side. I wondered just how many other people in the crowd knew about Kandi and Renee. Their love affair burned hot and cold, it appeared. The flame seemed to depend on some kind of weird hormonal surges that Kandi manifested through all types of odd behaviors. Her signals were positively epileptic at times.

Many months before, Billy had forwarded me a copy of an officer's report on a routine domestic disturbance call that he thought would be of interest to me. This particular report was special only because the participants in the lover's quarrel were Kandi and Renee.

A domestic call is a real pain in the butt for any police officer. It was even more of a pain because of a mandatory arrest policy that the city had developed before my arrival in Wichita. The policy was based on some university egghead's theory that if you arrested someone at the scene of every family fight or lover's spat; it would prevent the situation from escalating into violence and deter future disturbances. Every street police officer in America knew that the theory was bull shit. Invariably, just as soon as you started to arrest one of the combatants, the other one would turn on you. Even though only minutes before they may have been getting the holy crap beat out of them by their hubby, the battered wife would usually jump on your back and scream, "You son of a bitch, you can't arrest Bubba. I love him!" So much for protecting the innocent.

Due to the outcry from feminist groups, we had initiated a similar mandatory arrest program in Dallas. We immediately found that the numbers of arrests overwhelmed even our substantial resources in the bigger city. There just were not enough police officers to handle the other types of 911 calls while we were booking the "Battlin' Bickerson" families. The jails soon became so full that the sheriff had to stack the prisoners two deep on cots. The courts were backlogged years with these misdemeanor cases and the judges were so pissed-off that they refused to convict anybody. It was a major mess of the first order.

Even the feminists were not happy. We soon discovered that over half of all the arrests for domestic violence were women. Someone forgot to guess that the women were often the ones who threw the first punch or slammed the coffee table with the fireplace poker.

Kandi had been assigned as the City Manager's coordinator for Wichita's "Domestic Violence" program long before my arrival. At my first meeting on the proposed new procedures, she announced an estimate that about four hundred arrests would occur each year in Wichita. I took one look at the population of the city, which exceeded three hundred thousand, and the size of the police department and knew that she was terribly wrong in her estimate. I bluntly told Kandi that she was nuts if she thought that there would be only one additional arrest a day on average.

Apparently, questioning her sanity was the wrong thing to do. Kandi began a series of bizarre gyrations which included uncontrolled facial twitches, eyes rolling back in their sockets and the appearance of foam around her mouth. After I announced that we should call an ambulance, she recovered sufficiently to sputter that I was obviously from too big of a city and did not understand the type of people who lived in Wichita.

Maybe not, but I damn sure understood family fights and had my fill of them in the federal housing projects of West Dallas. There, we knew that we could not keep a man and woman from fighting any more than we could keep them from continuing to produce babies when they could not support the ones they already had. We just tried to keep them from killing each other as best we could.

We often times resorted to techniques which were not taught at the police academy. This included divorcing them right there on the spot and dividing up the property. No lawyers, no judges, no written decrees; just a simple ceremony handed down from one Dallas police officer to another. The process was very effective in dealing with semi-illiterate people who needed immediate judicial relief and expected the authority of the police to be used to solve all of their problems.

"Partner, you go out to the car and get the official book," my first training officer ordered. I dutifully retrieved the city issued map book of all the public streets and alleys in Dallas. It helped us find our way to calls in the often twisting and changing maze of roadways and new construction.

"Now Jimmy Joe, you and Betty Ann come on over here and put your hand on my badge. No, no, none of that yelling or I'll have to put somebody in jail," my trainer would direct.

"OK, partner, you got the official book?" He would ask and I would nod solemnly.

"Hold it here beside me. Okay. Jimmy Joe, put your left hand on my badge here on my shirt, see? Betty Ann, you put your left hand on top of Jimmy's here. No, Betty Ann, your other left hand. That's better. Now both of you raise your right hand and hold it up straight. Okay."

All during his often practiced speech, I marveled at my partner's judicial posture. He was a regular Judge Wapner of the "People's Court". It was all I could do to keep from busting out laughing and rolling on the floor.

"By the authority invested in me by the City of Dallas, the great State of Texas, and the grand high chief of police; I do hereby declare this here marriage null and void. Endibus, fightibus, nowibus." The bastardized Latin mumbo jumbo was always a great touch. It sounded so legal.

"Let no man put asunder what the law has resolved today. Amen," he said in his best Billy Graham voice.

An obvious wave of relief would usually appear on both of the weary spouse's faces. Suddenly, it seemed as if the weight of the world had been lifted from their shoulders.

"Now, Jimmy Joe, you get the stuff here that's just yours and you go. You don't get no furniture or nothin'. That's hers. You get your clothes and the car to go to work in and everything else is hers. That's my decree. Okay?" My partner would be rapidly wrapping up the bogus ceremony as I retrieved the "holy" book of maps. He sounded like a used car salesman fast talking his way to closing a deal on a Hyundai that leaked oil.

The settlement was almost always successful. On rare occasions, we would receive another call back to the same dreary apartment a few days later to re-marry the couple because they had kissed and made up. That was the way the world worked in simpler times.

But not in the more refined and researched world of the present. I estimated that there would be a minimum of four thousand additional domestic violence arrests each year in Wichita, and a possible maximum of up to eight thousand more arrests, if the new policy went into effect. Hearing this, Kandi went into her cyanide poison victim act again. Her theatrics won out and we were forced to launch the program based on her estimates. In other words, no additional officers or resources were provided to implement the new policy.

The first year we made over six thousand domestic violence arrests in Wichita under the new program. The biggest irony was that one of those included Ms. Kandi Maldonado herself.

When two young officers responded to a 911 call at Kandi's apartment they found both Renee and Kandi drunk out of their skulls. Both women were all scratched up like they had mated with a barrel cactus. Renee was clothed in a tee shirt and nothing else, demanding the car keys to her Volvo so she could drive home. Kandi sported an ugly black eye where Renee's knee had clipped her under the covers. Kandi was refusing to give up the car keys because her "wife" was too drunk to drive, so she told the officers.

When the officers found out that both of the women were city employees, they called their supervisor. The sergeant in turn called the Watch Commander, who naturally notified the Duty Chief.

We developed a system where each one of my three deputy chiefs rotated being on call each month. That way, there was always a high ranking command grade officer who could be summoned for serious incidents after normal office hours. On this night, as fate would have it, Pete Gant had the duty assignment and as usual he could not make a decision. Pondering what to do with the "Ruff and Fluff" twins, Pete called me at home at three a.m.

"Don't treat them any different than you would any other domestic call, Pete," I instructed, "You know the policy. Hook 'em and book 'em."

Pete reluctantly did as he was ordered. His butt hole was so tight from fear of retaliation from the City Manager that for a week afterwards you could not have driven a ten penny nail up his ass with a sledgehammer.

No one was surprised when the domestic violence charge was quietly dismissed by the municipal court for "L.O.P.—Lack of Prosecution." A nervous judge, practicing the time honored criminal justice tradition of "C.Y.A." or "Cover Your Ass", ordered that both Kandi and Renee pay a small fine for littering. The alternate charge stemmed from Renee dumping the kitty litter box over the apartment balcony during the fight. That way, the appearance that justice had been served was in place should any nosy news reporter uncover the real cat fight a week later. Thinking ahead, the judge reasoned that his resolution would also apply if a cat turd was suddenly found floating in the apartment swimming pool by the health department.

I kept a copy of the report as a testament to the efficiency of the American criminal justice system and in case I ever decided to write my memoirs. Occasionally, I would leave a copy of the highlighted report laying on my desk whenever Fluff or Ruff was dispatched to my office with another goofy instruction from the manager.

As I spied on Kandi and Renee doing their best to act normal, I heard Marla yell over the crowd noise, "Screw you Randy!"

She turned and stomped toward the front entrance by the overpriced gift shop. The fat businessman faced toward the crowd and grinned sheepishly.

"It's a female thing. You know, raging hormones," he declared. I joined everyone in the room in a loud groan of righteous indignation at his political incorrectness.

"Chief, you can't sit over here in the corner by yourself." Kandi had caught me trying to be inconspicuous and used her long legs to cross the crowded room. She completely ignored the "Randy and Marla Show" and some of the off duty police officers who were staring at her.

"Where's your pretty wife tonight?" Kandi rubbed it in as she glanced at the cheese dip.

"She won't be able to make it, Kandi," I said truthfully. We locked eyes for a moment knowing that the other would give no quarter in a fight to see who would be on top. She broke the staring contest first and smiled.

"Well, you know, mingle, mingle, mingle," Kandi fluttered her two bird-like hands in the air and stalked off with the distinctive rustle that her nylon panty hose made when her thighs rubbed together under her pleated skirt.

The party was starting to pick up steam. Someone had broken out a jam box that was tuned to Howlin' Hank's afternoon radio show of old country music. Hank was playing some seriously ancient stuff like Bob Wills and The Texas Playboys, Johnny Western and even Ernest Tubb moaning about "Walkin' The Floor Over You." The music brought back memories of sitting in front of a black and white television watching these characters in real life. I remembered that they all performed on a show broadcast "Live from Panther Hall" in Fort Worth, Texas. It was my hometown of the fifties and sixties. Officially proclaimed by the city fathers as "Where the West Begins", the Fort Worth of my youth was quite similar, in many ways, to the Wichita of the present.

If there was only some "Old Crow" in the punch bowl my dad would love this kind of party with its hillbilly music and loud talk, I thought aimlessly. Personally, I hated this socializing crap. I much preferred my own company than being around people. Any people. The best part of these engagements was the end. Attending was like hitting myself in the head with a hammer because it would feel so good when the pain stopped. For no reason that I could think of, I decided to stay just a little while longer and make a getaway by bending the bars on the restroom window and sliding to freedom on a roll of toilet paper. It seemed like a fool proof escape plan.

Employee parties were usually pretty crummy anyway. Water Department ditch diggers, with long hair and tattoos, never quite seemed to mix well with the spinsterly library clerks for some reason. Maybe it was the self-medication that some of those guys practiced on and off the job. Combine an assortment of mind altering chemicals, readily available on the street, with muscles built from swinging a heavy pick all day and you could come up with an interesting genetic mutation. Add in the fact that the mechanics from the city garage had a flat bed trailer with tubs of iced beer in the parking lot and this party had all the potential to be a mini-riot before it was over.

The annual "Employee Appreciation Week" was always a farce anyway. It was as if a few days a year of trying to be nice to the whole city work force would make up for 360 days of deviously trying to screw them in every way possible. Not even the dumbest sewer worker bought that bill of goods and the result was a complete waste of time. The city never seemed to run out of innovative ways to create resentment in its work force.

About once each year the City Manager would find himself needing a few thousand dollars for that extra special trip that he or the Mayor wanted to take to Cancun or Paris. The novel solution was to conveniently arrange for the finance computers to go down. This, of course, delayed the scheduled paychecks to all city employees for a few days while the technicians pretended to work feverishly to fix the problem. In the meantime, the multi-million dollar city payroll continued to accrue daily interest until sufficient "windfall" funds were credited to the city's massive account. Then the finance computers would miraculously be repaired and everyone would receive their paychecks a few days late with the sincere apologies of Tad Roadly, of course, for the minor inconvenience.

It was amazing how that happened over and over and no one seemed to care. It was even more amazing that no one noticed that the City Council adopted places like Cancun, Mexico and Paris, France as our cultural exchange "Sister Cities" so they could justify trips to these fun locales on official city business. I wondered why they did not adopt some prehistoric dump like Haiti, or maybe Istanbul, until I came to my senses and figured out the scam. I guess seeing the sights of a Turkish prison was not their idea of visiting a garden spot worthy to be considered Wichita's cultural equal. I was not so sure.

Another tricky aspect of employee appreciation parties was that the spouses of the employees were invited as well. This often caused some awkward moments between legitimate mates and office romance partners. There was so much sperm flying between fellow employees that meeting the "other woman" or the "other man", face to face, was guaranteed to make for at least a few tense moments during each get together. It always confirmed my belief that nature intended for each sex to have multiple spouses. If every man or woman had to put up with five or six mates of the opposite gender at home each night there would be no energy left to get into trouble. It seemed clear to me that if each man was required to keep a whole house full of women sexually satisfied, it would be highly unlikely to find that man out trying to nail some homely clerk in the supply closet on his lunch hour.

The Dallas Police Department's Planning and Research Division was blessed to have the all time queen of the lunch time two step. Her name was Rae Rae. She was a twice divorced secretary with cotton candy for brains and a body chiseled from marble. At least three times each week, Rae Rae would go to lunch with a male co-worker and return to work an hour later wearing different clothes. The evidence was so air tight that even the FBI could not have screwed up the case. Columbo could have figured it out blindfolded and with a hangover.

Being married to a police officer tested any marriage without the temptations of normal birds and bees stuff. Police wives usually fit into one of two groups; those that trusted their husbands implicitly and those that knew damn well that the son of a bitch was screwing everything in sight. I was lucky. My wife was in the first group and for some unknown reason I was never really tempted to cheat. Peggy was bright, funny, and loved me unconditionally. I do not know why my wife stayed with me through all of the trials and tribulations that had come our way in both cities. The stress often weighed just as heavy on her as it did on me. I was convinced that had I been my wife, I would have left my worthless carcass years ago.

One wild Saturday night when I was a Dallas lieutenant, my troops and I chased a stolen Camaro over half of the county at speeds in excess of a hundred miles per hour. Two men and a woman in the Chevy took turns shooting at us with a pistol and a shotgun every time we got a little too close to them. One of my officers lost control of his squad car and it flipped about three times just like on TV. Fortunately, he landed right side up in a marshy section of the Trinity River bottoms and was uninjured except for a compressed spine and a bruised ego.

We kept chasing the Camaro even after half of our flashing red lights and other emergency equipment on our cars burned out. Like the Challenger space shuttle, the government also bought our equipment on low bid. Just as my own car's electronic siren finally died a screeching death, the fabled Texas Highway Patrol blew the bad guys off the road just north of Denton. I mean that the troopers literally "blew" the Camaro from the highway with two clips from a fully automatic M-16 rifle. It was messy, but very effective. The Highway Patrol guys had a reputation for being short on smarts but long on armament. Finding a low yield nuclear device in the trunk of one of their squad cars would not have surprised me.

An hour after being involved in that incident, I was still feeling the pounding rush of adrenaline and the angry feeling of being scared to death. I was soon off duty and drove home in a daze to sit at my own kitchen table and ponder the meaning of life. Peggy was trying to show me the new wallpaper she bought. She began complaining that she had tried unsuccessfully to use the broken Weedeater again without success. The very same lawn trimmer that I had faithfully promised to fix two weeks earlier. Garden tool repair was never my strong suit.

Mentally, I was still chasing armed criminals bent on my destruction at warp speed, thirty miles away and in a different dimension. My mind was nowhere near my kitchen when Peggy interrupted my thoughts. In a flash, I charged out into the darkened back yard and took out my anxiety and fear on the Weedeater by beating it against a brick retaining wall that surrounded a giant oak tree. When I returned to the kitchen I felt oddly calm and serene. I handed Peggy the only recognizable piece of Weedeater that remained; about six inches of green plastic handle.

"Here," I said quietly. "It shouldn't cause you a problem ever again." I went to bed and Peggy never mentioned the incident. I guess I really showed that Weedeater who was boss.

Now that Peggy was sick, I painfully regretted all of the bad days I must have given her.

Mainly, I regretted December 7th. It was not because December 7th was the day that Japan had bombed Pearl Harbor in 1941. I was not old enough to be pissed off at the sneaky bastards for trying to take Hawaii by armed force. The Japs wound up owning the damned island anyway by just buying all the available real estate after the war. No, I remembered December 7th as the last Christmas party that Peggy and I attended together. The annual "Fraternal Organization of Police Christmas Party" had been well planned and attended. I was always sincerely honored to be invited by the line officer's union to attend the holiday function. Most police chiefs did not have that kind of rapport with the rank and file. Despite my occasional disagreements with the union president, the individual officers insured that I received a special invitation each year. It was one package from the labor union that was not usually ticking or required the bomb squad's examination before I opened it.

On the occasion of the last Christmas party with the officers, I was wanting to let off some steam and have a really good time for a change. The party would be limited to other police officers and their wives so I did not feel like if I dribbled mustard on my lap it would be on the front page of the newspaper. In other words, I wanted to be a normal person for just one night and not the police chief.

On the night of the party, Peggy was oddly quiet and irritable. I checked and the new Weedeater was hanging unmolested in the garage. When I slid up behind her and touched her shoulder while she was putting on her party dress, Peggy almost jumped out of her skin. I gave her what I thought was a tender hug and she recoiled like a forty four magnum. I coyly suggested a little roll in the hay before the party and Peggy gave me a look that would have melted the iceberg that ruined the Titanic's paint job. It was completely out of character for my usually bubbly, ever affectionate wife.

"What's wrong with you?" I asked with a complete absence of tact or diplomacy.

Of course, the blunt question was the absolute worst thing I could have said at that exact moment. I am really good at saying the wrong thing sometimes. Peggy whirled and promptly informed me that all I thought of was sex and that her life did not revolve around my testosterone levels. She ended all hopes of a negotiated cuddle by proclaiming that there was absolutely nothing wrong with her at all and that it was me who was all screwed up. I could not truthfully disagree with that analysis and I did not even try.

Things did not get any better once we were at the party. Peggy struggled to keep up appearances while sitting at the table with several patrol officers and their wives. The chilly atmosphere caused those around the table to struggle while trying to figure out how to act around the chief and his wife. It was awkward to say the least.

The highlight of the party was supposed to be a homemade video tape provided by one of the officer's wives. The film chronicled a large number of us attempting to clear a public street of about five hundred abortion protesters during the previous summer's outbreak of clinic blockades. The tape began by showing us bodily lifting protesters and, on my orders, none too gently throwing them in the back of yellow rental trucks. The whole room broke into loud cheers when the tape showed the looks of obvious surprise on the faces of the protesters. In the minds of most police officers, God intended us to handle civil disturbances the way it was taught at the Herman Goering School of Riot Control.

When the same tape showed me vainly attempting to pick up a heifer that probably outweighed me by fifty pounds, the crowd collapsed into hysterics. I could not seem to find a handle on the heavily perspiring woman who went completely limp as she had no doubt been trained to do in protester school. When the video showed me finally losing my grip on her sweaty wrists and falling flat on my butt, the crowd went wild with hoots and catcalls. I loved every second of my embarrassing failure that was forever immortalized on video tape. Peggy looked like she was having a root canal procedure without anesthesia.

I tried to change the mood by accepting the union president's offer to sing the first karaoke song. The sound system was set up by a professional dee jay that the union had hired for the night. It was brutal when I sang along to "Bad Man Jose", without much success in sounding like Jay or any of the Americans who had originally recorded the song in the sixties. Despite my off-key familiarity with the tune from our high school days, Peggy just stared at the wall. But when I broke into "Stand By Me", I thought Peggy would surely lighten up. She simply looked at me like great globs of goobers were flowing from my nostrils. When I finished the song, there were great cheers of relief that the end to my singing career had finally arrived. Glancing once again at Peggy's angry expression, I checked to see if my testicles had somehow become exposed and quietly returned to our table.

"Peggy, are you okay?" I asked.

"I have a headache. I want to go home," was all she said.

I confess that Peggy's demeanor did not sit very well with me. I was having a good time for the first time in a long time and beginning to feel like just one of the boys. Peggy wanted to spoil my fun and go home to a cold house and an obviously icy trend in our relationship.

"Okay, in a little while, okay?" I pleaded.

"No, now," she said sternly

"Damnit," I hissed. "Let's go."

On the ride home, the atmosphere inside the car was like driving in the back of an ice cream truck. Peggy's demeanor was confusing and frightening. "'De farther we drove, 'de meaner she got," my Louisiana friend, Dale Williams, would have said.

When we arrived at the baby sitter's house, Peggy stalked up to the door to pick up our daughter, Terri. She paid the neighbor girl, who we used on our infrequent nights out, and paused for a moment to button Terri's coat.

I sat sullenly in the car and listened to the crackle of the police radio. It was a crystal clear night. I picked out a bright star and stared at it.

"My job sucks. I'm getting old. I'm stuck in the middle of nowhere and now my wife is miserable around me," I said out loud to no one. "I really have a miserable life, God."

At three o'clock that morning the phone rang. It was my brother back home in Texas telling me that our mother had died of a sudden heart attack. Not my mom, I thought. Surely not "my" mom. I knew that she had not been feeling well lately and had developed some kind of strange skin rash that the doctors were treating with steroids; but people do not die from skin rashes, do they? Whatever the cause, the loss hit me hard.

At the burial service in the small country cemetery in Texas, I looked over and saw Peggy kneeling underneath a tree among the crooked headstones. She was bleeding profusely from the nose. In our twenty years of marriage, I had never before seen Peggy with a nose bleed.

Three weeks and six doctors later, her brain tumor was finally diagnosed. The lump was the size of a lemon when it was removed during an eighteen hour emergency surgery at the Mayo Clinic. No other hospital we tried would even attempt the procedure. The time was during what most people called the "Christmas Holidays". I called it agony. Our worst fears were soon realized. The tumor was cancerous and it was highly malignant.

When I complained to that bright star on December 7th, I did not know the meaning of a miserable life. I just thought I did. I often wished that I could turn back the hands of time, but I could not. Life went on and Peggy struggled to recover from the operation and the devastation of her illness.

Sitting on the boxes of cheap drinks inside Botanica and thinking about Peggy did nothing to improve my mood. I jumped down from my perch and sought the quieter confines of the office area to use the telephone. The closed door to the tiny office was marked "No Admittance", which I promptly ignored due to my high exalted position. I wearily collapsed at the cheap metal desk and reached for the phone. The desk top was a mess. On the left hand side was a half eaten sardine and apple butter sandwich and what appeared to be an unfinished biology experiment that had once been an edible substance from the garden center's cafeteria. A small television and a VCR huddled together on the particle board credenza. I could not resist opening the top desk drawer in the hopes of finding clues to locating Jimmy Hoffa or Amelia Earhart. Instead, I located a rather worn looking plastic vibrator and a tube of KY jelly. I imagined hearing the owner saying "Damn, I wonder where I could have left that thing?"

Deciding that I had done enough snooping, I quietly closed the rusty drawer and used my credit card to dial the EconoLodge in Rochester, Minnesota. Situated near the Mayo Clinic, this low price motel was Peggy's favorite refuge when she went to the Mayo for treatment. I envisioned how lonely and afraid she must be staying in that small room tonight. She always made reservations at the same location when she was receiving radiation, or other outpatient treatments, at the various hospitals that comprised the massive Mayo Medical Complex. Peggy was a creature of habit with simple tastes and a loyalty to friends that was unwavering. On one of her first trips back to the Mayo after her initial surgery, Peggy had happened by the EconoLodge and made friends with the night desk clerk who took the time just talk to her. The few moments of conversation was all it took for her to want to forever repay the motel for the clerk's hospitality.

The motel was a clean and safe harbor, in a sea of uncertainty, for a lot of very frightened patients who could not go home. I could only imagine how terrifying it must be to face those demons alone. I ached to be there with my wife, but the damned job would not allow me any time for an absence. I was convinced that if I were to be gone for more than a few days, the manager would use my absence as an excuse to change the name on my door. If that happened, we would have no insurance to pay the incredibly enormous medical bills that were piling up on my desk at home. I once considered just resigning my position to be with my wife and paying a few hundred dollars a month on the bills from our meager savings. It did not take me long to realize that I would have to live to be about a hundred and forty to payoff the debt we would accumulate without insurance. Not counting interest. Living to be a hundred and forty did not seem very likely to me, considering the damage that the stress of the job was no doubt doing to my heart muscle and other vital organs.

The usual night clerk, an elderly gentleman named Ted, had adopted Peggy like she was his own daughter. He took special pains to look after her to make sure she was doing okay. The phone rang until a young female voice, that I assumed was Ted's replacement on his night off, advised me that Peggy was not in her room. The stand-in clerk sounded far too chipper to match my mood. I left a message with the girl to tell Peggy that I had called. At least it was not an answering machine. I hated answering machines, even my own.

When I hung up the phone, I glanced around the small office. In the straight back chairs next to the wall were a stack of women's purses. The bags had obviously been casually tossed there by the people who had arrived early to set up the party. That was Wichita for you. The owners did not even lock the door to protect their own property. I immediately recognized Kandi Maldonado's enormous red bag. It also doubled as her briefcase at work. Sticking out of the bag's top was a stack of colorful post cards. I could not resist the temptation to see who would be sending Kandi post cards. The "All Girls Choir from Topeka", maybe?

Each post card bore a different date on its cancellation stamp and all had pictures of some less than monumental tourist site in Wichita. They all had the same message and signature.

"Kandi, I love you. Come back to me. John." Kind of a reverse "Dear John" letter, I thought.

John Maldonado was Kandi's ex-husband. Currently a non-recovering alcoholic, he had been a rather successful attorney around town at one time. John had won a big class action lawsuit against the city, and the previous police chief, for discriminating against minorities who applied to be police officers. The settlement was well into seven figures, of which John netted a cool five hundred thousand American dollars from Wichita's taxpayers. It was never clear on which point his marriage with Kandi split; his attempt to drink half a million dollars away in alcohol or Kandi's penchant for vaginas and clitori. I did not know if John knew about Kandi and Renee. Quite frankly, I did not give a hoot one way or the other.

I did hope that John did not try to come to tonight's party. It had been a long day and I did not relish it taking anymore weird turns. I laid back in the creaking swivel desk chair and tried to relax for a moment. My thoughts raced from Peggy to tomorrow's meeting with Mel. I was desperate to turn the Wichita Police Department into a first class organization. It was as if my own reputation depended on it, which it obviously did. To accomplish my self appointed mission caused Mel and I to fight on just about every issue. I had so far survived, but it was often not very pretty and always left me bruised and scarred. There was no question that the Manager was shopping for a new police chief. It was just a matter of time before he struck. I was trying my best to postpone the inevitable.

The Manager probed and plotted for a good excuse to replace me. At first, I tried to accept my ultimate demise in Wichita as a good thing. Maybe I could get out of this town and find another city manager that had not been the poster child for the Hitler Youth Corps. As usual, my over inflated ego and natural stubbornness just would not let me lie down and take what was coming. "Saint Rod", the patron saint of hopelessly futile gestures, would not walk away from a bad relationship even when I knew that it would be the best move to make in the long run.

In the early spring, we received notice that the "National Anti-Abortion Organization, Incorporated" was going to target Wichita for a week long series of demonstrations and clinic blockades. I inquired from Tim as to the extent of our officer's riot control and civil disturbance training. It did not surprise me to learn that the sum total of their previous instruction in this specialized area of law enforcement training was exactly zero.

It had been twenty years since the last Wichita police chief had to deal with a riot. The last spontaneous outbreak of civil disobedience consisted of hippies trashing a southside park. As is usually the case when serious situations are initiated by seeming trivial matters, the riot was caused by overzealous enforcement of parking regulations on a quiet Sunday afternoon. The chief proceeded to order his men to form a line abreast and march with nightsticks and shotguns at the ready toward the rock and bottle throwing long hairs. The chief must have thought he saw the tactic being used so successfully at a place called Kent State.

As the thin line of troops forced the hippies to retreat to the bank of a muddy creek in the rear of the park, the flower children were faced with a choice. They could escape the police by diving into the creek and risk glowing in the dark for the rest of their lives due to the pollution from the Vantage Chemical Company up stream; or they could turn and kick the asses of the heavily outnumbered officers. The rioters correctly guessed that the officers would not dare use their shotguns or pistols on half naked teenagers and turned viciously into the fight.

By the time the smoke cleared, about forty police officers required hospitalization and several squad cars had been overturned and set on fire. It was a classic bonehead mistake of crowd control. The FBI still taught the debacle in their police management classes all over America. It was cited as an example of the absolute worst tactic to use in a civil disturbance. If you pushed a rabbit into a corner where there was no way out, the cuddly Easter bunny would turn into a Tasmanian devil and fight ferociously to its last breath. People, no matter how docile or amiable, were the same. It was a good lesson to learn in life, as well.

I immediately began searching through all of my old lesson plans on civil disturbance training from my time as the Police Academy Director in Dallas. In short order, we had put together a brief, but hopefully effective, training program for the entire department. I did not want us to be on the Cable News Network getting our tails kicked by a bunch of little old ladies in tennis shoes. This would not be acceptable. Conversely, I also did not want our department to be perceived as a bunch of wild-eyed, club wielding Neanderthals in the eyes of the world. We were slowly building a good police department in Wichita, but the officers were not trained for what I knew was coming. After all the years in Dallas, dealing with everything from Ku Klux Klan marches to the Republican National Convention, I was the only member of the Wichita Police Department with any formal training in the basics of crowd control. I was determined to teach as much as I knew in the short time available.

At the Wichita Police Academy, we broke each class into two sessions. The morning session was textbook classroom fundamentals on the basic mission, philosophy of our plan, crowd psychology, and departmental organization during the protests. In the afternoon, we all adjourned to the drill field where we practiced, practiced, practiced. We worked on the fundamentals of getting into and out of the basic crowd control formations. The formations would allow us to safely keep order in a chaotic and highly emotional environment.

The City Manager stayed away from me completely during this time. He used my temporary absence from City Hall to seize the opportunity to cut ten police commander positions from the next year's police budget. The Manager replaced them with less expensive civilian administrative positions or eliminated their funding entirely. The bastard knew that I was too busy trying to prepare an entire department for an impending disaster. I had no time to pay enough attention to what he was doing behind my back. The Manager was shrewdly betting that our preparations to keep his city from burning to the ground would prevent me from organizing the kind of political coalition that I would need to fight his stupid meddling in our organizational structure. He was right.

Threats to bomb certain hospitals and clinics where abortions were performed gave me cause to initiate a special covert aspect of our plan. I had our Intelligence Section begin monitoring the cellular telephone calls and open radio conversations of some of the more radical protest groups that were forming in the city. It was all perfectly legal. As a surprise bonus, the detectives also intercepted Mel Michaels and Bob Showalter talking on their car phones about our "Storm Troopers" and how silly we looked marching around in riot gear. Our two leaders agreed that they would blame the whole thing on the police chief if there was any kind of embarrassing incident.

The detectives in the Intelligence Section were shocked at our manager's lack of appreciation for what we were trying to accomplish. Unfortunately, I was not. It did not take long for the whole department to know just how much support we did not have at the top. The written transcripts of Mel and Bob's conversations only made me sick. It was impossible to keep the information a secret within the organization. Preventing the department from mutinying was like trying to ice skate on Jello. The best I could do was to insure that our preparations continued unabated.

At the beginning of each practice session on the dusty field, the officers always looked like a gaggle of left footed geese. Some looked like they were trying to give birth while standing up. They were initially awkward in trying to form the simplest lines and riot control movements that they had seen drawn on the classroom chalk board only a few hours before. As they got a little better with their footwork, we introduced as much stress into the exercise as possible. This was important to test their emotional control and to prepare them for what they might hear and experience in a real riot situation. I had our department's helicopter fly over to make noise, kick up dirt and grass from the battered field and drop smoke grenades to simulate tear gas. The troops were impressed with the realistic exercises and told me that it was the best training that they had ever received. Almost all of them, that is.

One overweight female sergeant clearly did not want to be out of her air conditioned office in the Crime Prevention Unit. Since she usually wore only civilian dresses in her non-stressful assignment, the sergeant broke one of her fingernails trying to stuff her growing butt back into her police uniform for the mandatory training sessions. She also complained that she was offended that I had called her a "girl" during the simulation exercises on the drill field.

She was almost right. I had actually yelled at the whole mixed, male and female, class to "come on girls, let's get in line and do this right!" This seemed like a pretty tame stress inducer at the time. In fact, it served to be a good motivator in response to finding that some of my troops had problems chewing gum and marching at the same time.

Curiously, she did not complain about the same thing when the instructors were simulating crowd noise and yelling that the class all marched like the Rockettes. I guess the chorus line at Radio City Music Hall was more socially acceptable than being called a "girl". In any case, I exercised my command prerogative and removed her from the operational plan because she clearly could not handle even the least amount of stress that the assignment was sure to produce. I shuddered to think how her sensibilities would have been assaulted by what she was likely to be called in a real riot situation.

Ordinarily, the sergeant's removal from the demands of having to be a part of the dirty and thankless task would not have hurt her feelings. Trying to keep two opposing sides of a highly charged social debate from killing each other, in the name of "pro this" or "pro that", did not suit her desires in life. What really irritated the sergeant was that the other officers ragged her so much about not being able to cut it during training. She was truly embarrassed by their kidding and complained to fellow perennial whiner, Deputy Chief Pete Gant, that I had started the harassment of her by calling her a "girl".

When he told me about it, I broke out laughing. "Pete, tell her to file a formal grievance if she doesn't like it. But she's not going to cause an international incident, on world wide television, by shooting some poor nitwit in the crowd who calls her a bad name or makes her cry," I instructed.

The pressure was enormous and building. Thanks to our radio phone intercepts, I already knew that my career depended on our accomplishing the mission without major problems. I forgot the episode until my "loyal" deputy chief bypassed me with her grievance and hand delivered the document to the City Manager in record time.

The Manager quickly instructed his legal eagles, and the Personnel Director, that this was a "very serious charge" to be looked into right away. I was in stitches until it was leaked to the press that the police chief had been charged with "sexual harassment" by a female subordinate. There were no details released, just speculation and innuendo. Livid at the potential implications and damage that such a wild charge could generate, I contacted the City Attorney for advice on how to squash the rumors. He timidly advised me that I could not discuss the case publicly because the state law made any information about such a charge completely confidential. I said "bullshit" to that piece of great advice and wrote off the City Attorney as no help whatsoever.

I called the Equal Employment Office in Washington and the city's own hired consultant who conducted training on workplace harassment issues. They all thought I was making it up as some kind of preposterous "what if" academic debate. The image of Clarence Thomas in the press each day and night with his "Long Dong Silver" charges by Anita Hill was dredged up and applied to my situation by the media. Due to the press coverage, half of Wichita thought that Clarence and I were partners in some type of crime against humanity. I almost felt compelled to find an alibi for the Lindbergh baby kidnapping thing, as well. I began to hope that Peggy would testify that I was in a sixth grade history class with her when JFK was assassinated.

The City Manager finally called me for a rare meeting in his office about the charges. I hid my voice activated mini-tape recorder in my shirt pocket for protection against what he might later say about the meeting. At the outset, the Manager said he had ruled that I was guilty of sexual harassment and that he would be forced to discipline me. I knew what that meant and turned immediately on the offensive. I surprised him by presenting the written statements that I had obtained from the recognized experts who had dismissed the charge as "ridiculous". It did not hurt that all the statements recommended that the manager issue a "get a life" directive to the sergeant and announce the real facts of the incident. The sergeant, by the way, was now amazed at how much stink she had stirred and wanted to forget the whole thing.

When the Manager seemed to persist in his decision to find me at fault, I told him that I would fight in the press with the truth. We would see what the public really thought about all of his "serious charges" comments when they found out that the accusation was that a female had been called a "girl" and no one claimed I had my pants unzipped or attempted to molest their cocker spaniel.

"Who's gonna have egg on their face, Mr. Manager, when the public finds out that you have fed the mystery of all of this media firestorm because of a "get in line, girls" comment at a training session?" I charged. "They will want to know just what you have been smoking up here in your office and why you can't seem to have some balls for once and do the right thing without a bunch of political posturing."

The Manager countered that neither he nor I could comment because the facts of the incident were protected from public disclosure by Kansas law.

My face flushed and I instinctively turned to meet the challenge, telling him "Hide and watch, big guy".

The next thing I knew I was having an out of body experience, hovering over my chair and watching myself launch into a red haze tirade.

"To Hell with the Kansas state statutes about privacy! What about my rights not to be falsely accused and see my name and photograph in the newspaper every morning? Thanks to this being blown out of proportion by your actions and comments, some people are ranking me right next to Ghengis Khan and the Boston Strangler as a friend of women. This isn't the least bit funny anymore and if you haven't noticed, I am not laughing right now."

It was all so insane, but my blood was up. I could feel a good Weedeater session coming right there in his office using his scrawny neck as the handle. I would hand his secretary, Maria, what was left of Mr. Michaels on my way out the door, I fantasized.

When I did leave, we had accomplished nothing definitive. Three days later, my own secretary, Suzie, brought me an official letter from the Manager. It was mailed from nine floors above my office and included a formal reprimand from "his highness", written in complicated legalese and insulting language. It took me less time to run up the nine flights of stairs than it did to open the envelope.

I barged right past Maria, who looked confused and a little sheepish after having typed the letter no doubt, and waved the offending note in the general direction of his desk.

"I won't take this kind of crap!" I stated with a definite bravado in my voice. "You either take this reprimand back or we'll fight in public and that's that."

I was wearing my uniform and noticed immediately that the Manager kept staring at the nine millimeter on my hip. I realized that I had unconsciously placed my right hand on the butt of the Smith and Wesson. I angrily crumpled the offending letter and tossed it from halfway across the room as I turned and stormed out.

The manager officially withdrew the reprimand the next day and I learned a valuable lesson. I could back the bastard down if I was in the right and had hard evidence to support my facts. The gun helped too.

The one thing that such episodes did was to destroy my own concept of working together as part of a winning team. When you realize that the people you work with are adversaries, as much as the criminals on the street, it is a lonely and empty feeling. There was no team in Wichita, no loyalty to a cause, no supportive assistance and not a shred of sanity in any of it. Just me alone. Being police chief under such circumstances was drudgery. Having to put up with Melvin Michaels made it all the more painful each day. Success to our great leader meant his satisfying his own personal agenda, whatever that was. It was not about making Wichita a better place to live or even saving the taxpayers money. Our mission as department heads was to put forth the least possible effort without creating any waves. That obviously made the City Manager feel like he was in control.

Typically, police chiefs want to be in control all of the time as well. Deep down, I thought Mel respected that quality in me, but he 'feared it too. His fear made him all the more dangerous and determined.

Thinking about my close brush with false accusations, I decided to make a get-away from the small office before some one accused me of stealing their KY jelly. It would be hard to beat that rap.

"Super Sleuth Seizes Slippery Substance", the headlines would read above a five by eight smiling file photo of yours truly. I rolled out of the rickety chair and noticed that my back was becoming stiff from the golf game in the cold. Back out in the hall, I heard J. Frank Wilson and the Cavaliers singing "The Last Kiss" on the jam box in the party room. It had become another favorite of mine since I once discovered J. Frank begging for quarters on a street corner near downtown Dallas. At least, that was the name the grizzled old hobo gave when I identified myself as a police officer and asked for his identification. I believed him when he showed me some faded newspaper clippings from a tattered leather wallet.

I gave him two dollars for the cheap wine that he craved and never forgot the lesson on just how far you could fall in life without much effort.

Returning to the party, I found Fire Chief Lopez exactly where I had left him. I scrounged up a beat up straight-backed chair and turned it around so the back was in front of my crotch as I sat down next to him.

He looked at me with sad eyes and said, "You're doing a good job, you know."

"Well, thanks, Richard," I blushed. "That means a helluva lot coming from you," I said sincerely. "I've got a meeting with the Manager tomorrow morning. Any ideas on what it might be about?"

Richard turned away from me and stared impassively at the party goers who were getting a little bit louder.

"Good luck. You know, of course, that you are not getting a lot of help from your command staff. I hear things in the elevators and around the halls. It's not good what people say behind your back," he quietly stated.

Richard was a friend. I knew that he would not tell me any more information because he would not want to violate his own code of what were private conversations and what were not. I respected him for his convictions. Last year, Richard was the defendant in a law suit filed against him by one of his female fire fighters. He was accused of discrimination for not providing separate women's bathrooms in each fire station in the city. Most of the fire stations had, of course, been built long before there was ever such a thing as a female fire fighter. Quietly, Richard suffered the public ridicule and took the blame for the oversight in the media. All the while, he kept secret a confidential memo that he had vainly written to the City Manager five years before.

In the memo, the fire chief pleaded for the budgetary funds he needed to remodel his fire stations to accommodate the inevitable hiring of female fire fighters. Naturally, Mel had turned down the request without comment. It was certainly not Richard's fault that the fire stations did not have the appropriate toilet facilities. He had read the writing on the bathroom wall, pun intended, and predicted the future perfectly. Our less than brave City Manager left his fire chief twisting in the wind of public opinion without so much as a simple "thank you" for taking all the heat. The newspaper ran an editorial cartoon of Richard with a hangman's noose around his neck and his own fire fighters continued to be unaware of their chief's battles on behalf of his troops. Those few of us who knew the real story shook our collective heads and felt betrayed.

"Thanks for the clue, Richard. Don't let the bastards grind you down either," I said.

I gripped the chair's back and rose in the manner of an old west gunfighter pushing himself away from the poker table for a quick draw. Unperturbed, I patted Richard on the shoulder and headed for the safety of my perch atop the cases of cheap soft drinks. Through the glass walls on one side of the room, I could see people slow dancing in the gardens.

Pete Gant was holding court in the middle of the big room. He wore his gold badge and thirty-eight revolver on the outside of his polo shirt so that everyone could see that he was something special. Next, he would begin telling war stories about the time he was the only motorcycle officer who refused to go out on strike. It was reference to when the police union called a "blue flu" epidemic decades ago during a continuing dispute over low wages. I always wondered how you could have a "blue flu" when the Wichita uniforms were brown and green. "Brown flu" sounded so much more serious, I thought. "Green flu" sounded positively prehistoric, like the wicked virus that caused the extinction of the dinosaurs.

Most of the guys at the party looked at Pete's antics without much thought to the motivation for his efforts. It was hard to keep from staring at the guy who was obviously showing off for all the women around him. He was constantly fondling the walnut grips of his four-inch pistol. Knowing the people at the party, I had to guess that each one of them already knew of Pete's reputation with their wives. Keeping it from happening was another thing altogether.

I dragged my stiffening body back up on the drink cases and watched the party roll on into the evening. I killed time by carefully scanning the women in the crowd for the largest set of hooters. This small concession to wandering from the straight and narrow world of police chiefdom was a safe allowance, I rationalized. My game seemed safe unless there were any mind readers in the crowd. I quickly decided that there were four finalists in my fantasy contest. The lucky winners included the wife of the Chamber of Commerce president and twins who worked in the Health Department.

The Chamber president's wife looked very interesting. She was about twenty years younger than her graying husband and much taller. Her auburn hair also automatically made her a candidate for the other fantasy contest I played from time to time. This, of course, was the elusive search for the true blonde or the true red head. Only pubic hair that could not be tinted by Lady Clairol would decide admittance into this very exclusive fantasy club. In over forty years of life, I had not certified one legitimate member.

The twins were another story. They were never absent from each other's sight or reach. It was positively uncanny how they were never apart. I could only imagine the delicate amount of psychological surgery that would be required to convince one to leave the other alone long enough to enjoy a few hours of wild, passionate sex in the arms of someone who was not a mirror image of themselves. Most men probably were capable of the sex part, but not the surgical separation of these twins at the pubic bone. Plan B would have to be taking on both twins at the same time, I decided. Nothing special in that thought, just the standard male sexual fantasy. Probably only a set of male twins had any remote possibility of finding out whether or not their well endowed breasts were complimented by large, round nipples or the small, hard kind.

I finally chose Marty Sims' wife, or ex-wife I should say, as my fantasy contest winner. Jana Sims was sitting alone in a group of comfortable looking chairs in the room's opposite corner.

The son of a wealthy Kansas wheat producer, Marty had once been a member of the Wichita Police Department until he became involved in what started out as a routine investigation of a trivial matter. Ultimately, he was caught lying to the Internal Affairs investigators to cover up a bone head failure to report being involved in a minor traffic accident. Instead of reporting the fender bender, Marty attempted to paint over the scratched bumper on his squad car with typing paper correction fluid.

The clumsy attempt at subterfuge would have probably netted young Mr. Sims a few days off without pay if he had just admitted it. In the "go for broke" gamble of a Wall Street tycoon, like his father, Marty turned the simple infraction into a capital crime by claiming that he absolutely did not do it. Unfortunately for Marty, the Records Division secretary, who handed over six bottles of the chalky white liquid to Marty, thought it an unusual request and made an entry to that effect in the divisional log. Even as poor a report writer as Officer Marty Sims was, he did not need six bottles of correction fluid, she reasoned.

Faced with the evidence, Marty resigned rather than be fired for a serious violation of the department's honor code. "A Wichita Police Officer does not lie, cheat, or steal; nor does he tolerate those who do," the code read. It was a simple code to live by and obviously written long before gender specific pronouns were deemed to be politically incorrect.

Since leaving the police department, Marty had become a successful businessman in his own right. He built and operated two huge, multi-screened movie theaters on each side of the city. The theaters specialized in not quite first run motion pictures. They packed in the movie goers at a couple of bucks a head for the no-frills screenings. Once inside, popcorn was three dollars a box and a hot dog cost an amount equal to the national debt of Nicaragua. Nonetheless, parents spent a small fortune sending their pre-teen and post pubescent adolescents to the movies at Marty's "Regal Theaters". The price was still cheaper than hiring a baby-sitter when mom and dad wanted to go out on the town or play hide the salami without junior barging in the bedroom at a pivotal moment.

Marty Sims and Kandi Maldonado were friends. They spent hours at Marty's theaters and driving around in his Lincoln Continental talking on his car phone to politicians in Topeka and elsewhere. Kandi was also fascinated by Marty's collection of firearms. Despite not being a police officer any longer, Marty seldom went anywhere without a pistol. He favored a big nickel plated Colt Python in .357 magnum caliber. Marty had actually been arrested once by the Kansas Highway Patrol for shooting at road signs with the big pistol. Luckily for Marty, he was still married at the time and his wife, who was a Sheriff's deputy, got him off the hook by calling the troopers and getting them to drop the charges as a "professional courtesy". She then convinced the Sheriff to issue Marty a "Special Deputy" commission in return for a rather substantial contribution to the sheriff's re-election campaign.

Like Randall Anderson, Marty liked to stay buddies with police officers. They both set the troops up with off-duty jobs and, sometimes, with the older college girls from Wichita University who worked in their various business ventures. They also shared a habit of being constantly overweight and trying to dress like they had a lot of money, which they did. Right now, Marty had Tim David cornered over by the potted plants. He appeared to be seriously lecturing Tim over some important issue of foreign policy or the benefits of reservoir tipped condoms. In either case, Tim was trying his best to keep his famous inscrutable smile plastered on his face. At the same time, I could tell Tim was silently praying to practically every god he knew that Marty would be struck by lightning right through the overhead sky light.

I decided to go over and talk to Marty's ex-wife and get a closer look at the objects of my affection. Her white pullover sweater did nothing to conceal the obvious. What was the harm in that, I asked myself. When I did not answer my own question, I decided that it must okay.

"You can't hide over here all by yourself, you know. Can I get you something from the munchy table over there?" I asked in my best possible Sean Connery imitation.

Jana was caught a little off guard, but soon recovered. "Yes, bring me a Perrier with a slice of real lime in it please," she cooed as she handed me her empty plastic glass.

"A Perrier?" I made a face like sucking a lemon.

"Yes, please, and make sure it has plenty of ice and maybe a cherry in it. That would be nice," she repeated.

"No problem," I said confidently. "Nothing for a stepper," I added without any idea what that phrase really meant. I headed back toward the refreshment table trying to guess exactly how I was going to come up with such a drink from the cheap freebies that the Manager's lackeys had coerced from the community.

Renee Stark was standing near the ice bowl staring down at the melting cubes.

"Renee, have you found the stone out of my class ring? I lost it in there earlier when I was snorkeling," I asked.

"No," she said with a sigh. "Kandi is ignoring me." Just like Pete Gant, Renee could not stand being ignored. It was only a matter of time before she wiggled her tail at her lover to indicate that she had the ultimate power not to be ignored.

"Well, I wouldn't worry too much about it. I think you have something that no one else here has to offer Kandi," I said without thinking how "that" revelation would be received.

"What do you mean by that crack?" Renee flashed, sounding more hurt than angry.

"Oh, I'm sorry, Renee," I scrambled like Fran Tarkenton at his best. "It's just that she is playing hostess to all of these characters because she is subbing for the Manager who's not here yet. I'm sure she would rather be around her friends instead. You are her friend, aren't you?" I somehow managed to step out of the cow patty that I had made for myself.

"I guess so," she sighed. The ten milligrams of valium she had swallowed moments before I walked up had already taken the edge off.

"Well, don't get too stuffed on the punch and cookies to have fun later," I mentioned as Renee wandered away from the table to find someone more sympathetic to her troubles.

I spied a two liter bottle of Seven-Up sitting on the table behind the salted peanut bowl. Someone must have brought it special to mix with their own brand of vodka or gin. The odor of those drinks would not be too overt at an employee party where no alcohol was supposed to be served, I guessed. Filling Jana Sim's glass with Seven-Up and ice, I found myself an imitation Pepsi from the ice chest of cheap soft drinks and headed back to the corner where I had left my unsuspecting contest winner.

The trick would be to talk with her for awhile without being seen as too chummy. Being too obvious would start all kinds of rumors that I could ill afford. Jana seemed like she was in control of herself amidst this throng of less than normal party animals. I felt fairly confident that I could get by enjoying a few minutes of pleasurable interaction with a member of the opposite sex without causing a national scandal. It was a public place, after all.

When I made my way through the crowd back to her, the party had picked up steam. The clandestine alcohol consumption, and whatever other chemicals were being sucked down, was beginning to loosen everyone up.

"I think we're in for a wild night," I said as I set the glass down by her hand. "Sorry, but this was as close as I could get to a Perrier."

"No problem," she said gently mocking my previous promise to deliver as ordered. "Do these parties get louder, you mean?"

"I don't think it gets louder, actually. But it will definitely get more interesting as the night goes on," I ventured.

"Cool," she said, using a term once in vogue by people twenty-five years her junior.

"By the way, I don't think we've met before. I'm Rod Starr," I stuck out my cold hand to shake hers. It was body contact of some sort, at least.

"I know who you are, Chief," she said. "I'm Jana Sims. Deputy Jana Sims."

"Oh, yeah," I feigned ignorance of her background. "And what were you before you were a deputy?"

"A lot happier, mainly," she quickly replied. Her hand was warm, very warm. It was also thin and bony in a way that did not fit with the obvious over development of the soft tissues on her chest.

"What did you do before you were the police chief, Chief?" Jana returned my direct gaze. I was enthralled by her hair. It was a butternut color of blonde, shoulder length, with bangs that reached to her eyebrows. The left side of her styled curls was combed back from her face to reveal a perfectly sized ear. I fought the urge to lean over and nibble her earlobe.

"Well, I was a self-employed gynecologist," I pitched my favorite imaginary occupation. "I still have all of my own tools."

"I'll bet you do," she said, leaving me to ponder the hidden meaning of that comment.

Jana caught me staring at her and I looked deep into her brown eyes. Her smile faded and I tried to recover from being caught in the act. I had forgotten for a moment what it was like to get this close to an attractive woman, other than my own wife. The experience was exhilarating and oddly delicious.

"Would you like to take a walk outside," I asked innocently.

"No, I'm here with my ex," she countered.

"Well, if he's an ex, then he won't mind," I said.

"You don't know Marty very well," Jana whispered.

"Maybe I know Marty better than you think," I was beginning to enjoy this repartee.

"I don't have to go with you just because you're the police chief, you know. I don't take orders when I'm off duty and besides, I work for the sheriff, not you," Jana had her jaw set.

"Whoa, wait a minute," I protested. "I'm not trying to pull rank. I just thought that you might want to get away from these looney tune characters for a while, that's all." Somewhere in the back of my mind, I knew I should just walk away but I was enthralled and strangely curious to learn what might happen next.

"You want to show me your etchings, "Big City Chief"?" she sneered.

Well, there was the clincher. In a matter of minutes, I had been leveled by my lewd contest winner with the ultimate insult of being reminded that I was an "outsider". Crushed in round one, I could forge on or cut my losses as best I could. Like a fool, I decided to press forward.

I lowered my eyes and meekly said, "Look, let me start over."

"Okay," was all she said. Hope, like the Lone Ranger, leapt back into the saddle.

When I elevated my gaze from her knees to her face, the only thing I could think of to say was, "You are a very attractive lady." It sounded incredibly lame.

"Is that your best line?" Jana asked simply.

"Well, I don't use it a lot," I answered.

"Oh, sure, I know. You generally don't have to bother, being the "Grand High Poopah" and all. Women just throw themselves at you, I suppose."

"Yeah, that's me." I was starting to tire of the insults, no matter how big her tits were, and decided to play a little of her own game. "I've got the best job in the world and a million dollars in offshore Caribbean bank accounts. Governors and presidents call me by my first name, as in "Hey, shithead". It's a great life. Sorry you don't have a piece of it. What's your world like?"

Jana's smile returned and she joined in. "Let's see. I'm over forty, divorced, and I work for an idiot who was elected because his opponent was dumber than he was. I considered breast reduction surgery when I was thirty, but decided against it because I don't like pain. Now I'm glad I didn't do it because these things definitely help one stand out in a crowd, doncha' think?"

"Is that it?" I tried to cover my shock.

"No. Life has taught me that if it has tires or testicles, it will always let you down. On the other hand, I also know what pleases a man and how to do it. Other than that, I'm just a simple country girl from Russell, Kansas."

"I think I'm in love," I said. I was only half lying.

"I also don't like police officers," she said.

That stopped me cold and I was without a clever retort. Luckily, at that precise moment, World War Three broke out in the middle of the room.

"Damn you, Pete, your think your shit don't stink, but it does." I immediately recognized the shiny suit and ruffled cuff shirt of Randall Anderson, entrepreneur.

Pete had recovered Randall's date, Marla, from somewhere in the parking lot and had her in a lip lock on the make shift dance floor. Marla's tongue was definitely involved in returning Pete's oral invasion. In fact, it was hard to determine just who was invading whom. The sight was something to behold. There was Marla, who a short time earlier was crying and threatening to leave the party, now engaged in an strangely erotic bump and grind with Pete Gant in front of a hundred witnesses.

Unfortunately, one of the witnesses was Randy Anderson and he was seriously pissed off. The more Marla squirmed and humped, the more I became interested and the more Randy sweated and sputtered. Anderson reached across two other voyeurs and grabbed one of Pete's hands just as it was finding the crack in Marla's ass through the fabric of her tight skirt. Pete instantly stopped his one-on-one with Marla and looked at Randy like he had just beamed down from Pluto. Pete gave Marla a final affectionate squeeze with his left hand and grabbed the entrepreneur by the front of his throat in a right-hand strangle hold.

Tightening the grip on Anderson's larynx caused the fat man to loose control of his bodily functions. Urine dribbled down the front of his expensive slacks and pooled near his imported Italian loafers. Some people in the crowd laughed nervously at poor Randy's forced incontinence and the purple hue of his oxygen deprived face.

"You had better do something," Jana ordered.

"Not on your life," I said. I was enjoying watching Pete kill the asshole. It might be the only thing that Pete Gant would ever do to benefit mankind. This was history in the making.

"I think Pete will let him go before he does any permanent damage. They are probably longtime buddies who do this kind of stuff all the time. Randy has been supplying the fender lizards for a lot of years," I offered.

"Fender lizards?" Jana squirmed her nose at the phrase. "What exactly are "fender lizards?"

"Hey, don't get mad at me. I didn't invent the term. Some long dead big city policeman, of the type of people that you don't like anyway, coined the phrase. Believe it or not, there are women who have a fantasy of being draped over the hood of a police car and mounted by a man in uniform while the red and blue strobe lights flash. I reckon that it's a bonifide American tradition," I lectured.

"I assume you speak about this ritual from first hand experience?" she demanded.

"No," I answered truthfully, "but then I'm a little different from some of the older boys from the big city." I couldn't resist lobbing her previous insult back into her court.

Pete finally let go of Randy and the fat man fell in a gasping heap onto the urine soaked floor. Marla tilted her nose upwards and slowly sauntered towards the ladies room to repair her make-up. I absentmindedly followed her path to see if she was heading for the office and the dildo in the desk drawer. It was somehow disappointing to see that she was not going in that direction.

"Now what happens?" Jana asked.

"Absolutely nothing. Don't you understand? Tomorrow, "Handy Randy" over there, wallowing in his own piss, will be back at work wheeling and dealing like your ex-husband. Just like your ex, he will be available to Pete or any of these other police officers here because Randy can't resist being around people who have power. Just about whatever they ask for, Randy or Marty are willing to provide." I was on a philosophizing role and could not stop my mouth from staying in gear.

"I guarantee you that Randy will be at next year's "Employee Appreciation Party" with a few more coeds than he brought tonight, and definitely ones that are not so hormonal as Marla. That way, there will not be a need for as much macho, head butting conflict among the male attendees."

Pete was strutting around the room. "The son of a bitch attacked me. You all saw it. I should put his drunken ass in jail!" His eyes met mine and he stopped.

"Tim," I called across the room, "take Pete outside and check him for injuries."

Tim David nodded his acceptance of the order and waved the "OK" sign. He was grateful for the assignment, since it released him from having to politely listen to any more of Marty Sims' infantile babble. Tim went over and gently tugged at Pete's arm. They quietly exited through the sliding glass door towards the gardens beyond.

"Don't leave until we get to finish our conversation," I called over my shoulder to Jana as I left to assess the damage Pete had done. I politely nodded at Marty on the way out into the gardens.

"You're doing a great job, Chief," Marty called after me as I went out the door.

When I reached the gardens, Tim had Pete braced up against a sculpture of a nude Greek god; the male kind of nude Greek god. Judging from the size of his equipment, the long dead Greek who had modeled for the sculptor was a popular guy in the baths.

"God damn it, Pete. You better calm down right now or the Chief will have your ass," Tim ordered.

"Screw the Chief. And screw you, too, "Little Chief"," Pete slurred.

"If there's any screwing to be done here, I think I will do it," I announced my entrance to their counseling session with a little testosterone of my own. The statue of the semi-erect Greek stood as a silent witness while the party noises signaled that things had returned to normal inside.

"I don't think Pete loves you anymore, Chief," Tim whispered as Pete straightened his sweater and headed back to the festivities.

"I noticed that he's not exactly president of your fan club either, Tim," I countered.

"Well, it's the price I pay for hanging around greatness," Tim grinned. "Like Einstein wrote, "Great spirits have always encountered violent opposition from mediocre minds.""

"You've been hanging around too many of those other apple polishers in the party room, funny guy. Oh, I'm great okay," I said as I rubbed my increasingly sore neck. "I'm so great that no one will be seen associating with me for very long. No one but you, that is. The only way to get my dog to like me is to rub Gravy Train on my face. Yeah boy, I'm a real popular guy, I am. It's a great life, this "chiefing" business." I could become quite a whiner with just a little encouragement, I thought.

Secretly, I wondered what I would have done if Pete had grabbed me by the throat, instead of poor Randy. I concluded that I would have to shoot both Pete and Randy, as the dual executions would double my contribution to improving the world. My instinct to fight back when attacked was the difference between people like Randy and me, I guessed.

"By the way, Pete thinks you're screwing up the police department with all of your changes. He's also pretty sure that you and the Manager are out to get him," Tim confided.

"Yeah, right, and I guess he thinks Lee Harvey didn't do it either. He probably believes that Kandi and Renee are just tennis partners, too." Immediately I sensed that I had divulged information that was not already in Tim's data banks.

"What about Kandi and Renee?" Tim demanded.

"Nothing," I said, "just forget it." Tim dutifully dropped the subject and we both returned to watching the crowd again. It was apparent that just about all of the revelers were flying high on something.

"That Sims guy is nuttier than two kinds of fruit cakes," Tim broke the calm. "He wanted me to help him get the Mayor to put pressure on the Zoning Commission so that he can build a new, bigger set of Regal Theaters in a residential district on the westside. What a slimy toad."

"I'm sure that someone will soon build a new, bigger version of Marty's little wiener on his ex-wife," I said in reply. "That would teach him to try to get you to do his dirty work."

Tim David was about the only person I knew that I could safely verbalize a few of the normal male quips that most guys just tossed out without thinking about it. If I said something obviously ridiculous and totally void of any socially redeeming value like that around anyone else there was a better than even chance that my quote would wind up as the lead story on the five o'clock news.

"I'll go get us something to drink and meet you in the gazebo," Tim said as he pointed to the odd looking structure at the edge of gardens.

I could not put my finger on why I liked Tim David. He was not even a police officer. He was a civilian member of the department and had never been a sworn officer. As a civilian, Tim did not carry a weapon and had no enforcement powers under the law. His title was "Executive Assistant to the Chief" and he took his job very, very seriously. Tim told me once, during a long airline flight to a national conference, that he had the highest respect for anyone in the chief's job. He knew what went on behind the scenes and he wanted no part of it for himself. I guess that was the one reason why I not only liked him, but trusted him. He was not a threat. I believed him and never caught him telling me something that was not true. His prevarications to his wife, on the other hand, were something else. I did not get into his personal business and he and his wife, Sandra, seemed to be the perfect married couple.

When Tim found me in the gazebo, I had already reclined on one of the plastic lawn lounges that marked the building's use as a sun deck on warmer days. The sun was beginning to set behind one of the few full sized trees in the entire state of Kansas and my body was bone tired.

Tim handed me a real Pepsi that he had deftly uncovered somewhere and said, "Would you just look at those crazy people." He gestured back toward the party group.

Outside in the garden areas, there were several couples who had escaped the noise and were now strolling secretively among the rose bushes and gold fish pools.

"They're no crazier than we are, Tim," I tried to defend the human race. "We're all just trying to make it through to a better life, I guess."

"Well, I guess you're right. I've been hanging around police officers for almost thirty years and the one thing I've learned is that life is very short and it is very fragile. You can be here today and gone tomorrow, so you better make the most of it while you've got the chance." Tim sounded as if he was reading from one of my speeches to the Rotary Club.

"Take you for example," he continued. "You've only got so long to accomplish whatever it is that you want to do with this police department and then its "adios". You know that and so do I."

The bluntness of Tim's gloom and doom prophecy rocked me. "Gee, Tim, I didn't expect you, of all people, to join the opposition."

"Not me, boss, I'll be fighting right up until the last. If I know you at all, I think you know exactly what I mean." Tim knew me more than a little.

At that moment, Marla came running out of the party room with Pete in hot pursuit. He was about a foot off of her nice little ass when she tripped and fell head long into one of the garden's reflecting pools. Lilies and mottled gold fish were forcibly ejected up onto the concrete sidewalk in the accompanying splash. Pete stopped short of the water's edge and broke into a hearty laugh at the sight of Marla on her hands and knees in the green water.

"Sometimes I really do love this job," I said as I pointed toward Pete and Marla's attempt to replace cable tv as the most entertaining act in Wichita tonight. Pete held out his hand for Marla. As soon as she put her weight into his grip, Pete let go; sending Marla crashing back into the stinking water. She landed flat on her butt this time, with her legs splayed out in front of her.

Pete was the essence of helpful when he said, "You're not too graceful, are you baby?"

I watched the scene in detached amazement. "No wonder some people don't think police officers are so special," I told Tim. "If we were all like Pete Gant, people would hunt us down and make charcoal briquettes out of us with flame throwers."

Marla tried to stand up in the ooze that was once fresh duck dung. The slimy substance had now fallen even further down the food chain and served as the bottom coating for the shallow pool. She slipped again and fell on her increasingly sore butt for the second time in as many minutes. The curiosity had worn off for most of the crowd and they wandered back inside the building. I looked again toward the east as a giant B-1B bomber flew low towards its base on the edge of town. For a moment, I was sure that I saw the warplane launch a cruise missile, which arched towards City Hall, but then decided that the hallucination was just more wishful thinking.

"Do you think that Pete will nail Marla tonight?" I asked Tim matter of factly.

"Normally, I would say yes. However, not even Pete can abuse someone like that and expect to get laid," Tim answered. He pointed back to the pool in time for me to see Pete grab Marla by the hair and pull her up on dry land like a beached seal.

"Are you worried about your meeting tomorrow with Michaels?" Tim asked.

"Damn right I am. I vacillate between being afraid of the goof ball and wanting to arrange some big showdown with him to get it all over with. You know, kind of one of those "Shootout at High Noon" westerns. Only I don't know how much I look like Gary Cooper, although the Manager does look a little like June Allyson around the eyes."

"Uh, I don't think she was in that picture, Chief," Tim corrected me.

"And neither was I, my friend," I yawned.

When we turned back toward where we last saw Pete and Marla, there was no one in sight. They had either left the party or were bobbing for goldfish turds among the remaining lily pads. The likelihood of my desire for spontaneous combustion for the both of them seemed remote. In a concession to peace on Earth and to save the coroner some work, I decided to say a small prayer that they did not drown in the duck pond.

* * *

There was a blinding flash of light and I decided that maybe I was wrong about the cruise missile when I woke up in the lounge chair. I was as cold as I was stiff. I did not remember falling asleep. Tim was no where to be seen. I stumbled down the dark walk, kicking over the discarded cans and plates of half eaten cookies that someone had left on the steps, and into the still brightly lit party room. All the party goers had disappeared. The place looked like Miami after a hurricane. Someone had left their jam box behind to keep the clean-up crew company, I guessed. Roy Orbison was crooning "Pretty Woman" as I roamed through the debris. I wished Jana Sims had not left without us finishing our debate or whatever the encounter had turned into.

I tried to rub some feeling back into my frozen arms as I sleepily limped toward some sounds coming from the office area. As I got closer, the soft hum of the vibrator and a female voice in the background made me sure that I did not want to go inside to find out what was going on. The voice was set in the moan mode and it was so low that it was unrecognizable. Whoever was inside was definitely enjoying a much better "Employee Appreciation Week" than I was likely to have.

Just imagining what was going on inside the office reminded me of the first time I had ever encountered one of these plastic "marital aids." That was what dildos were called in the magazine ads before retail stores and the internet were specially designed to distribute such toys.

As a young patrol officer in Dallas, one of my first assignments after training was at Parkland Hospital. Parkland Memorial was the huge county hospital that took all types of people in need of medical care, including indigent cases. It specialized in gunshot wounds and was made famous when all the surgeons in Dallas could not pour President Kennedy's brains back into his head. Despite their best efforts, the young president died there in Trauma Room Number One in 1963. Since then, the room had become a shrine.

The primary job of the officer assigned to desk duty at Parkland was to take any police reports on crimes, or unusual incidents, that had not been reported to the police. Assigning a rookie to the hospital kept the dispatcher from constantly sending beat officers to 5201 Harry Hines Boulevard, Parkland's official address, to fill out the routine paper work. Actually, the assignment was good experience for a new officer, as well. The rookie could take his time asking questions and even use the telephone to call the station sergeant, or other officers, if he needed advice. This was not a luxury normally enjoyed by the officers in the field.

One night, about four in the morning, I was called to Trauma Room Two by a very matronly and very bored duty nurse. She wanted me to interview an obviously intoxicated middle aged woman who appeared to be in intense pain as she lay face down on the examining table.

"Ma'am, what is your name?" I asked the standard first question on all police reports.

"My name is eyeeeeeeeeee yaaaaaaaaaa llliss!" she half screamed, in a voice rising and then lowering in tone.

"Ma'am," I said remaining calm and professional as they taught me at the academy, "I think you said Alice. Is that right?"

"Oh, yeah" she exhaled quickly. "Alice Brooooooooooooooownn!" she started and stopped again.

"Okay, Alice Brown, what happened to you?" I asked standard question number two on the official Dallas Police "Miscellaneous Incident Report" form.

Before she could answer, a young male intern entered the room looking like he had not slept in the second half of the twentieth century.

"Okay, Miss Brown, we've got the x-rays back and the device is lodged rather deeply in your rectum," he said matter of factly. "It may be painful, but we will need to get it out of there."

"Get it out? Get it out?" Alice gasped incredulously during a rare moment of lucidity. "Don't take it out Doc. It took me too long to get it in there, just change the batterrrrrrrrrrrrrrrrrrrrieeeeeessssssssssss."

I looked confused and the young almost doctor mouthed the words "change the batteries" for my edification. Welcome to the big city, rookie, was the look the intern gave me. I never forgot his wise and weary countenance and decided that I did not want to be a part of changing any rectally inserted power sources in Dallas or in Wichita.

As I turned on my heel to get away from the moaning office, Kandi Maldonado opened the door. She almost swallowed her face when she saw me. The lights were dim inside and I only caught a glimpse of activity.

"I, I, I, uh, I, I, I don't think you should go in there, Chief," Kandi sputtered.

"Kandi, is everyone in there present because of their own free will? Are they all adults?" I asked in my best official voice. I was kind of enjoying catching Kandi with her red wool slacks on backwards and the brand name tag hanging in front.

"Yes. Yes sir," she answered quickly.

"Then you're right, Kandi, I don't think I should go in there. Try not to set off the fire sprinkler system, okay? And, oh, by the way, the rose goes in front big girl," I pointed at the back of her white crotchless panties peaking over the front of her disheveled pants. The absence of the standard embroidered pink rose indicated that she had managed to put her special undies on backwards, as well, in her haste to get dressed.

Kandi was still trying to mentally figure out how hot the room would have to get to activate the overhead sprinklers and what a rose had to do with anything as I headed out the front door. Outside, inhaling the cold night air, I stumbled in the dark towards where I vaguely remembered Tim leaving my car. I hoped it was still there.

TUESDAY

CHAPTER TWO

The alarm clock sounded just like the back up signal on a road grader. There is nothing more obnoxious than the raucous beeping the huge machines emit when they are in reverse gear. I woke up thinking that I had somehow fallen asleep in the middle of a construction project and would soon become a permanent part of Highway 54. The blue electronic digits of the clock read 6:30 a.m. and I was in the seductive warmth of my own heated water bed. It was a relief to realize that dueling with homicidal heavy machinery was only a dream, intensified by the continuous beep, beep, beep of the alarm clock. Where were the soothing sounds of the Howlin' Hank Morning Show, I asked myself? I made a mental note to change the alarm mode to radio, instead of that damn beeping noise. The racket was guaranteed to start your day off with a couple of aspirin and a mild concussion. Even Howlin' Hank selling burial plots for the sponsor of his early morning radio show would be better than the irritating beeping noise.

I slapped the clock with a wicked left hook that would have made Mike Tyson proud and connected with the sweet silence of the "OFF" button. Rolling to my left, I practically fell out of the bed and started the stiff trek towards the bathroom. Using the towel rack for support, I gingerly lowered myself onto the toilet to release an over abundant supply of Pepsi Cola that my kidneys seemed intent upon ejecting from my body. If I felt this bad in the morning, and I did not drink alcohol, how did the rest of the party goers feel, I wondered.

It was not that I had any heavy religious or moral objections to drinking. It was simply that the stuff always tasted like rifle bore cleaner to me. If the corporate moguls ever decided to make an alcoholic beverage that tasted like Pepsi, then there probably would not be enough Betty Ford Centers in the whole country for those of us who just never cultivated a taste for oven cleaner, or whatever the actual taste of bourbon was supposed to be.

Beer tasted no better, in my opinion. After the usual experiments in high school and college, I had long since decided that throwing up was no compensation for acting like a fool. Later, as a rookie patrol officer, I tried again to run with the big dogs and drink beer like the squinty eyed veterans. When we would get off the late night shift at seven in the morning, a lot of the "real" police officers would frequent a nasty rundown beer joint near the police sub-station called "The Outhouse." It was aptly named.

I watched my buddies pour tomato juice into a mug of icy beer and quickly suck down something they called a "Booger Red." The cultural rite of passage was out of my league. I tried, but I kept falling asleep; face down on the table in a shallow pool of slobber and spilled beer. Eventually, I would wake up and find my shoelaces tied together and a gaily colored condom rolled onto the six-inch barrel of my duty revolver on the table in front of me. The gun was supposed to stay concealed inside my coat when I was off-duty. It was all very puzzling to a young rookie.

I even tried drinking wine once. The occasion was a rather wild party that mixed police officers, airline stewardesses and a bunch of Dallas Cowboy's. The football kind of Cowboys, that is. Before Love Field closed due to competition from the new Dallas/Fort Worth International Airport, it was fashionable for airline pilots and stews to live in the up-scale apartments on Cedar Springs Road, just south of the busy airport. Many of the higher paid players on Tom Landry's team also called the apartment complex home. Included in the select group were a few police officers who worked off-duty as security for the team and obviously got to know the players very well.

The host for this particular party was a dashing young pilot for PanAm. His pencil mustache made him look like a dapper Errol Flynn. He had somehow secured a wide variety of old fashioned douche bags and filled them with various flavors of wine. The host had distributed these odd rubber bags strategically throughout the spacious apartment. They were designed to be conveniently tapped by the guests, using the handy flexible tube and appendage to pour wine into their wine glass, mouth or other body orifice. The scene was all very weird, even by police standards.

The football players seemed to have a great deal of trouble figuring out how to work the equipment; but the stews were excellent instructors, as I recall. In any case, wine from a feminine hygiene device did nothing to improve the taste for me. It still tasted like what was originally designed to flow out of the bags in the first place. I finally faced the fact that I was just not a drinker. It did not take me long to quit trying to act like I was W.C. Fields around other police officers, just to show that I was a regular guy. I just swallowed my pride and admitted that I was a wimp when it came to alcohol. Later, I became even more popular as the designated driver, after several of our fellow officers got fired for drunk driving off duty. In Dallas, driving drunk was a sure fire, one-way ticket off the police department. You might get by with three or four questionable shootings of unarmed suspects and still keep your job, but be caught behind the wheel with a blood alcohol level of .10 or more and it was curtains for your career.

After a quick shower and some posturing in front of the mirror to see how much of my worn body was suffering the effects of the earth's gravity today, I padded across the thick beige carpet to answer the plaintive ring of the phone.

Actually, I let our stupid answer machine pick the call up on the third ring. The machine was necessary so I could screen out any Libyan terrorist who might be calling to threaten to blow up the zoo because he mistakenly thought the locals abused the camels. In fact, most Kansans cared little about the camels. The sheep were a different matter.

"Hello," my own voice droned on the machine. "We're away from the phone right now, please leave your message at the tone."

"Hello, I'm not away from the phone and neither are you. Pick it up, dear," my wife Peggy instructed from the other end of the phone line.

"I was too away from the phone, Peggy, honest," I replied as I snatched the handset from its cradle. "The girls from Saint Mary's Home for the Sexually Promiscuous wanted me to rub strawberry jelly all over their bodies. We were about to take our early morning nude jog through the neighborhood when you called."

"Why not peanut butter?" Peggy asked, playing along with my perverted mania.

"Ouch. I don't think so. It doesn't lick off easy enough and, besides, what do you know about edible sex enhancement techniques anyway?" I asked. "What are they teaching you up there in that Yankee hospital, Mrs. Starr?"

"I'm coming home tonight and show you in person," Peggy said with a lilt in her voice.

"Great," I yelled loud enough to startle the cat. "What time do you want me to pick you up at the airport?"

"The flight gets in at 8:32 and I'll be on TWA this time, instead of Northwestern," she answered.

"That's fine, it will give me time to get the abused farm animals out of the living room and clean up all the used prophylactics from the gym downstairs. We are all out of rubbers, by the way. I went next door to borrow a cup of condoms from the neighbor lady and she pointed to her plastic Jesus on the dashboard of her Pope approved Fiat. I figured I was at the wrong house. Finally, she said she would just "give" me a dozen, rather than me "borrowing" some from her supply. It kind of hurt my feelings that she didn't want me to return them after they were used," I reported.

"I don't believe a word of it," Peggy said. "The neighbor doesn't own a Fiat."

"Okay, you got me, I made almost all of it up. By the way, why aren't you flying Northwestern Airlines, as usual?" I asked.

"Well, I had a coupon for a half-price ticket on a promotion that they sent me for being such a great customer this last year," she replied.

Boy, was that right, I thought. Peggy had logged more air miles than Santa Claus since her diagnosis. Our quest became trying to find some doctor or treatment that would cure her, or at least keep her alive until we could grow old together.

"When I went to buy my ticket they said all the seats were full. Well, I knew darn well that there has never, in the history of the world, been an airplane full of passengers land in Wichita, Kansas. Unless, it was a plane that crashed on its way to Dallas or L.A."

"Yeah, we call that a "Knute Rockne" here in Kansas," I retorted. The name was a historical reference to the famous Notre Dame football coach who was killed in a plane crash nearby. In the 1920's, the early model Ford Tri-Motor airliner, on which the great "Rock" was a passenger, crashed into the desolate plains about forty miles north of Wichita. There was a grubby little roadside monument, outside a McDonald's on the highway to Kansas City, to remind tourists that Knute had plowed up Kansas dirt on his way out of this world.

"When I challenged them on the fact," Peggy continued, "they finally admitted that they only had a few seats available for the half price promotion. While the airplane itself was practically empty, there were no seats for the special discount they sent me."

"Geez, Peggy, who are these people" I whined, "retired city managers? Or just assholes hoping to lie enough to earn recognition in the "Politician's Hall of Fame?"

"Anyway, I told 'em to keep their empty seats and fill them with the same kind of hot air they were trying to blow up my skirt," my spunky wife announced.

"Okay, baby, I'll meet you at the gate at 8:32 and I'll bring the strawberry jelly with me," I answered.

"We'll see," was all Peggy would promise as we said our good-byes.

The kitchen was spotless as I roamed in search of some orange juice and a chocolate chip cookie, my personal "Breakfast of Champions". I always kept things in order when Peggy was not at home. I never mentioned it, of course, but she was much more of a slob than I was and she hated to do house cleaning. We had cob webs in some corners of our home that had been spun by long extinct spiders before man had stepped on the moon. With our daughter Terri spending most of the week with Peggy's best friend, Carmen Hubble, and her daughter of similar age; I could really keep the house clean. I usually made one chipped coffee cup last all week as an orange juice glass. As long as the local super duper grocery mall stayed open all night to dispense sufficient frozen TV dinners, I was self sufficient. If the microwave ever broke down, I might have to commit suicide. Attempting to eat my own cooking would bring the same result.

Returning back to the bedroom, I pulled on my brown, long sleeve uniform shirt with the single gold star on each collar. I quickly buttoned it up over my lucky tee shirt. The white cotton undershirt had been a gift from my troops in Dallas just before my departure for Wichita. On the front, there was a bright blue and yellow drawing of a sinking passenger ship that looked vaguely like the Titanic. The scene depicted people jumping over the sides into a sea filled with hungry sharks. On the side of the sinking ship was written "S.S. D.P.D", meaning the Dallas Police Department. The bold caption at the bottom of the shirt was a declaration of promise as well as frustration at the time. "Don't get left behind," the black letters proclaimed.

I unconsciously fingered the gold star on my collar as I fastened a regulation clip-on black uniform tie to the top button. When I took the job as chief in Wichita, my predecessor had worn four gold stars on each collar as his symbol of rank. That was on the rare occasions that he bothered to put on a uniform. I quickly noticed that the deputy chiefs wore gold eagles and that there were no one star, two star or three star rank insignia in the entire police department. It seemed silly to wear all those gold plated brass stars. I quickly reduced the chief's official insignia to just one star. It would be hard enough keeping one star shining in this galaxy of the bizarre.

Three rows of award ribbons adorned my right chest, opposite the gold badge of "Chief" pinned above the left pocket. The ribbons were actually small, polished metal bars with brightly colored ceramic inserts. Each award bar was about an inch long and a quarter inch wide. The dark blue bar, representing the Medal of Valor, topped the rows of other lesser awards that had been earned in the course of my twenty-three year police career. I had earned four of the awards in Wichita, including the "Master Marksman Shooting Badge" for firing a perfect score with my duty pistol during the last departmental qualification session. The remainder of the citations had been earned on the sometimes violent, and always interesting, streets of Dallas.

At times, the ribbons did not seem like much to represent twenty-three years of my career. At other times, I worried that my uniform was beginning to look like a cross between Audie Murphy and Idi Amin. Of all the decorations, I knew that there was one ribbon that was always guaranteed to piss off the City Manager. The "Distinguished Service Award".

Despite the clumsy attempt by the Manager to scuttle me with the sexual harassment complaint during the training for the abortion protests, our department executed the plan that I had designed perfectly. Our procedures for handling the civil disturbances, pickets, marches and blockades of clinics and hospitals were executed with all the efficiency and skill that we could have ever hoped. When the six weeks of worry and stress in dealing with this complex social issue finally ended, we were elated. Newspapers around the country, and our own local paper that was seldom on our side, hailed what their editorial staffs called the "Summer of Professionalism" by the Wichita Police Department. It was quite an honor and our morale soared.

There was at least one honest member of the City Council for whom I had a great deal of respect. Councilman Steve Roberts was often left out of the discussions in the shady, behind the scenes dealings by the rest of the council. After the protests, he called me on the telephone to let me know that he would swing the political support necessary if I would request an official proclamation of commendation from the City Council. Steve thought it would be great for the council to honor the officers involved in controlling the protest activities. For sure, it would be little more than a symbolic gesture, but I liked the idea a lot. Mainly, it would let the troops know that their governing body was behind them for once and not attempting to stab them in the back or stick something else in their rear end.

When I suggested the idea to the City Manager, he about gave birth to a litter of kittens. "Why would we want to bring that damn abortion issue back up to the council for them to argue over it again. It would re-open too many old wounds," he cried. "What good would it do?"

I tried to explain the benefits but, unfortunately, I used the forbidden "M" word…morale.

"I'm sick and tired of hearing about morale around here. We're not paying these people to be happy, just do their jobs," Mel lectured me. I had heard the same tired line many times from him.

Losing the "Battle of the City Council Proclamation", I changed tactics. Would it be possible, I asked, for a few hundred dollars to be added to our budget? We could then buy all of the officers who participated in the operation a special "Distinguished Service Award" ribbon for their uniforms. I argued that this small symbol of recognition would signify the professionalism that had brought such high praise to the city, and the police department, from all around the world. In the wake of the Rodney King incident and riots in Los Angeles, it seemed like quite a feat to receive such accolades for policing in America. Naturally, the manager did not share my perspective. In fact, you would have thought that I had asked for the removal of his left testicle and half of the right.

"Hell no," he refused, "I'm not spending any money on any such nonsense. I'm sure that they would rather have the money in the form of a raise next year, instead of some stupid campaign ribbon."

The reply really made me see red. "First off," I said in rebuttal, "it's not a campaign ribbon. It's tangible recognition that they did more than just "do the job". They did a great job and everyone except you recognizes that!" My voice began to get louder as I finished with "and secondly, if I thought that two or three dollars would actually be allotted to each of them in the form of a pay raise; I would be all for it, but you know, and I know, that you're not about to offer the officers even a cost of living raise next year."

He hung up the telephone before I could slam the receiver down in his ear. Damn, I told myself, this is no way to run a railroad and certainly no way to go through life arguing with idiots for simple things that seemed so common sense.

I made one last attempt to get the awards for the officers. I suggested to the command staff that we pass the hat among ourselves and buy our officers the award bars out of our own pockets. The deputy chiefs and majors could not agree on whether they should kick in fifty or sixty bucks each for the awards. Pete Gant whined that he would not put any of his own money in the hat. If the city did not want to tell the officers that they did a good job, then he damn sure was not going to spend his money to do what the city should have done in the first place. I could not fight that kind of "cut your nose off to spite your face" logic and the whole idea fell through.

Privately, I knew that Pete was still angry that he had not shared in all the favorable attention that the successful operation had received. I had insured that he was not included in the actual operation for the same reason that I had removed the overly sensitive sergeant. Pete was just not trustworthy enough to be given an assignment where all of our professional careers were at stake.

Peggy and I talked it over and we withdrew eight hundred and forty dollars from our personal savings account to purchase the officers the awards. When they were delivered, I awarded each ribbon in a personal ceremony for every officer involved in the operation. No one, except Tim David, ever knew the source of the funds that were used to purchase the awards. The Manager inquired, via electronic mail, as to where I had acquired the money to buy the awards. I simply refused to answer him. He launched Tad Roadly and Renee Stark and their crew of financial auditors on a witch hunt to find out how we had illegally diverted funds out of our budget. I think they suspected a secret "arms shipment to Iran in exchange for the award bars" scheme. The auditors worked for two months on "Awardgate" and could not make a case, of course. When Tad reported to Mel that he was unable to pin an embezzlement rap on me, I do not know who was more disappointed, the Manager or Tad.

A few months later, the United States Department of Justice announced that I was their national "Police Chief of the Year" for our efforts in managing the civil disturbances. The Attorney General and the U.S. Marshall's Service were obviously impressed with our efforts in organizing the city's response to the massive abortion protests. The award provided for an all expense paid trip to Washington, D.C. for Peggy and me. The honor also included a visit to the White House for a ceremony in the Oval Office.

The President of the United States pinned the little blue and gold circular award on the lapel of my best gray suit and Peggy beamed with pride. Back home, my own City Manager, Mayor and City Council never acknowledged that I had been away or that they were even aware of the award, despite all of the media attention. Later, the Manager told me that he suspected that I had been given the award only because I was friends with a local federal judge. What an asshole.

Just as soon as Peggy and I got back to Wichita, I traded the President's medal for a Distinguished Service Award ribbon just like the ones the officers were now proudly wearing. Every time I met an officer in uniform, with his or her award ribbon pinned to their chest, I shared in their pride.

Pride was great, but right now I sure needed that eight hundred and forty dollars badly to pay medical bills. Maybe the City Manager had been right after all about morale being a losing battle. Certainly, my own morale was gradually eroding under a constant barrage of criticism and micro-managing that was inherent in the Wichita system. It was enough to cause a person to become an alcoholic. Maybe I could find an old douche bag and try drinking wine again.

Driving downtown was a breeze in Wichita. There was almost no morning traffic congestion. It was definitely unlike Dallas. Each day in Big D was a test of nerve and intestinal fortitude to determine if you could get to work without killing, or being killed, on the horrendously crowded freeway system. Parking in Wichita, on the other hand, was another issue altogether. When I parked the unmarked police car, under the green steel sign in the municipal parking lot that read "Police Chief", I felt very privileged. A free place to park, close to the City Hall building, was about the only truly important perk that went with the job. Since the parking garage had fallen down, most city employees were parking in Upper Mongolia or being dropped off by stealth helicopters each morning. The situation was a mess. It certainly did not make for more cheerful city workers. Many had to walk a half of a mile or more, with mud and snow seeping through the soles of their shoes, to get to their City Hall work stations.

Taking the slow moving elevator to my fourth floor office, I casually checked and saw that my name was still on the door. Being reassured of at least one more day of pay, I entered the outer office area where the secretary's desk was positioned. The paranoia had become a bad habit.

"Good morning, Suzie, how are you this bright and shining day," I asked with too much enthusiasm for an eight o'clock encounter.

"I'm fine, Chief." Suzie sleepily replied. "How was your night?"

"To be honest, I don't remember too much of it. But we need to check and see if Deputy Chief Gant was arrested for lewd and lascivious behavior with animals, not in his species, last night," I answered with a touch of seriousness.

Suzie was accustomed to stories about Pete, but she obviously wanted to hear the latest. "Now which jealous husband will I have to deal with over the telephone today?" Suzie asked.

"I think you will be spared that ordeal. However, if the director over at Botanica calls and wants to report a rash of duck rapings or sodomies of goldfish, I'm not in," I instructed.

Suzie dropped a stack of telephone messages on my desk. They had come in during the previous day, while we were golfing somewhere south of the Canadian border. She turned and left me to work my way through the in-basket on my desk that was filled to overflowing, as usual.

"Don't forget your nine o'clock meeting with the Manager," she called over her shoulder. Suzie casually waltzed out of my inner office toward her own desk, just outside the door.

"Don't remind me," I mumbled into thin air.

In the next forty-five minutes, I managed to handle most of the routine stuff in my tray. I signed what needed to be signed and delegated various assignments to my deputy chiefs for action within their specific areas of responsibility. Most importantly, I signed the bi-monthly payroll printout to insure that we would all be paid next week.

Signing the payroll printout was one of the many stupid requirements of my job. The fan fold computer generated report listed thousands of names, social security numbers and amounts. It was the itemized individual pay record for the over seven hundred current employees on the police department. The report also included thousands of former employees who were retired and receiving pension checks in the mail. I was required to sign at five specific locations on the report. My signature was supposed to signify that I had personally checked each and every entry. By signing, I accepted the responsibility from Tad Roadly, and the Finance Department, that the voluminous amount of information was correct.

I had no idea who was on the pension rolls before I took the job. It would take an army of accountants a month to completely check all of the entries. When I first protested that my signature was basically meaningless, I was sarcastically put in my place. Surely, Tad intoned, I would not sign something that I was not absolutely sure was correct. My response to this idiotic statement was to refuse to sign the totally unnecessary documents and just wait to see what happened.

For two years, no one in the Finance Department caught the fact that my signatures were missing from the forms. My own Fiscal Affairs Division clerks, who picked up and delivered the print outs to Roadly's office, marveled at our symbolic protest's success. When one of our clerks bragged to a friend in the Accounting Office about the subterfuge, our secret was out.

Tad called me, sputtering about my sabotage of his precious accounting system. I told him that he must be mistaken. Surely he would not have authorized our paychecks for the last two years if I had not signed the proper forms, I countered by repeating his own veiled insult from the past.

What goes around, comes around. One small battle won in a war where the winner was a forgone conclusion. I still hated the stupidity of signing the forms, but I obviously could not use the same tactic again. For the last four years, I had been signing the printouts "D. Duck". In a flourishing handwriting style that Warner Brothers probably would have approved for their impish cartoon character, I continued to circumvent the silly rules of Wichita's red tape. So far, no one had noticed the signature of exactly who was accepting written responsibility for millions of dollars of disbursements. I was dying to see how Tad would try to divert his own accountability to that well known financial genius, Daffy Duck.

At precisely 8:55, I caught an upward moving elevator to the thirteenth floor. The top floor was the exclusive lair of City Manager Melvin Michaels and his motley staff of assistants and ass kissers. At thirteen stories, Wichita's City Hall was not the tallest building in Kansas. It was just the second tallest building. A seventeen story office building, just south of City Hall, held the dubious honor of being the highest point in the entire state. King Kong would have picked both buildings out from between his toes like a couple of sand burrs, I figured.

Stepping off the empty elevator car, I found myself alone in a dark corridor. The decor and lighting was obviously designed to depress and intimidate even the most optimistic visitor. I groped my way to the north end of the building where the closed doorway to my leader's chambers stood. Curiously, there was no name on the forbidding oak door. Just a simple black and white plastic sign, that read "City Manager's

Office", was affixed to the dark wood. One could always hope that someone other than Melvin "Mohamar Khadafi" Michaels would be inside.

Before I opened the door and stepped off into the abyss, a quick stop at the men's room was necessary to quiet a pair of nervous kidneys. I reminded myself that you know you are getting old when taking a piss feels as good as sex once did. As the wave of relief flooded over me, I allowed my eyes to inspect the gleaming urinal. I faintly detected a line of tiny black letters carefully inscribed in the caulking between the blue tiles above the chrome plated flusher handle. A magnifying glass would have been helpful in deciphering the minuscule print. With some effort, I saw that it read "Mel Mickals Sux". Being a trained detective, I immediately identified the work as that of another loyal city employee. The spelling indicated a graduate of the Wichita School District. Or maybe Wichita University.

In the vacant hallway again, I made one last check of the small voice activated micro cassette recorder inside my uniform shirt pocket. With a deep breath, I pushed open the door to Mel's outer offices.

Maria looked up from the telephone to find me hovering over her cluttered desk. She was, without a doubt, the worst secretary in America, if not the entire free world. If it could be lost, Maria would find a way to lose it. She was referred to as the "black hole" and the name had no sexual connotation whatsoever. Things that went onto Maria's desk were never seen again. It was theorized that the missing TBF Avenger airplanes of "Flight 19", lost in the Bermuda Triangle off Fort Lauderdale, would someday magically fly out of Maria's desk and land on the roof.

Her reputation was hard won. Maria could not find her ass with both hands and she had an intelligence quotient that was in negative numbers. Normally, with that combination, a person would have a real problem keeping a job at any place other than Burger Whopper. But not Maria. She had been Mel's personal secretary since the Manager came to Wichita. To the chagrin of other, more talented secretaries; Maria's salary was set at an extremely high level on the clerical scale.

No one could understand the reason for Maria's longevity. Most employees made fun of her relentlessly and openly.

At a recent office party for the retiring Director of Parks and Recreation, his own secretary handed him a colorfully wrapped going away gift. Some of us had chipped in a few dollars to buy the director a retirement watch with the city logo engraved underneath the crystal. The city itself, of course, was too cheap to buy him anything. The director had worked thirty-five years for the city and got a punch and cookie send off. Not my idea of a first class organization.

As a joke, we had hidden our small gift beneath wadded up newspapers and placed it inside a very large cardboard box. The box was designed to hold a ream of computer paper and was huge. One member of the outgoing director's staff casually stated, "Gee, I wonder what could be in such a big box?"

To this inquiry, the newly liberated retiree stated matter of factly, "It might be all of my memos to the City Manager that Maria has lost in the last six months." Instead of laughing, the crowd all nodded their heads in solemn recognition of the trials and tribulations of working around the "black hole."

A few month's back, Dale Williams conspired to pull a very old gag on Maria. It was a prank that George Washington had probably tried on his own secretary. The premise of the joke was anciently juvenile. Nonetheless, Dale was absolutely certain that the bit would work to perfection on Maria.

My role in the prank was to be up in the manager's outer office, pretending to be waiting to see the manager, while Dale called Maria on the telephone.

"Maria, could you see if Mike Hunt is up there?" Dale inquired. "I know you know Mike and I really need to track him down right away." Of course, there was no real "Mike Hunt". He was as fictional as Maria's high school diploma; simply a character formed in the devious mind of Dale, the Water Department Director, to bedevil poor Maria.

Ever gullible, Maria asked Dale to please hold while she tried to locate Mr. Hunt. She put down the telephone and began asking around the office if anyone had seen "Mike Hunt."

Maria's slight Spanish accent worked perfectly in gently slurring "Mike Hunt" into "my cunt" at each repeated pronunciation of the name. Every time Maria would come back on the line and tell Dale that she could not find "my cunt", I would almost bust a gut. Dale continued to beg her to find the missing cunt, er, Hunt again. It was a matter of life or death that he speak with him right away, Dale pleaded desperately.

I kept the charade alive by playing along with the story line. "Oh, yeah, I think he went into the finance office a little bit ago", I would offer helpfully. Off Maria would go, waltzing down the hall, yelling "my cunt, my cunt, has anyone seen my cunt?"

People were falling out of their chairs and rolling under their desks from laughter. Maria appeared confused when people seemed to be avoiding her, slamming the doors to their offices as she wandered down the hall in their direction. To get a little more cooperation, she added emphasis to the request by announcing, "The Water Department needs my cunt right away. Can anyone help me find my cunt?"

The absolute pinnacle of hilarity in the charade came when Maria used the public address system in the City Attorney's office. At high gain volume, she inquired of an entire floor of incredulous lawyers and prim legal secretaries, "My cunt, my cunt, could my cunt please contact the City Manager right away." It was a question that begged answering. The roar from the thirteenth floor could be heard by the hot dog vendors down on Main Street.

Despite her ineptness, I knew at least one reason why the manager did not fire her. Maria knew about "The Apartment". In fact, it was Maria who was responsible for arranging the furnishing of "The Apartment." She also insured that the bills for "The Apartment" were paid on time from the manager's private checking account at the city credit union. The monthly statements for this account were not mailed to the manager's home, where his mousy wife might stumble onto the incriminating evidence. Instead they were sent to his office, where Maria intercepted them each month to keep anyone from learning about the arrangement.

"The Apartment" was a cozy little one bedroom furnished affair in the Fox Run Apartment complex, just a few blocks from City Hall. Carefully situated at the remote end of the second floor building nearest the park, "The Apartment" offered the City Manager seclusion, privacy and ready access to a quiet rendezvous. At any hour of the day or night, when he might arrange a quick sexual liaison with a willing partner, "The Apartment" was always available for use by the Manager.

Maria also made sure that the refrigerator stayed stocked with white wine and snacks for her boss and whoever might accompany him for a little horizontal two step between the sheets. For all the lack of her basic secretarial skills, Maria evidently did this one job very, very well.

I accidentally found out about "The Apartment" when I noticed the City Manager's car in a surveillance video of the parking lot that had absolutely nothing to do with monitoring his sex life. I had authorized the use of fifty thousand dollars from our evidence locker as "flash money" to show to a suspected major narcotic's dealer. The dealer, coincidentally, lived in the very same complex as the Manager's little love nest. When the deal went down, the dealer demanded proof that our undercover officers were actually big players in the Wichita drug scene. I was very nervous that the money would somehow "walk." In other words, be lost. In that case, I would be left hanging on a limb trying to explain how that much money had vanished from our protective custody. To say that the whole operation made me as nervous as a whore in church on Sunday was an understatement.

Our narcotic's detectives were trailing the suspected cocaine dealer around the clock. He promised to deliver twenty kilos of "blow", meaning powder cocaine, from a bigger dealer in Kansas City.

The only reason I noticed the Manager's car on the video was that Maria had asked me for a temporary loan car for the Manager from our seized vehicle garage. His regular city car was in the shop for maintenance, she said. The request seemed a little strange at the time, but Marie said the Manager wanted a very nice vehicle because he was traveling to Topeka to squire some state legislators around and wanted to impress them. I arranged for the former chief's Cadillac to be delivered to the Manager. Needless to say, I was very surprised when the gold El Dorado popped up on the surveillance video that the narcotics detectives brought to me to review.

A few discreet personal inquiries to the apartment manager, whose son had just applied to be a police officer, and the whole clandestine arrangement unraveled like a sweater made in Juarez. The woman who managed the complex seemed eager to regale me with "The Apartment's" entire history. She even included her own accurate guesses as to the apartment's purpose and Maria's involvement. Not all people are stupid. It was just one of Mel's flaws that he considered everyone but himself to be mindless. Being around Maria all day did nothing to dispel his theory.

The apartment manager told me that she never did buy the story of the city's need for a convenient place for visiting out of town dignitaries to stay. She had never seen Senator Bob Dole or Tammy Faye Baker spend the night there when they were in Wichita and therefore concluded that the whole deal was a sham. Of course, she was right.

I filed all the evidence away in a locked box in the trunk of my car and sincerely hoped that I would never need the information about the manager's extra-curricular sexual proclivities.

"I have a nine o'clock appointment with the Manager," I told Maria. She finally removed the telephone from her ear without resorting to surgical intervention, although she did momentarily get the cord caught in her hair.

"Oh, sure Chief, have a seat and I'll tell him you're here," she smiled and pointed to a row of stuffed chairs near the door.

Don Grady, the Building Maintenance Manager, came out from one of the many offices down the hall. He was obviously wandering in the general direction of the communal coffee pot.

"Hey Don, what's up?" I called as he passed me without noticing that I was sitting anonymously in the waiting area.

"Oh, Chief, boy am I glad I ran into you. Showalter is about to have a fit over that paint and carpet that you ordered," Don said.

"Darn, I knew he would come down on you over that. I'm sorry, Don, I'll try to get him off of your back," I offered.

"He's ready to blow his cork, Chief. He thinks that you're not a company man any more, big guy," Don smiled because he knew that neither he, nor I, could stand Assistant City Manager Bob Showalter.

"If he gets on you too much, Don, tell the knucklehead to kiss your big, hairy maroon and white Texas A&M butt and have him call me to witness it," I advised.

Don liked the reference to his engineering degree from College Station, where he had been a third string tight end on the Aggie football team. He laughed at the thought of Bullet Bob being humbled, just once.

"Okay, Chief, I'll do just that," he said as he kept going down the hall in search of a caffeine fix.

Actually, I thought I had been following all of the rules in ordering the carpet and paint to clean up the Chief's office. The whole floor was decorated in the early double knit leisure suit motif of the 1970's. The bright yellow walls did not go very well with the orange carpet and red plastic chairs, unless you were running a day care facility for the visually impaired.

When the entire City Hall building was finally budgeted for paint and new carpet, I contacted the company that won the bid to do the work and selected the colors for my office. Suzie and I picked a royal blue carpet and a muted, light gray flat paint for the walls. We intended to start a fire in the hallway with the plastic chairs. We knew that we could find better stuff in the hand-me-down storage room located adjacent to the Finance Department. The bean counters in that department had recently received all new modern office furniture. Despite every other city department being denied the same request by the Finance Department analysts for better furnishings within their individual budgets, the Finance Department had approved only their own request for new furniture. Imagine that.

In any case, the Manager elected himself as our interior decorator and decided to use a design of his own choosing. Unfortunately, the Manager had not bothered to tell any of his department directors of his decision. It was another manifestation of the Manager's uncontrollable desire to exert his influence over even the most mundane facets of city government. Mel selected a cheap gray paisley carpet and eliminated new paint from the plan. He preferred instead to keep the putrid yellow walls and save the funds budgeted for wall paint. This would allow him to access the money for another project he might find more interesting later in the year, like a trip to Europe.

When the contractor called Bob Showalter to ask if the City Manager would rather use the color scheme that I had chosen for my office, all hell broke loose. I was sure that Bob was giving Don a hard time, believing that we had conspired to give a little class to the obnoxious building design dictated by the Manager. The contractor was promptly informed that no one, except the City Manager himself, was allowed to chose the paint or the carpet. Individuality would not be tolerated. The irony did not fail to impress me. While, as a police officer, I might have the power to take a person's life in a deadly force confrontation; I could not be trusted to chose my own office decor. The absurdity was enough to make grown men cry.

"You can go in now, Chief," Maria called across the room. I put down my copies of "Soybean Review" and "The Kansas Government Journal" and walked in the direction of the Manager's inner office door.

"You should get some new reading material, Maria," I quipped. "I've read all of those magazines a dozen times. I have the articles memorized. Everyone gets killed in the end."

She looked very confused, trying to figure out how anyone could be killed in a monthly periodical about soybeans. I left her with the dilemma and walked through the Manager's open door.

Bob Showalter walked past me on his way out. Not to return, I hoped. Bob was tall and trim with prematurely thinning hair that topped a hawk-like nose. A flimsy set of wire rimmed reading glasses completed the impression of your stereotypical junior high school principal. Most people thought he was perpetually needing to take a good crap and just could not. I thought he was perpetually needing to take a good crap and just "would" not, because he hated to give up something for nothing in return.

Bob's primary function was to do the dirty work of the Manager. This tactic allowed Mel to distance himself personally from any decisions that were too controversial or unsavory. Bob was the consummate asshole. Although I understood his role, it seemed to me that he enjoyed screwing people, under the guise of following the Manager's directions, just a little too much. Between the Manager, Tad Roadly or Bob; it would be a toss up as to who would be pissed on first if all three were to catch on fire simultaneously. A mental image of Richard Lopez and his battalion of red helmeted fire fighters pissing on three burning bureaucrats was quite a vision. The imaginary scene evaporated as I walked into the chamber of horrors that was the City Manager's inner office.

Mel was conversing on the phone when I ambled in. I thought hard about how I might show some confidence during his hidden agenda meeting. He waved at the empty chair in front of his desk. Soundlessly, so the party on the other end of the telephone line could not hear, he mouthed the words, "close the door". Like a whipped puppy, I obeyed.

There it was. The six worst words in American management. "Come in and close the door". My first field training officer on the police department had taught me the significance of these words and the fact that whatever followed was never pleasant. He used to say, "Rookie, just remember the two simple rules of all "head hanger's". First, a "head hanger" is when you are getting your ass chewed out by the sergeant, or some other supervisor, and all you are expected to do is to hang your head and take it like a man. The lower you hang your head, the better. Hell, get your nose right down on the floor between your shoes, if you have to. Second, always tell the truth; unless it's something you've done that might get you fired. In that case, lie your ass off."

I had been fortunate not to have experienced too many head hanger's in my career, but I always remembered the two rules of conduct. I suspected that I would need this wisdom in Mel's office today.

The Manager looked tired but still a lot younger than his sixty plus years. His olive complexion was oily and pockmarked with hundreds of acne scars that must have made his adolescence a real nightmare. He was short. Very short. I guessed him to be about five feet five inches in his Thom McAnn leather wing tips. Mel wore a carefully tailored gray suit, with a white shirt and maroon tie knotted into a meticulous Windsor. No button down shirts or clip on ties for this guy. Not a hair was out of place and he had on enough "Brut" cologne to deodorize a dozen outdoor portable toilets. I had to give it to him, though. While most people his age were fighting to keep their weight down, Mel looked trim and fit. I knew that he did not have the physical stamina to stay in shape. Therefore, I suspected that the Manager cultivated a massive tape worm, about a mile in length, as his weight control program.

He began shuffling through a stack of papers on his desk. At the same time, he kept the telephone receiver balanced between a slightly oversized ear and his left shoulder. Finally, he said into the phone, "I'll have to call you back later". The Manager set the handset in its cradle without looking up from the cluttered desk top and turned towards me. I was spared the slimy handshake that would have caused me to wash my palms with chlorine bleach afterwards.

"Oh, hi. How are things going?" Mel asked innocently as if he was surprised to see me.

"Terrific. How are things up here?" I answered his question with a question and left the ball in his court.

He smiled faintly and looked down at his messy desk again. "Too much work and not enough time to do it all, you know," he said.

The smile threw me off track. I was beginning to feel like any control I had was about to be lost. Once again, it was that same damned feeling I had with used car salesmen. If Mel had offered me a great deal on a pre-owned Yugo, I would not have been surprised.

"What can I do to help you?" I offered, trying to sound as sincere as possible.

"Nothing really, its all stuff I've got to handle myself," he replied. It was foolish for me to think that he would allow anyone to help him, other than swing an ax. "How's the police department?" he asked.

I stifled a strong urge to tell him about some of my own problems and decided to be gentle. "Well, Mel, you know, running the police department is a piece of cake. It is fighting this damned city bureaucracy that drives me nuts."

He frowned and softly replied, "I know your job has not been easy. Frankly, I don't know how much help you are getting. Maybe its professional jealousy, but you need to try building better relationships with your law enforcement peers."

I hated these willowy references to anonymous people and said, "I think I've got a pretty good relationship with most of the people that I interact with each day, particularly the Feds at the FBI, DEA, and U. S. Attorney's Office. On the county side, I let the sheriff think he is in charge of everything so his political ego won't get bruised. You know what the sheriff's nickname used to be, don't you? I mean, when he was in the police department, before he retired to run for sheriff?"

"No," Mel replied simply.

"Captain Cuckoo," I answered. "Can you imagine having to deal with a person who goes crazy at the drop of a hat. It's like walking on egg shells to be around the nut case. His own troops are afraid to get near him because they are likely to be assigned to the "lost cow" detail that stomps around out in the boonies looking for stray heifers."

"How do you get along with the District Attorney?" Mel asked.

"Fine, as far as I know. We don't agree on some occasions. Naturally, I want her to prosecute all the cases that we send over there and she only wants to pick out the sure winners. "Sitting Ducks Dora", or "Don't File Dora", is what the detectives call her. She only wants to try the cases where there are a dozen eyewitnesses, a video tape of the crime in progress, all ten fingerprints, some toe jam left at the scene for DNA analysis and at least three confessions. We don't get too many cases like that, unfortunately. But we both understand our roles and I like her personally. Plus, she smells good," I replied.

"You know she has a history with some of your command staff?" Mel tested the waters to determine the depth of my knowledge of the closed door secrets he possessed.

"Sure," I answered. "It doesn't come up."

I did not take the bait on Mel's inquiry about Dora Davenport's past sex life. Long before she was elected District Attorney and long before I came to Wichita, Dora was a hot young civil lawyer who made a reputation for herself in divorce and child custody cases. Being unmarried, she indulged her fetish for screwing the lights out of just about every male police officer on the Wichita P.D. The arrangement was very convenient. As the "other woman", Dora could be the catalyst for the marriage breakup and then handle the divorce case after the split.

There was something about the gun, badge and handcuffs that attracted some women. A wise, old veteran police officer in Dallas told me early on, "Son, that badge will get you a lot of pussy; but it only takes one pussy to get that badge." My career was always more important to me than a piece of ass. I carefully avoided any temptation that might blow up in my face. Besides, corny as it sounded, I liked my wife's ass just fine.

Now, many years later, Dora was married to a very successful architect in town who treated her like a queen. Her past was just that in my mind. Her past. The only bad part was that several of the then low ranking patrol officers she had played doctor with fifteen years ago had been promoted during their careers and were now members of my command staff.

Of course, Pete Gant was a prominent member of the "I Diddled Dora Club". I suspected that anything Dora wanted to know about what was going on inside the police department, she could readily access by calling Deputy Chief Gant and reminding him of the "good ol' days". One mention of a nut gurgle to Pete and he promptly forgot all about loyalty to the department or anything else in his life. That was assuming that Pete had ever felt any loyalty to anything or anyone in the first place, which was very doubtful.

"Well, to be frank, the word I get from your counter parts in the law enforcement community is that you are not very well liked," Mel advised me.

I fought the urge to tell Mel just how well liked he was around town. "Mel, I'm not running a popularity contest. I'm trying to run a police department. As far as my popularity goes, most of the crap I take from these people, and inside my own department, comes from implementing decisions that you have handed down."

Oops, I've done it now, I thought. I could see Mel's complexion change immediately. This was a constant sore spot for both of us. I constantly badgered him to allow me to run the police department and make the decisions, and "he" was constantly trying to run the department and make the decisions. I often felt like a Heisman Trophy winning "Run and Shoot" quarterback, who had been the highest draft choice from a winning college program who suddenly finds himself on a last place pro team that runs the Pop Warner straight tee offense from 1915. In Wichita, it was an antiquated system where the coach called all the plays and not the quarterback. To say that I chafed in the system would be like comparing the scruffy Flint Hills of southern

Kansas to the Rocky Mountains. Politely, the system was frustrating. In truth, it sucked pond scum.

Mel's jaw tightened and there was a long pause as he gathered steam to nail me. "I have consciously made an effort not to get involved in police department affairs," Mel said with a straight face.

"Come on, Mel," I exclaimed. "Just yesterday, I got this e-mail message from you instructing me to promote Tanya Murphy because, you said, it would increase the affirmative action ratio of command personnel in the department. Who, why, and how I promote members of my executive staff should be my prerogative, for heaven's sake. I have to live with these people and build a team that can get the job done the way I want it done. That's what being a police chief is all about."

I knew exactly why the Manager wanted Tanya Murphy promoted and, for once in the mind of Mel Michaels, it had nothing to do with her gender.

Two years ago, after all of the positive publicity over handling the abortion protests, I had been tentatively offered the job as the police chief in Tampa, Florida. The job came with a huge compensation package, more than twice my salary in Wichita, and it was a much larger department. The only drawback was that Peggy was not so sure she wanted to move to Florida. We made arrangements to visit the city before I made a definite decision.

While all of this was in the papers about my possibly leaving Wichita for greener pastures, an anonymous letter was received by the District Attorney. The unsigned note alleged that I had personally beaten a wounded suspect who had been shot by the police. This, of course, was a complete and total fabrication. Nonetheless, Dora felt the political need to call the state Attorney General and request a full investigation of the letter's false allegation.

I was outraged that I would be put through an inquisition over a piece of paper on which no one had the courage to sign their name. The timing, of course, was a death blow to the Florida job and the letter's motivation was beyond coincidence. My protests did nothing to change Dora's mind. I really did not expect her to have the ovaries necessary to call it the cheap political shot that it obviously was. In a way, I understood her playing the time honored "Cover Your Ass" political game. But it certainly did not make the ensuing media feeding frenzy any easier to take. The job offer from Tampa was quickly withdrawn by a nervous mayor in that city. Being honest with myself, I could not blame him, either.

Of course, the City Manager seized the opportunity as another way to get rid of me. Actually, he had been sending me little e-mail messages encouraging me to take the Tampa job by telling me what a great place Florida was and blowing enough hot air up my pant's leg to decrease my sperm count. When the D.A. called for an official investigation, the Manager figured he could not lose either way. However, when he had the City Attorney discover that the source of the rumor was an anonymous letter, Mel knew that much more would be required to make the false charge stick. That was when he recruited Tanya Murphy to spy on me from inside my own police department.

Tanya was a bright, intelligent woman who was extremely ambitious. She was also as homely as a mud fence. Tanya had been a "Kansas High School Rodeo Champion" in her youth and still looked like something only a horse could love. I liked Tanya because she did not shy away from hard work and I appreciated her desire to get ahead in this world. Because of her talents and motivation, I had promoted her to lieutenant and assigned her to the Internal Affairs Section. This was an area that I placed my most trusted and competent personnel because of the sensitive nature of their work in investigating allegations of misconduct against police officers. The job required access to the entire department. The Internal Affairs' offices were near my own so that we could confer on a regular basis. Like me, the Internal Affairs lieutenant had a pass key to any lock in the department.

Late one night, during the nightmare investigation of the trumped up charge, I could not sleep. I tossed and turned and tried counting harpooned district attorneys until after midnight. Finally, I got up, dressed and drove downtown to my office to get some routine work done without the constant interruption of some muck raking reporter. I wandered down the hall to the I.A. offices, in search of a personnel file I needed to complete a performance evaluation. Being ever curious, I noticed that there was a pink message slip on Lieutenant Murphy's desk to call the City Manager. This certainly aroused my curiosity further and I searched her desk top.

Underneath the full size calendar, on my "faithful" subordinate's desk, I found a half completed report addressed to the City Manager and titled "Surveillance on the Chief of Police". The report detailed my own activities for the last three days and included a detailed list of the current paperwork on my desk. Documents that were inside my own locked office.

The report was carefully structured under headings such as "Lunch Locations and Time", "Meetings", and "Out of Department Contacts". The espionage report had stopped before the section on "Incriminating Statements" had been completed.

I returned the report to its hidden location and never said a word about my findings to anyone. It was a real blow, personally. I had just rewarded Tanya with a promotion to lieutenant and given her my trust and a prestigious assignment, but it obviously was not enough for her. I decided that Seven-Eleven would be selling ice slushies on the sun before I would ever promote Tanya Murphy again. When the situation was finally resolved, Tanya found herself transferred out of Police Headquarters and back to a patrol division. I also made sure that her pass key was returned. To make certain, the locks on my office were changed.

Knowing how ambitious Tanya was, I figured that she had been pressuring Mel for another promotion in return for her spy efforts. This payoff for services rendered was due, despite the fact that I had been totally cleared of any wrongdoing. In fact, I had received an official letter of apology from the Kansas Attorney General for getting involved in what was a shameless political attack in the first place.

"Murphy's an up and comer and she deserves to be promoted," Mel insisted.

"Maybe," I said, resisting the urge to throw her treachery in his face. "But that's the police chief's call and not yours, Mr. Manager."

"Okay," he sighed. I knew that this did not signal his agreement with my position; only that he was tired of debating the subject with me. "The bottom line is that there are a lot of people who do not think you have the skills to do the job. I am getting a lot of complaints from members of your own department, as well as the community. There are members of the City Council who are getting nervous over our inability to eliminate crime in this city and they are pressuring me to do something."

"How about approving my budget requests for additional police officers, for one thing, instead of sending me secret instructions that I must prepare a "no increase" budget request to show to the city council? That makes it look like I don't have sense enough to know that we are woefully understaffed. Every cocktail waitress and taxi cab driver in Wichita knows how few police officers there actually are in this city," I pleaded. "We're spread thinner than a gnat's ass stretched over a box car."

"We can't just keep throwing money at our crime problems, there's not enough tax dollars to go around," Mel insisted.

"Not if we keep buying land we don't need, that's for sure." I retorted.

"What's that supposed to mean?" Mel shot back.

"You know damn well what that means. You used part of the police department's budgeted funds last year to buy land up on Twenty First Street for a new police sub-station. A station that we don't need. Hell, we don't even have the officers to staff it. Another sub-station is not even in our own long range plans for expanding the police department over the next ten years. Just who owned that property up there, Mel? Tell me that," I demanded.

Actually, I did not need Mel to tell me who owned the land. City Councilman Ray Gondorf owned the parcel of land through a dummy real estate corporation. I also knew that the city had purchased the property for ten times its appraised value. The bogus holding company rented the run down shacks, currently on the property, to illegal aliens and crack dealers for huge monthly rates. Councilman Gondorf made a small fortune on the deal and, of course, would insure that Mel had his political support on the council whenever it was needed. That was one vote that definitely would not go my way in any showdown, I reasoned.

"That has nothing to do with our conversation today," Mel slammed the door shut on any further exchanges of who knew what about whom.

"You need to improve your relationships and start acting like a real police chief, instead of some crusading Boy Scout," he concluded icily.

I bit my tongue again and sat very still as I looked squarely at the top of his head. Mel continued to stare at his desk top. He had not looked me in the eye for the entire time that we spoke.

"You're right, Mel" I finally said. I stood up from my chair and rose to my full six feet, one inch frame. The leather of my gun belt creaked when I got up. "Is that all you need me for today?" I asked.

My sudden humility confused him. "Well, just try to do better," he sighed, never looking up.

I turned on a polished heel and strode out of the door in my best imitation of a West Point cadet. Mel was right. I should try to do better. The question was whether or not I wanted to be a better Boy Scout or a better asshole like he wanted.

Riding the elevator back to my fourth floor office, I tried to think about my meeting with Mel and where my life was heading. There was no question that my relationship with my boss was terrible. The real problem, as I saw it, was my inability to bend to his controlling, manipulative style of management. The longer I worked under the system, the more I hated everything about it. The issue was not just my desire to control the police department anymore. I kept finding out things that did not fit with my underlying belief that people in authority should be fundamentally good and honest individuals. Mel was right. I was a damn Boy Scout at heart.

The office was quiet when I returned. It was 9:30 a.m. Just in time for our mini-staff meeting that we held each morning. The mini-staff was a variation of a full scale staff monthly meeting, only a lot shorter. It was designed to start the morning off with a brief exchange of information and plans for the day among my senior staff members. Attendance by my three deputy chiefs and Tim David was not required, but it was expected.

I tried to keep these meetings light in content and in the twenty minute range. Deputy Chief Gant was always the last to arrive. We usually spent half of our brief time together each morning repeating what was discussed before Pete appeared. If we did not, Pete pouted and claimed that we excluded him from important decisions. I graded him down on his last performance evaluation because of his chronic lateness and it caused a minor explosion.

"I'm not late to anything important," Pete had complained.

"Do you ever think, Pete, that when I call a meeting, I have a tendency to think that the purpose might be important?" I responded. "Chiefs are funny that way. They think they have the right to expect their closest command staff members to follow their directives."

"Pete, you were even ten minutes late to this meeting concerning your performance evaluation," I continued. "I'm having a hard time swallowing your excuses when you are late to a scheduled meeting about your own performance. An evaluation, I might add, that is grading you down for being late. Do you see a connection here?"

It all did no good, of course. Pete would continue to be late to everything as long as he lived and probably afterwards. I pictured Saint Peter tapping his foot, waiting to review Pete's application to heaven. Meanwhile the ever tardy and recently deceased Pete, would be stopping along the way to trim his nose hair.

Tim David was already in the office when I arrived. He was smiling and looked rested. Billy Wade came in right behind me. He looked like hell. The circles under Billy's eyes were a testament to a lack of sleep and the abuse his wife must have given him when he got home late.

Jack Denson came in just as I sat down behind my desk. Jack rounded out my trio of deputy chiefs who, combined with Tim, comprised my senior command staff. Deputy Chief Denson was a quiet, almost shy man. I had promoted him twice in the last six years, not because he was black, but because of his ability to follow my directions without argument. Mel Michaels delighted in sending me instructions about where to assign Jack. When Denson had been a captain, Mel wanted me to assign him to command the East Patrol Division because of the large numbers of blacks in northeast Wichita. I tried to point out to the Manager that patrol divisions were commanded by majors, not captains. Besides, I did not believe in assigning people based on their skin color.

Mel responded by eliminating the rank of major from the authorized strength structure in the next year's budget. It was a typical over-reaction that he reasoned would solve the problem. When we all pitched a fit, the Manager held firm. He did not like the rank of major anyway, he countered. When he was in the Army, he told me, he never saw a need for majors.

It was hard to fight the impressions of a nineteen year old draftee from over forty years ago. In the dawn of the atomic era, Mel never rose higher than private during his less than illustrious two year hitch. Now, he was in charge, by God. If the rank of major stood in the way of something he wanted done, he just wiped it away. That was how his mind worked.

After months of arguing, the best I was able to salvage was a minor concession. I would not be required to demote the three current majors right away. The Manager allowed them to keep the rank for another year. If they did not retire in a year, they could keep the title but there would be no extra pay for the position. In addition, captains and any remaining majors would be equal in authority and responsibility, according to Mel. The idea was managerial and organizational insanity. It was like telling the surgeon and a nurse that they were both in charge of decisions in the operating room. If you can imagine that chaos, then you would have a good idea how the system worked in a para-military organization like the police department.

I sat down in my high backed leather office chair and swiveled to gaze mindlessly out the window. The chair was a present from Peggy on my first anniversary of being chief. She had visited my office one day and observed me attempting to wire back together the worn out chair the city provided me. Her present did not arrive soon enough to keep me from first humiliating myself in the city's chair.

I had been meeting with the president of the First National Bank when the rickety chair collapsed for the umpteenth time that week. The damn thing dumped me unceremoniously on my embarrassed posterior. I fell in a heap behind the desk. Body, soul, badge, gun, uniform and all just disappeared from the view of my office guest. I was a disembodied voice to the bank president while I cussed the piece of junk city chair.

I felt like an old Chevy Chase skit of Gerald Ford on "Saturday Night Live." When I crawled up from the floor, the banker was in stitches. Prior to my ridiculous prat fall, we had been discussing my request for a donation from the bank to buy bullet proof vests for a new class of recruit police officers. The bank president was skeptical of my assertion that the city did not buy body armor for its new officers. After all, the ballistic vest protection was a standard piece of police equipment all over the country, he rightly assumed.

After falling out of my broken chair, the bank president quickly wrote me a ten thousand dollar check for the vests. Every time I tried to sit back in the chair, it would fall apart again. Tears of laughter were rolling down his cheeks.

"Jesus Christ, Chief, stop it," he cried between guffaws. "I get the picture. If the city won't buy its police chief a decent chair to sit in, how will it protect its police officers. You've convinced me. Here, take the money quickly before I have a heart attack from laughing so hard."

Peggy did not think the whole embarrassing episode was so funny. She picked out a classy maroon executive chair, with tufted leather and brass accessories, and had it delivered to my office. It was a great present but it hardly matched the early 1960's bomb shelter decor of my office. I loved her protective gesture as much as the chair.

"What's going on in patrol this morning, Billy?" I asked as I glanced out of the dusty office window. The blue Kansas sky was an awesome sight in the morning, I thought.

"Not much, Chief. I'm still digging through my paperwork from yesterday," he replied.

I turned back to the group and saw Tim still smiling. "And where did you vanish to last night, Tim?" I asked.

"Oh, Chief, I decided to go to midnight mass when you fell asleep in the lawn chair. You weren't much fun to be around after that," he countered.

"I guess not," I admitted. "Has anybody seen Pete this morning?"

"Yeah," Billy said. "He's here somewhere but it's Tim's day to watch him, not mine."

Tim rolled his eyes at Gant's tardiness again and I turned to Jack for a report of his day's plans.

"You got anything going in investigations, Jack?" I inquired.

"Well," Jack carefully began, "We've got a couple of big cases that appear to be coming together that I need to brief you on, Chief. Also, I've got a kinda, uh, unique personnel situation that you should know about."

Tim broke out into a large grin. As usual, he already knew about everything long before it got to me. Glancing to my right for any other reaction, I noticed that Billy just looked hung over and was his usual clueless self.

"Okay," I groaned wearily, "Let's hear it."

Deputy Chief Denson never changed his expression as he said, "Well, if you don't mind Chief, I would like to bring down Lieutenant Manson to give you the details first hand. It's a very, uh, unusual case, Chief, and I think you should really hear it from someone else."

"Come on, Jack," I protested. "You've got me dreading the worst with this story. What's the deal?"

"Chief, you'll just have to see the report to believe it," Jack replied. "I've got Manson writing it down in black and white before we schedule an appointment with you. That way we will have all the facts documented and the story straight."

"Give me hint, huh, Jack?" I pleaded. "Just so I can feel like I'm not the only one in this department that doesn't know what's going on."

Tim interrupted before Jack could compose a reply and said, "Chief, let's just say that it's out of this world."

Jack squinted his closed eyes into a grimace and Tim's grin got even wider. Before I could say anything else, the mayor walked in the open office door unannounced.

"Mr. Mayor, what a pleasant surprise to see you up here," I offered.

"Good morning, gentlemen," Mayor Ben Cole announced. "Don't let me interrupt you. I just stopped by to say "hi".

My staff and I all rose from our chairs like we were attached to the same string. "No problem, Mayor," I chimed. "Come on in. I think you know my command staff, don't you?"

"Oh sure," the Mayor said. "I've known most of them for longer than you have, Chief." He was not smiling as he nodded at each member of my staff. I thought I detected a questioning gaze at Billy's glowing hangover, but I could not be positive.

Tim took the hint, and the lead, and said, "Mayor, we were just finished with our meeting. Chief, if you don't need us anymore, we have to start work on that assignment now if we are going to have it ready for you by the end of the day."

Billy looked puzzled. For a moment, he wondered what assignment he had missed. When Billy finally figured out what Tim was doing, he followed Tim and Jack out the door as my staff carefully brushed past the Mayor.

Ben Cole had just been re-elected a few months previously and was the consummate politician. He talked a great line about family values and his vision of "getting the community back together." In truth, Ben's vision was to get Ben into higher office. He was a Wichita native who grew up being the nerd picked on by the other kids in school. Ben dropped out of high school and joined the Coast Guard at seventeen. Returning home after his hitch, he somehow met and married the daughter of a rich real estate developer after convincing her that he was a bonifide war hero of the first order.

For the last thirty years, Ben tried his hand at several different honest jobs without success. Finally getting his G.E.D. high school equivalency degree, Ben failed miserably selling real estate in his father in-law's company. Also, he had not prospered being a bank teller, a short order cook and a mail order Chinchilla rancher. All the furry little creatures died; leaving Ben's wife with another large debt from her shiftless husband's latest get rich quick scheme.

After awhile, Ben discovered what he did best was sell bull shit. He projected a humble, unassuming posture before the public that endeared himself to the voters. Behind the scenes, Ben's ego was as enormous as his big red nose. The broken blood vessels, from many years of alcohol abuse, gave the mayor an appearance that was a cross between Saint Nick and Karl Malden. In his mind, Ben thought he was more popular than both with the public. He was probably right.

"Rod, how are you doing," the Mayor asked, using my first name like any good politician.

"I'm fine, Mayor," I replied. "Thank you for asking."

Ben nodded and wiped an imaginary speck from his new double breasted suit. "I got a great deal on a new wardrobe down at Buck's," he admitted.

"I can see that, Mayor. It looks very nice." No one knew where Ben Cole got his money, since he did not have a real job. The mayor's position paid five hundred dollars a month in recognition for what was supposed to be a largely ceremonial job in the city manager form of government.

"You should go down and see them for some new clothes yourself," the Mayor said, as he looked disdainfully at my brown uniform with the forest green stripe down the side of the pants.

"Thanks, Mayor, maybe I will," I mumbled. I had as much intent on going to "Buck's Custom Haberdashery" as I did on becoming a sperm donor.

"Victor called this morning and asked how you were doing," the Mayor continued. "He was especially concerned about your wife."

Victor Pasqual was the former police chief who retired just before I took the job. Ben Cole treated him like a little brother. They had obviously been connected politically for many years. Victor was a drunk, plain and simple. He had been a young man when he rose to the chief's position, after the previous chief suffered a nervous breakdown in office. Now in retirement, Victor found religion for the first time. At least that was what he told the judge after his last drunk driving arrest.

Most members of the Wichita Department covered for their former chief when they found him drunk and passed out at all hours. Unfortunately for Victor, he had wandered up the highway to Salina where his former position cut no slack with the local police. They found him driving around and around in circles, on the parking lot of a Methodist church, at four thirty in the morning. The Salina officers were not able to stop Victor until he ran off the pavement and crashed into a swing set by the church's day care facility. Victor's blood alcohol level that morning was 0.24. The amount was three times the legal limit for drunk driving in the state of Kansas and about ten times more alcohol than Victor could handle, despite his long history with the bottle.

Victor paid his fine and quietly served his probation. In the meantime, he turned into a religious fanatic. His wife of forty years left him. Not because of his drinking, but because she could not stand the constant muddled lectures about sin and repentance. I felt sorry for Victor and treated him with the utmost courtesy out of respect for the position that he had once held. Regardless of his skills as a police chief, or lack of them, it was a job that would drive anyone to drink.

"Victor likes you," the Mayor said. "I think he really likes your wife and wants to become a part of your family, so to speak."

"Mayor, my wife and I already have a family. I don't think we want to adopt Chief Pasqual," I quipped without too much sarcasm.

"That's not what he means," the Mayor explained. "His spiritual family is what he calls his friends now. I'm afraid I've already adopted him. It's just that he is really trying to change his life for the better. I've asked him to stay around City Hall and give me advice from time to time."

The odor of cow manure was overpowering. Terrific, I thought. Just what I needed. The Mayor was going to get his advice on how a police department should be run from a reformed alcoholic whose last original thought had been during the era when service station attendants actually pumped gasoline into your automobile.

"You ought to think about changing your life around a little, too, Rod," the Mayor suggested.

"I don't know, Mayor," I hedged. "I kind of like who I am. It's the assholes around me that I would like to see changed. Could you arrange frontal lobotomies on some select people that I chose? Maybe wrangle a group discount rate over at the med school to re-section a little brain matter for a few members of the city organization."

Cole ignored my hazy reference to his ability to obtain cut-rates on things like new suits and mind altering surgeries for a few people around City Hall. "Just remember, Rod, there will be life after you've been the police chief. You need to think about where you are going after your tenure is up. There might be some good opportunities right here in Wichita later on for a person with your experience."

I blinked and did not reply. I wanted to tell the Mayor that I planned to open up a prophylactic recycling center in his neighborhood when I retired, but I decided he would not appreciate the humor. I also wondered if "prophylactic" was too technical a term for a politician with a G.E.D. to understand. They probably failed to cover that word on the exam.

Ben kept me from committing further political suicide when he finally said, "Well, gotta go and run the city. See you, later, Chief."

He drifted past Suzie and out into the hallway by the elevators. I followed him with a quizzical gaze while I pondered his visit. Billy Wade interrupted my self-imposed trance.

"You know Chief, I really like that guy," Billy said.

"Where did you come from, Billy?" I asked. "I thought you were gone."

"Oh, I was just standing around out here in the hall," he replied. "I think the mayor is the one guy that keeps the manager off of our ass."

"Well, Billy, you know "his honor" a lot better than I do," I answered. What I really thought was "Billy, you are either incredibly stupid or full of it". However, I had an uneasy feeling that Billy was just a little too close to our mayor. I did not want to make any more enemies right now. I still had not figured out what to make of Cole's last statement concerning "good opportunities after being police chief" when Billy brought me back to earth.

"Chief, I really do need to talk with you about the Guenther hearing," Billy said.

"What about Guenther?" I asked.

"Well, he's got a disciplinary hearing on the rude conduct complaint coming up and he's not out of the hospital yet. It kinda makes things awkward," Billy lamented. "You know, suspending a guy who's been shot and all. Are you sure we should go through with the punishment hearing?"

Carl Guenther was one of those police officers that was missing some minor element in his overall construction which would have made him a really great officer. He was hard working, aggressive and had a great nose for finding bad guys. Unfortunately, he was also full of the John Wayne syndrome and believed himself to be God's gift to American law enforcement. Too much the hot dog, I feared, and sometimes the mustard leaked out.

It seemed that Guenther was always in trouble. During the abortion protests, we tried desperately to keep him out of the line of fire. Deputy Chief Wade had placed him in charge of the command post security detail. It seemed like a relatively safe assignment and worked well for most of the major demonstrations. Just when the major protests finally fizzled out, a group of about fifty demonstrators stayed in Wichita and decided that they would picket the police department instead of the clinics.

Before we could realize our mistake in assignments, Officer Guenther was on the defensive line to greet the protesters, along with about six other officers. The crowd began giving the officers a hard time, shouting insults and calling them names. From out of the crowd, one rather elderly lady, wearing red high top tennis shoes and a "Save the Whales" tee shirt, moved directly at Officer Guenther. She carried a sign that read "Down with Hitler's Police in Wichita."

Guenther officiously blocked her path and motioned that he wanted to talk with the woman. This was a direct violation of his instructions and his training. Officers on the crowd control line were not allowed to engage in conversation with the protesters, lest it lead to debates and emotional involvement with the specifics of the social issue. Our job was simple. Enforce the law. That was all we needed to do.

For whatever reason, Officer Guenther decided to disregard his training on this particular day and we would all live to regret his decision.

"Ma'am," he politely told the tennis shoed granny lady, "I'm extremely offended by your sign."

"Oh really," the lady said. "You don't like being called a Nazi, huh?"

"No ma'am, I sure don't. It brings back painful memories in my family," Officer Guenther said in his best hurt little boy voice. "You see, I lost a relative in the concentration camps at Auschwitz."

The woman was stunned. She was completely humiliated at her own insensitivity. Like most of the protesters, the woman was basically a good, honest person who felt strongly that abortion was an affront against God and should not be allowed in a civilized nation. Unfortunately for her beliefs, the law said otherwise.

The lady began crying. "I'm so, so sorry young man. I don't know how I could have been so inconsiderate. I'm a Christian, you know. I'll pray for your relative's soul. Did he die in the gas chambers?" the repentant woman asked.

"No, you stupid bitch," Guenther shot back quickly. "He got drunk and fell out of a guard tower and broke his neck."

With that, Officer Guenther began guffawing in laughter and left the woman standing knee deep in gullibility.

The Channel 12 news crew that caught the entire exchange on video tape was headed by a friend of mine from my church softball team. Unbelievably, he gave me the video rather than show it on the six o'clock news. I was very grateful.

The Internal Affairs investigation did not take long to sustain a violation of our departmental regulations against Officer Guenther. He was charged with failing to "treat each citizen with dignity, courtesy, and respect while utilizing good judgment in every situation". We called it "Rule 999". It covered just about every eventuality when officers acted like complete fools.

Deputy Chief Wade recommended a three day suspension without pay. I had concurred with the recommendation and ordered that the suspension begin immediately. However, as usual, Billy was slow getting the paper work done. Before Officer Guenther could be officially disciplined for the granny lady affront, he became involved in another incident which was even more serious.

Since Guenther had extensive military training, he had earned a slot on the SWAT team as a demolition expert. It was his duty to handle the need for flash grenades, smoke canisters or other diversionary devices that might be necessary.

I had formed the "Special Weapons And Tactics" team shortly after coming to Wichita. Before my arrival, it was an unorganized free for all at the scene of any type of major incident. In training a hand-picked unit and equipping them with the essentials of special police operations, we had saved a lot of civilian casualties.

Most assuredly, there were several police officers whose lives were saved due to SWAT's expertise.

Getting the equipment was not an easy task. Predictably, Mel refused to provide any funds for the project. The National Guard donated some thirty-seven millimeter tear gas guns and an assortment of gas and smoke rounds. It was the best equipment that France made after the war, the National Guard captain had assured me. Which war, no one knew for sure.

The first time we used the gas gun to fire one of the ancient projectiles, it was a classic study in the effects of bargain basement shopping. I ordered the army surplus tear gas round to be launched into a second story window to flush an armed robbery suspect who had barricaded himself inside a small apartment and refused to surrender. The missile shaped projectile actually bounced off the double pane glass window and rolled back toward our perimeter. The damned thing was smoking and whistling when it exploded at my feet and showered us all with fifty year old tear gas. The suspect was laughing so hard, from watching our antics out of the cracked window, that he surrendered without a fight.

After that adventure into military hardware, I went to nearby McConnell Air Force Base to see if they had any surplus military helmets for the SWAT team to wear. I figured that there must be thousands of the heavy "Kevlar" brain buckets just laying around all over after our country's many foreign excursions into the Middle East, the Balkans and just about every other third world hot spot on the planet. My efforts to acquire some of their surplus junk became quite a chore. Finally, the Base Commander made me execute a "Temporary Loan" form, in quadruplicate, assigning twelve of the olive drab helmets to my personal custody. Each year, a Staff Sergeant from the air base called me to verify that I had not sold the helmets to the Russians.

A couple of weeks previously, Officer Guenther and the rest of the SWAT team was called out for a barricaded person call on the north side. Some wacko had been out drinking and came home to argue with his wife after the bars closed. It was a typical drunken family argument. The point of contention was probably something of less than vital importance, like the size of the wife's ass or the dog's breath. Who knows. After hundreds of these types of calls, no one cares.

Anyway, the drunk threw his wife through the screen door just as the first patrol officer rolled up in response to the neighbor's 911 call of a disturbance. The drunk pulled out a pump shotgun from behind the front door and pointed it at the officer. Displaying more valor than was expected, the young patrolman managed to drag the crying wife to safety behind his squad car and avoid being shot by the husband.

Responding to the SWAT call out, Officer Guenther decided that he would try talking the drunk into surrendering before the rest of his team, or the duty chief, arrived. Totally against all accepted police procedures, Guenther abandoned his protected position and took two steps into the drunks yard. The bad guy came out of his house, naked and yelling wildly. The suspect was wearing nothing but a twelve gauge, the report would later say.

Officer Guenther turned and ran for a nearby tree just as the drunk fired a load of number eight bird shot into Guenther's exposed buttocks. Before the drunk could chamber another round, the patrol officer who had saved the wife fired a full clip from his nine millimeter Smith and Wesson. Out of a total of fifteen shots, the patrol officer struck the suspect four times. One round blew a testicle onto the neighbor's front porch. Two other shots from the patrolman's pistol grazed the suspect in both legs. The fourth hollow point bullet gave the naked warrior a third eye socket right in the middle of his forehead. The drunken fool never felt the pain of the detached testicle.

By the time the neighbor's cat was pawing at what was left of the blue and pink reproductive organ, which landed with a sticky splat on the neighbor's wooden porch, Officer Guenther had told his story to the Homicide Division detectives and Internal Affairs investigators. It was clear Guenther thought that he was a hero. The young patrol officer, who had been forced to kill the drunken husband to save Guenther's ass, was devastated and curled up in the front seat of his patrol car and bawled like a baby.

The American Civil Liberties Union refuses to believe it, but most police officers are terribly effected by having to use deadly force. I have seen some officers become so emotionally torn by the experience that they had to be hospitalized. Some require psychiatric counseling for years afterwards when the ghost of the guy they killed keeps appearing night after night at the foot of their bed.

The patrol officer later discussed his own personal demons with our "Critical Incident Stress Debriefing Team" and our departmental psychologist. During the same week, Guenther had tiny bits of lead picked out of his pimply rear at Wesley Hospital.

"Tell me what you suggest, Billy," I answered. "I'm not real high on suspending a guy that's hobbling around on crutches, either."

"I don't know, Chief," Billy whined. "I just thought you may have thought of something better."

"I know, I know. You thought I'd come up with a better way to cut the baby in half. But, hey, guess what? I'm running out of Solomon-like ways to deal with these same nutty characters that cross my desk each week. It's always the same ones that get into trouble," I lectured. "Why did Chief Pasqual and you guys hire nitwits like these? It is going to take us years to weed the nut cases and loose cannons out of the department."

"I'll tell you what, Billy," I continued. "You go down to the hospital and tell Guenther that his disciplinary hearing on the abuse of the granny lady has been placed on hold until he returns to full duty. That should take some of the pain out of his sore ass."

Billy seemed relieved with the decision and waved good bye as he shuffled toward the hallway elevators. I could not claim it was a great decision, but it was the best I could come up with on short notice. I had visited Guenther in the hospital the night he was shot, as was my practice whenever any officer was injured. He really was a likable guy, but damn it, he acted like an idiot with the old lady protester and this latest incident was just plain stupidity.

If Guenther had not tried to charge in there like Arnold Swartzeneger, there was a great probability that our trained negotiators on the SWAT team could have talked the poor drunk out of the house. At the very least, the duty chiefs had strict instructions from me to wait out those kinds of situations. Chances are very good that a drunk will almost always sober up and then surrender when they realize how serious things have become. If not, they usually pass out. When this happens, the snoring adversary is easy prey for a blinding stun grenade blast, followed by a swarm of heavily armored SWAT officers leaping from all directions like Ninja warriors.

I wondered if Guenther was still trying to impress his new wife. The new Mrs. Guenther was also a police officer. Her nick name was "Rambolina". No one remembered what her real first name was. Her appearance was a cross between Sylvester Stallone's body and the countenance of Samantha's mother on "Bewitched". Older than Carl, Rambolina was a female body builder who delighted in pumping iron and balancing her under the counter steroid levels with health food.

On the eve of their marriage, Rambolina went to a local sex toy store and picked up a few items for the honeymoon. She bought six pairs of leather underwear, with zippers, and a couple of leather masks with small air holes for minimal oxygen acquisition. An assortment of other kinky accouterments included a soft leather whip and some dog collars with stainless metal studs. No one on the police department would have ever known about her strange shopping habits if she had not pulled out her badge and police identification card to show the clerk. When Rambolina asked if there was a police discount available, she crossed the line of ethical behavior. The sex shop clerk did not believe Rambolina was a police officer. She called 911 to report an impostor posing as a police officer to receive special favors. Soon the shop was full of uniforms and supervisors who heard the call come out over the radio and just had to see what kind of dildo would try to impersonate a police officer in a sex shop. Pun intended.

Rambolina's shopping spree did not seem to embarrass her in the least. The five day suspension she was assessed for her own violation of "Rule 999" was used as unpaid honeymoon leave in Bermuda for the newly married couple. Since then, there had been reports that both members of the Guenther family had reported for work with black eyes and bruises. It was only a matter of time before one went too far in their games and seriously injured the other. At best, the first officers on the scene would likely have a hard time deciding who bit whose ear off first.

I returned yesterday's telephone call from Howlin' Hank, who wanted me to appear on his tv show, and drove toward a hastily arranged luncheon date with him at 11:30. We agreed on a little Mexican food restaurant on North Broadway simply because it was close.

"La Estrelita" was a fairly nice restaurant, tucked in between a Pizza Hut and a beer joint, just a mile or so north of City Hall. I liked the place because of the name, not the food. "La Estrelita", translated from Spanish, means "Little Star". It seemed like an appropriate place for the police chief to eat. The little stars on my collar fit the name, if not the decor.

The eatery was run by a Lebanese guy who could not speak a single word of Spanish and very little English. I was sure that he had no idea what the name of his restaurant meant. He bought the building from the previous owner a few years before and decided not to change the name to save a few dollars on his Yellow Pages ad.

"What can I bring you today?" the waitress asked. She was Hispanic, about seventeen years old, and very, very attractive. In fact, she was quite a stunner.

"Can you just bring me a Pepsi?" I asked. "I'm waiting for a friend before I order."

"Sorry, all we have is Coke," she replied with a smile.

"That'll have to do, I reckon," I answered. I hate it when a place sells Coke, but not Pepsi. You would think after all of these years of brutal competition that the two biggest soft drink makers in the world would just let their vendors slug it out, face to face, in the free market. Oh well, one of life's little speed bumps, I guess.

"Okay, one Coke coming up," she said cheerfully.

I looked out the front picture window at the dismal surroundings on North Broadway. It was not a very impressive sight. Used car lots dotted the landscape right and left. The street ran north and south, almost exactly dividing the town in perfect halves from city limit to city limit. Most Wichitans thought of themselves as either "Eastsiders" or "Westsiders", depending on which side of Broadway they lived on.

The restaurant was filled with an assortment of noon time diners. The tables held a combination of men and women in business suits, as well as truck drivers in

Levis and denim shirts. Eating establishments can be real melting pots of society, I mindlessly observed.

"You better quit daydreamin', pardner," Howlin' Hank slapped me on the back with some great advice.

Damn, I was loosing my police instincts. Somehow, Hank had slipped through the side door without me seeing him. It was a good thing he was not an armed robber with a sawed off shotgun. In that case, my guts would now be splattered all over the walls and become the primary cause for finally redecorating "La Estrelita".

"You're right, Hank, daydreamin' is a bad habit and it causes warts," I stood up in reply.

Unknown to me, Hank had brought Mickey Blake with him. She would certainly spice up the lunch, I thought.

"You remember Mickey, don't you Chief," Hank introduced the underground sex goddess. "We just finished taping a show and she was hungry too, so I brought her along. I hope that's okay."

I nodded at Mickey and we all sat down. "That's great," I lied. "How have you been, Miss Blake?"

"Fine, thank you," was all she said. Wichita's undisputed queen of oral sex gingerly took her seat. I was not certain how it would be perceived being seen in a public place with Mickey. I hoped that Hank's presence would cancel out any wild rumors that might get started. At least half of the restaurant patrons had already noticed her. The other half did not recognize Mickey with her clothes on and nothing in her mouth.

The waitress returned with my substitute Pepsi and took our orders right away. As usual, Hank tried to order the "Kansas Sheepherder's Special" from the confused girl.

"I'll take a glass of water and a piece of ewe, darlin'," Hank smiled devilishly. The young waitress actually blushed, probably more at Hank's obligatory "darlin'" at the close of his sentence rather than understanding the connection between the imaginary special and "ewe".

Hank finally relented from teasing the waitress and picked the spiciest item on the menu. Mickey ordered the same dish, but with extra hot sauce. I chose the traditional standard fare for gringos, a "Mexican dinner". I knew this would insure that I received whatever leftovers remained in the kitchen, but at least it would not be heavily peppered with jalapenos. Despite my Texas heritage, I really did not like Mexican food or anything spicy. I had protected my taste buds from the assaults of tobacco and alcohol. Unlike a lot of other people, my sense of taste did not require a jolt of liquid fire to activate its function. I assumed, from personal observation, that Mickey Blake probably had no sense of taste in her mouth whatsoever.

Hank eyed the cute waitress as she retreated toward the kitchen.

"It's a pity," he said, "she'll be just like all the other "senoritas" from south of the border. They're only good lookin' between the ages of fourteen and nineteen. When she gets past twenty, her body will start to change into the shape of a bag of wet cement. Add in about six kids in quick Catholic succession and her life expectancy will dwindle to about fifty," Hank sighed wistfully. I purposely failed to comment on his oft expressed sociological theory.

"How are you and the City Manager getting along?," Hank cut right to the chase.

"Not at all, as usual," I replied quickly.

"Boy, he sure is one tough guy to be around," Hank said. "When they were passing out personality, Mel was playing with himself in the closet, that's for sure."

Mickey did not even flinch at Hank's crude remark. I did. Hank was not the country bumpkin that he portrayed himself to be. He was really an extremely powerful influence in local politics, but his forte was in behind the scenes maneuvers. For this reason, I made it a point to keep him in my corner.

I tried to get back to the subject of the meeting. "Hank, when do you and Mickey want me to be on your show?"

"Well, let's see," Hank dug a pocket calendar from his western style leather coat. "We've got every Wednesday clear between now and Christmas. Just pick a date and we will set you up."

"That's what I'm afraid of," I replied. "You will set me up, that is."

"Oh, come on Chief," Hank's feelings were hurt. "You know we don't do that on our show."

He was right. I had appeared on their television talk show at least six times and a dozen more on Hank's radio show. They had always been the model of cordiality. In fact, Hank often tossed me beach ball size questions, that he knew I would hit out of the park, on issues I wanted to explain to the public.

"You're right, Hank," I made amends. "Because of that, I never turn you down. When you've interviewed all of the local hog callers and tin foil collectors in town, I'm always good for an update on the latest spiffy new crime fighting sensations from Wichita's finest. How about a week from next Wednesday, then?"

"Great, we got you penciled in at the usual fee," Hank said as he scribbled a note into his little calendar book. The usual fee was a Pepsi before and after the show. I wondered how much Daryl Gates, the former Los Angeles Police Chief, got for doing the "Larry King Live Show". Maybe he got a Snickers bar to go with the soft drink. I made a mental note to ask Hank for a raise.

"Any special subject you're interested in for the show, Hank?" I asked.

"Yeah, you could tell us how you are controlling the hookers on South Broadway, if you want," Hank answered.

"Yeah, Chief, I hear that you've wiped out all that nasty sex on the streets," Mickey chimed in.

"That would be a trick, no pun intended, Hank," I retorted.

"No Chief since Caesar has solved prostitution."

"In that case, let's talk about your new budget request. I'm sure the audience would be interested in the firestorm that will erupt over that little honey," Hank stated with a very serious tone which was not his usual style.

"How did you know about my budget request, Hank?" I asked. "I just turned the damned paperwork in to Michaels."

"Oh, you know, I hear things around town. By the way, if I were you, I'd be watching my backside right now. The word is that your boss has been bad mouthing you to the City Council. It looks as though he's trying to lay the groundwork for another move to send you packing, my friend." Hank was getting even more serious and his voice lowered. He leaned across the table and whispered, "If there's a way to get rid of Mel Michaels instead, you let me know and I will help in that endeavor any way I can."

"Thanks, Hank. I believe you would. But right now, I've got things under control," I lied wistfully. "If things turn sour, I'll let you know. In the meantime, I can talk about how we solved the latest series of armed robberies. How's that for the show?"

"Great idea, Chief," Hank changed gears and broke into his usual hokey grin. "It's been in the papers and everybody's been talking about the "Pillowcase Bandits". What do you think, Mickey?"

Mickey Blake was not following our conversation very closely. She only caught the word "pillowcase" while she fumbled in her purse for a cigarette. Looking up, she was obviously confused.

"Uh, I'm not sure what kind of subject bed linens would make, but we can make anything work with the Chief on the show," she smiled.

The "Pillowcase Bandits" had been a group of ex-convicts who wore Halloween masks and brought their own pillowcases to carry away their loot. The FBI provided the money to pay an informant who fingered the names of the three bad guys. We were keeping them under surveillance, hoping to follow them to a crime and catch them in the act. Unfortunately, they gave our stakeout team the slip before we had any hard evidence.

We formed the Crime Analysis Unit a few years earlier to analyze crime trends and predict potential targets. This unit was very helpful in identifying where and when we should deploy our limited resources for the best effect. The unit had become especially adept at picking the most likely locations and potential times for armed robberies. Their specialty was identifying groups of dumb crooks who used the same pattern over and over again.

Our detectives took the crime analysis predictions for last weekend and chose the six convenience stores most likely to be robbed. The plan was to put a "shotgun squad" in the back room of each store. A "shotgun squad" is comprised of two officers, armed with the standard Remington 870 twelve gauge pump shotgun. Their job it is to monitor the store clerk behind one way glass or a spy hole. If the robbers hit, the officers are in position to make the arrest. Hopefully, they can do so before the clerk gets killed by a nervous, or especially vicious, bandit.

Sure enough, the "Pillowcase Bandits" could not resist a small "Stop N' Rob" store on the south edge of town. It turned out to be a bad night for the bad guys. Two robbers entered through the front door. One was wearing a "Bart Simpson" Halloween mask and the other wore a rubber gorilla head, complete with black fuzzy hair.

When he came in the door, Bart yelled, "Its a hold up, you cock sucker! Gimme all the money before I blow your fucking head off!" He punctuated his demands by pulling a large black pistol out of his belt and pointing it directly at the clerks head.

"Gorilla Face" stayed by the door, as the lookout for roving police cars, while the third suspect kept the getaway car running at the side of the building. Out of sight, the wheelman driver did not rate wearing a mask.

Staring down the barrel of Bart's ugly pistol, the clerk remembered to do just what the nice detectives had told him to do. Fall down on the floor and cover his ears.

When the clerk seemed to vanish behind the counter, Bart Simpson was confused. He pulled his rubber mask up above his eyes to get a better view of what made the clerk disappear into thin air. At the same time, he tugged a pink pillowcase from his coat pocket. It was very considerate of him to bring the pillowcase for the clerk to sack up his cash withdrawal.

With a knack for great timing, Detective Tom Malone chose that precise moment to step out from behind the toilet paper isle.

"Trick or Treat, Motherfucker," Detective Malone called out.

When a confused Bart Simpson turned to see what fool was talking to him like that, the officer fired a blast of number four buck shot into the luckless robber's mid section. At the ten foot range, even the plastic wad that held the lead pellets inside the shell was lethal. The coroner would later find the round's inner plastic shot sleeve imbedded between two of Bart Simpson's shattered ribs.

"Gorilla Face", seeing his partner's liver escape through his lower back, broke for the front door and safety beyond. Detective Amos Black pushed over a display of

Kotex to get a better shot at the fleeing gorilla. A stubborn box of maxi-pads caused his aim to be a little high. Most of the heavy lead pellets struck the gorilla in the back of the neck and head. A spray of blood, brain matter, and fake gorilla hair doused the magazine rack and ruined the store's entire stock of Penthouse and Hustler. As soon as "Gorilla Face" lost his face, Detective Black yelled in his most authoritative voice, "Stop! Police, don't move!"

The fake gorilla never heard the warning. Predictably, the blast of hot lead through the back of his skull caused his ears to stop working, along with every other part of his body. The clerk would later swear that, even though he had kept his hands tightly clamped over his ears as instructed, he definitely heard the officer identify himself as a police officer and yell for the suspect to stop. The clerk just was not sure of the sequence of the events between the shots and the command. As far as he was concerned, it did not really matter.

Both officers ejected their spent shell casings and chambered another round in their Remingtons. They looked at each other, took a deep breath, and charged through the smashed front glass door to find the getaway car and driver they knew would not be far away.

The third robber had the tape deck in his Buick tuned to its highest level to match the blower of the car's heater. His chills were getting worse as his last shot of Mexican brown heroin was wearing off. Snoop Doggy Dog was blasting some mean rap tunes on the tape about killin', and gang bangin' and whorin' and shit and the lookout was oblivious to the carnage inside the store.

Wow, the getaway driver must have thought, who are these motherfuckers sticking big guns in my face?

Detective Malone jerked open the driver's door and pulled the dumbest getaway driver in robbery history out onto the pavement. The Buick, which was in gear with the motor running to keep the heater blowing, rolled driverless toward the front of the convenience store. Detective Black fell heavily on the robber's spinal column with a knee drop that he learned from watching "World Federation Wrestling" on tv with his kids. The driver expelled air from a collapsed lung, just as his precious Buick rolled into the line of gas pumps thirty feet away.

The ruptured gasoline lines spurted fuel onto the Buick's hot manifold with catastrophic results. In a matter of seconds, the Buick was a molten hunk of junk. The Snoop Doggy Dog tape had vaporized and about fifty thousand dollars worth of damage was done to the front of the convenience store.

The N.A.A.C.P. and the local A.C.L.U. protested vehemently when they learned that Bart Simpson had been armed with a air pistol that was designed to look like a forty five automatic. Boy, we all thought, you just can not trust these criminals anymore. First we found out that he was not the "real" Bart Simpson cartoon character and then we learned he did not even have a real gun. Geez, what a kidder that guy was. Oh, well.

Neither "Gorilla Face" nor the getaway driver was armed. The professional complainers called it excessive force. I called it damned good police work. The liberal hearts called for an investigation by the FBI. I called for an investigation by O.S.H.A., the federal "Occupational Safety and Health Administration", since my assessment was that getting shot while committing a robbery was an "occupational" hazard. We sparred in the press for a while, but when the getaway driver confessed to sixty five other robberies that the trio had committed; it ended the debate in the community. Score one for the good guys.

After lunch, I drove back to the office for more routine paper work. I tried to clear the electronic messages from my computer, but they poured in faster than I could catch up. The damned machine had replaced the telephone and required absolutely no personal interaction between the sender or the receiver. I hated the system. To me, it took all of the humanity out of management. Dealing with people is what being a leader and a good manager is all about, I thought. The infernal machine was just too impersonal and made too good of a crutch for assholes to use when they had no people skills whatsoever.

My less than widely accepted theory is that the whole electronic communication age has contributed to a severe lack of leadership in America. Most current heads of organizations are incapable of leading a bunch of drunken sailors into a San Diego whorehouse.

Many just seem to have never been required to learn with their own hands just how to work with human beings on a day to day basis and there is no college program available for the skill. Have you ever heard of a Bachelor of Science degree in "Leadership"? Think about it.

As a watch commander in Dallas, I had a simple and reliable system to determine if the sergeants under my command had any innate leadership ability.

Harry Hines Boulevard runs north from downtown Dallas to the city limits, many miles away. Like Broadway in Wichita, the street acquired a well deserved reputation for prostitution, drugs, power drinkers and some hellacious bar room brawls. The wide street was lined on both sides with topless, bottomless, middleless, and you-name-it-less beer joints. If you did not have a knife or a gun when you paid your cover charge at some of these places, the bouncer issued you one at the door.

Whenever a new sergeant was assigned to my unit, I would instruct the sergeant to arrange a "bar check" of one of these establishments for a specific time that I selected. A "bar check" is a visit of five or six police officers, in mass, to check the bar's licenses, look for drunks passed out on the tables and search for underage patrons. Often the officers would order the lights turned on inside the dimly lit or blacked out night clubs as soon as they entered. The tactic allowed them to see the pistols that had been thrown on the floors by ex-cons who could not afford the felony rap. The house lights were also very useful to identify just who were getting blow jobs under the tables. In essence, the checks were a tool to show the bar owners and their sleazy patrons that the police were still in control of society and the law would be enforced.

At the appointed time, I would sit across the street, out of sight, and watch how the sergeant would organize his or her troops in the parking lot. A bar check is a fun break in the routine for most police officers. There is a safety in numbers feeling and the nude dancers and waitresses in most of these joints are always an interesting sight. In fact, most officers would usually argue to see who went in the door first. The initial officer always had the best chance to observe the most bizarre illegal sex act, undetected, before someone yelled, "Shit, the poo-leeece are here!"

The leadership test was based on a simple premise. If the sergeant was unable to motivate a group of red blooded American police officers to practically run through the doors to see what naked perversity was occurring inside, then the sergeant failed the leadership test. When the officers hung back, unsure of their sergeant's instructions or support, I knew I had problems. The worst failures in leadership were those supervisors that ordered their officers to go inside and check the bar, but stayed outside in the parking lot by themselves.

There are a few of these types of supervisors and commanders in every police department, but I found multitudes of them in the other facets of city government.

I left City Hall at exactly five o'clock feeling that I had done little to earn my daily pay. I drove in silence, listening to the standard calls on the police radio of traffic accidents and burglary reports. People were returning home from work all over the city. Some were crashing and dying before they could get there. Some were being welcomed home by finding their front doors kicked in and all of their possessions missing. Actually, in naive Wichita, most of the burglary victims had left home with their doors unlocked and then were amazed to discover that someone would actually steal from them. None of the mundane radio calls caught my attention or interest.

The empty house was a reminder that my life was incomplete without Peggy. I dug into the Antarctic waste land of our freezer for another frozen TV dinner. Vaguely toying with the idea of just eating this one like a Popsicle, I finally relented to conformity and electronically activated the appropriate amount of microwaves to heat it. The computer enhanced color photograph on the package looked positively scrumptious. I decided to eat the box and throw away the gooey mess in the microwave, which had only a passing resemblance to the picture on the package. I am such a sucker for buying an item based on its packaging. Just as soon as the food additive scientists stumbled onto a way to vitamin enrich cardboard, I would be much healthier.

Time seemed to hover close to a complete stop until the reluctant clock finally released me to head for the airport to pick up my wife. Not bothering to take off my uniform, I unclipped the stupid black tie and wandered down the stairs to the den. The remote control for our big screen tv set had become the highlight of my evenings. In my own darkened lair, surrounded by stereo sound and flipping through a hundred channels at the speed of a finger twitch, it was a great feeling to finally be in control of my life. Even Mel would appreciate this moment, I thought. Mel probably had two tv remotes. One for each hand.

I knew for a fact that the City Manager had an electronic mail computer terminal installed in his bedroom. That way, he could get up at any hour and begin clicking away on the machine to his black heart's content. At first, I was puzzled by the odd times, late at night or in the wee hours of the morning, that were digitally time stamped by the computer on some of the stupid messages I received from him. Finally, his homely wife had a little too much white wine at a formal banquet and confided to me that the "God damn computer", as she put it, had replaced sex in their bedroom. I resisted the temptation to tell her about the twenty other women I could name, and probably a herd of llamas from the city's petting zoo, that had replaced sex in their bedroom. It seemed safer to let her blame the "God damn computer."

As usual, I was early arriving at the airport. And, as equally usual, the plane was late. The waiting area for gate seven was practically vacant. There were few people meeting travelers from Minnesota and points north and east. An airport police officer and I wiled away the time, by talking shop, until Peggy's plane finally touched down.

"I hope your wife gets to feeling better soon, Chief," Officer Alvarez completed our talk. "We're all praying for her at my house." Despite Peggy's initial insistence that no one know about her illness, it was impossible to keep a secret for very long in Wichita.

"Thanks, Eddie," I answered sincerely. "We appreciate it a whole lot. You take care of Mary and your new baby girl, okay?"

Eddie grinned and waved good-bye as Peggy's flight began to disembark. I made it a point to keep up with all the officer's families. Whenever a member of the department or their spouse would have a baby, Suzie would highlight the entry on the daily departmental bulletin each morning. I sent each family a special gold embossed

"Welcome to the World" card for the baby and a personal note. It seemed like the thing to do for an organization that I was trying to build into a bigger "family". I was determined to counter the overall city philosophy of treating the employees like galley slaves all of the time. The troops appreciated my gesture as much as the birthday letters they received each year from me. Their own moms might forget their birthday, I overheard an officer confide to his partner one day; but not the chief, by God. The sentiment and the confidence made me feel like a part of the team and not an outsider from the big city.

Peggy appeared in the jet way looking tired and worn. The bright multi-colored silk scarf pulled loosely around her head was a new one. It was her concession to fashion in hiding the surgery scars and a severe lack of much in the way of hair. Peggy's smile grew into a huge grin when she saw me, standing at attention like a toy soldier, across the waiting room.

"Welcome to the "Twilight Zone", ladies and gentlemen," I greeted the sleepy horde of lost and road weary travelers.

"Hey, tall and handsome stranger; wanna wrestle?" Peggy asked.

"No, I'm sorry, ma'am, I'm waiting for my wife," I answered with a straight face. "You didn't see a woman on the plane, about your height, with long curly brown hair did you?"

"Yeah, I did. She wanted me to give you this," Peggy said as she gave me a big hug and a warm and wet kiss. "Don't you like my new look?" She put a fingertip on top of her scarfed head and twirled in a circle like a ballerina.

"Oh, yeah, it's definitely hot. Let's go, Madonna, you're under arrest," I ordered.

"Oh, pleeeeese mister big policeman, don't hurt me," Peggy squealed just a little too loud. About six of the sum total of nine passengers, who stepped off an airplane designed to hold two hundred, turned and stared at us. Soon, due to Wichita's lack of ability to attract visitors, we could replace the airport with a stage coach stop, I guessed. Maybe Roy Rogers' scruffy bearded old side kick, Gabby Hayes, could run the place. He and Mel would get along fine. Neither one could understand the other.

One benefit of living in a city no one wanted to fly in to was not having to wait long at the baggage claim. In less than five minutes, Peggy and I were loaded in the city car and driving directly across a nearly empty parking lot to the exit gate. I gave the attendant my "get out of the airport free" card, a small perk that went with the city owned vehicle, and signed the parking toll ticket.

The elderly female attendant smiled and revealed only one front tooth to complement her bright orange hair. "Thanks Chief. By the way you're doin' a great job. Don't let those politicians get you down. Keep doing what you're doin'," she said.

"Bless you, ma'am," I said in my best Texas accent, "We're trying real hard." Immediately, I wondered who "we" were.

"I know you are," the attendant testified. She leaned down closer to the open car window and called, "And welcome home Mrs. Starr, we're glad to have you back." Peggy waved a gloved hand and returned the smile with one of her own that could melt even the hardest heart.

"How does it feel to be famous?" I asked Peggy when we drove away from the toll booth.

"A little odd. How do these people know so much about our business?" she answered.

"Damned if I know. It just goes with the territory of being the chief's wife, I guess."

We were home in a matter of minutes and dropped the luggage in the living room like last week's trash. Peggy summoned up another large smile, from her seemingly inexhaustible pool of optimism, at the "Welcome Home" banner draped across the entrance to the bedroom hall. Our daughter, Terri, worked for hours on the elementary school computer to design the perfect message. It read "Hi, Mom, tomorrow is the bestest day."

"I'll go get Terri the first thing in the morning," I offered. "In the meantime, lie down and do whatever the nice policeman tells you to do."

I gently pushed her toward our bedroom with a hand placed strategically on each side of her posterior. It was like holding a sack of kittens. In a matter of minutes, Peggy was soundly asleep in my arms.

WEDNESDAY

CHAPTER THREE

Peggy was up long before I awoke to the sensual voice of Patsy Cline growling about "Sweet Dreams". I reached across Peggy's vacant side of the bed and switched off the alarm radio before Howlin' Hank had a chance to try to sell me on the merits of Preparation H. If Preparation H reduced the swelling of hemorrhoids, what did Preparations A through G solve? Maybe "A" took care of Alzheimer's or assholes. I should buy some to see if it would work on city managers.

Peggy was downstairs riding her stationary bike in our converted gym in the basement. When we purchased the house, the entire basement was finished out except for one room. Chad and I worked during our off time for most of an entire summer to panel the walls in the unfinished room, install carpeting and build some recessed storage cabinets to transform the space into a really nice extra room. When Peggy became ill, she purchased a stair machine, a stationary bike and a treadmill. She was determined to get her body into the best physical condition possible to fight the disease. Only a fool would bet against her. Or someone who did not know how determined Peggy could be when she resolved to accomplish something.

I hated the idea of exercising, particularly indoors, but Peggy seemed to thrive on the experience. It was the first time since junior high school she had attempted any type of physical exercise at all. Peggy arose each morning she was home at 4:30 a.m. and dutifully began her assault on the agony machines downstairs. The thought of sweating and grunting before dawn did not appeal to me in the least. I might drag myself out of a warm bed if the Kansas State University's women's water ballet team was downstairs…naked.

Maybe.

When Peggy and I first met in high school, I was the captain of the track team and fancied myself pretty hot stuff in the quarter mile. In college, the daily workouts became a real grind and I soon lost all of my boyhood belief that track was fun. Running was a serious business at the major college level. The thrill of winning a race evaporated and was soon replaced by a corporate philosophy of input and profit margins. It was all I could do to keep my body together to maintain my scholarship for four years.

A strange phenomena occurred, however. The older I got, the better I was. It seemed like that as the years went by, my athletic career somehow became brighter. The improvement was amazing. Each year I seemed to mentally drop another tenth of a second off of my fastest quarter mile time. What was once a university record of 46.8 seconds in the four hundred meter dash was replaced in my memory with a 44.8. Heck, by the time I died, I would have the world record. At least in the recesses of my ever improving memory enhancements. I wondered if all old athletes remembered themselves a lot better than they actually were. Probably.

I pulled myself out of the heated water bed and lurched wearily toward the kitchen. Peggy was slowly and deliberately climbing the stairs from the basement as I passed the carpeted landing.

"Oooh, cute butt," she cooed in response to my nakedness.

"Thanks, but I bet you say that to all of the guys you sleep with," I replied.

"What was your name again?" she asked. "You fellows all look alike after a while. Here one day, gone tomorrow."

"Well we just can't resist a woman with ear to ear stitches in her head and sweat dripping from her nose," I replied, as I tossed her a hand towel from the kitchen rack.

"Oops," she rubbed her flushed face. "How about some breakfast?"

"No way, Peggy. How many years do we have to live together before you understand that I refuse to eat chicken embryos before noon? It's a violation of the United States constitution, I think. If it ain't, it ought to be," I lectured.

"Okay, how about some orange juice then?" Peggy asked, knowing that O.J. was about all my stomach could handle early in the morning.

I made a U-turn back toward the bedroom and a hot shower. Half way down the hall, I called over my shoulder, "There's room in the shower for two. When you find the orange juice, bring some in for both of us."

Unfortunately, Peggy did not show up to play any early morning water sports in the shower. It was just as well. There was probably a little known Kansas law that prohibited sex in anything other than a bed. Kansas has some strange laws. It is practically the only state in the union that continues to list adultery as a criminal offense. Fortunately, District Attorney Dora Davenport did not think the biblical sin was high enough up on the criminal priority list to prosecute any of Wichita's strayers from marital purity. The list would have been long and illustrious.

Absentmindedly, I contemplated the amount of wasted hot water that swirled down the drain during my early morning shower. When the city went through a period of water shortages a few years ago, the city council passed ordinances to try to conserve water. A law was instituted prohibiting the watering of lawns except on certain days. The permissible days were established according to last two digits of a person's home address. The system was very complicated and was, of course, completely ignored by every one in town except the techno nerds at Wichita University who used a mainframe computer to determine their watering schedule through the year 2130.

Furious, Mel called me and demanded that we use police officers to enforce the water ordinance.

"Come on Mel, you've got to be kidding," I replied. "Its not the citizen's fault if they are violating your ordinance. No one can understand the stupid scheme you guys have developed. Heck, the best I can figure is I can water my grass on alternate Thursdays, during the full moon, in months with the letter "R" in them. Is that about right?"

"I don't know what your watering schedule is and I don't care," Mel replied. "I can't even figure out what mine is, but we must have some enforcement or else the city will be forced to buy the water from the state."

Ahahhh, the almighty dollar is behind this as always, I thought. "Sir, I'm looking out of my office window right now," I answered, "and the damn sprinklers for the City Hall lawn are spraying hundreds of gallons of your precious water out onto the concrete parking lot. No one is going to take this law seriously until we learn to conserve in our own house. It's silly for me to take officers off the streets just so we can scare people with the "Water Police". We're stretched too thin with real crime and I just won't do it."

Mel and I had been down this ugly road before on a couple of occasions. Once, when Mel received a report from the Library Director with a problem collecting fines for overdue books, I received a memo instructing me to use police officers to track down and arrest the book crooks. Naturally, I refused to establish the "Library Police" to track down the delinquent borrowers. The manager was really pissed off then, too.

In my hazy crystal ball, I could just see the whole scenario unfold.

"Up against the wall, bitch. It's the "Library Police" with a search warrant for missing books," the heavily armed assault team would yell as they kicked in the front door of some little old lady's town house.

"We know you've got that copy of "Moby Dick" you borrowed in 1958 in here somewhere. Now where is it, Granny; before we throw the book at you?" It was a worse idea than it was a pun.

The city was also engaged in a long standing feud with local bar owners over the issue of topless dancers. One member of the City Council, Reginald Newman, took up the cause of the moral majority to continuously develop ordinances aimed at controlling nude dancing. Every time a new city ordinance was passed preventing the showing of any skin, the bar owners would immediately hire an attorney to successfully assert the unconstitutionality of such a law. In the meantime, Mel would get pressure from Reginald to enforce the latest version of the ordinance before a judge could strike down the law. It was such a ridiculous waste of time and effort. We just did not have the officers to devote to being the "Breast Police".

I admit that the idea to institute a "Hooter Patrol" was unique. To his only credit, Reginald Newman was thought of as somewhat of a free thinker. Which is to mean that absolutely no one understood most of the gibberish rolling out of his mouth. Reginald's true claim to fame was that he was sole heir to a large fortune his family had accumulated over several generations in the Kansas banking industry. Genetically, Reginald was unquestionably of a diluted strain. To say that he was dumber than dirt was an insult to mud. Reginald was perennially re-elected by the citizens in his district because he was thought to be likably harmless.

Reginald's questions during City Council meetings were usually so long and twisted in their construction, that no one knew how to answer them. Mel allowed me only rare appearances before the Council. I was only permitted to address relatively safe issues that would not allow me to expound on our city's real problems. A few months before, I was forced to endure one of Councilman Newman's questions that took more than fifteen minutes for him to formulate and verbalize in his usual convoluted fashion. When he was finished, I looked up in total confusion from the oak podium in front of the council chambers where I was standing. In the infamous pregnant pause, I looked towards the seat reserved for the City Manager hoping that Mel had some idea what Reginald was trying to ask. He kept his head down, staring at some imaginary piece of lint on his zipper, and was absolutely no help.

"Mr. Newman," I said, "with all due respect, I don't have a clue what you are talking about."

The other council members and the sparse crowd in attendance broke out laughing. The City Manager turned blue. Newman looked incredulous, as if he could not understand what the joke was. After fifteen minutes of uproar, the Mayor finally took control and said, "Chief, we know just how you feel. We don't have a clue what Reginald asked either."

Reginald Newman and the "Breast Police" became synonymous with stupidity in local government.

Peggy strolled into the bathroom with a glass of semi-fresh frozen orange juice and the local section of our daily newspaper, the Wichita Eagle, also known as the "Eagle Beagle" for its usefulness to toilet train puppies.

"Congratulations," Peggy announced. "You made the editorial cartoon."

"Great, just what I need," I moaned as I toweled the water from my hairy legs. "How bad is it?"

"Well, it's a great picture; that's for sure," Peggy proclaimed. She handed me the folded newspaper and I managed to drip shower water on only part of it.

The cartoon depicted a classic image of Superman from the 1950's television show. Standing with his hands on his hips, cape flowing, Superman was defiant in his posture as he stood in front of a spinning planet Earth. Everything was the same in the cartoon except that Superman was sporting a remarkable likeness of my face. The background was filled with the barely recognizable skyline of Wichita; what little there was of it. The caption read, "Truth, Justice, and the American way. Starrman to the rescue!"

"Cute", was all I could think to say.

"It's a nice play on your name, don't you think?" Peggy asked.

"Oh, yeah, it will be a nice play on my faltering career, too, when the Manager and his psychotic syphilitics see it," I countered.

The accompanying brief editorial praised me for standing up to the City Manager and asking for more police officers in next year's budget. It quoted anonymous City Hall sources as saying that my budget request defied a direct order that the city manager had given to all of his department heads. The order was that no budget requests were allowed to include any increase in personnel. For once the paper had printed the true facts. Someone had obviously leaked Mel's directive to the newspaper. Mel would be fit to be tied. He hated leaks more than Richard Nixon. The body of the article asked, "Does Wichita finally have a real police chief?", and postulated how the City Manager would react to such a change from the previous "do nothing" administration of Chief Pasqual.

I knew exactly how Mel would react. He would not just shit a brick, he would crap an entire fucking wall. Maybe even a whole building.

As much as the city leaders talked about change and progress and improvement, they definitely did not want anyone rocking the boat. A new idea was a one way ticket to being labeled disloyal. I found myself wanting to continually apologize because my mind would not turn off just because I had a Kansas address on my drivers license. It was a constant source of friction.

I read the article more closely hoping to see the print fade into invisibility. It was the kind of article that would look great in my scrap book, but would only pile more baggage on my back at work. A former police chief in Dallas had given me a great lesson in the "Baggage Theory". He said the job of a police chief was one where you accumulated "baggage" as time wore on. Every time you disciplined or fired a member of your department, that person had friends who threw rocks in the bag you carried. A bad media report added more rocks. Political battles fought, won or lost, added even more "baggage". Practically every action you took and every decision you made as the chief, added to your load. When the bag became too heavy to carry, you fell. It was as simple as that. Right now, my bag felt like it weighed more than Switzerland. The Alps and all.

The sports page was much more to my liking. The University of Texas had once again beaten Oklahoma in their classic meeting each fall in the Cotton Bowl. I fretted that the corporate sponsorship of bowl games would eliminate a hundred year old tradition of gridiron warfare. Growing up in Fort Worth, I was instilled with the belief that the University of Texas was "The" university. Coupled with this instinct was a inherent dislike for O.U. and everything Oklahoman. If O.U. were to play the "Hitler Youth", my Texas heritage would force me to root for the boys from Germany.

Each year, the two teams met in October to establish bragging rights for the rest of the year. The game was always played at the Cotton Bowl near downtown Dallas. The site was supposedly chosen as being neutral ground, laying geographically halfway between Austin and Norman. Only an Oklahoman was stupid enough to believe that Dallas was neutral territory.

Despite having some great teams, Oklahoma always seemed to find a way to lose to the Longhorns. I always suspected that the referees made the O.U. players wear shoes and the unfamiliar equipment interfered with their game.

After a series of high profile criminal investigations involving Oklahoma players, another theory was popular within the police department in Dallas. The latest explanation for Texas' invincibility held that O.U. was hampered by not being able to bring their full squad to Dallas. Crossing the state line would violate parole restrictions for most of Oklahoma's players. Instead of off sides or a personal foul penalty, the referee would announce over the stadium's public address system, "Parole Violation, defense, fifteen yards and loss of liberty. First down, Texas."

Personally, I felt the real game was played the night before in the streets of downtown Dallas. Each year, the fans from both sides would begin gathering about dusk in downtown to party, raise hell and shout their support for their favorite team. It was a tradition. It was a ritual. It was the one night a year that the Dallas Police Department turned out in full force. We called it the "planned riot", since we always knew the date, time and location of the confrontation.

Decades ago, Dallas would bring in extra police officers from surrounding cities to help out. The first thing the out of town officers did was remove their name tags from their uniforms. This allowed them anonymity and a free reign to "kick ass and take names", without fear of any Internal Affairs investigation. It was a wild scene for the police and the partygoers. After too many participants in the festivities wound up in body casts from being stomped by police officers from towns with names like Midlothian and Waxahachie, the city stopped inviting the outside officers and the mayhem turned considerably less violent.

In my early career, it was expected that the police department would arrest six or seven hundred people during the affray. The Chamber of Commerce people loved the pre-game ritual, since it was great for the economy. As long as no one went too wild and tried to burn down the Neiman Marcus store everyone was happy. The Dallas Police Wives Association would rent a ballroom in one of the downtown hotels and serve the police officers with sandwiches and cold drinks to keep up our strength. The department mobilized several hundred officers and each of us made dozens of arrests for public intoxication, disorderly conduct, urinating in public and general public lewdness. It was not uncommon to see two overly stimulated college students coupling in the middle of Commerce Street, thereby proving their worthiness to attend dear old U.T. or O.U.. Whichever.

The whole thing started to get a little too dangerous when a group of O.U. students and alumni became a little too excited and pushed a piano off a balcony from the twentieth story of the Adolphus Hotel. Luckily no one in the teaming mass of people below was killed. I decided right then and there that the little plastic construction worker's helmet the department issued me for the occasion was completely worthless as protection against falling pianos.

Later when I became a jail sergeant, Texas/O.U. night was always a challenge. We struggled to determine how to house and control the hundreds of drunken prisoners. For one thing, it would have been a very bad idea to put Texas Longhorn fans in with supporters of the Oklahoma Sooners. Deaths in the city jail were not good for our departmental image or for one's individual career if you were supposed to be in charge. Therefore, we went through a process of segregation at the time of booking.

"Are you for Texas or O.U.?" a bored jail guard would ask the drunk.

"Huh?" the guy would usually reply.

"You know," the guard would ask, "which team do you want to win tomorrow?"

"Fuck, I don't give a shit. I just came up here from Corsicana to act like a fool and get laid. All I got was a little stinky finger before you assholes busted me. I hate it when that happens," was the standard reply.

The next morning's arraignment, for those arrested during the rally, was a page right out of Judge Roy Bean's "Law West of the Pecos". The jail guards would slowly bring a string of ten hung over prisoners handcuffed to a long, shiny chain to stand before an equally hung over judge.

"Okay, Mr. Elwood Nosepicker, I see that you are charged with public intoxication," the judge would read from the arrest report. "How do you plead? Guilty or not guilty?"

"Guilty, your honor," the now humble hell raiser would usually answer.

"Okay, the Court accepts your plea of guilty. Guard, how much money did Mr. Nosepicker have in his possession last night when he was arrested?" the judge would ask.

The guard would turn over the back of a yellow form which listed all of the prisoner's property that was taken away from him during the jail intake process and carefully inventoried as the man's total net worth.

"Let's see, your honor, oh, yeah, here it is. Elwood here had six dollars and twelve cents in his pockets."

"Mr. Nosepicker, the court finds you guilty and fines you six dollars and twelve cents. Pay the Court Clerk and you will be released immediately. Next." The judge continued down the line until the group of miscreants was processed and the guards brought in another string of ten prisoners. Whatever amount the prisoner had in his or her property was the exact amount that the judge set as their fine. Two dollars or two hundred dollars, it did not change the system.

If an arrestee wanted to plead "not guilty", justice was not deterred.

"Okay, your bail is set at, huh, huh, guard how much did this here "not guilty" feller have in his pockets?" the judge would ask the bailiff.

Whatever the amount was, it became the same amount of bail required for release. Another court appearance was set for six months in the future for those who plead not guilty. Of course, most failed to return for round two and their bail money was forfeited to the City of Dallas municipal coffers.

Some of my favorite memories of Texas/O.U. night were of the "one way sidewalks" and the water trucks.

As we began attempting to control the violence and chaos a little more, it became apparent that some method had to be found to reduce the confrontations that usually resulted in a fist fight or cutting. One of our brighter "up-and-comer" captains proposed installing wooden sawhorse barricades along the street curbs. Manned by police officers, the wooden barriers would keep the revelers out of the traffic flow of honking automobiles and half naked coeds fornicating in the back of pick up trucks. He also suggested that we enforce a rule that all the pedestrians had to walk clockwise, in a big oval like scheme, throughout downtown. Any stupid shit caught walking counter clockwise, against the flow of the other stupid shits, would be immediately arrested by the officers monitoring the crowd from behind the barricades.

It was a great idea! Even the dumbest Okie could not pick a fight if all they saw was the back of a person's head. Other than a little more doggie style public sex than usual, the results were a tribute to pure genius. Unfortunately, fate was not kind to the captain who came up with the idea. As luck would have it, he was fired several years later for getting drunk in a city car and crashing it into an adult book store in a misguided, but totally futile, gesture of showing his love for an aging porn star. But, for one shining moment, the captain had the idea of the century that forever changed the "planned riots" in downtown Dallas.

Each passing year the rally became less and less intense with fewer and fewer people arrested. As further encouragement to hold down the festivities, the police department set a limit of 2:00 a.m. for the street party. At the appointed hour, the streets were closed to all vehicular traffic. The street and sanitation department brought in four large water trucks, followed by four large street sweepers to clean up the mess. But the best part of the plan was that the water trucks had their high pressure nozzles pointed directly at the sidewalks to blast a torrent of icy water on any die hard partygoers who were either too stubborn or too drunk to go home.

In what was to be my last assignment at the annual event, I climbed through the rusted stairwell to the roof of the old Police and Courts Building and watched the trucks and sweepers do their work. Located at the corner of Harwood and Main Streets, the ancient building housed the City Jail and functioned as Police Headquarters.

It had witnessed history and heroes, made and destroyed.

Precisely at two o'clock, I looked west down Main Street. There, in the hazy distance, was a wedge shaped line of police motorcycles with their red and blue lights flashing; leading the procession of green painted water trucks and orange street sweepers. On they came, spewing water left and right, in a carefully planned maneuver to clear the streets. Even seven stories above the street, I could hear the screams and squeals of the crowd below as the cold water forced them to run for cover. Everyone seemed to be having a good time, especially the water truck drivers.

Just below me on Main Street, across from our building, stood a row of two story buildings used as offices by bail bondsmen and soon-to-be disbarred attorneys. Like every other city in America, bail bond companies in Dallas sprang up like weeds near the City Jail. The bondsmen wanted their telephone number to be the last glimpse a prisoner might see before entering into the bowels of hell. The bond companies raked off a neat ten or fifteen percent of the bond amount to insure temporary freedom for a person who was otherwise left to sit in behind steel bars awaiting his or her trial. It was a lucrative business for someone who did not want to do any real work. Except for breaking a few arms or legs every now and then when a client "forgot" to appear in court for his trial, it was easy money for the bondsmen.

I watched as an enormous pink Cadillac pulled up and parked in front of Chino's Bail Bonds. "You bust 'em, we trust 'em", was the slogan painted in bright red letters on the glass office front. Chino's telephone number was mounted on the wall above the entrance in fluorescent digits six feet high. Ray Charles could have read the sign. Remembering the phone number to dial with your one precious jail house phone call might be another matter. Hopefully, "Hooked on Phonics" was working wonders with the youth of America so they could better remember their bail bondsman's telephone number.

The south Dallas pimp parked in front of Chino's and went inside, ignoring the red "No Parking Due to Special Event" sign mounted on the parking meter. The top was down on his Caddy convertible, revealing its beautiful white leather upholstery and the blue shag carpet installed on the dash board. The owner was obviously a student of the "Elvis School of Interior Decorating". The steering wheel had a matching blue fur wrap. A pair of fuzzy pink dice hung elegantly from the rear view mirror. I bet he won those at the State Fair this week, I thought.

I had a perfect view down into the interior of the car and strained to see something illegal like a pistol or baggy of grass. Watching the pimp argue with the bondsman through the clear office glass, I almost forgot about the crowd dispersing in all directions. Soundlessly, the pimp waved his hands and flapped his gums while the heavy-set bail maker stood with his meaty forearms folded across his chest. There was obviously an argument over the release of some of the pimp's "ladies". The women were bringing in no revenue sitting on their butts in jail, rather than moving their butts on Industrial Boulevard; a Dallas street known as "Hookerland".

When the water trucks and sweepers slowly arrived at the intersection below, they stopped about a hundred feet before they reached the pink Cadillac. The Caddy was blocking one of the four lanes that the trucks needed to continue in their line abreast march. After a few quick words with the police motorcycle sergeant, one water truck driver forged ahead of the rest and pulled along side of the convertible. It was a nimble little maneuver reminiscent of the Navy's "Blue Angels" precision flying team, only with a five ton green water truck at ground level.

The driver raced his motor and positioned the high pressure nozzles directly at the Cadillac. In a flash, a thousand gallons of Dallas' best Trinity River water roared into the convertible's interior.

It was hilarious. Water poured into the open top car until it would hold no more. The flood cascaded over the sides of the car and onto the sidewalk and street. The pimp ran out, cussing and screaming at the truck driver seated in his elevated cubicle behind heavy glass five feet above the street. The driver grinned and waved a middle index finger at the pimp and drove off down the street with his yellow revolving lights flashing in happy rhythm.

The pimp ran back inside the bail bond's office, with his multiple gold chains and ear rings jangling.

Then the next water truck drove up. All four trucks proceeded to dump their remaining loads of murky water into the Cadillac. Inside the bail bond office, people were building improvised sand bags from old coats and sweaters to keep the water from coming in under the door.

When the free car wash was complete, a motorcycle officer pulled up behind the overflowing Caddy and wrote the pimp a ticket for illegal parking.

As I turned away from my bird's eye view of real life, the last thing I saw was a pair of pink fuzzy dice floating down the middle of Main Street, Dallas, Texas. Who says the American criminal justice system does not work?

Peggy watched as I finished toweling off in front of the mirror. What little chest I had was sagging down toward my waist and my complexion was a cross between the "Pillsbury Doughboy" and a beached jelly fish. Only my legs still looked strong and muscular. Too bad I could not make a living doing panty hose commercials.

"What did you fix yourself for breakfast?" I asked.

"Waffles, two eggs, and bacon," Peggy answered. "You sure you don't want any?"

"No, thanks," I replied. "Throw me my robe from behind the door, will you?"

Peggy retrieved the heavy, dark blue bath robe from its hook and tossed it my way. The robe, a Christmas present from Chad, was a real luxury on cold Kansas mornings and had the official Naval Academy logo embroidered on the chest pocket in gold thread. I slipped its warmth over my still damp body and started to tie it closed with the attached cloth belt.

"Hey, don't I get any attention around here anymore?"

Peggy puckered her lips like a little girl who wanted her daddy to buy her an ice cream cone.

I opened the robe's front and wrapped it around her as she stood in front of the shower stall. I pulled her inside the robe with me long enough to notice that close body contact awakened a long suppressed physical reaction.

"Where did he come from?" Peggy asked as her eyes wandered down my naked body.

"Oh, I think he smelled the bacon from the kitchen. Usually, I only feed him once a month," I quipped. "He's a real low maintenance pet."

"Poor baby. Something's got to be done to build up his strength, before he withers and falls off," Peggy announced.

Peggy turned serious and looked up into my eyes from the eight inch difference in our heights. "I know my being sick is tougher on you than it is on me," she said.

I hugged her harder and a tear mixed in with some of the shampoo I had failed to get out of my hair. "You're something else, kid," was all I could say.

* * *

An hour later, I finally steered the unmarked car out of my garage. It was eight o'clock. I was late for work. I really did not care.

It was another gray and overcast day in "Doo Dah Land". The cloud cover seemed to hover about twenty feet above West Kellogg Avenue as I pushed the car forward through light traffic. As usual, the wind was already screaming its defiance to anything that stood in its way.

There were no weather vanes in Kansas. If a person wanted to know which way the wind was blowing, he just looked out the window and noted which direction his car was leaning in the driveway. The wind was strong enough to bend metal.

Traveling quickly down Kellogg, I turned on "National Public Radio" to pick up the news about what was happening in the bigger world outside of "River City", Kansas.

I just caught the tail end of a story about a plastic surgeon in Hollywood, Florida who seduced one of his female patients. He went to her home three times weekly for a twenty minute sex session and then charged her insurance company a thousand dollars per visit for the "physical therapy house calls".

It certainly seemed as if the doctor was getting a little too greedy for just twenty minutes, even by Florida standards. My natural curiosity caused me to wonder just how the scheme was finally uncovered when the newscaster mentioned that it was an insurance claim processor who first noticed the "house call" notation on the doctor's charges and said, "Whoa, no way a doctor makes house calls these days." She pointed the abnormality out to her supervisor and the doctor was caught with his pants down and his greed hanging out. In flagrante delecto, so to speak.

Peggy and I chose a big, modern house on the far west side of Wichita to make our home. It was as close as we could get to the "panhandle" region of Texas and still meet

Mel's requirement that I live inside the city limits of Wichita. Actually, Chad picked the general area. We let him choose which high school he wanted to attend during his senior year. We then made sure our house would be in the correct district to match his selection of schools.

We knew it would not be easy to leave all of his buddies behind in his last year of high school. Chad's interest in attending one of the military service academies meant he would be required to start the application process over again when we moved to Kansas. I convinced him there would be a lot less competition in the smaller state. Compared to Texas, Kansas was practically deserted. Only 2.8 million people populated the entire state of Kansas. In comparison, there were over three million people living in the Dallas/Fort Worth metroplex alone.

He did not seem too happy about the move until I finally said, "Look, Chad, think of it this way. There will be a whole new set of girls you haven't met yet."

I was right. Within forty eight hours of unloading the moving truck, a petite blonde was at our doorstep with a plate of "welcome to the neighborhood" brownies. She lived three houses down and was exactly Chad's age.

"Well, Louie," I told Chad, trying to imitate Bogart in "Casablanca", "I think this is the beginning of a beautiful friendship." I was right and he flourished at his new high school; in and out of the class room.

The campus radio station at Wichita University was the only station in town to carry the syndicated "National Public Radio" broadcasts. I liked the network because it was the unvarnished details without any attempt at slanting the information. Jack Webb would listen to N.P.R., I told myself. "Just the facts, ma'am," Sergeant Friday would say. The radio station was a shoe string operation, to be generous. It seemed they had a particularly anemic squirrel running inside their little treadmill powered generator this morning. I could barely pick up the signal from less than twenty miles away. The whole station was funded by donations and some of the most bizarre corporate sponsors ever to grace the American air waves.

"Don't forget our "Begging for Bucks" pledge drive underway now," Durwood Hamilton intoned. Durwood was the balding owner, manager, operator, reporter, engineer, and janitor for the station. I had once liked Durwood but I had learned the hard way not to trust him. At all.

"The news is brought to you courtesy of Doctor P. Michael Rose at the "Rose Hand Center", located in the Park View Shopping Center. Doctor Rose specializes in all types of injuries to the hand, fingers and wrist. Drop by to see him today for a complete check up," Durwood read the ad card with perfect diction.

"Hey Durwood," I yelled at the dashboard radio while trying to send my voice back down the FM radio waves like a telephone. "What do you think Doctor Rose's wife asks him after a hard day at the office? Well, honey, tough day, huh? How many hand jobs did you do today, sweetheart?"

It was almost too much to think about. The good doctor probably made three hundred thousand a year playing with people's fingers and infected hang nails. The best part was that if he scratched the crack of his butt at a baseball game, no one would notice or care. I was envious of his salary and his anonymity.

Thinking of being under the microscope made me notice the lady driving next to me in a teal colored Lexus. She was staring at me as we waited for the signal light to change. It took me a minute to realize she was wondering why this person in a policeman's uniform was shouting into thin air when there was no one in the car with him. My game with the radio would be difficult to explain. I rolled down my electric window and she did the same. Great, I thought, dueling electric windows. The ultimate status symbol conflict.

"I finally arrested the Invisible Man. Got him in here with me now. Don't worry, we're all safe again," was all I could think of to say.

The woman nodded, winked, and gave me a thumbs up. She drove off when the light changed. Claude Rains, the actor who played the part of the invisible man in the old black and white movie, would have been proud to know his transparent character was still alive and doing well in Wichita, Kansas.

I made a mental note to curb my mania in public view more often. Who knew what kind of story the lady would tell at her country club breakfast?

As I topped the rise leading into the downtown area, I could not help but feel a sense of pride in Wichita. Despite everything, the place was a clean and modern place to raise kids. In the spring and summer, we loved to go to the minor league ball park that passed in view through my left side window. Lawrence Dumont Stadium was an old ball yard which had been completely refurbished recently. The Wichita Wranglers were a Double A farm team of the Kansas City Royals presently, although they changed affiliations almost every season. It was not that the Wranglers played great baseball. They did not. It was the ball yard. An artificial turf infield meshed perfectly with a lush green grass outfield to give you the impression that the game was old and new at the same time. I loved being down on front row, the stadium lights illuminating and vividly defining every square inch on the field of honor. To smell the grass and throw peanut shells at the umpires made for a small slice of heaven in any league.

I persuaded the stadium manager to provide the police department use of the facility for our first annual, and first ever, "Inner-Departmental Softball Championship

Game". Last year, I decreed that each division in the department was required to field a softball team to compete in a tournament for the newly established "Chief's Trophy".

There was a lot of whining and groaning by the command staff, but I essentially ordered that it would be "mando-fun". In other words, it was mandatory that everyone participate and everyone have a good time. Or else.

I appointed a lieutenant from our Traffic Section, who was crazy about softball, as the league commissioner and asked him to set up the schedules. He did a great job and the whole department was soon caught up in the fun of the games. It did a lot for all of our morale. I even invited Mel to the championship game, but he did not bother to reply to the invitation. He probably suspected an assassination attempt.

The deputy chiefs and I were the umpires at the final game in the grand old stadium. I purchased the trophy out of my own personal money without even bothering to ask Mel for a budgetary appropriation. At the end of the game, the players dumped a bucket of ice and Gatorade on me as I presented the winning team their trophy. I loved it. In fact, there was so much about Wichita that I loved. It was not the city that was killing me, it was the job.

When I reached my office, Suzie looked worried.

"You're late, Chief, what's wrong?" she asked.

"I'm sorry, Suzie, I know I should of called, but Peggy got in late last night and we kinda spent a little time getting re-acquainted." Despite my best efforts I failed to repress a wink.

Suzie smiled coyly and looked a little embarrassed. She was about ten years older than I and came from a small town in western Kansas. I often forgot my own telephone number, but not the name of Suzie's hometown. Ellinwood. I delighted in asking Suzie for the answer to her hometown's secret question. She feigned to not know what I was talking about while we played the game.

"You know Ellen would, Ellen would, Ellen would what? I'm dying to know. What would Ellen do?" was my part in the opening scene.

"Not much," was all she would say with another patented school girl smile.

Suzie was the perfect secretary; loyal, efficient, and trustworthy. I loved her like a big sister. When her father passed away with a heart attack, it hurt me almost as much as when my own mom had died.

"Chief, we need to talk about office security", Suzie got back to being serious. "When I got here this morning, all of the stuff had been moved around on my desk."

"What kind of stuff, Suzie?" I asked.

"You know, the Scotch tape, pens, paper clips; that kind of stuff," she replied.

"Is there anything missing?" I questioned.

"Not that I can tell, but I'm sure we locked up all the doors last night. You need to check your desk, too," Suzie advised.

I looked through the papers on my desk and the near empty in-basket. At first, I could not determine if anything was missing. Then I remembered I had left two quarters on my desk for an afternoon Pepsi that I never got around to buying from the machine next door. The coins had vanished. It was possible to attribute the minor theft to a thirsty clean-up lady the night before; although such a pilferage had never occurred previously.

When I turned on the computer to answer my morning's accumulation of electronic mail, my blood turned cold. There, on the blue monitor screen, was a listing of three unsuccessful attempts to access my computer files. The computer automatically listed the last log off time and date. It also memorized any attempts to enter back into the system. The screen listed three attempts at 0012, 0015, and 0017 hours. The log showed that someone had tried to break into my electronic files shortly after midnight and they had used this very terminal inside my locked office. The only reason they had failed was that I had changed my password the day before.

I never thought too much about computer security and picked "log on" passwords that were simple and easy to remember. My Wichita badge number, 1409, was a favorite. My Dallas badge number, 3442, was another one I used. The system demanded a new password each six months and you could change it yourself any time you wished. Before yesterday, my password had been "Peggy". It was hard to forget your wife's name, even for someone as forgetful as me. For some unknown reason, I decided to change the password the previous day as a sarcastic commentary on how my life was going. I picked "GreatYear" as my new password. Maybe it was wishful thinking. In any case, my whim had apparently prevented whoever was stalking my office from reading my electronic mail traffic and the sensitive materials stored in the computer's electronic memory.

Whoever the suspect was, he or she must have known the old password. Otherwise, they would not attempt to log onto the system; knowing the computer would automatically record their attempts. I could have easily missed the zero's in the time listing on the opening screen which quickly flashed on the monitor during the log on process. But it would be difficult to overlook three failures on the automatic log, even if I had not been searching for such evidence as I was this morning. The suspect must have become frustrated, feeling confident that he or she had the right code word, and continued to type in "Peggy" three times before finally giving up.

Not even Suzie knew my password. Who could have access to a code that I had made up from my imagination? I knew it would not have been difficult to guess that

I might use my wife's name. But, no, whoever turned the machine on was not guessing. They knew. Or thought they knew the right password. If they had been on a guessing expedition, they would have tried more than three times to break the code. The only place where the password was electronically stored and accessible to anyone with the right clearance was in the city's Central Computer Data Center. The electronic data repository had to be the link. The data center was a part of Tad Roadly's Finance Department.

I was confident no one could have correctly guessed my spontaneous change to "GreatYear". The spy was probably very shocked when "Peggy" did not provide instant access. The only reason the password did not give them entrance into all of my correspondence logs for the last six years was the irony of my game playing the day before. Once more, a sense of humor had overcome adversity. The thought failed to make me feel any more comfortable.

"Suzie," I called on the office intercom, "call Don Grady, up in Building Management, and have him send someone down to change the locks on all the doors to our offices again."

"Okay, Chief," was all Suzie said.

"And ask him to make sure that no one, even the clean up crew, gets a copy of the key. Thanks, Suzie," I punched the off button and turned back to my computer screen.

There was some great stuff in my computer files which could be highly damaging to some of our most prominent citizens and public officials. I kept all of the crazy, and sometimes semi-illegal, orders Mel sent me during the last six years. I also kept electronic copies of all of my replies and warnings. While a number of my responses bordered on insubordination, they would prove that I was definitely not a willing participant in the Manager's questionable activities.

One file in particular was a hot potato for which the statute of limitations had not yet expired. I checked and the "Pistol Range" file was still intact. I decided to print a paper hard copy of the file, just in case. In scanning some of the documents while the laser copier hummed in Suzie's outer office, the whole ugly episode was replayed on the screen.

The Wichita Police Department operated their own firearms training range for almost fifty years. When it had been built shortly after World War II, the range was situated on the outskirts of town and away from any business or residential areas. The parched grass land, on which the range was originally constructed, was considered practically worthless in 1945. Even when the municipal airport sprang up nearby, no one envisioned a time when the relatively small outdoor shooting facility would interfere with anything important.

Slowly over the years, the city's airport expanded and became a major terminal for cross country airline traffic. Most of the airplane manufacturers in Wichita began building hangars and test facilities at the fledgling airport. The aircraft industry soon became Wichita's largest single employer and received generous tax abatements from the city as the companies acquired new land or planned expanded facilities.

Still, the police department continued to use the pistol range to train its police officers. Each year, thousands of pounds of lead was fired into the earthen berms surrounding the wooden framed targets. As the department slowly grew, more police officers were trained on the range and they regularly practiced with their handguns at the sight. Wells were dug to provide water to clean the facility and sprinkle what little grass could be coaxed to grow in the lead saturated soil. The Rangemaster also used the well water to wet down the bullet backstops to keep the ever present Kansas wind from blowing lead tainted dust clouds during firearms qualification sessions.

Whenever it rained, thousands of gallons of water filtered past the decaying lead and into the underground aquifer. To make matters worse, a succession of police range personnel used the wells to dump their toxic wastes. Since no one in their right mind would drink the gray well water, the officers assigned to the range would pour used cleaning solvents, leaky tear gas canisters or just about any other toxic refuse that came their way into the wells. Of course, no one could conceive of the future "Environmental Protection Agency" when this disposal practice began in the 1940's. Because the area was secluded, there were also no grotesque two headed babies or other mutated genetic manifestations of lead pollution to reveal the ground's deadly secrets.

When I first toured the pistol range, I caused a halt to any future dumping into the wells. Unfortunately, the damage had already been done. In fact, Wichita was discovering other large areas within the city where ground water contamination was a major problem. The city and local industries were struggling to find solutions to clean it all up without federal intervention. It was not that the city was being a nice guy in removing the nasty toxic waste before we all began to glow in the dark. Nooooooo. The banks simply refused to lend money to people who wanted to buy land on top of the polluted water when the issue of who was responsible for cleaning up the mess was still in legal limbo. No bank loans meant no new businesses and no new businesses meant no tax dollars flowing into the city's coffers.

Our own little contribution to melting the planet was not a problem until a big manufacturer began coveting the land we were using for our pistol range. They were determined to build a new office and maintenance complex to service their business jet customers. Arab sheiks and movie stars flew into Wichita regularly to get a fifty thousand mile tune up on their personal jets. The wealthy moguls landed, took one look at the desolate surroundings, and wondered how in the hell Wichita, Kansas ever became the center for aircraft manufacturing in America. So did I.

One day, completely out of the blue, Mel sent me an electronic mail message announcing the impending sale of our pistol range to the aircraft company. He gave us sixty days to vacate the premises. When I asked where we were supposed to do our weapons training, Mel said he had no idea. That was my problem, he replied. Put up some sticks in the mud in a farmer's wheat field out in the county and shoot, was his suggestion. I tried to explain that modern police firearms training was a little more complicated than shooting at sticks. It was useless. I might as well have been talking nuclear physics with a three year old.

Since he had already made the deal with the aircraft company, Mel washed his hands of the whole issue and turned over the details to his assistant, Bob Showalter. Bullet Bob bluntly ordered that all police department property be removed from the sight within the week, when the construction bulldozers would flatten the area.

My file memo in reply was pretty blunt, as well. "Bob, if your bulldozers begin pushing over buildings out there before we give the go ahead, you better be sure that they have some great burial insurance. We have enough old, leaky dynamite and other assorted military explosive goodies stored there to scatter their atoms all over creation. Remember the space shuttle explosion? The pilot had blue eyes, one blew left and the other blew right. The results will be the same at the range if you shake the ground too much."

This bluff bought us a little time to plan how to move the equipment, but no relief on where to conduct our continuing firearms training. The State of Kansas mandated that all officers become qualified with their weapons during recruit training and then be re-tested at least once each year thereafter. It was a little matter of being able to hit what we aimed at during a gunfight. Innocent bystanders with police bullets in their bodies were bad for the state's economy. Not so surprisingly, the city had given absolutely no prior thought as to where to relocate the pistol range before Mel consummated his deal with the aircraft company.

Neither Bob nor Mel offered any assistance in money or ideas on how to move the equipment or where to store it. Our only option was to take a recruit class out of their studies for a week and use them as manual labor. We distributed the ammunition, reloading presses, targets and a myriad of other essential items all over the county in the homes of various individual officers. I am sure the wives loved it when they came home and found they could not park the Toyota out of the snow because ten thousand rounds of thirty-eight caliber pistol ammunition was were stored inside the garage next to the water heater. It was all so ridiculous.

I lit the match to a real firestorm when I inquired if the city had requested E.P.A. approval for the transfer of the property. I had prior experience with this federal requirement in Dallas. We tried to move our pistol range when I was the Police Academy Director. There were grand plans and the money was already set aside in the city budget to build a huge new facility with all the latest equipment to train Dallas' finest.

Unfortunately, getting rid of the old range facility stopped us cold. The Feds had been very specific. "If you pick up one tablespoon of this lead contaminated dirt," they had ordered, "you have to clean the lead out of it before you put it back down somewhere." The clean-up cost would have been millions of dollars. Needless to say, the City of Dallas, which had a funny fetish for following the law, was still using the old range. The fetish was old fashioned, I know, but I liked it a lot better than what Mel had planned.

"Complying with Federal environmental regulations is not your concern," Bob's angry e-mail replied.

I retorted with a "cover your ass" e-mail of my own. "I admit that I am not an expert in E.P.A. regulations or environmental law. However, as the chief law enforcement official in this city, I am warning you. My best advice is not to proceed with the sale until you have consulted with the United States Attorney. In the meantime, we can use the time to better plan an orderly phase out of the current facility and construction of a new one to take its place."

The warning and advice fell on deaf ears. We were unceremoniously kicked out on the appointed date specified in Mel's contract with the aircraft company. The corporation quickly built their new complex on the site, complete with a picnic area and day care playground for their employees and their kids. It was all very nice. Every day I expected Godzilla to rise up out of the ground and begin swatting flying jets overhead. Maybe the mutated monster would just bite the heads off of a few corporate executives and politicians, I hoped.

For the last four years, we had been without a firearms training facility. I scrambled to borrow small private gun clubs and used the small sheriff's department range to keep the state from de-commissioning the entire Wichita Police Department. We shuttled our officers from their beats and sent them miles out of town to the other ranges so that they could meet the state's minimum qualification standards. Routine practice or safety training was impossible. As the largest police department in the state, it was humiliating as well as extremely risky.

We were chancing a negligent training civil lawsuit that would have choked a whale. If one of our officers was involved in a questionable shooting, my computerized file would convict the city manager of criminal negligence without much room for a defense. The money that was paid to Rodney King by the Los Angeles Police Department would be bubble gum change in comparison to what Wichita would owe for Mel's stupidity. Other memos in my computer files argued this very point, without much success. The paper trail of my correspondence and Mel and Bob's insufferable stupidity would be like driving a wooden stake through Dracula's heart if the file ever surfaced during a legal action.

The pistol range file was by no means my only "CYA" file stored on the computer system. I made a mental note to begin printing all of the files into a paper format as a back up. Kansas might loose a few more trees from all of the paper, but these files were my life insurance policy in case of an all out nuclear exchange with Mel Michaels. A war that was becoming more and more inevitable.

By the time I had worked through printing a few of the more juicy files, it was time for our 9:30 mini-staff meeting. Billy, Tim, and Jack were on time as usual. Equally as usual, Pete did not arrive until five minutes after we began the meeting.

"Chief, I asked Suzie to set a three o'clock meeting with you and I on that personnel matter we talked about yesterday, if that's okay," Jack Denson noted.

"Sure, Jack, that will be fine," I answered. "You guys have got me intrigued on this one anyway."

"You mind if I sit in on this one, Chief ?" Tim asked. "I might learn something."

When I looked at Tim David as he spoke, it was clear that he could barely keep a grin from spreading across his face.

"Sit in on what?" Pete Gant asked as he walked in the open office door.

"Jack's spaceman problem," Tim answered Pete's question. "He's going to brief the Chief on it today at three."

"Oh boy," Pete said. He rolled his eyes toward the approximate location of Saturn, as if he could see into outer space through the ceiling of my office.

"Spaceman? Tim, as far as I'm concerned you can sit in on any meeting you want," I asked and answered at the same time. "Jack, do you see any problem with Tim hearing the briefing? He seems to already know a helluva a lot more about this thing, whatever it is, than I do."

Jack slowing shook his head in the negative and meekly said "I don't see a problem with Tim, but we will need to keep a tight lid on this one, Chief."

Pete Gant frowned but did not say anything. He hated my use of Tim David as an equal to the deputy chiefs. Pete felt that since Tim was a civilian and not a police officer, he should not have the same level of access, prestige or influence as the sworn command staff. Except for the Chief of Police, the Deputy Chief position was the pinnacle, in Pete's mind, in the paramilitary hierarchy of the police department. I disagreed and since I was the chief and not Pete, he was forced to grudgingly accept Tim's role in my administration. My decision did not stop him from whining about it every chance he got, particularly behind my back.

"Chief, have you decided what you are going to do with Todd Bradley?," Billy asked. It was another one of Billy Wade's wayward problem child police officers. Bradley's case carried another complicating factor. He was the president of the police officer's union.

Todd Bradley was notorious for his temper tantrums, on and off duty. Once, while working an off duty security job at a local high school football game, he pitched the all time bone head fit. One of the cheerleaders, with "Buffy" carefully stitched across her spiffy new cheerleader sweater, made up an impromptu cheer which sent him into adrenaline overdrive.

"Romp 'em, stomp 'em, kick 'em in the chops", the high school cheer went, "Beat 'em, club 'em, like the big fat cops."

Officer Bradley marched over to the fresh faced young cheerleader and curtly asked her not to do that cheer again. Despite the fact he was not smiling, the petite seventeen year old must have thought that the round bellied officer was just kidding. Ten minutes later, Buffy started the cheer again.

"Romp 'em, stomp 'em, kick 'em in the aaaaaauuuugggghh," was all she got out of her mouth before Bradley had grabbed her from behind and clamped a meaty paw over her mouth. The enraged officer then proceeded to drag Buffy along the sidelines like a mop. Infuriated, he smashed the cheerleader's megaphones, kicked the pom poms into the stands and whacked the microphone table for the cheerleader's portable loud speaker system with the night stick in his free hand. Horrified parents began pushing their way from the stadium bleachers to rescue their little darlings from the policeman gone berserk. On the fifty yard line, the players stopped the game to behold the bizarre spectacle.

When Officer Bradley pushed over the "Fighting Terrapin's" mascot, the student inside the costume lay on his back and could not stand up because of the huge green plastic shell. The kid in the suit flailed about helplessly in the midst of the turmoil boiling around him. That was the last straw. Obviously, nobody insults the team turtle and gets away with it.

The remaining cheerleaders, assisted by the Terrapin's third string offensive line, charged Bradley in a scene from Custer's Last Stand. The weight of bodies crushed

Officer Bradley to the ground where he was finally subdued by two other off duty officers who had rushed to the melee.

That night, on national television, Wichita became infamous again. The sight of half naked cheerleaders and helmeted football players rolling around on the ground with Officer Todd Bradley was immortalized as ESPN's "Play of the Day". The mascot flailing around on his green turtle back was a nice touch, the announcer thought.

That was last year. Bradley served a record sixty day suspension without pay. The incident became known in W.P.D. folk lore as "Todd's Terrible Turtle Tumble". The suspension was so long that Todd had to get a job unloading trucks at the Dr. Pepper bottling plant to pay his bills. The only reason I did not fire Bradley then was that he only needed a year and half to go for his pension. I just knew I would live to regret the decision. I was right.

Todd Bradley's latest addition to his Internal Affairs file was a little more serious.

After his suspension, Deputy Chief Wade transferred him to the evening shift. The transfer was to serve as a continuous reminder of his punishment for making us all look like fools on national television. One freezing cold night about seven o'clock, Bradley decided that he would stop by "Super Bill's Barbecue Palace" for ribs. His intent was to surprise his wife by bringing home dinner so they could eat together as a real family while he took his authorized thirty minute meal break. It did not seem to matter to Todd that his home was fifteen miles outside the boundaries of his assigned beat.

Officer Bradley parked his squad car in the drive way and carried the overstuffed white paper bags of barbecued ribs, ranch style beans and cole slaw to the front door of his home. He lied when he radioed the dispatcher that he would be off the air to write up a report. Free from any bothersome call answering responsibilities, Todd then switched off his portable radio.

When the officer used his key to enter the locked front door, he noticed there were no lights on in the house. There was, however, a fire built in the living room fireplace which gave the house a warm, romantic effect. Perfect for his surprise love offering to his wife, Bradley thought.

What the fireplace did not accomplish for atmosphere, the lit candles throughout the house did. Bradley noticed his favorite Frank Sinatra record playing softly on the old style stereo and wondered how his wife knew he was coming home to surprise her.

While he was pondering the meaning of life, and whether or not the ribs were getting cold, his attention was drawn to a glimmer of movement by the fireplace. In the dim, flickering light of the burning logs Officer Bradley squinted his eyes to add some definition to the motion that caught his interest. A sofa was blocking most of his vision and the officer eased forward for a closer look. Bradley's police instincts told him to move as quietly as his two hundred and fifty pound overweight frame would allow. The two paper sacks of high cholesterol fast food did not add any to his stealth.

Halfway to the sofa, Bradley froze in his tracks. The glowing fireplace and candle power combined to produce enough lumens to provide a definite form to the movement that he had detected. The shape of a naked ass bobbing up and down was unmistakable.

Due to the sofa's position, the bare butt appeared to be unattached to any other body parts. The ass rhythmically peeked over the top of the intervening furniture and then disappeared below the sofa's back and out of sight.

Up and down, up and down, over and over in a strangely erotic peak-a-boo fashion that was made all the more surreal by the soft lights of the flickering candles.

Officer Bradley immediately figured out the scenario and he was sorely pissed off. His fifteen-year-old daughter had been in heat for months for the juvenile delinquent motorcycle punk next door. Bradley had tried about every parental trick he knew, including slapping some sense into the girl's dense skull. All she did was pout about how her daddy was ruining her life, since her love for "Bobo" was deep and everlasting. Besides, she thought without divulging to her parents, Bobo provided her with some killer weed that was dynamite shit.

The officer gently lowered the now forgotten food bags and carefully unsnapped the strap on his worn leather pistol holster at his side. "I'll scare the shit out of the no good son of a bitch and break 'em both of this habit," Bradley thought to himself. He lowered his profile as much as his beer gut would allow and began to creep closer to the couch.

As he got closer, the sounds of the one-on-one encounter next to the fireplace competed with Sinatra's scratchy "Strangers in the Night" on the ancient turntable. "Oh, baby, oh, baby, oh, baby, oh, baby, oh, oh, oh, ooooohhhhhh" came softly from behind the sofa. Vaguely, the voice did not seem quite right, but Bradley was too close to pouncing and he concentrated on picking the right moment to leap on the unsuspecting lovers for the maximum fright effect.

When he decided that the timing of the "oh, baby's" and his proximity to the activity was perfect, Officer Todd Bradley rose to his full five feet nine inches and inhaled deeply. He jerked his rusty four inch thirty eight revolver from its moldy holster and shouted in his best police voice, "Freeze, asshole, don't move!"

The asshole and the rest of the connecting tissue could not freeze. The precise pivotal moment was at hand and nothing short of a nuclear blast could stop what was coming. Literally "coming".

Bradley got an eyeful. Sure enough, the little doper from next door was the culprit. His long, stringy hair did nothing to improve his pimply, nineteen year old face. The homemade tattoo on his left forearm, courtesy of his prowess with a sewing needle and a laundry marker during a recent thirty-day stretch in the county jail for shoplifting, identified him forever as "Bobo". At least the stupid hairball did not misspell his own name, Bradley thought.

The copulating couple was not on the sofa, as the officer originally suspected. They were on the carpeted floor between the couch and the brick fireplace hearth. The female part of the duet was crouched on her knees and elbows with her head supported by a garish red throw cushion from the K-Mart collection. Bobo was humping her, doggie style, with his oily face pressed as close as possible to his lover's back. With his tongue, Bobo was licking her spinal column as she offered her rear entrance to his young passion. Heavy breasts yielded to the force of gravity and were swinging wildly in the narrow stretch of space between the woman's chest and the floor. The nipples brushing against the carpet only heightened her orgasm and made her oblivious to Officer Bradley's approach.

Bradley grabbed an edge of the cheap, light weight sofa and threw it halfway across the room. "I said freeze, motherfucker!" The officer screamed.

He was exactly correct in his identification of Bobo as a "motherfucker".

Frightened completely out of his wits, Bobo stood straight up and displayed the final moments of what was intended to be a glorious sexual finale to his terrific command performance. Despite his brief life, tonight's sexual encounter was already memorialized in Bobo's personal fantasy highlight film as an all time show stopper.

Officer's Bradley's wife, Lucille, rolled over onto her back and screamed. When she saw her husband standing over her with pistol in hand, Lucille knew that life as she knew it had just ended. She tried desperately to hide her entire forty-seven-year-old body behind the small red couch pillow.

Standing over Lucille and dripping with sweat, Bobo stood with his own "pistol" in hand, as well. The problem was that his weapon had fired its only shot as evidenced by the harmless dribble oozing between his fingers. The crazed police officer obviously had at least six extremely lethal rounds of high velocity thirty-eight ammunition at his disposal while Bobo's weapon wilted completely out of sight in a matter of seconds.

As Lucille continued to scream, Bradley slowly assessed the situation; pausing only briefly before he went completely nuts. Upon later review, I thought the short delay was a tremendous improvement in controlling his behavior. The shock of finding the mother of his children being boned by Bobo took Bradley a few seconds to alter his tactics. He had been so sure of catching his hormonal surging teenage daughter in the act. Instead, the sight of his own wife, flushed and glistening with perspiration in the glow from the fireplace, took him by total surprise.

The hysterical woman could not seem to stop. Screaming, that is. Lucille had long since forgotten about "Oh, Baby" Bobo and his magic wand.

Hearing the blood curdling screams and believing Charlie Manson had somehow escaped from his California prison cell to perpetrate multiple gruesome murders at the Bradley household, the neighbors frantically dialed 911.

Bobo was frozen, just like the officer ordered, and could not speak. It was just as well that he had nothing to say because Bradley thrust his revolver directly into Bobo's face. Like Errol Flynn lunging with his sword in an old pirate movie, the force of the heavy barreled pistol carried a lot of momentum when it collided with Bobo's lips and crooked front teeth. Bobo's two main incisors snapped in half like pieces of chalk. Three lower front teeth were smashed back from the gum line as the steel barrel of the revolver bored into Bobo's oral cavity.

Officer Bradley raised his arm ever so slightly until the serrated front sight on the top of the pistol's muzzle carved a neat little niche in the roof of Bobo's mouth. Blood spurted all over the officer's gun hand from Bobo's smashed mouth. The would be sex god opened his lips wider so more oxygen could get past the intruding pistol barrel. Bobo was desperately sucking air through the bloody froth when Bradley raised his arm even more, forcing Bobo to stand on his tip toes lest the offended husband twitch and end the whole affair by pulling the trigger. Already, there was eight pounds of meaty finger pressure on a ten pound trigger pull.

Lucille continued to scream at the top of her lungs. The neighbors called the police emergency line again. This time they mentioned to the 911 operator that there was a police car out in front of the house. The result of this little bit of information was electric. The routine "Disturbance" call was immediately upgraded to an "Officer in Trouble" emergency. In police departments all over the world, Lizzie Borden hacking up the neighborhood would have a much lower priority rating than an "Officer in Trouble" call. Every police officer in Wichita began roaring, with flashing red lights and wailing sirens, towards Todd Bradley's house.

In the meantime, Officer Bradley's vision was impaired by a fuzzy red haze due to his dementia. He was completely oblivious to Bobo's blood streaming down his arm, his wife screaming uncontrollably or the family dog nervously licking his balls in the corner. The odor of spilled barbecue sauce and ribs was noticed only by Rover.

"Now, you worthless piece of shit. I'm gonna' blow your fucking brains out," Bradley announced.

"Naugggghhhhh," was about all Bobo could manage to croak. Bobo's vocal cords were temporarily out of commission due to a combination of fear and the lethal weapon jammed in his mouth. The rusty old Smith and Wesson, manufactured before Bobo was born, was rammed halfway down his throat.

Bradley raised his gun arm even higher and instructed Bobo to "Move, asshole!"

The teenager carefully backed a couple of steps on the top of his toes, as the hysterical Mrs. Bradley scooted her bare butt across the carpeted floor and out of the way. The officer marched Bobo backwards across the room toward the front door. Along the way, Bradley gave a vicious kick to the bags of ribs and beans that he had carefully laid on the floor only moments before. The officer's sudden movement caused Bobo to lose control of his bladder and yellow rivulets of pee trickled down his legs. Even the dog began to howl.

Out the door the two went, until they stood alone in the front yard. The pair were brightly illuminated by the high powered sodium vapor street light. It was below freezing outside in the Kansas night but neither Bobo nor Bradley noticed the cold.

Only a block away, Officer Joe McCarthy pushed his "Special Police Package" Chevrolet even harder to get to the "Officer in Trouble" call. He had already run over enough curbs and lawn furniture to blow out all four steel belted radial tires. The shaking vehicle was now running on the tire rims, kicking up dirt and sparks along the way. McCarthy was determined to get there first and do whatever it took to save his fellow officer, by God. The other officers did not call him "Dirty Joe" for nothing.

"This is it, dickhead," Bradley calmly stated. His eyes gleamed in the yellowish glow cast by the street light as a thumb slippery with Bobo's blood cocked the pistol's hammer. Bobo closed his eyes and lost all control over his bowels.

The odor of steaming Bobo crap was overwhelming in the frosty air.

The image of Dirty Joe's grinding squad car distracted Bradley for just an instant. From a half a block away, the bizarre apparition came steadily onward. Along with a lot of other miscellaneous automobile parts, the siren and light bar had long since been shaken loose from the car's roof. The sparks and smoke pouring from the melting engine and tire rims more than made up for the missing emergency equipment in both noise and visibility. What were once four special order brake drums on the vehicle's wheels were on fire due the excessive friction.

Dirty Joe did not let the car stop rolling before he jumped from the moving vehicle. He hit the ground rolling like a paratrooper and charged across the front lawn of the Bradley home. McCarthy could not have stopped the car even had he tried, since the brakes were totally useless in their melted down state. The heavy duty brake pads were designed to withstand five hundred degrees of heat. That benchmark had been surpassed about a half a mile back. The entire pile of overheated junk, which only minutes before had been a beautiful piece of sleek automotive engineering, careened to a stop against a fire hydrant. The overtaxed radiator exploded and enveloped the wrecked hulk in a plume of steam and sticky green anti-freeze.

Everyone later agreed that it was Joe's best tackle since he played linebacker for Wichita's Northwest High School "Grizzlies". Joe blind sided Bobo from a full gallop. As an unintended result of the violent collision, the pistol was torn from Officer Bradley's hand, along with six more of Bobo's molars. The old gun's front sight also sliced a four inch chunk of flesh from his cheek where the serrated rib cut a sideways exit. Miraculously, the revolver did not fire. When the pistol was later found under the rose bushes in the front yard, the rusty hammer was still cocked. The fact that Bradley had not oiled his service revolver since he was in recruit school was probably the only thing that kept Bobo's brains from fertilizing the front lawn.

Dirty Joe fully intended to destroy the bad guy to the best of his physical abilities. He had only vaguely caught a glimpse of the person the officer was confronting in the yard. No matter, an "Officer in Trouble" call practically required that someone get the crap stomped out of them. The over aggressiveness was a prevention technique, as much as anything else, to deter the suspect from ever attacking a police officer again. There was a kind of unofficial "Code of the West" thing among police officers on this particular issue.

In this case, it did not really matter that Joe failed to find out poor Bobo was guilty of nothing more than laying a little pipe in the wrong house.

However, when Officer McCarthy raised his heavy, non-departmentally approved metal flashlight to smash the bad guy's face in, he was shocked. There was not much of a face to whack. In fact, the guy was completely destroyed already. Naked, spurting blood and with feces and urine smeared all over his shaking legs; Bobo rolled into a fetal position and groaned incoherently. Despite his reputation as "Dirty Joe", Officer McCarthy had never beaten anyone who was not fighting back or getting their just deserts as pay back for an assault on an officer. All was considered fair in a game of playing "catch-up" after the suspect had gotten in the first blows, but this was different. Joe was not exactly sure what was going on, but his instincts told him that something was very much amiss. In any case, Bobo was no threat to anyone now.

Even Officer "Dirty Joe" McCarthy knew when to stop.

The neighborhood began raining police officers in a matter of seconds. It looked like the D-Day invasion of Normandy with all of the uniforms and weaponry. By the time the whole situation was figured out by the sergeants and lieutenants on the scene, the watch commander had already notified the Internal Affairs detectives to come and take over the investigation.

An ambulance hauled what was left of Bobo to Riverside Hospital and several subsequent dates with an oral surgeon. Lucille began claiming rape almost immediately. She was having a difficult time explaining Frank Sinatra, the candles and a half consumed pair of edible underwear still wrapped around one ankle. Despite the mounting evidence against the rape angle, Lucille clung to her story.

When the smoke finally cleared and all of the paperwork was done, Bobo was coerced into not filing assault charges against Officer Bradley by Dora Davenport. The District Attorney coolly explained to Bobo that she would be forced to charge him with rape, based on Mrs. Bradley's insistence about her chastity. The only way around the charge against Bobo, Dora explained, was if the whole sordid affair was just forgotten. Bobo's medical bills were paid by the county and he swore to himself to stick to women closer to his own age. Or at least those who did not have a crazy husband who carried firearms like Officer Todd Bradley.

That only left the Internal Affairs investigation to resolve Bradley's multiple violations of departmental policy. Every one of the Officer Bradley's supervisors and commanders recommended Bradley's termination, including the usually reticent Deputy Chief Wade.

"Billy, I confess I'm having a hard time on this one," I announced.

"Chief, what's to worry about?" Billy asked. "This is our chance to get rid of this bonehead once and for all. You are always harping about cleaning out the bad apples. Isn't that what you have been preaching since day one?"

"I know, Billy, but, in all fairness, my job is to focus in on the specific violations of our rules and regulations that were sustained by Internal Affairs and render a decision based on the facts," I declared.

"Bull, Chief," Pete interjected, "the facts are that Todd Bradley is a raving lunatic and should be fired."

"Don't forget, guys," Tim David added, "this lunatic is president of the police union and there are political and morale issues to consider."

I ignored Tim's information, even though he was right on target with his concerns as usual.

"Pete, what would you do if you came home and found your wife of twenty-five years being mounted on the living room rug by some pencil necked geek from next door?" I asked.

"First, Chief," Pete grinned, "none of my wives would ever need to hunt a trouser snake from outta the house, if you know what I mean. And second, I'd be smart enough to kill both of 'em and dispose of the bodies where you couldn't find them."

"Yeah, Chief," Billy jumped in, "Pete has a heavy duty garbage disposal at his house that could grind up an elephant."

For the first time in a long time, all of us laughed together at the image of Pete grinding up a pachyderm.

"Well, I'll tell you what, Billy." I finally announced decisively. "I am not inclined to fire Bradley for this one. I'm not sure I would have done anything differently since I don't have a heavy duty disposal like Pete's." I winked at Gant and he returned the smile. "But we absolutely do need to get his attention or else the dumb bastard is never gonna' make it another six months to get his pension."

"Okay, so what do we do with Bradley then, Chief?" Billy asked. "We've already suspended him so long on the turtle deal that we set a new departmental record. Besides, I don't think they will hire him again down at the Dr. Pepper plant. He ran a forklift off their loading dock and smashed a gazillion gallons of diet drink last year, the clumsy oaf."

"Call the Personnel Director and set up a pre-termination hearing here in my office for next week," I instructed. "Make sure the proper notice is served on Bradley, according to the labor contract, and that he understands the purpose of the hearing is to review command recommendations for his termination. If he gets scared and resigns, fine. If he finally realizes his entire career and his pension are in jeopardy and gets his act straight, fine. If he comes in here and acts like a fool, then I will fire him for being more than stupid and that will be fine, too."

There was a chorus of "fine" which greeted the end of my short speech. Most everyone seemed pleased with the decision. Everyone except Pete. Pete Gant would not be pleased with any decision I made. I had once given him a ten percent pay raise for grudgingly accomplishing all of his yearly performance goals. The increase was twice the amount the other deputy chiefs had received and a hundred times what I received from my boss, the City Manager, which was nothing. Pete complained that it was not fifteen percent.

They all assumed there was a better than fifty/fifty chance Bradley was such a mental case that he would make me mad enough at the hearing to fire him on the spot. I just hated to terminate people for stupidity. It was not a problem when an officer clearly broke the law or simply could not do the job. I had a hard time cutting people loose who became involved in situations which could generate a topic for any one of the tabloid style daytime talk shows.

We adjourned our meeting and I scratched around in my desk drawer for another pair of quarters to replace the stolen change. My morning Pepsi was an office routine. I had purposefully not informed my staff about the security breach. Other than Tim, I was not certain if any of them could be trusted. In fact, I was not sure that one of them was not the suspect who had attempted to break into my files the night before.

Retrieving the Pepsi from the machine down the hall, I returned to my office to find a full tray of mail awash on my desk. I poured half of the Pepsi carefully into my favorite coffee cup. The white mug was a gift from Peggy. In precise black letters, the cup was stenciled with the world's surest truth. "Politics is not the oldest profession, but the results are the same." I was not certain of the grammatical correctness but drinking Pepsi out of the cup gave me a strange feeling of being above the daily ugly political interactions that my job required.

By eleven o'clock I had burrowed my way through most of the routine paper work and returned a half a dozen telephone calls. Peggy called to let me know she had picked Terri up at her friend Carmen's house and had driven our daughter to school. Not much else was bubbling in the office. The telephones were oddly quiet.

"Suzie, I'm gonna go get some lunch and wander around on the streets for a while," I announced as I passed by her messy desk on my way out the door.

"Okay," she called back. "Don't forget your three o'clock meeting and your speech tonight."

"Oh, yeah, thanks. See 'ya," was all I could muster in enthusiasm for a reply. I had almost forgotten the speech. I gave so many speeches in the community that it was hard to keep them all straight. Luckily, Suzie did a great job in scheduling and coordinating my appearances. The talks were usually about crime in general or my home-spun philosophies on just about any subject. I rarely took any prepared notes to assist me. To keep it interesting for me, I much preferred to spend some time in conversation with the audience before my comments. My impromptu remarks were then built around any humorous issues or information which came up in the pre-speech warm up. That way, each speech was a fresh one.

I spoke to Lions, Kiwanis, Optimists, Baptists, Methodists, Catholics and Druids. It did not matter. All were part of the community and all wanted to meet and hear the police chief. I liked the feeling of being on stage and the excitement of a live appearance. I truly had no idea what I might say from one moment to the next. That was what made it fun.

The City Manager hated my speech making appearances because he could see that I was building a large and powerful support base among the citizens. He had Bob

Showalter call me to his office and suggest that my speeches to the community were interfering with the time that I should be spending to concentrate on crime. I pointed out that the time I spent with the various community groups was usually after regular working hours and therefore on my own time. Bullet Bob retreated into the protection of saying, "Well, some members of the Council have expressed a concern." Yeah right, I thought sarcastically. That was about as likely as finding a virgin in Hugh Hefner's house.

The City Manager then issued a city regulation requiring all department heads to notify him before they made any speeches. We called it Mel's "Mother, May I?" rule. The regulation stipulated that we notify the City Manager of the date, time, location and subject of any community speech. The stated purpose of the rule was to insure that "subjects in conflict with official city policies" would not be addressed. Besides being a perfect example of Mel's flaming paranoia, the directive was a patent violation of the first amendment of the United States Constitution; not that Mel ever gave any thought about the Constitution.

I continued to average about three speeches during my eighty to ninety hour work week. There was never a single reply to any of my e-mail messages notifying Mel of my appearances. Nonetheless, I dutifully continued the notification process to prevent the manager from using any violation of the silly rule as grounds to ax me.

During the last year or so, I had begun to mix in some pretty wild topics as the reported subjects of my speeches. It was an effort to try to get a reaction or at least some notice that the manager was even reading what he required to be sent to him. I notified Mel that my speech to the Retired Military Officer's Association was titled "Sexual Hygiene in a Combat Zone", although the real subject was "Advances in Police Technology". The speech scheduled for tonight was to the Citizen's Police Academy Alumni Association. The title of the speech was printed on their brochures as "Community Partnerships Against Crime". I reported to Mel that the subject would be "Practical Techniques to Retard Premature Ejaculation". I could not resist adding a postscript and a hyphen so that the complete title was "Practical Techniques to Retard Premature Ejaculation—a Hands On Approach". I feared the hyphenated addition might finally catch his eye and the game would be up. Oh, well.

It had started raining when I reached the parking lot. Several "Parking Control Checkers", or "P.C.C.'s", were huddled around one of their little Suzuki Samurai vehicles talking and laughing. The PCC's were not armed or commissioned police officers, but they wore uniforms and smaller badges that identified their function as regulators of the thousands of parking meters which infested Wichita's downtown. There were twelve PCC positions authorized in the police department and all were women. They took pride in their work and felt themselves an important part of the police team. If you called them "Meter Maids", they would kick your teeth in.

The laughter continued as I walked to their group in the cold drizzle.

"Hey, Chief, nice hat," one of the women called.

"Yeah, Chief, I don't think that tilt is allowed by regulations," another chimed in.

The group all jumped on me, picking on my battered uniform cap as the rain pelted down. I liked hats and always wore a baseball cap of some description when off duty and casual. On duty, I had grown up with a system in Dallas where we were required to wear our uniform caps at all times; even inside the squad car. Since I was taller than most officers, this had forced me to learn to wear the cap at odd angles so that the curving slope of the car's interior headliner could be accommodated. The cap's jaunty angle became a habit and, eventually, a personal trademark of mine in both departments.

In Dallas, an older veteran officer had taught me a trick to avoid the "Cap in Car" regulation. We went to the Property Division and persuaded a plump civilian clerk, that the older officer was screwing just enough to keep her friendly, to issue each of us an extra uniform cap. Every day that we worked together, both of us tossed one of our caps in the back seat to use whenever we got out of the car. Each of our second caps were pinned to the overhead fabric liner of the car's roof. The second cap rode about an eighth of an inch above our heads inside the car and we never had a concern about its location. While minor discipline for the petty infraction was common among our fellow officers, my veteran partner and I never worried about the sergeant jumping our case for not wearing our hats in the car. The caps were always in place, according to regulations, when the supervisor passed by. We never failed to wave and grin, safely confident in knowing that there was always a way to overcome stupidity.

"Beverly, it's not the cap that is crooked," I answered, "it's my head that is off-center."

All the PCC's laughed even more. "Chief, you're the only person, other than my mother, that calls me "Beverly". Why don't you just call me "Bev" like the rest of the girls?"

"Gee, Bev," I feigned digestion of a large slice of humble pie, "I didn't think I knew you well enough to be so familiar. Anyhow, the last time I called anybody a "girl", the City Manager tried to get me in a lot of trouble." I broke out into a broad grin to signal we were still having fun.

"Chief, you can call us girls any time you want," Beverly spoke for the group. "If that little short piss ant of a manager gives you any more trouble, we'll write him so many parking tickets he will need a wheel barrow to carry them to court."

While the girls all laughed at Bev's vivid picture of our boss loaded down with thousands of parking tickets, the cutest of the bunch joined the verbal fun. Mandy was a small, petite young woman who was barely twenty one. She was the daughter of a local minister I knew from his attendance at several of my speeches. Mandy's father was a big supporter of my philosophies and he often sang my praises during his sermons. Consequently, I looked after Mandy like she was my own daughter. She was of legal age but appeared sixteen. The other PCC's looked after her too, like a baby sister.

"Chief, don't you know you're just one of the girls?" Mandy asked. "Didn't we give you a pair of shorts to make you a member of our club?"

"You sure did, Mandy," I answered. I broke out into a big, deep laugh at the memory. It felt good to laugh.

Before my tenure in Wichita, the city had ordered the rag top Suzukis for the parking checkers to drive. They were intended as replacements for the old Cushman three-wheel scooters which had fallen apart due to age and a lack of spare parts. Unfortunately, Mel refused to allow air conditioners to be installed in the new vehicles. He believed that since the PCC's obviously did not have air conditioners on the scooters, they would not need them in the little Suzukis. The money for the air conditioners was diverted to another location in the massive overall city budget that was known only to Mel. There was no question in my mind that the ability to siphon off the funds played the major part in Mel's decision.

It was obviously a decision made by someone who did not have to wear a heavy uniform and ride in the Suzukis for eight hours a day. Particularly on hot summer days in Kansas, when the temperature was always over a hundred degrees.

Shortly after my arrival, I made it a point to ride with as many of the field personnel in the department as possible. To the chagrin of many traditional police commanders, this included the lowly parking control checkers. It was on my birthday in July when I found out just how hot the inside of one of the little white parking control vehicles could get. As my PCC partner made her rounds among the rows of downtown parking meters, I sweated along with her and vowed to do something to get the poor women some relief. Proctor and Gamble did not make enough deodorant to compensate for the effects of no air conditioning on a summer day in Kansas.

All my efforts to get vehicle air conditioners for the PCC's failed miserably in the budget process. Shifting my tactics, I tried to change the uniforms for the PCC's to a lighter and much cooler "skort" type of shorts, instead of the regular wool uniform pants worn by police officers. This attempt was again dashed on the rocks of Mel Michael's tight fisted budgeteers. Finally, in desperation, I authorized the parking control checkers to cut off a pair of their uniform pants and have them altered into shorts for summer duty wear.

It was not a big victory, but the PCC's were grateful. Mainly, I think they were just surprised that anyone cared about their welfare. During their squad meeting one morning, they asked me to attend the regular briefing for a special event. When I got there, Bev, Mandy and some of the other girls presented me with a brand new pair of regulation uniform pants in my exact waist size. How they found out the size, I never learned. I was a little confused about the gift until I held the tan colored trousers up to show the rest of the group. We all quickly noticed that the legs had been professionally altered into a pair of shorts, complete with the standard forest green stripe running down each side of the pant's leg. They were perfect. It was all I could do not to put them on right then and there and march up to Mel's office to show off my trophy.

"Thanks, Chief. Thanks for trying," Mandy had said. "Thanks for everything you do for us." I remembered the words vividly. I continued to treasure the shorts more than any other award I was ever given.

"Look, ladies, we need to break this up," I said, still refusing to call them "girls" lest Mel crawl out from under a parked car and yell "gotcha". "We better get to work, before the lieutenant comes by and yells at us," I suggested.

We all smiled, waved, and shared our "be carefuls".

Despite the rain, I was warmed by the encounter and disappointed when the PCC's took my hint to go back to their dreary task of writing parking tickets. The revenue flow into the city's coffers was important, I reminded myself, because the Mayor might feel compelled to add more custom made brick sidewalks downtown next year.

I drove around aimlessly for awhile just listening to the police radio. Nothing but fender benders and burglar alarms caused by the rain came across the air waves. With my garbage gut stomach rumbling, I ventured upon a McDonald's on the east side of town. I decided to go inside and sit with the customers, instead of continuing the aimless patrol around the city.

I chose the "Super Value Meal Deal", which was probably a healthy dose of monosodium glutamate shaped into two hamburger patties, French fries and a large Dr. Pepper. These guys did not have Pepsi, either. I decided the whole anti-Pepsi thing was a communist plot to undermine the youth of America.

The price on the colorful banner promoting the burger package sale was $4.95. I pondered why the scrumptious picture on the advertisement never looked like the smashed pile of bread dough and ground beef that came in the sack with your order. The high school age clerk brought me to reality by saying, "Okay, officer, with your discount, the total comes to two dollars and forty-eight cents."

I hate it when clerks do that. Its an unwritten rule in most fast food places that uniformed police officers pay half price. The theory by the owners is to encourage the officers to spend their unpredictable meal periods at the location, which is a sure fire method to prevent robberies or disturbances. It is very cheap security for the businesses. It is also damned embarrassing when the clerk announces the discount to the entire world.

"That's okay," I replied. "I don't mind paying full price." All the while, I was hoping that we could keep our negotiations off the front page of the National Inquirer. Like most other departments, the Wichita P.D. had a regulation against accepting gratuities. I damned sure did not want to be seen violating my own rules.

The clerk looked very confused. "Huh, I don't think you can pay full price," he stammered. "We have a rule here and I don't think I can break it."

"Look, we have rules, too," I stated, sensing the hungry line behind me growing and becoming more and more interested in what was causing the slow down. "Here, just take the money," I ordered and handed the clerk a five dollar bill.

The clerk's striped brown and orange uniform shirt carried an official plastic McDonald's name tag identifying the young Einstein as "Burt". Burt was having a very difficult time with the decision. He fingered my five dollar bill nervously and stared into the sad eyes of Abraham Lincoln on the currency's portrait in hopes of receiving presidential guidance. His computerized cash register instructed him to give me $2.52, an amount that was exactly half of the purchase price. On the other hand, here was an adult authority figure who did not want the money. To further complicate matters, the combination of D's and F's that Burt had received in all of his junior high school math courses did not prepare him to make the complicated subtraction in his head. That was why McDonald's had their machines programmed to automatically make the calculations for their employees. It was corporate America's answer to the failure of our public school systems. I decided to call the phenomenon the "Burt Syndrome" from now on. For a moment, I thought Burt might pull off his shoes and start to work on the problem by counting toes and fingers right there in the middle of the restaurant.

Clearly without a clue, Burt finally gave up trying to figure out whether he should carry the one or move the decimal point in his head. "Officer, just reach in here and get what you think you're owed," Burt instructed as he pointed to the open cash drawer.

I had to smile and resist the urge to look around for the television cameras. "No thanks, son. Look, I'll tell you what. You just keep any change left over from that five dollar bill. If you decide later I owe you any money, I'll be right over there by the window. You can come and let me know, okay?"

With another major decision in life made, I scooped up my bag of pre-mixed chemicals and dead cow extract and made a hasty exit to the dining area. Burt seemed only mildly relieved. He finally put the five dollars in the cash register and nodded his fuzzy head in compliance.

Safely barricaded behind the salt and pepper shakers on my table, I munched the fries and cheeseburger as slowly as possible. It was important to give Burt the necessary time to develop any new formulas in quantum physics that might be required for his calculations. He struggled to solve the tricky mathematics problem I had presented and finally gave up. I figured the extra nickel was well worth the show.

After leaving McDonalds' version of the Midwest campus of M.I.T., I wandered north to our newest police substation. As always, the place was practically deserted. Since there were not enough police officers to establish any new beats for the station to service, we were forced to staff the shiny new building with only one desk officer per shift. Even then, we really could not spare the officer for the unproductive fixed post assignment. The alternative was to just lock the building and leave an "Out on the Streets" sign on the front door. Even I realized that such a step was hardly a politically palatable option. The desk officer's job was to keep the lights on and handle any walk-in traffic. It was boring duty. When I came in the front door, the officer was watching re-runs of "Gilligan's Island" on a small portable tv which he had brought from home.

"Hi, Dan, any business?" I called out.

"Not much, Chief. It's slower than frozen snot around here," the officer answered. "We just got another load of hate mail about the decor outside. Other than that, there's nothing going on." The decor the officer referred to was a headache for me that even an entire bottle of Excedrin could not conquer. As usual, Mel Michaels was at the center of my pain.

When the new building was proposed and approved in the budget without us even requesting it, Mel hired an architect and contractor with no input from the police department. This was standard practice. After all, what did the police know about designing a police station?

During the final phase of construction, the workers began affixing large bronze plates to the outside of the building. The ornaments were about two feet in diameter and looked like round shields. Each cast plate was unique and held the artist's interpretation of an example of "Wichita's Culture", whatever that was. They were mounted about ten feet up along the top of the building's exterior walls with large bolts that fitted flush into the design.

The sculptor, who had been hired by Mel to design the artistic plates, was the daughter of Ray Gondorf. City Councilman Ray Gondorf. City Councilman Ray Gondorf, who previously owned the land where the police station now stood. City Councilman Ray Gondorf, who made a small fortune on the inflated sale of the land to the city. A one hundred thousand dollar design fee was awarded to Councilman Gondorf's daughter from a little known line item in the city's operating budget called the "Public Art Fund". The award was just another excellent example of how important it is to get a good quality education in the fine arts, I theorized.

Most of the designs looked like my twelve-year-old had scratched them out on her red plastic "Etch-a-Sketch" machine. They had all the creativity of oatmeal. The damned things were mounted at intervals of every ten feet along the outside walls and encircled the entire building. The primitive attempts at art included engravings of airplanes, wheat shocks, and a flowing river. These symbols had obvious connections to the city's industry, agriculture and geography; but the big problem was the swastika.

Young Miss Gondorf thought she needed something to signify Wichita's American Indian heritage. She checked out a book from the university library and found an odd shaped good luck symbol which was used by several tribes of plain's Indians. Unfortunately, the talentless moron had either never taken a world history course or just did not foresee a problem when she copied the six crossing lines from the textbook on Indian artifacts.

To make matters worse, the engraving had been randomly affixed by the construction workers to the building's most visible position centered above the front door. It did not matter that the direction of the swastika's lines were pointed exactly opposite of Adolph Hitler's Nazi symbol. The similarity to the universally hated logo was too damned close. Anyone who was not undergoing lithium treatments knew all bloody hell would break loose just as soon as the bronze orb became public knowledge.

Even before the official opening of the building, I tried to tell Mel there would be a big problem if we went ahead with the unveiling. Too late, he countered, the engravings were already installed. Besides, he replied in an e-mail that I kept in my "I can't believe he is so stupid" file, it was art and what the hell did I know about art? That was why he had hired a professional artist, he said. I replied that I did not know a damned thing about art, but I did know a little about history and could point out many instances where wars had started over smaller issues than how the swastika would be perceived. After all, I did have a college degree in history to prove I had at least heard of the Holocaust, which was more than little Miss Gondorf obviously knew. Mel angrily blew me off, as usual.

To make sure I would not be there to cause a problem, Mel hurriedly re-scheduled the official opening of the new police building for a time when he knew I would be at the national police chief's conference in Miami. It was difficult to imagine opening a police building without the police chief present. Of course, the slight was intended as a public insult. Instead, when the shroud concealing the bronze plates was dropped in the unveiling ceremony, it became a public outrage and my absence was noted by the media as some sort of ethical protest. Jack Denson, serving as the "Acting Chief of Police" while I was out of state, was forced to represent me at the ribbon cutting. When the swastika was first revealed, Jack said that the gasp of the crowd sucked enough air out of the atmosphere to ground the space shuttle.

By the time I returned from the conference, the debacle was at full boil. The police officer's union was up in arms and demanding that I do something. The newspaper was fanning the flames with articles about the division in the American Indian community over being represented by a swastika. The reporter noted that some unidentified patrol officers wondered aloud if it would be okay to put little Confederate flags on their squad car antennas, in recognition of their own cultural heritage or Robert E. Lee's birthday. One detective brought a plaster bust of Mussolini and placed it on his desk top. When asked by his supervisor, the detective claimed that the Italian dictator was a long, lost first cousin. I figured it was only a matter of time before we had a full scale holy war on our hands within the department.

I tried to talk to the City Manager about damage control, but he had firmly tied his decision to Councilman Gondorf's daughter and her artistic talents. He refused to budge. The Jewish police officers on the department were threatening to refuse to enter the building, even if assigned there. For once, the ACLU sided with the police officers and offered to file a civil law suit in their behalf. I could not say I blamed the officers, but I seemed powerless to do anything that would not make the situation even worse.

When a Jewish sergeant filed an official departmental grievance, I was forced to act. The sergeant cited a city regulation which prohibited "offensive gestures, words, or symbols in the workplace" and listed the City Manager as the offending party. As redress for his grievance, the sergeant demanded the City Manager be disciplined and that the swastika be removed immediately. I did not have the power to do either, but I was required to act on the grievance.

After telephone consultations with half a dozen employee relations experts from around the county, most of which could not believe how stupid our city manager was, I ruled that the sergeant's complaint was a valid grievance under the city's regulations. I forwarded my findings, along with a strongly worded "I told you so" admonition, to Mel. In an effort to soften the blow, I continued to suggest to the City Manager various ideas he could use to gracefully exit the dilemma without causing World War Three.

His response was to eliminate the city regulation which he had violated. He went so far as to pre-date his elimination of the policy to two months prior to the complaint and blamed me for not recognizing that the rule I based my grievance finding on was no longer valid. Privately, he told the City Council members I was at fault for not properly inspecting the designs prior to their installation and that I was stirring up my own department against him. The council all agreed that nothing should be done about what the Manager called my "failure to properly manage the department" at present or else they would all lose face. The Manager assured them that he would deal with me later.

In the meantime, the plate was still firmly bolted to the wall above the substation door. At times, I thought about sneaking up late at night and unscrewing the damned thing myself before someone started using it for target practice. The controversy raged on in the press and in the community like an open sore that refused to heal.

I made my way through the deserted squad room and found a telephone on one of the back tables. I dialed my home number and Peggy picked it up after two rings.

"Hey, kid, what's up?" I asked.

"Oh, hi, there's nothing going on here 'cept I'm trying to remember what I did with my dry cleaning," Peggy answered. Since her multiple surgeries, her short term memory loss was becoming more and more of a problem.

"Have you tried looking in the microwave oven?" I countered.

"Very funny, smart guy," Peggy replied. "Oh, yeah, Victor Pasqual called to check on me and see how I was doing. He seemed very concerned."

"Yeah, I bet he did," my voice hardened a bit. "What else did Chief Pasqual want?"

"Nothing. He said he was really worried about us, that's all. Are you coming home at the regular time?" Peggy changed the subject.

"No, babe, I'm sorry. I've got a speech tonight at the police academy and it will be late before I get home," I answered.

"Do you want me to go with you?" Peggy asked.

She often enjoyed the socialization for which I cared little.

"Heck no, you've heard all of my funny lines already. I'll pat you on the head when I get home." I knew Peggy would be sound asleep by nine o'clock, when her energy level was depleted to practically nothing. She was an early riser but when her batteries ran low each evening, it was lights out for Mrs. Starr.

We said our good-bye's and I sat staring at the beige telephone for a moment longer. I was disappointed that I could not spend more time with Peggy. We were uncertain as to when she would be jetting off again to the Mayo Clinic for some other type of treatment or more tests. The disease put a funny spin on the amount and quality of time we spent together. While we were together a lot less, it seemed; we were more than close during the time we did see each other. It was hard to explain.

My reflections were interrupted by the disembodied electronic voice of Dan calling on the intercom from the front desk. "Chief, Mr. David is holding for you on line two."

I punched the blinking line and asked "Tim, how the hell did you find me here?"

"It was just a wild guess, Chief," Tim answered. "When I couldn't raise you on the command radio channel, I thought I would try one of the substations. You're not that hard to track down, you know."

"Well, before you ask, the answer is no. I am not out here painting over that damned swastika," I announced.

"Surely, some of my own highly creative, innovative staff will figure out how to solve the problem without my personal involvement." It was a hint I had been dropping around the department for weeks. So far, no one had taken the bait.

"I just wanted to let you know that Deputy Chief Denson called the office. He needs to postpone the three o'clock meeting until nine in the morning due to some new information about the situation," Tim's voice lowered conspiratorially. "That's one meeting that you will not want to miss."

"Tim, you guys have got me nervous on this deal. What's the big secret?" I demanded.

"Can't say over the phone, Chief. You know my boss is a stickler for security. Besides, I wouldn't want to ruin the surprise," Tim countered.

"By the way," he continued, "I need to leave a little early today, if that's okay."

"Do you still want to sit in on the mysterious meeting with Jack in the morning?" I asked.

"I sure do, but something important came up this afternoon. I'll tell you about it in the morning. Okay?" Tim repeated.

"It's all right with me, Tim. I guess you're gonna' to miss out on my speech tonight also," I stated petulantly.

"Chief, no offense, but I already know most of your speeches by heart. They're great, don't get me wrong. I don't think you will need me in the audience tonight, anyway," Tim answered cryptically.

Our conversation ended and I wandered through the vacant building toward the front desk. Gilligan and the Skipper were slapping each other around on the small tube when I rounded the corner.

"Dan, if you keep watching that crap, your brain is going to turn to mush," I advised.

"I know, Chief, but there's not much to do around here," the officer moaned. "I've already played with myself twice and sharpened all of the pencils in the desk." As proof of his efficiency, he held up a handful of yellow number twos which had been ground down to half their original length.

"Well, just make sure you don't get those tasks confused," I retorted.

Dan changed the television to the PBS channel which was airing bits and pieces of a nostalgic video depicting aging stars from the early days of rock and roll who were re-enacting their original hits for posterity, and a few royalty dollars. It was the pubic television station's semi-monthly fund raising drive which I called "Begging For Bucks".

"Hey, I remember that group," Dan called out as he pointed to a group of three very heavyset female singers on the tube. The trio was dressed in bright red flowing robes of sequined silk that added the appearance of another fifty pounds to their already hefty bulk.

The "Chantalls" were performing their "one hit wonder" from 1960 which was only vaguely familiar. "I thought there were four girls in that group. I guess one of 'em musta died," Dan lamented.

"Yeah, from the size of them, it looks to me like they ate the other one," I commented. At that moment, the lead singer dedicated their next song to the departed member of the original quartet, although she said that "a little bit of Annabelle remains inside all of us".

Dan grinned. I waved a "be careful" and exited out the front door to my car. I was a little disappointed that the swastika did not fall on my head and put us both out of our misery.

As soon as I unlocked the car door, I knew something was wrong. My side handle police night stick was laying on the passenger side seat cushion and not wedged in between the two bucket seats where I always kept it. The glove box was closed, but a stack of giveaway baseball cards were scattered in the floorboard. I usually carried a supply of these in the glove box to hand out to the kids I met while patrolling the streets. Since the cards were of the relatively inept Kansas City Royals, I knew they did not have enough energy to jump out of the glove box by themselves. I could not find anything missing but someone had definitely been in my car while I had been inside the substation.

"Hey Dan," I called when I opened the front door just wide enough to yell inside, "Did you see anyone in the parking lot while I was inside?"

"Huh?" Dan answered. I immediately knew that it was hopeless. He had changed the tv back to Gilligan's Island. The castaways had Dan's attention more than the parking lot. It was no wonder. I was forced to admit it; Ginger was a knockout.

"Never mind," I said with enough disgust to make Dan wonder what he had done wrong. He snapped off the tv and began to shuffle papers on his desk.

All of our police cars used the same key. It was a safety measure I had learned the hard way in West Dallas. On a family disturbance call, we had an officer shot in the stomach by a fourteen year old runaway. While some of the officers chased the shooter into an upstairs bedroom, none of the other six officers at the scene could find the right keys for the only police vehicle that was not blocked in to get the wounded officer to the hospital.

I held the officer's hand and cradled him in my lap to reassure him we would quickly get him to the doctor and everything would be just fine. Neither the wounded officer nor any of the rest of us thought the little .22 caliber bullet that the kid had fired could do serious damage. Hell, it didn't even hurt, the officer who was shot said. While we waited for an ambulance, he bled to death in my arms. The tiny piece of lead had severed his aorta.

When the SWAT team finally busted in the door they cut the juvenile killer to ribbons with automatic weapons fire. The kid had just one bullet in his cheap "Saturday Night Special" and he had used it to kill the officer. Of course, the SWAT team did not know the kid was out of ammo and they did not care. Neither did any of the rest of us who had watched our friend die.

It took a long time to wash the officer's blood off my hands and out of my dreams. In response to the memory, I made sure that any police car key would fit every vehicle in our fleet in Wichita. There had never been any downside to the practice. Until now.

I started the unmarked car and made a right turn onto Twenty First Street, toward the Wichita University campus. Some people thought it was the single most fouled up college in America. The professors and administrators were rumored to spend more time arguing about the size of the nameplates on their office doors than they did teaching. In fact, the students seemed to be an annoyance to the professors; who appeared more interested in getting grant money from the city, state and federal governments for their pet research projects. They seemed to vie with each other to develop the most useless, idiotic academic trivia on which to write scholarly papers that no one ever read, much less used. One of my favorite examples was a forty thousand dollar grant to study "The Cultural Impact of Poetry by Blue Eyed Women in Guatemala". I wondered if the report could possibly exceed two pages. Double spaced. In large type.

What few students did attend the college, called the place "Hilltop High". The highest crime beats and lowest income area in Wichita surrounded the campus on three sides. Enrollment was steadily declining and the university elite pretended they could not figure out why. I concluded that the school's reputation around the country was probably a joke. The current student body president was allegedly a twice convicted felon. During the last campus election he admitted that he had a "minor" continuing heroin habit. The young lad won office in a landslide; no doubt solidifying a promising future in politics. I would not send my dog to the place; much less my child. Anyone who would come down out of the clouds of Kansas academia for one minute would see that a degree from Wichita University was considered worthless to any employer who was looking for graduates with a quality education. A degree from "Hilltop High" was death to a career in anything other than "animal husbandry" or "hotel/motel management".

The best part of the campus was the golf course. The course was built in 1897 as a swank country club and now made up the eastern boundary of the college. I was not much of a golfer. It was a game that I decided I would learn to play when I retired to some south Florida beach.

I drove slowly past the rusting football stadium where the university's now defunct football team had performed twenty years earlier. The football program was ultimately dropped due to yawning apathy. The slowly decaying stadium stood as a silent reminder of long afternoons getting embarrassed by schools with "real" football programs.

On the golf course nearby, a group of young female students were obviously getting a lesson from their golf instructor. The women were dressed in tight fitting black and gold stretch pants with white sweaters and matching knit caps. The girls looked to be a lot older and more mature than I remembered the coeds appearing during my collegiate days at the University of Texas. I concluded it was the diet of corn fed beef and fresh milk which enabled these wholesome looking Kansas farm girls to grow the major league "yahbows" that stretched beneath their sweaters. My mind wandered to thoughts of self pity. Where were girls like these when I was young and single, I asked myself. The answer depressed me. Twenty years ago, they were all un-united egg and sperm cells in men and women who were now well past forty, like me.

The afternoon passed slowly. I showed up at a few dispatched calls to chat with the troops and made repeated phone calls to the office to check for messages. Suzie claimed it was the quietest she had seen the office in a long time. The weather was deteriorating. I told Suzie to take off work a little early to beat the almost non-existent Wichita rush hour.

I was watching the windshield wipers keep time to my aimless driving when I was suddenly surprised to see the Police Academy building pull up on the right. I was not sure how it got there, since I had been daydreaming for the last hour or so about coeds with large breasts and mysterious car burglars who did not bother to steal anything. Glancing at the watch my troops had presented me when I left Dallas, I realized my arrival was about thirty minutes premature. The gold and blue Dallas Police badge logo under the timepiece's crystal was a constant reminder of Big D. I was tired of driving and parked in the half filled lot.

"You're early, Chief," the officer who coordinated the "Citizen Police Academy" program held the door open. The rain was coming down harder. "Some of the audience are early too, though. I guess they are excited to hear you speak."

"Tony, at my age, I'm excited to hear me speak," I said.

"Huh?" the officer looked confused at my comment. He obviously was not reading my mind. For the last hour I had been feeling sorry for myself and believing that I was old and over the hill. Young people were beginning to depress me. Those coeds would never perform lewd and obscene acts on my aged body, I was sure.

"Never mind, Tony," I told the young officer who looked like he had been shaving since last Thursday. "You wouldn't understand."

The Police Academy building was another one of Mel Michaels bargain basement deals. It was an old converted elementary school. The local school district leased the unused building to the city for one dollar a year, as long as we kept up the maintenance. The city was four years behind in paying the lease. Someday, I knew it would be my responsibility to pony up the four dollars out of my own pocket to keep the school district from foreclosing on the cheap bastard that was our city manager.

One good thing about the building was that it contained a small gymnasium. The gym was designed to be easily converted to an auditorium, complete with stage. It was an excellent location for very large meetings, recruit graduation exercises and pot luck get togethers like tonight. The biggest drawback of the building, other than its age, was that the water fountains were mounted two feet from the floor. After all, they had been designed to quench the thirst of five and six year old cookie crunchers.

The rest rooms contained the same type of miniature "Shoot low, sheriff; they're riding Shetlands" equipment. I made my way toward a door with a white hand lettered

sheet of white typing paper that identified the entrance as the "Male Room". Few people knew that underneath the paper signs on both entrance doors were ornate brass
letters that permanently identified the rest rooms as "Boys" or "Girls". The cover-up of
the original designations had been ordered by Mel. He cited the use of words "boys"
and "girls" on the doors as clear indications that a pattern of institutional racism and
sexual harassment existed in the police department. It did no good to remind him of
the building's origin as a school built in 1940 for children. We were all guilty as
charged in the police department and that was that.

A large man with big, thick glasses and a day old growth of beard greeted me as I
pushed open the swinging door to the newly designated "Male Room". An oddly
coifed toupee did an extremely poor job of covering his bald head.

"Hey, Chief," the man said as he moved towards me. "How you been? You probably don't remember me, do you?"

I fought the urge to tell baldy that not only did I not remember him, but I doubted
if his own mother could recognize him in the ridiculous hair piece.

"Gee, you look familiar," I lied. "you're, you're…"

"Hubert, Hubert Coggins," the man helped me answer. "I was in the first Citizen's
Police Academy class. Yeah, boy, that was a while back. Right after you first came to
Wichita. I still remember everything you said on the first night."

Hubert stuck out a mangy paw to shake and I noticed that his fly was unzipped.
Despite my better judgment and with full faith in modern science's assurance that I
could not get HIV or Lou Gehrig's disease from the ritual, I reluctantly shook his hand.

"We're gonna have a big crowd to hear you tonight, Chief," Hubert continued. "Are
you gonna tell us what the real scoop is on some of your big cases? Huh, Chief, are ya?"

I pulled my hand free without resorting to deadly force and tried to smile. I walked
past him and sought refuge in a stall. Like every other restroom toilet stall in America,
the sliding bar which latches the stall door was mounted two inches above the slot that
it was supposed to slide into. The lock refused to close properly.

"You'll just have to wait and see what we talk about, Mr. Coggins," I called out. "It'll
be a surprise that way."

I gave up on attempting to lock Hubert out of my life and concentrated on deciding beforehand just how many times I would shoot the ignorant bastard if he tried to
follow me onto the toilet stool. I flushed the toilet twice in rapid succession in hopes
that he would get the idea and leave. I did not feel safe until I heard his booming voice
emanating from outside in the hall. Luckily, he had captured another victim.

The gym was filling up when I made my entrance. Six long rows of tables had
been placed end to end; leading from the elevated stage to the back of the cavernous

room. White paper table cloths had been draped over the tables to form a reasonably attractive eating surface. The food was spread out on another row of tables at the rear of the room. Obviously, everyone in the Alumni Association had been told to bring a covered dish.

I heard some laughter and sat down next to the sound before I realized that the source was Kandi Maldonado. Seated on her other side was her estranged husband, John. The same John who was bombarding the reluctant muff diver with post cards begging her to move back in with him and rebuild their marriage. Oh brother, I thought to myself, this night ought to be fun.

I recognized most of the other people at the table. Kandi's current room mate and live-in lover, Renee Stark, was there. She was with a guy who looked a lot like the punk rock singer, Alice Cooper, but I could not be sure. Dale Williams, the Water Department Director, had left his southern belle of a wife at home and was there in the company of his blonde bombshell secretary named Norma something or other. I was pretty sure they were not an item. Yet.

Deputy Chief Billy Wade was in attendance with his wife, who looked terribly uncomfortable. I suspected vaginal itch as the source of her discomfort and was about to prescribe an over the counter medication when I noticed Randall Anderson sitting at the end of our table. Randy was the self-styled entrepreneur that Pete Gant almost strangled to death at the "Employee's Appreciation" party. He did not look any worse for the experience. I purposely chose not to say hello to anyone. I decided to keep my mouth shut and observe the interplay of my fellow guests.

To cover my silence, I took out a small pocket notebook and gave the impression I was hastily preparing my after dinner speech. Glancing up from my scribbles, it was easy to note that Renee was heavily self-medicated. Her eyes were glazed and her speech was slow. I suspected either Valium or one of the more potent newer anti-depressants like Zoloft or Prozac. Better living through chemistry again.

Kandi was just plain drunk. I could smell the sickly sweet smell of cheap wine ooz-ing from her pores. Her adoring husband, John, seemed not to notice or care. He kept giving her deep, affectionate looks which Kandi either did not perceive in her alcoholic haze or simply refused to return. For once, John was the sober one of the pair.

To round out a perfect dinner group, Randall Anderson was seemingly as obnox-ious as ever.

His boisterous laughter sounded like a water buffalo in heat.

Billy Wade and his wife clung to each other in mutual defense against the outside world. They were observing the show at the table and were clearly uneasy over the seating arrangements. Mrs. Wade squirmed a little more and I mentally changed my unsolicited diagnosis from vaginal dryness to pin worms.

Stoned out of her mind, Renee rose from her seat unsteadily and announced to the whole world that if she did not eat soon, she would puke and pass out from hunger right then and there. I learned long ago to never stand in the way of a doper, even a minor league prescription drug abuser like Renee, when they wanted to eat. The whole table seemed to waver between accepting Renee's proposal to start the food line or individually melting through their seats.

Renee put her finger in her mouth and started to gag. I turned my head so that any undigested bean sprouts or cottage cheese would not smack me in the face. I slowly rubbed an imaginary speck from the corner of one eye, as if Renee's gagging had already discharged a chunk of lung.

To everyone's relief, the Alumni Association president took the microphone and announced that the buffet style dinner was ready. We were all encouraged to take the paper plate and plastic utensils in front of us and "dig in". I expected Renee to pull out a shovel from underneath her dress.

Renee removed her finger from her mouth long enough to shout a loud "yessssss!", with a lot of hissing on the delivery. Alice Cooper, or whoever the unlucky guy was escorting Renee, tugged at the sleeve of her blouse. He whispered a few choice words to the hungry wench which seemed to calm her down a bit. Kandi, equally blasted from another type of chemical, blissfully blew a snot bubble and staggered to her feet. For the moment, the alcohol seemed to be controlling her usual odd facial twitches.

I stood up just in time to see Marty Sims come through the open gym doors leading into the main hallway. Walking some distance behind him was his ex-wife, Jana. I was beginning to wonder about this "ex" business. It seemed like I had seen her more with Marty lately than before they were divorced. I stared at her long enough to send a telepathic lewd message. Physically, she was even more stunning than I had allowed myself to notice before.

Marty and Jana picked a spot two tables over from my seat to put their coats down and found a place at the end of the fast filling food line. When Jana turned, our eyes met and she smiled from halfway across the room. I hoped the change in her facial expression was not just gas. Worse, I thought, maybe she really could read the telepathic brain wave message that I was unconsciously emitting. My private thoughts could be an outline for a full feature article in Penthouse Magazine.

As we received our food, I could see that Randall Anderson had brought two young college age women with him. He pointed out several items on the table they should eat or avoid, like a father guiding his kids. Randy abandoned the coeds as soon as he saw Renee Stark. Randy whispered something to Renee and she followed him into a corner, leaving Alice Cooper to hold both plates. I tried to move a little closer hoping to pick up any juicy tidbits of conversation. While Randy and Renee were exchanging low volume verbs underneath the massive gymnasium scoreboard, Kandi staggered up behind Randy and stuck a stubby pink Vienna sausage in his ear.

"How does it feel to take it in the ear, Randy?" The late, great inebriated Miss Maldonado queried. Both Kandi and Renee broke out in hysterical laughter while Anderson used a meaty finger, adorned with a diamond pinkie ring, to pry the slimy meat by-product out of his aural canal. He seemed totally disgusted. Evidently Randy did not like getting screwed in the ear with a squishy little dildo made from pig lips.

"Jesus Christ, Kandi!" Anderson yelled. He dug a chunk of pink meat out of his ear and threw it on the polished gym floor. "Don't act like such a bitch. We're in public, for Christ's sake." For a moment, I thought he might cry.

Richard Lopez and his wife put down their empty paper plates and quickly made their way back to the table. Retrieving their coats and Mrs. Lopez' purse, the Fire Chief and his wife made a hasty exit through the gym door.

"Ear sex!" Renee screamed as she tried to punch a half eaten piece of celery into Kandi's unprotected ear. Kandi was drunkenly watching Anderson remove the Vienna sausage when she belatedly sensed Renee's assault with the celery. As Kandi lurched away, she whirled headlong into her estranged husband, John, who was coming up to her with two plates of overdone meat loaf, mashed potatoes and green beans.

The two crashed together and food went flying all over poor John and a couple of innocent bystanders. In drunken parties or real life, innocent bystanders always get the worst of it.

"Oh, crap," John moaned as a hunk of gravy coated meat loaf slid down his trouser leg. "Kandi, watch what you're doing."

"Fuck you, Bozo," Kandi slurred. Her eyes started rolling and the nervous twitches of her mouth returned to make her seem maniacal.

"Baby. Kandi. Sweetheart. You shouldn't talk like that," John answered. He was trying desperately not to offend his pickled semi-wife. With mashed potatoes dripping down his chin, he looked like a wimpish Colonel Sanders.

"I'll talk any fucking way I please, dickless," Kandi announced. "And let me try to make this clear to your stupid little brain, keep...the...fuck...away...from...me!" Each syllable was louder and more precise than its predecessor.

John Maldonado was in great pain. He hung his head and slowly shuffled back to the table. John's retreat trailed food parts along the floor like Hansel and Gretel leaving bread crumbs to find their way. In more ways than one, the guy was lost. As soon as John sat down, he buried his head in his hands and began to cry like a baby.

I waited for someone to go over and console the shattered attorney, but no one made any effort. I heard someone in the still moving food line crack a joke, "You know what looks good on a lawyer?"

"Meat loaf?" The other person countered. A dozen people laughed.

"No, a Doberman," the jokester answered with the real retort in a very old routine. Only a half a dozen people laughed at the second punch line, originally written by Jack Benny around 1930 and promptly discarded as not very funny.

Renee and Kandi hugged each other in an odd display of triumph. I almost expected high fives or bumping butts together.

"He's an asshole," Renee said. "All men are worthless assholes." I was in no position to disagree.

In any case, arguing with Renee right now would be downright suicidal.

In an attempt to act like nothing out of the ordinary had occurred, we all got a plate of various unlabeled concoctions and returned to the table area to devour the bland looking food. I remembered Peggy telling me once that women used pot luck dinners as the time to experiment. Usually, they were new recipes in the cookbook they received for Christmas, but were afraid to try on their own family. If no one fell over face down in the noodles, then the creation might be safe to serve at home.

Everyone ate quietly, ignoring John who continued to hide his face in his hands and sob. It made me feel sad and angry at the same time. I wanted to slap the top of his head and tell him to get over it. Kandi Maldonado was about a five on the Rod Starr's "good looking women" scale; and I had very low standards in my rating system. Surely an attorney who had won a half a million dollars in one case could find a replacement for the drooling bitch who had just publicly humiliated him.

After about two bites of something that was green and oozing, I got up and pushed back from the table to escape "Fluff and Ruff" and all of their misery. When I stood, Renee had picked up another Vienna sausage and begun the search for a new victim. I gave her a look which dared her to try it. No amount of Valium in her blood stream could cloud the message in my eyes. I fully intended to break her arm if she got within ten feet of me. As I walked away, I felt ashamed of the entire human race.

Like a magnet, I was drawn to the table where Jana Sims was seated. Marty was there, of course, and had leaned his chair back against the wall to face the stage. There was an empty chair at the table and I eased into it.

"Mind if I sit here?" I asked.

"Heck, no, Chief," Marty seemed thrilled at the attention. "We'd be honored to have you sit at our table. What's all the commotion going on over there with your group?"

"They're not "my group", Mr. Sims," I answered. "I don't know what color the sky is on the planet they live on, but they seem to be enjoying the view."

"You know my wife, don't you, Chief ?" Marty asked.

"Jana, this is Chief Starr."

"Yes, we've met," Jana stated. "And how are you this evening, Chief?"

"Well, things at my table were getting a little too intense for me," I replied. "I'm just a homebody, you know, and all of this excitement is just too much for me. Would you like to go over and join the fun?"

"I would," Marty jumped at the invitation with no hesitation. "I need to talk to Kandi about a senate bill that's coming up pretty soon in Topeka. It's bad for business and we need to kill it before it's born. You know kind of a legislative abortion, huh, Chief?" Marty broke into a hearty laugh at his weak attempt at humor. His metal folding chair scraped on the hard wood floor as he stood to leave.

"You comin', Jana?" Marty asked.

"We'll be right over," I answered for both of us without taking my eyes from Jana's gaze.

"We're getting some dessert first," Jana said, waving toward the chocolate cream pies on the nearby food table.

"Okay, I'll see you over there before the speeches start," Marty called over his shoulder. When he walked away, I could see the unmistakable bulge of a pistol on his right hip, underneath his suit coat.

"Are you guys married or what?" I asked bluntly. My ability to talk to women while using some measure of tact and diplomacy was non-existent.

"What business is that of yours, Chief ?" Jana shot back. "I didn't ask you if you had a wife and kids waiting for you at home."

"As a matter of fact, I do have a wife and a daughter waiting at home," I answered truthfully. I slowly turned my head and watched Marty join the group of fun lovers at my old table.

The drone of their laughter grew louder.

"Let me guess, Deputy," I ventured back into the conversation. "You keep good old Marty around just to carry your gun for you, is that it?"

"Very perceptive, Chief," Jana answered. "No, I'm afraid the pistol is his own. It's the only thing he has that shoots regularly."

I was a little taken aback at her obvious implication that Marty used his Colt more than he did his reproductive organ.

"That definitely sounds like a serious personal problem for poor Marty," I stammered.

"Well, when I was married to the guy, it was a problem for more than "poor Marty", as you call him," Jana stated. Her voice was hard and cold, with sarcasm dripping on every syllable.

"Is it still a problem for anyone other than poor Marty?" I asked with raised eyebrows. I knew I was getting deeper and deeper into this dangerous conversation, but I could not seem to stop myself.

Before Jana could answer my leading question, Kandi and Renee broke out in more peals of laughter. It appeared, from the frantic movements at their table, as though another assault on a body orifice was about to occur.

"Now what's going on over there?" Jana asked.

"My guess would be that Renee or Kandi or both are trying to stick a little weenie into your ex-husband's ear," I observed with all the dryness of court testimony.

"A what?" Jana asked incredulously.

"A little weenie. You know. One of those gross looking little sausages, pickled in grease, which are actually all of the parts of a pig that no one really wants to eat," I explained. "They grind all of the parts up, cook it under a lot of pressure until it turns to pink mush and you can't tell the pig's anus from his scrotum. When it's thoroughly disgusting, they shape it into little weenies and pack 'em eight to a can."

"Sounds yummy," Jana commented without much conviction.

"Yeah, people don't buy them to eat, just to play with,"

I observed. "Kandi and Renee must go through a case of the things a week, by the looks of how much fun they are having tonight."

"Well, it must be cheap entertainment," Jana said.

"It won't be cheap if they stick the weenie in the wrong person's ear," I scowled.

Thankfully, Jana steered the conversation towards more interesting waters as I turned to look into her face again. "Aren't you afraid to be seen in public talking with a divorced woman?" she asked.

"No, are you worried about my reputation or yours?" I queried back.

"I've been worried about what my actions would be around you ever since I first saw you," Jana said as she dropped her eyes to gaze into her lap.

There was a brief, uneasy pause filled with a lot of static electricity as I tried to figure out exactly what Jana's comments really meant. As usual, I was without a clue. All I could think of was Mel Michaels telling me I needed to work on my interpersonal relations. In Mel's definition, I supposed it meant I should grab my groin and flop my equipment up on the table for Jana's inspection and reaction. I had definitely decided that I would pass on that option when there was an obnoxious screech and the unmistakable whine of electronic feedback from the portable microphone and speaker system at the other end of the room.

Renee had climbed onto the elevated stage and was clumsily unbuttoning her blouse. Only her escort for the evening, the Alice Cooper look alike, and the Citizen Police Academy Alumni officials appeared very concerned. When the president of the group tried to escort Renee off the stage, the little woman gave him a powerful elbow right in the middle of his fat stomach. The blow doubled him over as he gasped for air. While three or four other members of the civilian group tried to assist their leader, Kandi staggered up the steps to join her soul mate, Renee.

Renee managed to undo most of the snaps on her J.C. Penny original top when Kandi lurched to her side. "God, I'm hot!" Renee breathed into the microphone.

"Let's do a little number to loosen this crowd up, what do you say folks?" Renee rasped. I held my breath and prayed both women would be beamed aboard the starship "Enterprise".

Enthralled by the scene, the crowd turned their full attention to the potential duet on the stage. There was a little wave of nervous laughter rippling across the room. Renee and Kandi whispered to themselves for a moment and then broke into a horrible rendition of the Supremes' "Baby Love". I could almost hear the neighborhood dogs howling outside.

Another woman on the Alumni Association's "Board of Directors" tried to gently urge Kandi and Renee to relinquish their budding new singing careers. Kandi stunned the heavyset woman with a stiff arm to the face which should be enshrined in the "Pro Football Hall of Fame". The lady stumbled backwards until she fell on top of the guy that Renee had elbowed. He was still bent over in excruciating pain about ten feet behind the imitation Supremes. The jostle of the collision with his less than mortally wounded board member was the final impetus the president's stomach needed to eject everything that he had eaten in the last twenty four hours.

About a gallon of what looked like green pea soup and cottage cheese poured out of his mouth and nose. The mess splashed onto the polished oak boards and ran in rivulets all over the stage. All hell broke loose then. People ran for the exits in pandemonium. In spite of the distractions, Kandi and Renee tried gamely to keep the tempo of "Baby Love" going. What troopers. The show must go on, I thought.

"Let's get outta here," I commanded over the rising uproar and grabbed Jana's hand.

"I can't go. I have to find Marty. I came with him," Jana yelled back as she glanced around the room trying to locate her ex-hubby in all of the confusion.

"Forget him, we've got to get the hell out of here while the getting's good," I practically screamed over the pandemonium exploding all around us. Jana's answer was lost in the noise and I dragged her outside through the emergency fire exit door.

We were in my car pulling out of the parking lot before either of us realized what we had done. Jana brought us back to earth by asking, "What about your speech?"

We both laughed. "I don't think that there will be a speech tonight," I chuckled. "In fact, I think the whole meeting was about over when we made our getaway. As I remember it, the Alumni Association president made a very forceful motion for adjournment."

Our laughter turned to howling. "Yeah," Jana gasped between convulsions of guffaws, "His motion was so forceful, I think I have some of his "Robert's Rules of Order" on my sweater."

I glanced over at her chest and stopped myself from brushing an imaginary green pea from the front of her heavily laden bosom. My use of control sobered me a little and my laughter dwindled slowly to a giggle.

"Is there any particular reason, mighty police chief, why we ran out of there like a couple of scared rabbits?" Jana finally asked.

"I think you could safely say that my career cannot afford a personal association with a riot at the Police Academy right now," I answered. "The officers there will probably handle it without resorting to calling out the National Guard. If we're lucky, there were no media representatives present. They usually don't attend these get togethers, since our functions are supposed to be a good news kind of thing without a bloody beheading or an Elvis sighting which would help their station's ratings. Just in case some newsy took a wrong turn and was there tonight, I don't want to take the chance on being involved."

"Well, if the reporters weren't there, they won't know what they missed tonight," Jana correctly stated. "What do you have planned for next month's meeting to top this one?"

"I was considering something along the lines of a human sacrifice next month. What do you think?" I asked with a straight face.

"Can I pick the victim?" Jana played along with the game.

"Sorry, we've already got a list of viable candidates. In fact, we might need to have a whole series of sacrifices." Mentally, I could see the scrolling names of potential victims on the inside of the car's frosted windshield.

"Don't you have to sacrifice virgins?" Jana asked with a straight face. "There are rules to sacrifices, you know."

"Uh, hmm, I hadn't thought of that. I think you're right. Do you know any virgins that will allow us to carve their hearts out?" I asked.

"None come readily to mind. By the way, where are you taking me?"

Jana looked up and tried to find a familiar landmark on the darkened highway.

That was a good question. I had no conscious knowledge of where I was going. Subconsciously, I was driving towards my home. It could be a little awkward to show up at home with Jana and her hooters. "Peggy, I rescued this girl from a riot at one of my speeches and she followed me home. Is it okay if she stays with us? Can I keep her, huh, huh?" I imagined myself asking.

"Well, since I can't take you home with me and hide you in the spare bedroom until Christmas, how about I take you to your home?" I offered.

"That's fine with me, but it's a long way to my house," Jana replied.

"Where do you live? Oklahoma?" I asked.

"Almost," Jana said. "I live in Clearwater."

"Clearwater? Geez, that's thirty miles from here," I whined.

"You're the one who guessed Oklahoma. Besides, you kidnapped me from the meeting just when things were getting interesting. Do you want to go back there and bash heads or take me home?" Jana inquired. "For a ride home, I might just forget that kidnapping is a federal crime."

"Yes ma'am, whatever you're heart desires. Do you have a special route in mind or will just the downtown business district of the thriving metropolis of Clearwater do?" I bowed to the better logic of Jana's request.

The population of Clearwater was probably less than a thousand mostly dirt poor citizens. It was a very sleepy little town located west and south of Wichita, but still inside the county's borders. Staying within Sedgwick County was an important consideration. I did not want to violate Mel's rigid rules on how far I could take my city owned car. Despite a streak of non-conformity, I followed the rules whenever possible.

"I can give you directions when we get closer," Jana interrupted my silent thoughts.

We sped south down the loop of highways encircling Wichita and I turned west onto Kellogg Avenue. Kellogg was the main roadway that cut the city into the north and south halves. It was also known as Highway 54 and met the other primary dividing roadway, Broadway, just south of downtown to form a sort of "X marks the spot" center point for the city.

We passed the airport entrance and were soon nearing the city limits. The streets were still slick from the rain and I reached under the dash to turn the volume of the police radio down so we could hear the oldies radio station from the rear speakers. It was a trick that police officers learned early in their careers. You listened to the police frequencies in front and music in back. I could never explain how the mind filtered the sounds, but I knew that if my call number came over the police radio, I would recognize the call as mine even in the middle of a Chuck Berry twin spin.

Instead of Chuck on the oldies station, we were subjected to a watered down version of the national news first. The federal government had temporarily shut down because of another argument between Congress and the President over a balanced budget.

"That's just great," Jana said. "Our government is putting up a closed sign and going out of business. That makes me feel so confident."

"Don't sweat it, Jana," I used her first name somewhat clumsily. "It's just a political game. Besides, the temporary furlough of government employees will give the postal workers time to clean their guns before they go back to work and start shooting fellow employees."

We passed Restland Cemetery on the right and I glanced quickly at the spot where I knew the Police Officer Memorial Monument was erected. The memorial's hidden location always irritated me. The statue and engraved plaque honoring Wichita police officers who had given their lives was located in an obscure cemetery located on the very outskirts of the city.

Prior to the erection of the monument, the police department had led a campaign to purchase a suitable memorial using citizen donations. That was the easy part. When we raised the money, I argued with the city manager about where the memorial should be situated. It was my contention that the monument should be placed in a prominent location where people would be reminded every day of the police officer's sacrifices. Mel did not see the sense in using up valuable city property for a "silly stone marker", as he called the memorial. I suggested using a portion of the lawn in front of City Hall, along Main Street. Mel said the monument would detract from the beauty of the building. Bull shit, I replied. It was hopeless. How do you argue with a heartless moron who has no sense of duty or honor? Luckily, the cemetery owner offered us a home for our monument or else I guess it would have been stored in my front yard. Even the cemetery's owner agreed the memorial should be displayed someplace more fitting.

Jana pulled me back from the bad memory before my stomach acid level increased, as it usually did when I began thinking of the Manager. "Turn that up," she commanded. "I love that song."

I adjusted the volume until Nat King Cole and his daughter softly crooned their "Unforgettable" duet through our rear speakers. The song was courtesy of modern electronic science, since the father had died of cancer long before his little girl grew up to be a great singer in her own right. The sounds of a dead man and a living, breathing beautiful woman singing together sent chills up my spine. The song always does that to me.

"If you turn left up here, we can cut off some mileage," Jana instructed.

"Okay," was all I replied as I turned the heavy Chevy onto a less than solid looking dirt and sand road. "Are you sure this road will be okay with all of the rain we've had?", I asked.

"No problem, I come down it all of the time in all kinds of weather. Of course, I have a four wheel drive Jeep Cherokee," Jana answered.

"Great." I swerved the car in the mud to avoid some big furry animal in the road. I was not quite sure if the obstacle in the road had been a werewolf or a collie. In either case, I missed it and managed to get back onto the crown of the roadway.

"Do you drive the back roads very often, Chief?"

Jana asked with a note of humor in her voice.

"Not if I can avoid them," I answered honestly. "I don't know very many people who live out in country."

"It's peaceful out here and I'm happy," Jana smiled in the darkness.

We made a few more twists and turns at Jana's directions and I began to wonder if I could find my way back to civilization. When grass began to grow down the middle of the road, I really became concerned.

"It's not much farther. Just down the road a ways," Jana pointed over the top of the Chevy's hood ornament.

"Boy, I'm glad. I thought you were taking me out here so I would run out of gas in an abandoned spot and you could have your way with me. For your information, I filled up with gas today. I'm too smart for you," I boasted.

Two or three more dark figures darted out of the bushes beside the road and ran after the car. I comforted myself in the knowledge that there had never been a confirmed sighting of "Big Foot" in Kansas and drove on. I thought of a story one of our assistant chiefs in Dallas had told me about my ambition to be the police chief in a major city.

"You remember when you were a kid growing up out in the country?" the assistant chief had asked me.

"Sure, Chief," I answered. Actually, I had only spent summers with my grandparents in the country. The rest of the time my home was a four room frame house in a low income neighborhood on the south side of Fort Worth.

"I bet you had an old dog that laid up on the porch each day, not doing much but sleeping. right?" the chief asked again.

"Yes sir, we had an old dog named "Mutt","" I answered truthfully, wondering where this story was going.

"I bet every day the mail car went by down the dirt road you lived on and that old dog ran out to chase the postman's car, didn't he?" the chief asked.

"Right again, Chief," I played along.

"Everyday that damned dog laid on the porch and dreamed all day of catching that mail car; just like you have a dream you think about all the time of being a police chief. Now, I want you to think about what happened to that dog when he finally caught up with the car he dreamed about so much," he commanded. "What happened to your dog named "Mutt"?"

"He was run over and killed," I remembered factually.

The chief's eyes softened a little as he gave me the fatherly advice in the punch line of his story. "That's right Rod, he got run over. And if you don't watch out, your dream of being a police chief will run you over too. Be careful of what you wish for, it might come true and you might not like the results."

I thought about the assistant chief a lot. Next to my father, he was probably the wisest man I ever met. He was right on target with the dog story. I had caught the mailman's car by landing the police chief's position and now it was a constant battle of dodging and fighting to keep my dream from running over me.

"I can't figure out how you have lived this long without learning to drive on dirt roads," Jana stated. "Are all the roads in Texas paved?"

"Oh, shoot, little lady," I shifted into my John Wayne accent. "We got all the modern conveniences down home, wah hah. Why soon, they're gonna have water that comes right inside the house and paper on a roll, so's you don't have to wipe your butt with a page from the Sears Roebuck catalog, wah hah."

"Wow. How about keeping your eyes on the road? Maybe it will help your driving." Jana countered. "Try focusing both eyes forward this time."

I noticed that I had turned and was staring at her again. I tried to continue the John Wayne voice, but it was starting to sound more like Humphrey Bogart with a cold. "I especially like the parts in the Sears Catalog with ladies undies, wah hah."

"I bet. Try to keep your fantasies in check for a few more miles, okay?" Jana pleaded.

"Okay," I gave up on John and Humphrey. "You don't have anything against a guy that gets aroused by a catalog, do you?"

"Not as long as you don't get aroused over the farm implement section. I think there are one or two tractors parked along this road," Jana answered.

"How about you, Jana. What got you excited in your bygone youth?" I queried.

"Well, let's see. I thought I was fat and ugly in high school and gave myself to the second string tight end in my junior year to see if I could really be loved by anyone," she replied.

"Was it?" I asked slyly.

"Was it, what?" Jana sounded confused by my question.

"Was his end tight?" I asked and immediately regretted my weak attempt at humor.

She sighed at my juvenile interruption to her story. "I don't remember. Anyway, I wore black horned rimmed glasses and scored so high on the SAT tests I won a scholarship to Emporia State College. Do you know where that is?"

"Let's see, I'll take a stab at guessing Emporia, Kansas. Am I right?" I asked.

"Very good, Sherlock," Jana awarded me points for knowing my basic Kansas geography.

"Sure, I know Emporia State. The home of the "Fighting Honeybees" or some other odd mascot like that. My friend Tim says all of the best looking women in Kansas go to that school," I remembered.

"That's not completely true. After all, I went there. But he was probably right about the other girls," Jana tried to sound humble.

"Well, I wouldn't know for sure. I've never been to Emporia, actually. I went to college at the University of Texas, you know. Austin was full of good looking girls. I just never got to know any of them. In a biblical sense, that is", I hedged.

Jana did not pay my ramblings any notice and continued with her own biography. "When I graduated, I got a job teaching junior high school English in Derby, Kansas. The college placement office thought it would be perfect for me. I guess they thought I exemplified what a Kansas school teacher should look like."

"You certainly don't look like any teacher I had in junior high," I interjected, while letting my eyes wander down to stare at her enormous chest again.

"Well, I was a real late bloomer, so to speak. When I arrived in Derby, I met Marty on a blind date. I thought he was cute and he was a big policeman from Wichita and all. I chased him and begged him to marry me and...," Jana stopped in mid sentence. "Why am I telling you all of my life story?"

"I don't know. Maybe it's because I'm such a great listener. I am having a hard time picturing you chasing after Marty. There must have been hundreds of guys who were trying to give you manual chest x-rays," I declared.

"No," Jana glanced down at her chest. "These didn't really turn into works of art until after my baby was born."

The news that she had a child surprised me. I do not know why the thought had never occurred to me, but I never considered the fact that she might be a mother.

"I didn't know you had children, Jana. That's great. How many kids do you have?"

"Not so great. I don't have any children. Not anymore, that is. My daughter was killed by a drunk driver when she was two years old," Jana's voice lowered to a whisper.

"Oh, damn, I'm sorry. Believe me I really am sorry, I didn't mean to bring up bad memories." Now, I really felt like a fool for playing games with this woman's past. What right did I have to delve into her previous life? In fact, what in the hell was I doing with this woman in my car, a long way from home, and without a clear picture of where this adventure was going to end, I wondered to myself?

"It's okay," Jana let me off the hook. "The accident was a long time ago. I quit teaching school because I couldn't stand to see other people's children being happy all day and joined the Sheriff's Department. I guess it was my attempt to do something about the type of person that had killed my little girl. Who knows. I'm not sure I understand all of the psychological ramifications caused by the death of a child. In fact, I don't think I want to understand."

We drove on in silence for a few minutes. I could not think of anything witty or even semi lucid to say. Finally, Jana broke the somber mood and announced, "Well, it could be worse. We could be lost."

"You mean we're not? I hope you've been dropping bread crumbs. If there was a damned tree in this county, I would climb it to see if I could get a bead on the Epic Center's lights downtown. The state is so flat, we should still be able to see them from about fifty miles out," I guessed.

"You mean you don't like Sedgwick County?"

Jana pretended to be hurt at my jab at her home district.

"How can you like a county named for one of the most monumental screw-ups in Civil War history?" I asked.

"I don't guess I've heard that story. Since the war's over, you can let me in on the secret," Jana pleaded.

"It's no secret. General John Sedgwick was a Kansan who served in the Union Army. He was an egotistical asshole who received his officer's commission in the army through his political connections with the governor back home. Actually, his wife supposedly screwed half of the Kansas legislature to get her hubby's appointment to general approved."

As if on cue, the radio broke into Tammy Wynette's old country classic, "Stand By Your Man". We both stared at the radio and then looked at each other with wide eyes.

"Now, that's spooky," Jana said.

"Yeah, well, anyway," I said, while trying to shake off the image of General Sedgwick's ghost riding in the back seat with us. "At one of the war's major battles, the good general was riding astride his white horse along the front lines. His own troops, who obviously had more sense than John, were seeking cover in their muddy foxholes from the Confederate snipers who were firing at them from across no man's land."

"Keeping from getting shot sounds like a good idea to me," Jana commented.

"Yeah, that's the object of the game; in war and life. Anyway, the general's troops were pleading with the pompous idiot to get off his stupid white horse because it attracted a lot of enemy fire. Of course, being a politician and from Kansas, General Sedgwick refused to listen to anyone's advice. He turned to one of his lackeys and said, "Don't worry, Stephen, those Rebs couldn't hit an elephant at this dis…'"

"At this dis…? I don't get it," Jana quizzed.

"The pompous bastard never finished saying the word "distance"," I explained. "A fifty caliber minie ball from some cross eyed Alabama backwoods Confederate soldier caught him right in mid-word."

"Ouch, I bet it hurts to get hit in mid-word," Jana grimaced.

"I don't think it hurt him too much," I sighed. "The shot blew most of his silly head off and that was the end of a promising political career. Who knows, with sense like that, maybe he could have been mayor of Wichita. Or at a least a city manager. Instead, they just dug a muddy hole for his worthless hide right there on the battlefield and his troops all lined up to piss on his grave. He was apparently not very well liked."

"I can tell," Jana stated.

"The folks back home named this god forsaken county for their hero and that's how we come to find ourselves lost in the middle of Sedgwick County, Kansas, U.S. of A," I put the finish to my story.

"We're not lost. Turn left here," Jana pointed to a gravel drive way next to an orange plastic mail box. The mail box was marked with the initials "J.M.S."

"Who's J.M.S.?" I asked, my police curiosity never quite abated.

"That's me, silly. Jana Marie Sims," she answered. "Instead of "Jana Marie", my daddy called me "Jamboree" when I was little. He was a big fan of the "Grand Ol' Opry" radio show. I think he was very disappointed to discover I couldn't carry a tune in a bucket. He always wanted to hear me sing on the radio."

"I bet you sing better than you think," I said as the gravel crunched underneath the heavy car's steel belted radials. We drove up to the front of a white, two story frame farm house that looked as old as I felt. The porch light immediately snapped on and a young woman with long brown hair came out into the yellow light.

"Can I help you?" the woman called as I stopped the car next to Jana's Jeep and a red Saturn parked at the side of the house.

"It's okay, Beth. It's me," Jana called in return.

"I didn't recognize the car," Beth said as she sauntered down the front porch steps to meet us.

I immediately stuck out my hand to introduce myself, lest Beth begin to get the wrong impression. Whatever that might be.

"Hi, I'm Rod Starr," I offered in my best professional voice.

"Hello. I'm Beth Miller. Glad to meet you," she returned the greeting with an impish smile. "Rod Starr, as in Chief of Police Rod Starr?" she added.

"Yeah, I guess so, but tonight I'm just returning a lost child to her home for a glass of warm milk and a plate of cookies," I answered. It always embarrassed me when people recognized "what" I was, before they knew "who" I was.

"Well, I'm one of your big fans, Chief," Beth replied. "We're glad to have you. Come on in the house."

The porch was painted a shade of battleship gray which seemed to complement the gloss white of the home's exterior. A wooden porch swing hung by rusty chains to the left of the entrance to the old frame house. I thought I glimpsed an old style wooden barn at the rear of the house, but it was too dark and misty to be sure. Beth held the front door open while Jana and I both scraped the mud and grass off of our shoes before seeking refuge from the chilly night air.

I followed Jana into the cozy kitchen area and she set about rummaging through the cabinets. "Beth, why don't you take the chief into the living room and I'll see if I can find some coffee or something hot to drink. Chief, what do you want? We've got some coffee here somewhere, I know, or I can make some hot chocolate."

"Well, to be honest, Mrs. Sims," I answered, reverting back to the formal address in front of Beth until I knew exactly what role she played in this drama, "I'm not much of a coffee drinker. The hot chocolate sounds awfully good, though. I admit that I have a sweet tooth. It's my only vice."

"Your only vice? Chief, you must be a very dull guy," Beth chimed in. "Let's go into the living room and I'll see if we can warm you up."

The living room was not very large. I guessed that the house was at least a hundred years old, judging from the high ceilings and the hand carved woodwork around the door frames. In the center of one wall was a huge stone fireplace which seemed to dominate the rest of the room. Beth took out a poker from the old style brass rack mounted on the hearth and stirred at some coals that were already glowing below the iron grate. She tore a piece of newspaper from the stack of "Wichita Eagles" on the coffee table and used the crumpled paper to get a flame going. I noticed the editorial cartoon of me in my Superman suit was being used to start the fire.

"About time I did something useful," I commented.

"Huh? What's that, Chief ?" Beth asked.

"The fire. That's me you're using to start the fire with," I pointed to the enlarging flames as my cartoon face melted into black ash.

"Oh, yeah," Beth laughed. "I told you we'd heat you up."

"Are you and Jana family?" I asked, trying not to sound too nosy.

"No," Beth continued to laugh, "just roommates. When she and Marty split up, I moved in to help her with the house payments. I don't know why she didn't move into one of those modern apartments in Wichita. It would be a lot closer to work and more "in circulation", if you know what I mean. This "Green Acres" country living puts a damper on my love life, that's for sure."

"You mean you don't get too many callers out here, Beth?" I asked.

"No, every now and then we get a traveling salesman passing through. We generally lock him up in the barn or chain him to the bed until he's completely used up and then bury him out behind the septic tank," Beth dead panned.

"I think I saw that movie on the late show," I replied. "Kind of a reverse "Arsenic and Old Lace" with Cary Grant, huh?"

"Yeah, that's it." The fire was going good and Beth tossed a log from the wooden box in the corner of the room onto the blaze. "That should do nicely, don't you think?"

"It feels great to me, Beth. I hate this cold weather. Another damned winter in Kansas is about all that we have to look forward to anytime soon," I observed caustically. I sat down in a blue velour covered easy chair and scooted it a little closer to the fire. The polished hardwood floor hypnotically reflected the dancing flames.

"How do you like being the police chief?" Beth, still standing, turned her butt to the fire and rubbed the back of her jeans with her hands. Her long brown hair made her look about ten years younger than Jana. I guessed that Beth was around thirty-five. She was attractive, but she would definitely be a loser in the "Rod Starr Fantasy Large Breast Contest". Beth's nipples were about the only rise I could see from under her cotton pullover turtleneck.

"It's a crummy job. That's not for publication, but it's the truth. The best thing you can say for being chief is that it beats picking up cans along the road for a living," I allowed myself a little self depreciating sarcasm.

"I work at the Sheriff's Department, too, you know," Beth surprised me. I did not picture her in law enforcement, any more than I pictured Jana as a sheriff's deputy. "Yeah, but I'm not a real officer like Jana. I'm a civilian. I work in Records. It's not very exciting."

Beth sounded as though she was apologizing for her job in the Records Section. Standing in front of the fire, I could see she was tall and almost fragile in appearance compared to Jana. A five by seven inch color picture of Beth and her roommate standing in front of the Sedgwick County Sheriff's Department logo at the County Court House was prominently displayed in a silver frame on the fireplace mantle.

"Hey, there's nothing wrong with the Records Section. I spent a lot of my time in Dallas assigned to that job," I said, speaking only the partial truth. I had been assigned there twice. Once, as the late night lieutenant for over two years and then again as the Division Commander during my punishment phase in retaliation for seeking the chief's job. The Records Section did not hold too many fond memories in my dusty attic.

Beth turned to face the fire and show off what little ass she had. Her faded jeans were tight, but there just was not a lot of meat on the frame.

"How do you like the sheriff?" I asked. It was a stupid question, but I had run out of things to say and did not want to lie any more about my love for the Records Section.

"You mean "Captain Cukoo?" Beth laughed. "If his brains were gasoline, he wouldn't have enough to power a piss ant's motorcycle two laps around a BB."

I laughed too. Beth's description accurately summed up my own assessment. "I didn't realize that your sheriff was so well known in his own department," I observed.

"He's just a politician who's learned how to survive," Beth sighed.

"Well, I'm sure my own troops say the same kind of things about me," I said.

Beth turned back to face me. "No, Chief. Would you like to know what they say about you?"

I was not so sure I really wanted to know, but I could not resist the opportunity to hear Beth tell me what she had heard. "Sure," I said as I braced myself for the inevitable criticism.

"One of your officers came in last week to get some copies of a mug shot we had on file. We got to talking and he said it best. The guys think that you have balls," Beth confided in her best conspiratorial voice.

I was a little embarrassed by this woman I hardly knew talking about my sexual parts, even in an analogy. Self-consciously, I stared at my lap where I hoped my balls were currently safely stored.

"The officer said you had one ball about the size of a basketball and another one that was really big," Beth laughed.

"You know what else he said, Chief?" I did not answer for fear of hearing more about my phantom anatomy. "He said you were going to get your balls cut off by the City Manager sooner or later because no one could keep standing up to that maniac without running into a buzz saw. That's what he said. So, I think we both work for the same kind of person. Only, I don't have any balls to cut off."

I pondered the information solemnly. The officer's observation about my demise was probably a pretty accurate prediction.

"Don't worry about not having any balls, Beth. For your information, I think they're grossly over rated. They also get in the way when you trying to ride a bicycle."

"Chief, are you bragging about your balls again? I swear, Beth, it's all he's talked about all night," Jana chimed right into the conversation as she came into the room carrying a big metal tray with three ceramic mugs of hot chocolate.

"Pardon me, Madame, but it was your roommate who brought up the subject of my private parts. Personally, I think God had the right idea with women. He put the important parts inside so they would not get caught in heavy machinery," I answered.

"Well, gang, some of us have to work tomorrow. I think I will snuggle up to a warm book and enjoy this chocolate in bed by myself. Good night all," Beth announced.

Both Jana and I returned Beth's "good night" with ones of our own and I stood up for some unknown reason as the younger woman left the room.

"She's a good friend," Jana said as we both watched Beth's exit up the stairs.

"I can tell," I agreed. "She seems like a very nice person."

Jana crossed the room to the stereo and flipped through some compact disks. "Anything in particular that turns you on?" she asked.

"Whatever. Any girl that likes Nat King Cole has got great musical taste. Surprise me," I challenged.

She did. Jana found a CD of Chad and Jeremy's classic album from the sixties, "On Distant Shores". Soon the sweet, gentle harmonies of these two soft spoken singers from my youth filled the room. I closed my eyes and a pair of expensive Bose speakers transported me back in time.

This is crazy, I thought. What am I doing here? I'm a married man in the middle of no where with another man's wife. Hell, I still was not sure whether or not Jana was still married to Marty. In either case, I knew damned well that I was still married. And happily married. I opened my eyes to see Jana staring at me. I could tell by the look crossing her face that the situation was becoming more complicated in a terrific hurry. She was extremely attractive in the fireplace light. Heck, the truth was that Jana would have been attractive in the glare of a search light.

I was near panic trying to decide in my own mind exactly how I was going to get out of the predicament that I had made for myself when Beth came back down the stairs. The room mate was dressed in a long cotton night shirt and carrying a hardback copy of a Joseph Wambaugh police novel.

"I just saw a car start to pull into the driveway, but it backed out and left. Are you guys expecting any company?" Beth asked.

"I don't think so. Probably just another lost soul traveling the back roads who decided to make a U-turn and go back where he came from," Jana replied.

"That's a neat trick, if you can do it. Go back where you came from, I mean," I babbled.

"Okay guys. Good night again," Beth called as she turned on a heel to re-climb the stairway and find out if Bumper Morgan, or whoever was Wambaugh's latest fictional cop hero, could survive the dangerous world of being a big city detective.

Jana and I allowed our eyes to meet again and the panic returned. She bit her lower lip and removed a small portion of her pink lip stick. It was the perfect color to go with her blonde hair.

"What about Marty?" I asked.

"What about him?" the muscles in Jana's soft face tightened just a little.

"You know what I mean. Are you guys married or what?" I was grappling for some issue to bring myself back to reality.

"We're legally divorced," Jana confessed. "There wasn't much of a marriage after our little girl died."

"Well, why do you continue to hang out with him?"

I pressed on with the only semblance of a conversation that seemed in the least bit innocuous.

"I don't really know," she answered. "I guess its because he's safe, you know."

"No, I don't know. Marty seems about ten bricks shy of a full load, carrying that damned gun around and all. He doesn't appear very safe to me," I observed.

Jana walked over the stereo and adjusted the volume just a tad lower. I took the opportunity to regroup my thoughts. I rose from my chair and tossed another log on the fire. Jana floated back towards the big sofa which matched the fabric of my chair and patted the seat cushion as a signal for me to join her.

"Tell me about your wife," Jana said when I sat down. The question floored me temporarily but I soon recovered and leaped at the opportunity.

"I have a great wife. We've been together for about twenty-five years. Same old story. High school romance that continued through college. We fell in love and have stayed there forever. The truth is that she's the only girl I've ever really been with, if you don't count a couple of awkward high school experiences in the back seat of my old Nash Rambler at the drive-in. I wouldn't know how to act with another woman."

Jana picked up my hand from the sofa cushion and held it. Her touch was electric. The body contact caused me to feel an instant physical reaction. It was all too real for comfort. One side of me wanted to run out of the door and another side wanted to bury my face in the perfumed aroma of Jana's tempting breasts.

Weighing my choices, the guy with gonads as big as basketballs, according to his troops, turned into a cowardly eunuch.

"I'm sorry, Jana. I've got to go. I'd like to stay a while longer, but I just can't," I stammered.

Before I knew it, I was out the door and crunching my way through the gravel towards my cold car in the drive way. I did not look back as I cranked up the engine and made my getaway like a thief in the night. The only thing that was stolen was a small piece of my armor plated reputation as a straight arrow.

Somehow, I made my way back to Highway 54 and re-discovered the route home. The entire trip home was a daze. Long before midnight, I was back in my own bed with Peggy. She did not even notice when I crawled under the covers. I hoped she did not notice my shivers, either.

THURSDAY

CHAPTER FOUR

Dawn was no where near breaking through the dark Kansas night when I arose and quietly got dressed for work. I might as well get up, I reasoned, since there was absolutely no likelihood that sleep would invade my soul. The few times I allowed my mind to slip towards unconsciousness, I quickly awoke amid dreams of the final scene at Jana's house. No matter how hard I tried, I just could not picture myself doing anything differently than what I had done. That disturbed me greatly. One thing was for sure though, Jana Sims had given me a tremendously exciting and terrifying moment to remember. The thrill was strangely addictive and I was drawn to experience the sensation again. The feeling was like inching up to the edge of the Grand Canyon and spitting over the side. Only in my case, I had only slobbered on my shoes.

Peggy stirred once and mumbled something that sounded like, "What's going on at four o'clock?"

I was honest when I said, "Go back to sleep, baby, I've got some work to catch up on at the office and I can't sleep."

Thirty minutes after leaving my warm bed, I was dressed in my uniform and maneuvering the Chevy out of the garage into the frigid Wichita morning. The heater soon began to blow warm air. Like me, the engine probably did not have enough time to cool down since being taken for a spin to Jana's house last night.

I flipped on the university radio station to catch the news from National Public Radio. The Boeing Aircraft workers were on strike again. It was a game they played every year or two. Another congressman had been caught getting oral sex from a teenage campaign worker. The Congressman claimed he did not know that the girl was only sixteen when the nut gurgle occurred. Besides, it was the night before the election and he was under a lot of stress, for gosh sakes. Locally, the Wichita City Council was set to debate the merits of recycling versus building another land fill. The Mayor was threatening to strongly oppose the latest suggested location for the new trash dump. His voiced opposition meant the Mayor's potential kickback from the land sale by the current owners was not yet high enough. Blustering was the Mayor's best political tactic and the surest method to increase his percentage of the action.

I usually did not wait for the sports scores, but my mind was too numb to hit the off button. The Dallas Cowboys defeated the Detroit Lions at Texas Stadium on the previous Sunday. The newscaster reported the Dallas newspaper story of the game began with the definitive put down, "Would the lady who dropped her eleven kids off at Texas Stadium, please return and pick then up now? We can't keep them any longer. They played in the second half and only scored thirty-five points against the Lions."

While I was trying to figure out how Detroit could be so inept against the Cowboys, a car blew by me so fast in the adjacent lane that all I saw was a red blur. Instinctively, I floored the accelerator to catch the speeding vehicle. By the time I caught up with the traffic violator, we had passed Ridge Road and were flying down West Kellogg at speeds approaching mach three. I checked my seat belt and shoulder harness out of habit and laid the radio microphone in my lap.

The driver in the little red Ford Mustang paid no attention to my unmarked police car rapidly closing the distance from behind. It was easy to slide into the vacant lane behind the vehicle's right rear side because there was no other traffic on the road at the early hour to interfere with the pace. In this position, I was in the violator's blind spot. The driver of the other car could not see me in his rear view mirror. I was all but invisible in the right side door mirror, as well. If he could have seen my reflection there, the printed notation on the mirror would have cautioned the driver that I was closer than I appeared.

I was about to be a lot closer.

Police officers are trained to maintain a constant distance behind a speeding vehicle and then get a reading from their patrol car's calibrated speedometer. This technique provides a highly accurate "clock" of the violator's speed and usually holds up in court if the officer can testify that the distance did not vary between the officer's car and the speeder's car during the "clock". In the days before police traffic radar became so widely used, the speedometer "clock" was the primary method of speed enforcement. The skill was honed to an ultra fine art by most officers who wanted to keep their sergeant happy by providing him with a few speeding tickets to report on his activity sheet each day. The standard rule in Dallas was that "a ticket a day keeps the sergeant away." I learned the skill of "clocking", but I rarely wrote a ticket without special circumstances.

In fact, my personal rule of traffic enforcement during my entire career had been one that reserved citations for assholes and people who I arrested for some other charge. The theory was based on a relatively simple principle of mathematics. I quickly found there were sufficient assholes in the world for me to encounter on random traffic stops to fill any quota that my sergeant might set. If a violator was polite, answering "yes sir" and "no sir" in reply to my questions and had made an honest mistake with whatever the violation might be; I never issued a citation. Fortunately for the city's revenue stream, there were numerous people who started out the encounter with, "What the hell did you stop me for?" or "Why didn't you get that other guy who was going just as fast as me?"

The corollary to the rule was that if I arrested the driver for another charge, such as warrants or driving under the influence, I filled up their pockets with citations for all of the traffic violations they committed. My reasoned justification for piling on the charges was that the person being arrested was already pissed off for going to jail. So, it was unlikely I was going to further reduce their opinion of police officers by giving them multiple examples of my autograph on their traffic tickets. Also, I knew most offenders were not likely to receive the full range of punishment they deserved for whatever charge that precipitated their arrest. Therefore, the extra tickets just kind of made up for the lack of true justice in the great scheme of things.

Safely tucked into the Mustang's blind spot, I glanced down at the green glowing digits of my own speedometer. The display confirmed what the Chevy's vibrating chassis already told me. We were going too damned fast. My speedometer read 97 as I eased off the accelerator and applied a slight left pressure on the steering wheel to put me directly behind the Mustang. I allowed myself to fall about five car lengths back just in case the fool driving the Mustang decided to slam on his brakes. Keeping my right hand firmly clinched to the wheel and my eyes glued to the Ford's tail lights, I fumbled with my left hand for the plastic rocker switch on the dash that would activate the red and blue flashing strobe lights concealed from casual observation behind the Chevy's grille.

Naturally, I had purchased the lights myself since there was no money in the budget for emergency equipment on unmarked vehicles. Don Grady's mechanics had done a great job of installing the grille lights at the city garage. The mechanics had even scrounged up a neat piece of electronic equipment which made the headlights flash on and off in a "wig wag" pattern whenever the rocker switch for the other emergency lights was activated. Don admitted that a salesman had sent him one of the headlight flashers, as a free sample, to encourage the city to buy them for the whole fleet of police cars. Don rightly decided the likelihood of Mel Michaels purchasing the extra emergency equipment was similar to his chance of being elected "Miss Teenage Prom Queen" or getting any recognition in the current century for his dedication and hard work in service to the city.

When I finally found the rocker switch, the light show began. I did not need the glowing red indicator light on the dashboard to tell me that all of the vehicle's emergency lights were working properly. The reflections from my red and blue grille lights, and the alternated flashes of high beam head lights, bounced off the guard rails, trees and buildings along the side of the highway in the pre-dawn darkness. The driver of the Mustang responded quickly to the dazzling behemoth behind him and the flare of his own brake lights added to the blaze. Slowing down dramatically, he carefully put on his right turn signal to indicate that he was pulling over. Judging from his complete disregard for the speed laws, I figured he rarely used the turn signal. In fact, it was probably an even money bet as to whether or not the turn signal bulb had received an electrical charge since the car left the factory test grounds.

I picked up the microphone from my lap and keyed the red plastic button. "Number One, I'll be stopping a car," I said calmly, as our speed fell to below the posted limit.

"Go ahead, Number One," the sleepy dispatcher responded. All over the city, I could hear eyeballs clicking open as officers wondered what in the hell the police chief was doing awake at this hour, much less stopping a traffic violator.

"Number One," I said, continuing to repeat my designated radio call sign according to procedure. "We are East bound on Kellogg approaching the Meridian Street exit, on Kansas license K-king, W-William, L-Lincoln, nine, three, eight. A red Ford Mustang, unknown occupants."

The policy called for the dispatcher to immediately send a back up unit on all traffic stops during the hours of darkness as a safety procedure. In my case, it was not necessary for the dispatcher to select a unit to respond. An electronic hash of radio emissions scratched over the speaker as numerous officers talked on top of each other to volunteer for the back up assignment.

"One Twenty Six, I'll back Number One," a transmission finally came across clearly.

"Ten four, One Twenty Six. He's East bound on Kellogg approaching Meridian. Number One, what's your location now?" the dispatcher asked.

The Mustang was braking quickly and pulled over to the right side of the highway at exactly the spot where the off ramp began its descent toward where Meridian Street crossed underneath the freeway.

"Number One, he's going to stop right here at the Meridian exit," I repeated into the microphone.

"Ten four. One Twenty Six is en route to back you," the dispatcher advised.

The Mustang rolled to a stop on the shoulder of the roadway and I positioned my vehicle about ten feet to the rear and about a half a car width to the left. The offset space to the left of the speeder's vehicle made my car stick out slightly in the traffic lane. It was, however; a tried and proven method to protect me should another vehicle sweep down the side of our cars and unknowingly smash me while I stood outside the Mustang's driver's side window.

I hung the microphone on the dash mounted clip and began my pre-stop check list. Most people think a police officer just gets out of their car and writes a ticket, but there is a lot to be done to stay alive in this business for any length of time. First, I put the parking brake on. In case someone did hit my car from the rear, the wreckage would not go quite so far. Second, I turned the wheels to the right for the same reason and flicked on the car's standard emergency flashers to add to the already intense display of colored lights. The next step was to locate my uniform cap, night stick and flashlight.

Only a fool took their ticket book with them on the first contact. The folder was something else to carry in a hand one might desperately need free of any encumbrances. One secret to living a long and injury free life as a police officer was to approach every traffic stop as if "Machine Gun Kelley" was the driver. Sometimes he was.

I saw the effects of the danger of "routine" traffic stops on numerous occasions in Dallas. One cold night in East Dallas, my friend Woody Akins and his partner stopped a car to inform the driver his tail lights were out. That was all, just tell the guy to put in a fuse at the next service station and go on. What Woody and his partner did not know was that the fuse was okay. It was the naked woman, bound and gagged in the trunk, who managed to use her toes to pull out the tail light wires of her kidnapper's car and cause the malfunction. The driver shot Woody eight times with a sawed off thirty caliber carbine. One copper jacketed military style bullet struck Woody squarely in the top of his head as he crumpled to the pavement. When the shots rang out, Woody's partner was sitting in the warm squad car, unprepared, because it was too cold that night for both officers to get out for just a tail light. The task was just a "routine" traffic stop.

My assignment that night was to guard the crime scene while the rest of the city searched for Woody's killer. It was extremely cold and the blood froze on the pavement before the crime lab investigators could get there. They photographed the reddish brown pools and chipped it up with metal scrappers. I never forgot the vision of the wind blowing ice crystals across those pools of frozen blood.

The most important piece of equipment for a nighttime traffic stop is an officer's flashlight. We had adopted a rechargeable plastic light which was designed to generate fifty thousand watts of candle power for illuminating the far side of the moon, if necessary. The lights were great when they worked. Unfortunately, the company was back east in one of those cold Yankee states and the manufacturer did not care if their products were ever repaired after they were originally sold. We returned several broken models to the factory for repair and they never re-appeared. It was like the reports and requests I sent to the city manager. Somehow, somewhere, all of my memos, the flashlights and Flight 19 were trapped in the Bermuda Triangle together. I once asked the manager's secretary, Maria, if she had any relatives working for the "Stronglite" Company. Maybe there was another "black hole" at the flashlight company that had migrated from the Caribbean and Wichita.

When I exited my car, I took my time walking toward the Mustang. The flashlight beam showed only the driver, who appeared to be watching me in his left outside mirror. I always checked the vehicle for bumper stickers to give me a clue on what I might expect. For example, if there was a sticker that read, "You'll pry my cold dead fingers off my Winchester when I die", I would probably use my car's public address system to ask the driver to step out of his car first with his hands where I could see them. That way, I could get in the first shot, if necessary, and more easily pry his cold dead fingers off of his Winchester before the ambulance got there.

In this case, the Mustang was very clean and new. The only sticker was a small blue decal in the rear window that gave access to the County Courthouse parking garage. I guessed the driver to be an attorney as I eased up on the car. I was wrong.

The back seat was clean and empty in the white glare of the Stronglite. My next check was of the driver's hands to see if they were as empty as his back seat. Noticing that he continued to stare at me in his outside mirror, I purposefully flashed the Stronglite beam directly into the mirror. The resulting splash of high intensity light into his pupils temporarily blinded him long enough for me to safely check out his hands and the front seat for any obvious weapons. There were no howitzers or other heavy artillery that I could see, but I did not relax when he rolled down his window.

The sickly sweet odor of burning sweat socks hit me full in the face and I tried not to give any recognition that I noticed the unmistakable smell of marijuana.

"Yes sir, officer," the young man said. I guessed the driver to be in his early twenties or maybe late teens.

"May I see your driver's license and insurance card, sir?" I opened with the standard line.

"Sure, Officer, but what did I do wrong?" the driver asked.

"We'll discuss it," I said firmly, "just as soon as I see your drivers license and insurance, sir."

It was always best to get the driver's identification before any argument started. It leveled the playing field somewhat.

"Okay," he said. The young driver handed me a Kansas drivers license and reached for the glove box. I stepped back about two steps and kept my flashlight in my left hand, shining the beam directly at the glove box latch. I slipped my right hand from the front of my gun belt, where I had rested it, to the butt of my pistol. I thumbed the holster's break top and leaned down slightly to get a clear view of the glove box through the car's side window. For only a moment I thought how ridiculous it was to think that this kid might try to kill me. Then I remembered Woody and the frozen blood pools. If the driver grabbed a gun from the closed compartment, I would see the weapon and have a precious few seconds to react. As further protection, I would not be standing in the same spot as I was the last time the driver had seen me. All combined, the survival tactics might give me just enough edge to throw a hail of nine millimeter rounds through his back window before I ran screaming into the night. When it came to the possibility of getting killed, I tried to be very, very careful and preferred not to be remembered as a dead hero.

Instead of revealing a weapon, the flashlight beam showed that the glove box was practically empty. The driver retrieved a white envelope and closed the plastic latch on the beige dash. I again advanced along the car's side and took the insurance card the driver dug out of the envelope.

"Thank you, Mister, er, Mac Ghoulie. Am I pronouncing that correctly, sir?" I asked.

One of the oldest tricks in the police profession is to mispronounce a person's name to see what kind of reaction is elicited. Most bad guys or people guilty of something did not complain if you butchered their names. An honest citizen usually did not like it when you called them by something other than what any dimwit could pronounce.

"That's close enough officer. What did I do wrong?", the person identified by his drivers license as Wilbert Leonard McCoole answered. I knew damned well his last name could not be pronounced as "Mac Ghoulie", but he did not seem perturbed. Add another point toward his potential guilt score, I thought. I wondered just how much grass he was holding.

"Sir, the reason I stopped you was that you were speeding," I answered. "Do you know how fast you were going?"

This question was another old police trick to obtain a statement which could later be used in court. After first being stopped, a driver might tell you he was doing a hundred, or better yet, he might blurt out that he did not have a clue as to how fast he was going. At trial, the driver would swear to the judge he was only doing fifty miles an hour. When that happened, his first statement on the street was admissible to impeach his perjured testimony.

"No, not really. I thought I was doing the speed limit, but I could be wrong," the young man said. He tried to produce a lopsided grin, but his lips did not want to cooperate. The inside of his upper lip stuck to his teeth, indicating a very dry mouth. His nervous throat was so parched I could have sold him a sip of water for a hundred dollars.

"Well sir, I clocked you at ninety-seven miles an hour in a fifty five mile per hour zone," I replied, revealing some of the cards in my deck.

"Gee, officer, I didn't think I was going that fast, but I'm not used to this car. It belongs to my dad," he said. That was when I recognized the name and put it together with the County Courthouse parking decal.

Jonathan McCoole was the County Treasurer. His name was on all of the tax statements one received in the mail informing homeowners that taxes had escalated again. Of even more notoriety, the elder McCoole was responsible for running the County Tag Office where people registered their automobiles and paid the obnoxious state personal property tax Kansas levied on all cars and trucks. The Tag Office was the single most hated governmental bureaucracy in the land. If the place ever caught on fire, the Fire Department would not be able to hose water on the building for all the people roasting marshmallows in celebration.

Like every other citizen of Kansas, I too had experienced the misery of the County Tag Office. When my mom died, my father gave me her car because he had poor vision and was too old to drive anymore. It was a high dollar automobile, for sure. An ancient Ford Pinto, with all of seventeen thousand original miles on the odometer. My mom drove it once a week to town for groceries. It was the classic "only driven by a little old lady to church on Sundays" car, except my mom drove the little four cylinder to the Piggly Wiggly church of the double coupons.

After my mom's death, my dad came to stay with Peggy and me for a few weeks until he became restless and wanted to return to his home in Texas. Before he left, he signed over the Pinto's title and my secretary notarized his signature on the unfamiliar document.

I took the paper work down to Jonathan McCoole's tag office and walked into another dimension in time and space. Rod Sterling was the only thing missing from the nightmare experience. After standing in line for almost an hour, the clerk informed me I needed a sales receipt for the car before I could obtain a Kansas license plate.

"Ma'am," I said, "I don't have a receipt. My father just gave me the car, he didn't sell it to me."

I was tempted to tell her I traded a bag of beans to my dad for the Pinto's title.

"I'm sorry, sir," she said. "I've never seen a situation like this before. You must have a receipt so we will know how much to charge you in sales tax for buying the car."

"Excuse me ma'am, but I'm not driving back to Texas to get a receipt from my dad for something I didn't buy. There must be another way," I implored.

"Oh, sure," she said. "Just take this form back to your dad and have him fill it out in triplicate, notarizing it here and here, stating the car was a gift. That way the gift tax will be much lower than the sales tax."

"No ma'am, I'm afraid that gives me the same problem. I'm trying to avoid a sixteen hour road trip home. My father doesn't live in Kansas, don't you see?" I pleaded.

She did not see. It was a typical case of blind Kansas justice. She informed me that if I wanted to appeal her decision, I could see her supervisor. Naturally, being the stubborn type, I promptly requested the appeal route.

I stood in line to see the harried supervisor for almost another hour. The woman had a phone in each ear and there was obviously no room for me in her mental gymnastics. Everyone in Wichita was complaining to her about something. I was beginning to understand how the office had received its infamous reputation. Controlling my rising frustration, I carefully explained my story to the supervisor and she obliged me with a solution.

"I've never seen a situation like this. You can just pay the sales tax on the standard book value of the car," she stated flatly, "and then pay the license fee and property tax."

"Great, that will be fine," I said. How much could the tax be on a Pinto that Ford ceased manufacturing decades ago, I asked myself.

"The total will be four hundred and twenty seven dollars," she answered my unspoken question.

"Holy cow, Ma'am. The whole darn car is not worth four hundred and twenty seven dollars," I protested.

It did no good to whine. This was the best deal I could make. Take it or leave it. I looked around to see if there were any disgruntled postal workers standing in line that might exact some measure of revenge on the odious system. Just my luck, there was never an armed mental case around when you needed one. I was beginning to write the check when the supervisor said, "Uh, oh, wait."

"What is it now?" I asked with a sense of dread.

"This Texas title does not conform to federal regulations for certified odometer readings. I'm sorry, but it's not acceptable," she stated officiously.

I was becoming a little angrier but maintaining remarkable control, I thought. "What the heck do you mean, it's not acceptable. It is an official document issued by the State of Texas and the odometer reading is right here on the back of the title, according to Texas State Law. It's been notarized and not only that, but your own vehicle inspection department has checked the damn speedometer and certified that it's correct." I shoved the required Kansas odometer certification form so far in her face that bright red lipstick was smudged on the yellow paper.

"I'm sorry, sir, but we do have to follow the law, now don't we?" the supervisor smiled sweetly. I wanted to pull her red lips up over her blue hair.

I demanded to see "her" supervisor and that action landed me on a hard wooden bench outside the Office Manager's office. I waited for a third hour to plead my case. I needed F. Lee Bailey to handle the appeal. Vaguely, I had an uneasy feeling that with a little luck, I might be able to parlay this license plate affair into the gas chamber.

"I'm sorry, sir, I've never seen a situation like this," the Office Manager said. "I'll tell you what. I'm going to waive the odometer title requirement if you will have your father prepare a notarized statement declaring that the reading is correct."

"Ma'am, you don't understand," I whined. "My father is in Texas. I need the license plate now. I'm not driving six hundred miles to get a signature on a piece of paper that signifies the first piece of paper was correct." Despite my best efforts, my voice was rising in volume and tone. The other people in line just nodded knowingly.

"Well, okay, sir," the woman finally admitted. "We'll waive it for now, but you will have to send us the form when you return home to visit your father so we can have all of our paper work correct."

"Fine. Great. Terrific. Whatever," I declared. She began to type the information into the computer and reached to hand me the ugly purple, white and yellow Kansas license plate. As soon as my hand touched the precious metal object, she jerked it away.

"Uh, oh," she said seriously, as if she had just found an unexplained rash on my scrotum.

"Let me guess," I ventured, "You've never seen a situation like this. Now what?"

"Well, your notary signed on the wrong line on the back of the Texas title," she stated. "See right here? It's supposed to be signed there." The woman pointed a bony finger at a spot about a millimeter below the line where Suzie had notarized my dad's aged scrawl.

"What difference does that make?" I fairly screamed.

"Well, the form has to be correct," the woman stated flatly.

"You will have to go back to Texas and get a new title issued and start all over by signing it on the correct line."

That was just about all I could stand. At this point, I seriously, but fleetingly, considered going nuts and shooting everyone in the room. I promptly decided I did not need the obligatory insane postal worker to do my killing for me, I would do it myself. The newspaper headline in the morning's addition would scream, "Crazed Chief Commits Carnage". If everyone in the county had to put up with this type of crap at the tag office, I seriously doubted there would be a jury of my peers that would convict me. In fact, there was a greater possibility they would award me the Nobel Prize for making the world a better place to live by reducing the surplus population of idiots.

My next appeal was directly to the head man himself, Jonathan McCoole. I waited in his outer office for almost another hour before he came out to see why some one with the same name as the Police Chief was wanting to see him.

I went through my song and dance for the umpteenth time in a cool, calm, professional manner. Only once did I call his staff a bunch of "ignorant slime sucking gutter sluts".

At least he did not say that he had never seen a situation like this. In less time than it took to repeat my sad tale of woe, Mr. McCoole handed me my license plate and wished me a good day. Needless to say, I was impressed with the County Treasurer.

Now, I had his doper son in the middle of the freeway at four o'clock in the morning, driving ninety miles an hour in his dad's new Mustang. It's a small world, especially in Wichita.

"Well, I'll tell you what Wilbert," I started. "By the way, what do your friends call you? They don't call you Wilbert do they?" I smiled. It was another old police trick to give people the impression you wanted to be their friend by addressing them in a familiar fashion.

"No, er, officer," Wilbert seemed confused by the smile. "I go by my middle name, er, Lenny. Most people at school call me Lenny. I go to Butler County Junior College."

It figures, I thought. The school was famous for producing some of the best marijuana growers and chicken ranchers in the Midwest and Lenny did not look like he knew much about chickens.

"Okay Lenny, you wait here and I'll be with you in a second," I smiled again.

I backed up along the side of the car until I reached its left rear. I then turned sideways to ease back toward my own car, while glancing at on coming traffic and keeping one eye on my new friend, Lenny. I could see my back-up unit roaring toward me from a distance. The officer had already activated his roof mounted red and blue flashing lights and they were highly visible on the nearly deserted roadway.

The blue lights were another minor victory in the great war against Mel Michael's micro-control style of management. When I first came to Kansas, the state law only allowed red lights for emergency vehicles and all of our squad cars were so equipped. For some arcane reason, blue lights were actually prohibited on police cars. I soon joined a small lobbying group of police chiefs in the state that wanted the flexibility to use both red and blue lights for greater officer safety in the urban environment. The individual officers were very much in favor of the change and we had several scientific studies attesting to the greater visibility of the combination red and blue display. A law was proposed and soon signed by the Governor. The politicians at the state level loved that kind of law. It made the police happy and did not cost them any state tax dollars.

When I suggested to Mel that we should include money in a future budget to add one blue plastic lens to each car's light bar, he pitched a fit. Mel demanded to know what was wrong with the color red and accused me of manipulating the law to get better equipment for the police department. Of course, he was absolutely correct in his accusation.

In response, I proposed we buy only the blue lens as replacement parts when the original equipment became damaged during normal operations. Using the attrition method, we would take about ten years to complete the change over, but at least we would finally get into the twentieth century about the time the twenty-first century started, I reasoned. No soap, Mel said. He liked red and that was that. Not by a long shot, I thought.

When the tornado came through Wichita and obliterated the city parking garage, the funnel cloud was also accompanied by an ungodly hail storm. With hail the size of horse apples, the barrage completely destroyed all of the windshields and light bars on the entire fleet of police cars. Mel was forced to buy replacement equipment although he hated the thought of spending the money. We contacted the manufacturer to insure our new light bars would be shipped directly from the factory with the red and blue light combination. In addition, I personally renovated any light bar that had somehow escaped the hail storm by using a five pound sledge hammer on the old red plastic lens side. When he discovered my scheme, Mel was livid. Fortunately, Don Grady's mechanics had all of the new light bars installed before Mel could change the order. Now, every time I saw a blue light flashing in Wichita, I remembered one small victory. Most of the officers never knew of Mel's paranoid intransigence or why their chief had taken a sledge hammer to some of the lights on their cars.

Don Grady knew and we shared the secret with a smile and the Atlanta Brave's "hatchet chop" hand sign, to emulate my proficiency with a sledge hammer, every time we passed each other in the hallway.

The back up officer pulled up behind my car as I reached for my driver's side door handle. I waved him to have a seat with me in my car. Officer Rocky Jones was soon sitting in my passenger side front seat while he beat his gloved hands together to warm his frozen fingers. I changed the police radio frequency to check young Lenny for any outstanding arrest warrants.

"Number One, traffic for Spider," I spoke into the microphone. This was our not so secret police code meaning that I wanted to speak with our computer desk in the Records Section. "Spider" was an acronym representing "Special Police Information Data Entry Retrieval." I could not claim credit for the catchy name. It was a moniker attached to the unit long before I came to Wichita. I gave the clerks permission to hang a life-size cardboard cut out of the comic strip hero, "Spiderman", over their radio console. The cartoon character was the civilian clerk's mascot and a symbol they were involved in the fight against crime as well, just like the fictional super hero dressed in red and blue tights.

"Go ahead, Number One," the Spider clerk answered. Spider was actually located in the Records Section and not in the Communications Center with the other radio dispatchers. This physical separation of radio consoles was done so the Spider clerks could do any additional research which might be required to personally verify warrants or information in our voluminous paper files.

"Number One, I need a wanted check and a driver's license search on a subject, last name McCoole, spelling m,c,c,o,o,l,e; first name, Wilbert, common spelling, white male, date of birth, eleven, twenty-two, eighty."

"Ten four, Number One. Stand by," the Spider clerk replied. I guessed she was probably turning to the other Spider clerk next to her and asking why she thought the chief was checking subjects and wanting drivers license records at four o'clock in the morning.

"Chief, what the hell are you doing out here stopping cars at four o'clock in the morning?" Officer Jones asked. He was curious, but obviously impressed I knew how to make a traffic stop.

"Heck, Rocky, you're out here, aren't you? Why can't I come out and have some fun, too?" I joked, nodding at his clumsy attempts to get the blood flowing back into his frosted digits.

"Some fun, Chief," Rocky laughed. "I thought you Texas guys didn't like this cold weather, much less traffic enforcement. It's so damned cold that the lawyers have their hands in their own pockets for a change."

I liked Rocky Jones a lot. He was an intelligent, hard working police officer who took a great deal of pride in his performance and the department. He was the only child of an Army second lieutenant who did not come back from Vietnam. Probably due to the lack of having a father around the house when he was growing up, Rocky knew absolutely nothing about sports and the other officers kidded him unmercifully about it. The guys around the police station were all the time asking Rocky how many touchdowns he thought the Royals might score in the last round. Rocky did not know who was the better boxer, Muhammad Ali or Ali McGraw, and he did not seem to care. Through it all, Rocky just grinned and went on about his job of being an excellent, caring police officer. Truly one of Wichita's finest.

"Well, Rock, I wasn't really planning on working traffic this morning, but this clown about blew me off the road," I said. "I clocked him at ninety-seven and the interior of the car smells like a virtual reality advertisement for "Guatemalan Giggling Grass"."

"Have you got him out of the car yet, Chief?" Rocky asked.

"No, I wanted to wait until you got here. He's very nervous about something. I'm not sure if it's the dope or something else," I confided. "Let's see what Spider tells us about him." I purposely did not tell the officer that I had deduced the nervous kid was the son of the County Treasurer. I still was not sure what relevance that small bit of information might play in the equation, if any.

It was oddly pleasant to have the chance to talk to a real police officer about real police work; and not administrative decisions or political bull shit. I admit that the comfortable sensation of being around the street officers was the reason why I tried to do a little actual law enforcement from time to time, unlike just about every other police chief I knew. Most chiefs despised the time they had spent on the street as patrol officers and vowed never to return to the drudgery, boredom and panic which comprised a street officer's daily life. I loved all aspects of their job and longed for the simpler, black and white world of street policing.

"Number One," the Spider clerk called me on the radio.

"One, go ahead," I answered.

"Number One, Wilbert Leonard McCoole is signal thirty, however, his drivers license is suspended by the state for excessive violations," the clerk replied. "Signal thirty" meant that young Mr. McCoole did not have any outstanding warrants issued for his arrest. However, driving on the suspended license was an arrestable charge if I chose to enforce it.

"Ten four, thank you Spider. Hold the license information print out for me, I may call you for a copy of it later," I instructed.

"Well, Chief, there's your probable cause for arrest and search of his car," Rocky pointed out. "You probably had enough P.C. to search his car with just the odor of marijuana, but now we can impound the car if we arrest him and do an inventory search."

"Very good, Rock, you should take the sergeant's test next year," I said. "And by the way, I will make sure there will be no sports questions or painting tests on the exam."

The first jab was at Rocky's well known lack of knowledge about anything having to do with athletics and the second swipe was intended as a departmental inside joke about my predecessor's promotional procedures. It seems Chief Pasqual was famous for "inviting" people he liked over to his house to help him rake leaves, clean gutters or put multiple new coats of baby blue paint on his house. The popular theory was that whoever spread the most paint got promoted. I changed the system to a written examination based on professional source text books and promoted right down the list, according to exam scores, without any favoritism or regard to who did a better job with chores around the house.

"Okay, let's get him out of the car and see what we've got here," I suggested.

Rocky and I both exited my car and walked slowly toward the Mustang. As the back up officer, Rocky took up his designated cover position at the right rear of the car and added his own Stronglite beam to further illuminate the interior of the car. Rocky began his guard assignment by lightly tapping the right side of the Mustang and quickly flashing his light directly into the driver's mirror. These actions served as an announcement to let the driver know that another officer was on the scene. Rocky was a pro.

After once again checking to make sure the driver's hands were visible and empty, I motioned for him to roll down the window.

"Lenny, can you step out of the car for me?" it was an order as much as a request.

"Sure, officer, what's wrong?" Lenny asked as he opened the car door.

"Let's step back here out of the road a minute, so we can talk," I answered. I pointed towards a spot where Rocky was standing on the curb side of the car. Only police officers who were really stupid or lazy stood in the street or between their cars while they talked to traffic violators. It was a great way to loose about twenty four inches in height due to traumatic amputation of your lower legs. More than one police officer had been transformed into an instant midget by having their legs crushed between their own front bumper and the rear bumper of the violator's car due to a collision by another vehicle approaching from behind. At four o'clock in the morning, the chances were even higher that a drunk driver would wander off the road and try to mate with the rear end of my Chevy. It was just one more hazard to worry about.

When we joined Officer Jones, Lenny began to shake noticeably. I was cold, too, but Lenny's shivers were caused by something else.

"Lenny, did you know your drivers license is suspended?" I asked.

"Oh, shit, damn, I knew the state was out to get me, but I, uh, I didn't think it would be so quick. Look, I'm sorry officer. If you write me the ticket, I promise I will pay it right away. Okay?" Lenny pleaded.

"Well, Lenny, it's not quite that easy." Some survival instinct caused me to pause and watch Lenny more closely. "Are you carrying a gun in your car?" I asked.

This abrupt change in the direction of the conversation was another basic tactic which Rocky and I had learned years ago. The techniques served to do two things. First, it forced the suspect to mentally change gears and allowed him the opportunity to say something incriminating like, "No sir, I don't have no gun, just a flame thrower." Secondly, if you followed up correctly with the next standard question, your search of the vehicle was unimpeachable later in court when the suspect had acquired enough legal assistance to draft the United Nations' charter.

The question really rattled Lenny. "Uh, what, uh, gun in car? Uh, who me? No, I, uh, there's no gun in the car, officer."

His lips said no, but his eyes said yes. Lenny began to sweat in temperatures where the wind chill registered a balmy five degrees above zero.

"Okay, I believe you Lenny," I lied. "You don't mind if I look in your car do you?" I played the next follow-up question perfectly.

"No, uh, I mean no, uh, I don't mind. Go ahead and look. There's no gun in there," Lenny announced nervously. Eureka, the magic "consent to search" was obtained so we would not run afoul of the Fourth, Fifth, Sixth and a half a dozen other constitutional amendments which protected Lenny's rights, even though he had never read the constitution in his young life. I doubted if Lenny could spell "constitution".

I nodded my directive toward Rocky, who started towards the car to search it. Actually, as Officer Jones had correctly surmised, we really did not need Lenny's consent since the odor of burning marijuana provided sufficient probable cause for a search. We could simply arrest Lenny for the suspended driver's license and search the car in accordance with what the courts called an "inventory search", as Rocky had also suggested. Remembering the assistance of Lenny's dad at the Tag Office, I wanted to keep all of my options open if we were not forced to arrest his boy for a criminal offense more serious than a suspended license.

Something flashed into Lenny's eyes that made the hair on the back of my neck stand up. I do not know exactly what triggers the response. You can not describe the feeling. It is just intuition. Even the U. S. Supreme Court had validated the uneasy suspicious feeling, calling it an officer's "Sixth Sense" in a famous court case that all new police officers were required to study in the academy.

"Wait, Rock," I called out. The officer stopped as he was about to open the Mustang's passenger side door.

"Turn around, Lenny, and put your hands on the side of the car," I commanded. Lenny hesitated and I took a hold of his right elbow to turn him. I could feel his muscles tense through the light jacket he was wearing. I added pressure to my hold on his arm and spun him into the side of car. Rocky rushed up to my side and slammed Lenny's right arm up on the trunk of the Mustang, pinning it there.

With practiced hands, I began a pat down of Lenny's clothing. As I ran down his right leg, my gold college class ring clanked audibly against a hard metallic object. I knew at once the bulge around Lenny's ankle was a handgun. In seconds, I jerked a semi-automatic Glock nine millimeter pistol out of Lenny's custom designed cowboy boot.

"What's this, huh, Lenny?" I asked.

"Fuck you, you son of a bitch, I ain't saying shit. You can't put nothing on me, you bastard. Do you know who my dad is, cocksucker? I'll have your badge, motherfucker," Lenny screamed while little flecks of spittle quickly froze on his chin.

"Gee, Chief, where have I heard that before?" Rocky grinned and took the pistol from me as I completed handcuffing our suddenly irate prisoner.

It was down right amazing how fast Lenny's attitude toward us had changed, I chuckled to myself.

I took Lenny back to Rocky's squad car and seat belted him into the front seat. While I guarded the livid prisoner, Rocky completed a search of the Mustang. Lenny had been truthful. There was no gun in the car, just in his boot. Unfortunately for Lenny, there were ten baggies of marijuana in the car's trunk and a set of scales. In addition, the Mustang's ashtray was full of half smoked joints. Young Mister McCoole was traveling up the road to success as a low level dealer and enjoying the ride along the way. Only in America could a kid from a successful family parlay a bright future and comfortable life into the horrible existence of a no class little drug dealer. What a country.

Lenny screamed bloody murder and began bouncing his head off the seat rest when Rocky read him his "Miranda Rights." "You planted that shit on me, you son of a bitch," Rocky yelled. "That's not my dope, you musta' put it in my car. You motherfuckers do that shit all of the time. I'll beat this rap!"

"I think this kid's been watching too many re-runs of the O.J. trial, Chief," Rocky grinned. "It never ceases to amaze me how the old "consent to search" trick works every time. If you ask about a gun, people will give you their consent to search their car and forget all about the headless torso in the back seat or the hundred million in counterfeit twenties under the seat. Damn, Chief, you haven't lost the touch."

"I don't know, Rocky, I almost forgot to pat him down before you got into the car. All those paper cuts sitting at a desk job have caused me to slip a little, I think." Just as I said that, Lenny began tossing his head at the confining shoulder harness and the handcuffs he reluctantly wore behind his back. He continued to scream about how we had manufactured a big conspiracy to frame him.

"Hey, kid, did I plant this on you, too?" Rocky asked as he leaned across the front seat and plucked a hand rolled marijuana cigarette from behind Lenny's left ear. I had not noticed the joint buried beneath Lenny's long curls. Lenny thrashing about in the front seat revealed his hidden stash to my eagle eyed partner. Rocky held the evil weed up in front of Lenny's face so our recently captured felon could get a good look at the latest nail in his coffin.

"Shit. I'm fucked," was all Lenny would say from then on. I had to agree with him.

It took us two hours to get a tow truck for the Mustang, write up all the arrest reports and drop the gun, marijuana and scales in the evidence locker. In the meantime, I used my cellular phone to call Lenny's dad and inform him of the arrest. It was the least I could do as a professional courtesy. The father's telephone number was unlisted, but Spider had the listing catalogued in their emergency contact computer. Mr. McCoole was very drowsy when I woke him up with the bad news about his son's arrest. I suggested that he might want to come down and bond Lenny out of jail before the media got wind of the story and met him at the front door with tv cameras blazing.

"Keep the little bastard," was Mr. McCoole's final comment after thanking me for making the call. Ah, a father's love is a beautiful thing at five in the morning. I could not say that I blamed him one bit. The elder McCoole did want to know how to get his new red Mustang out of the police impound lot. At least he had his priorities straight.

It was a little after six a.m. when I finally arrived at City Hall. The building was deserted, with only the "Badge On the Floor" officer in sight. The "BOF" was a regular police officer who was pulled from his patrol duties to baby sit a desk at the rear entrance to City Hall between the hours of 5:00 p.m. and 8:00 a.m. each day. The totally unproductive assignment was at Mel's insistence, of course. It was ridiculously boring duty for a highly trained police officer to basically answer an occasional telephone call and act as a security guard at a fixed post assignment. Try as I might, I could not get the City Manager to hire private security for the mundane job. Better yet, I recommended we lock the doors of City Hall at six o'clock each night and not open them again until seven in the morning. This was the protocol used by the County Courthouse located just across the street, but it obviously made too much sense for us to copy. Silly me.

Mel had once tried to use the BOF as delivery boys to take papers and other items out to the homes of individual City Council members, pick up visiting dignitaries at the airport or go out for burgers when the Manager or his staff worked late at the office. When I caught a whiff of those types of assignments by the City Manager, I promptly pitched a small fit. Such functions, I complained, were not in a police officer's job description and with the help of the police officer's union; we put a stop to the demeaning duties.

My resistance did not deter the City Manager from his idea of how to effectively use city employees. He promptly assigned the same menial tasks to fire fighters assigned to one of the fire stations near downtown. Instead of complaining to their own chief, the fire personnel called the Channel 12 news room and gave the entire city a televised view of the Wichita Fire Department using a huge red hook and ladder fire truck to deliver pizza to a city councilman's home. Of course, Mel somehow blamed me for causing the whole problem. The public stink over his stupid blunder was enormous and lasted only until the Council voted the City Manager a ten per cent pay raise for the great job he was doing. Go figure.

When I made my way up to my fourth floor office, I found the door to my outer office unlocked. I thought about going downstairs and bringing the BOF up with me as backup, but decided that maybe I was becoming too paranoid. I carefully opened the door and looked inside. Asleep, in the middle of the room was the Executive Assistant to the Chief of Police and last year's "Non-Sworn Police Employee of the Year", Tim David.

I let the office door slam shut behind me. The noise brought the snoring executive to a sitting position. He looked at me without any recognition showing in his eyes.

"Who is it?" Tim croaked sleepily.

"Santa Claus and I'm not very happy 'cause there's no chimney in this damned building," I answered.

"Eat shit, Santa," Tim mumbled. "I never did get the blow up doll I asked for last Christmas." Tim rolled onto his back atop the gray speckled carpet.

He stared at the ceiling and wiped drool from the corner of his mouth with the back of an unwashed hand.

"You're never gonna get any presents if you don't go home every now and then to check under the tree, big guy," I preached. "What are you doing here? Perhaps, the better question is, what are you doing passed out on my office floor?"

"Ugh, I've sure got a awful taste in my mouth," Tim moaned. "Have you got anything to drink?"

"If you mean like coffee, the answer is no. What do I look like, the Maxwell House delivery boy?" I asked. "I'll check the refrigerator and see what I can find."

I went into the little anteroom near the office which held a small sink, cabinets and an old, hand-me-down refrigerator that someone had donated to the police department when Eisenhower was in office. The secretaries and some of the other office staff used it to store their lunches and other perishable items. Occasionally, the ancient ice box held a liter bottle of Seven-Up or another type of soft drink someone had brought for their own enjoyment at work. Tim stumbled along behind me like a Roman slave on his way to a crucifixion.

"Ramona is sure gonna be angry if you drink her diet "Big Red"," I offered as I surveyed the refrigerator's sparse interior.

"Screw Ramona, this is an emergency," Tim replied.

"I think screwing Ramona is too severe a punishment for stealing a little of her soda, but it's your body," I observed dryly.

Ramona Hamilton was a grossly overweight woman that worked in the Employee's Credit Union office across the hall. She had a wart on her cheek which grew daily. Right now, the probable melanoma was about the size of Cleveland.

"What-da-ya-mean, my punishment? I'll just tell her that the Chief was thirsty. She likes you," Tim's scratchy voice sounded pathetic.

I poured a half a glass of Ramona's strawberry diet drink into a white Styrofoam cup. The foam cup was illegal around city hall since Mel declared the little drink holders a danger to the world's ecosystem because they could not be recycled in accordance with the city's official position on saving the environment. Actually, the city purchased a hundred thousand "paper" cups from the company where the Mayor's wife worked and they were stored all over the place. The Manager was very anxious to use the paper versions up or get them out of the building before someone asked too many questions. In the meantime, all other drinking utensils in Wichita's City Hall were deemed "politically incorrect".

"You know," Tim asked, "how is it that a woman who is two hundred pounds overweight and probably dying of the African face eating virus, drinks diet soda? I mean, what difference can it make? Surely, she doesn't like the taste of this stuff." He sipped the red liquid and made a face that indicated he had just swallowed a mouthful of sweat from the back of a hairy wrestler.

"I heard the guys up in the lab decided to do an experiment to see which stinks the worse, a wet goat or Ramona," Tim croaked. "They set up their instruments and got all prepared for the big test. When they brought in the goat, the laboratory technician fainted from the smell."

"Very funny," I dead panned. "Ha, Ha."

"No, that's not all," Tim continued. "Then the lab guys brought in Ramona and guess what. The goat fainted."

I wandered back to my inner office door and was pleased to note it was locked. When I gained entry, Tim followed me inside, uninvited. He plopped down in one of the worn out office chairs in front of my desk and sighed heavily.

"Last night was simply incredible," Tim admitted.

I wondered how he knew about my evening so quickly. Then I realized that he was talking about his own activities. Tim seldom bragged about his exploits, but when he did you knew it would be something right out of a triple X rated video.

"Incredibly unbelievable, Chief," Tim re-asserted his conviction that the previous evening had manufactured a memory which would revive his limp sex drive deep into his old age. He smiled a crooked grin and staggered to his feet stiffly. Tim disappeared out the office door and I could hear him rummaging through the battered fridge for another hit from Ramona's stash. When he returned, Tim had scored two cups of Ramona's crimson diet soda. I realized he did not want to feel guilty drinking the stolen soda alone and wanted to share the responsibility for the minor transgression.

"Tim, you need to make this up to Ramona," I mentioned. "I don't know about the goat thing, but I do know that when the city took her mug shot for her official ID card, the photograph weighed ten pounds. You've got your work cut out for you just finding the right wrinkle to put your hand in. Or another part of your body which would satisfy Ramona. How 'bout your leg?"

"Incredible, simply incredible," Tim kept repeating. He slumped down in the same chair he recently vacated. "I don't know how much longer I can keep this up. My body just won't take the abuse too much longer and there's a history of heart disease in my family, ya know."

"You're the only guy I know who was born old, Tim," I said. "You had a beard before you were eight and had lost your virginity by ten. From the size of your equipment, I'd say you've been in demand ever since your below waist baby pictures were printed by Ripley in his "Believe It or Not" column. Now what have you done to humble the rest of us mere mortals?"

"Simply incredible," Tim moaned and closed his bloodshot eyes in a futile attempt at protection from the over head fluorescent lights.

"Uh-huh," I responded in anticipation that we could some how move past the introduction. "Tim, I'm not getting any younger waiting for your story. I can feel my own arteries hardening as we speak. You think we could move on while my clothes are still in style?"

"You know your buddy, Harvey Cagle?" Tim asked solemnly.

"You screwed Harvey Cagle?" I asked incredulously. "How could you do that? He's my best friend."

"You don't have any friends, Chief," Tim answered with the harsh truth. "Relax. No, I didn't attack your buddy Harvey."

"Thank God," I feigned enormous relief at the news. Actually, I did consider Harvey a good friend. He was an elementary school principal I had met by playing on the church softball team. As far as I could tell, he was one of the few male members of the Wichita School District I had met that was not a homosexual.

Our Vice Section was forever arresting members of the school district administrative staff in the local parks with someone else's penis tightly tucked in their mouth or other body orifice. The previous school superintendent was a controversial lout who embraced every liberal theory that came along and he was a card carrying member of the ACLU. Whenever I would call him about the latest arrest of one of his staff members for homosexual lewd conduct, the superintendent's attitude was, "So what? Is that a crime?"

Eventually, the liberal educator's contract was finally bought out for a huge sum of taxpayer's dollars so someone a little less radical could guide our children's lives. I really missed him. Coverage of his outrageous actions was often the only thing keeping me off of the front page of the newspaper. Unfortunately, the person chosen as his replacement was as dim as a fifteen watt bulb. From the deep south, his staff joked that they had to limit their written reports to the new superintendent to only one page so his lips would not get tired when he tried to read them.

"No, your buddy is the principal at that small elementary over on the eastside. I forget the name of the school. Any way, it's not important. What's important," Tim finally admitted, "is one of the teachers that works there."

"Oh, yeah?" I asked, becoming a little interested in Tim's tale.

"Yep. Do you remember when I went over to the school a couple of months ago to coordinate your speech to the kids and their parents on the dangers of drug abuse or pre-teen masturbation or some other similar evil?" Tim answered.

"Vaguely," I answered.

"Well, while I was there I got to talking to Doctor Cagle about you and he introduced me to this sweet young thing who teaches the third grade at his school. By the way, you know he's not a real doctor, don't you?" Tim asked.

"Yeah, Tim, it's called a P.H.D. I don't think they let him do surgery or anything like that." The ends and outs of the American educational system was not Tim David's forte. Telling incredible sex stories was.

"Whatever. Any way, yesterday I got a call from the little angel right out of the blue. She invited me over to the school after a P.T.A. meeting for a conference. When I asked her what kind of conference, she said the subject would be sex education. Well, hell, how could I resist such an intriguing invitation?" Tim pleaded.

"You couldn't resist, right?" I played along with Tim's story.

"Right. I took the afternoon off and went home to spend some time with the little woman so she wouldn't complain that she hadn't seen me all day. Around dark, I told her I had a late night assignment at work so not to wait up," Tim continued.

"I hope you didn't tell her that I ordered you to work late last night. Don't bring me into your schemes. I don't lie well enough to pull them off," I admitted.

I remembered a time as a lieutenant in Dallas when the wife of one of my sergeants called me on the telephone and cussed me out like I had long ears and a tail. She wanted to know just how long it had been since I had an "old fashioned country ass whuppin'" since she was about to come down to where I was and put such a hurt on me.

Her husband had been on the police department for ten years, she said, and had always been allocated two consecutive days off each week. Now that he was working for me, his days off were split to Monday and Wednesday according to Mrs. Sergeant.

After she accused me of ruining her marriage by breaking up their family life, I told her that her husband was assigned Mondays and Tuesdays off and had those days for over a year. She called me a lying son of a bitch and hung up in my ear before I could get another word out.

When the sergeant showed up for work that night, it was my turn to chew his head off. The bastard told his wife that I split his days off because I was such a hard ass. The real reason for his absence from his family was so he could screw the nymphomaniac blonde secretary from the Investigative Unit every Tuesday night. It seemed like Tuesday was the only free night the secretary had to fit my sergeant into her busy schedule. To cover his tracks with his wife, the sergeant had been taking one vacation day off each Wednesday for several months. The asshole told me he was taking a night school college class on Wednesday nights so I would give him the time off. Boy, was I trusting.

The sergeant and I had a little "Come to Jesus" meeting in my office and I considered opening up a big can of "whup ass" on him right then and there. Instead, I told the sergeant to call his wife and confess while I observed the conversation. It was his wife or his stripes, I threatened. The sergeant decided to keep his rank and trust that he could figure out some way to justify his philandering to his wife. From listening to the phone call, I think it would have been easier for him to take the demotion.

"When I got to the school it was closed," Tim got back to the story, "but the teacher that called me was waiting inside to unlock the front door. She was wearing a yellow rain coat, like the kind those school crossing guards wear. I mean that's ALL she had on. A yellow rain coat with nothing underneath."

"Come on, Tim, I'm not buying this line of hooey," I protested. The image of my own third grade teacher, completely nude and wrapped in a yellow rubber rain coat, popped into my mind. It was an ugly sight.

"Wait it gets better. I'm not lying. Listen to this. Before we can get down the hall, she goes down on me right there in front of a picture of George Washington. Can you imagine that?" Tim demanded.

"No, Tim, quite frankly, I can't say that it is easy to imagine any of this," I declared.

"It's true, I swear," Tim whined. "After a long period of incredible resistance on my part, I'm afraid that I couldn't hold it any longer. She swallowed it all right there under the picture of George Washington. That's when she wanted me to call you."

"What?" I stopped gently rocking in my leather chair and snapped forward at the mention of my involvement in Tim's sexual fantasy. "No way!"

"Yeah, that's what I told her. I tried to explain that you wouldn't be interested, seeing as how you are such a straight arrow and all," Tim answered.

"Okay, Tim, not that I'm believing any of this but just how old of a woman are we talking about here? Was she like, a Hiroshima blast victim, or what?" I could feel myself starting to be drawn into the story.

"Chief, I swear this girl could not be over twenty-five and she had a body that would melt lead. Maybe a little plump, but not so you'd notice. She had the cutest little smile, just like an angel," Tim explained.

"This is getting a little hard to swallow, Tim," I said, immediately realizing my choice of words were not the best.

"Well, it wasn't hard for her to swallow last night. But wait, that's not all," Tim promised.

"Somehow, I suspected the story wouldn't end there under George Washington's picture," I answered.

"After our first encounter, she leads me off down the dark hall until we found the entrance to the library. Once inside, she tells me that she has this thing for books and would I please mount her right there on top of the Dewey Decimal System," Tim explained.

"That's it, Tim. This is not like you to make up stories. You're beginning to sound like Pete Gant. More than half of what he says is fantasy and the other half is stolen from some one else," I said.

"I swear, Chief. How could I make up shit like this? It has to be true; it's too weird to be made up," Tim pointed out.

"Well, that makes sense, in a twisted sort of way," I admitted.

"She went totally crazy when we climbed on top of one of those little round tables in the library," Tim described. "You know those miniature tables where kindergartners sit while they color pictures and pick their noses. The kids who sit at those tables can't stay in the lines and I couldn't either last night. She was bouncing all over the place. I bet we fell off that damned table at least a dozen times."

"Well," he continued, "I rode that bronc for about four hours. There was a lot of nipping and sucking and licking going on, in between a few very brief rest stops. About midnight, I collapsed from exhaustion and a severe need for fluid replenishment. Maybe even a sperm transfusion, if there is such a thing."

"There isn't, at least not in Kansas, I don't think," I counseled. "What time did you escape from this Amazon?"

The elevator bell rang out in the hallway, signifying some other early riser was coming to work ahead of the crowd.

"You better hope that's not Ramona, hot rod," I cautioned. "I don't think you're in any shape to pay for the Big Red you drank. At least, not in trade. Maybe she will take money or an I.O.U. You know, one of those "I'll gladly screw you on Tuesday, for a drink of your soda today" letters of agreement. As your agent, I don't want ten percent of the action."

Tim ignored me and launched into round two of his story.

"After I dozed off for a little while, this angel washes me down with a stack of those brown paper towels they have in school rest rooms and puts my clothes back on me. I was as helpless as a newborn baby. The next thing I know, we are in her car and she's taking me over to her apartment at the "Fox Run". You know, the ones right down the street from here?"

"Yeah, great, Tim, I know the place," I noted. "So does just about everybody else in town. I hope no one saw you."

"I doubt it," Tim said. "We were inside her car. Anyway, we go up to this apartment and her roommate is inside with some other guy I'd never seen before. They're screwing like a couple of dogs in heat, so the angel and I join in."

"Come on, Tim, I'm having a hard time believing all of this debauchery, much less your claim to have set the all time endurance record," I stated.

"It's a fact. But I'm coming to the thrilling conclusion," Tim promised.

"Thank heaven for small favors. I don't think my heart could take much more of this baloney. As a matter of fact, I don't think my Bulova is crap proof." I held my left forearm and wrist above my head to protect my official "Dallas Police Department" imitation gold retirement watch from the imaginary pool of bovine dung flooding the room.

"Well, I'm pumping away in this foursome, see, when I catch a glimpse of myself in this wall mirror they had mounted in the bedroom," Tim paused for a minute to catch his breath. "That's when I noticed that I've got bites and scratches all over me from the "Battle of the Books" back at the school library. Holy shit, I thought. How am I going to explain this to Sandra? The thought really shriveled my timbers and I just couldn't do much more for that angel after that. So, I grabbed up my clothes and made a hasty retreat out the door. I wound up walking here in the rain and falling asleep on the floor."

"Tim, I'm not believing a word of this B.S.", I vowed. "Write it up and send it in to the Playboy Forum, but I don't think that they will believe it either."

"Yeah, well maybe I should send them photos with the article." With that statement, Tim peeled off his tweed sport coat and unbuttoned his pink shirt which was once starched in an earlier life.

His entire chest and back was covered with a colorful combination of hickeys and scratches. There was no mistaking the fingernail gouges that tracked Tim's flanks and shoulders. The purple suck marks all over his body were already turning that peculiar yellowish tint.

"Damn, partner, you were telling the truth. Are you going to tell Sandra you got into a fight with a crazed octopus? I don't think she will buy that line, since Kansas is at least a thousand miles from the nearest ocean. You want us to arrange a break in at Sea World and claim you wrestled some radioactive freak of nature back into its cage; thereby saving all of Wichita and human civilization as we know it?"

"Very funny, Chief," Tim whined. "Besides, I've already thought of that. Wichita doesn't have a "Sea World". This is serious. I can't go home looking like this. I'm so damned stiff and sore from falling off that table and sleeping on the floor here, I can hardly move. Not to mention that my mouth tastes dryer than the Gobi Desert. Oh, shit! I almost forgot, my car is still in the elementary school parking lot."

"Calm down, Tim. You will think of something. You always do. Just think of your new "angel" as one of your usual motel clerk affairs and offer one of your patented tried and proven excuses for not coming home last night. Pick one of your lines that's worked before. It's as simple as that," I offered.

"Yeah, that might work," Tim peeked at the ceiling for a sign of confirmation. "Sandra's pretty trusting. I'll go downstairs and get the first officer I find to give me a ride over to the school to pick up my car. Maybe I can get it out of the lot before the other teachers start arriving for work."

"Good plan," I ventured as encouragement.

"Hey, but what about these damned scratches and bites on my cute little body?" Tim asked. He had the worried expression of a little boy caught reading his father's Playboy.

"I can't help you there, Timmy boy. If I were you, I'd either check myself into a leper colony or try to keep my clothes on around my wife until Christmas. The evidence should fade by then, I would think," I said with a whimsical smile.

"Thanks, Chief. Gotta go," Tim waved as he staggered out of the door. "What a night!"

"You can say that again," I commented to an empty room.

* * *

"What brings you in so early, Chief?"

Spinning around at the sound of Suzie's voice left me temporarily dizzy. I had fallen asleep in my overstuffed chair while staring out the dark window. The room was filling with the dim light of another dreary October dawn trying to break its way through the Kansas cloud cover.

"Geez, Suzie, you snuck up on me," my startled answer failed to hide my sleepy voice.

"Do you have a big day planned, or what?" Suzie asked again.

"Oh, let's see. Yeah, I have a conference call with the United Nations and then later on I'm jetting to Washington to offer the President some advice on this Balkans' thing. Other than that, I'm trying to complete a normal day in the big city," I proclaimed wishfully.

"Uhmmm," Suzie played along. "I don't think I have any of those appointments on your calendar for today, Chief. How did last night go?"

"You wouldn't believe it if I told you, Suzie. The Citizens Police Academy meeting was a complete and total fiasco. As a matter of fact, I'm not sure I was really there. If anyone calls and inquires about the event, tell them that you think I was scheduled to speak in Tibet last night," I ordered.

"Who was in Tibet last night?" Tim David asked as he came through the door looking a lot happier than I remembered from earlier in the morning.

"I was, if anybody asks," I commanded. "Are you back already?"

"Nothing to it, boss. Oh yeah, I forgot to ask about your night," Tim said. Suzie gave him a confused look as if to say, "What part of this movie have I missed already?" and walked back into her own area.

"Well, I don't think I could top your night, even if I tried. Did you get your car?" I asked.

"Yep, and I called Sandra and told her I got involved in a big vice raid while I was working on a special hush, hush project you had assigned. She said she understood. What a wife," Tim praised the woman who would cut his heart out with a plastic spoon if she knew what her husband had really done last night.

"Damn it all, Tim! I told you to leave me out of your little white lies to your wife. If she asks me about it, I am not going to lie for you. This is not "small island rules" stuff here. You are in your own home town, Bud. Not even a buzzard craps in his own nest," I announced in my best Will Rogers' analogy.

"My, aren't we philosophical this morning," Tim observed. "So what did you do last night that brings you into the office before dawn today in such a good mood?"

"Kandi and Renee put on a stage act at the Citizens Police Academy meeting last night which brought the house down. Literally. I managed to make my escape with Jana Sims before any shots were fired," I answered. "On my way into work, I arrested the County Treasurer's son on a "Felony Intent to Distribute Narcotics" charge and your basic concealed weapons possession rap. That's about it, I think. No, wait, not quite. I found this bum passed out on my office floor and rescued him from the clutches of a hideous space alien who tried to suck his blood out through his belly button and other various other spots on his body. That about covers my boring night."

"Congratulations Chief, you said the secret words and won a hundred dollars. "Space aliens" will be all you can think about in just a few minutes when Chief Denson gets here for your nine o'clock meeting," Tim prophesied.

"That's right, I almost forgot," I admitted. "I am finally going to hear this mysterious tale of woe, aren't I?"

"Before last night, I thought this story would be the highlight of our week, Chief; but now I'm not so sure anymore," Tim mused. "I'm going down to the cafeteria for a real breakfast before the meeting. You want me to bring you anything to eat?"

"No thanks, I've got my breakfast," I said, pointing to the can of cold Pepsi Suzie had brought into the room and placed on my desk. She performed the daily Pepsi ritual for me only when she thought I had a particularly grueling day scheduled.

When Tim left, I busied myself on the computer waiting for the designated hour of my meeting with Jack Denson and his staff member. I sent the Manager an e-mail alerting him to the McCoole arrest just in case the political wires started buzzing across the street at the County Courthouse. I always tried to keep him informed of any police activities that had political implications. That way, the Manager could play the big shot with the City Council and Mayor by informing them first hand, before they read about it in the newspaper or heard it on the radio. The City Manager expected the information from me, but never acknowledged his appreciation for the source of the brownie points it earned him. I did not tell him about the antics of his Inter-Governmental Affairs Officer and his City Auditor last night at the meeting. I decided to let him find out about that debacle from someone else. Besides, my story would be that I was in the "Male Room" trying to repair the defective stall door latch during the entire episode and I did not see a damned thing. It was safer that way.

At precisely nine a.m., Suzie buzzed me on the office intercom. "Chief, Deputy Chief Denson and Lieutenant Manson are here to see you."

"Great. Send them in, will you," I instructed. Except for the routine morning mini-staff meetings, Jack Denson never just walked into my office. He always announced his presence to Suzie and received permission to enter before coming through my office doorway. As a symbol of my openness with departmental members, I rarely closed the inner door. Just about everybody in the department knew they were welcome to casually wander in and say "hi", or transact business directly with me if they had followed the proper chain of command.

Jack Denson knew the door was always open, but he insisted on respecting the formality of my position. It was a little too much pomp and circumstance for my tastes but Jack was comfortable with the arrangement. I once tried to match his formality for a week or two in our telephone traffic. I would call his secretary's number, rather than Jack's direct line at his desk, and say something like, "Please give my compliments to Deputy Chief Denson and advise him that the Chief of Police desires his presence in the Chief's Office at two o'clock." This went on for a while and I tired of the game. I soon went back to calling him on his direct phone line and saying, "Hey, Jack, when you get a few minutes this afternoon, can you come down and see me about the Rogers case?"

Jack and Lieutenant Norman Manson appeared in my doorway looking as if they were both constipated. "Come on in the house guys and make yourselves at home," I said. I stood and shook Manson's hand since I had not seen him in a week or so. Jack waved with an open palm and sat in the same chair from which Tim David had spun his lewd tale a few hours earlier. The lieutenant pulled another battered office chair closer and piled a stack of papers on the edge of my carefully ordered desk.

Norman Manson was a strange kind of duck. He was a tall, stocky man with sad eyes and a slow southern drawl. When I first met Norman, he insisted on telling me his entire life history which included the intimate details of two marriages and divorces caused by excessive drinking and impotence. Manson was personable and articulate, but prone to saying the wrong things at the wrong time. I had appointed him as our department's first "Public Affairs Officer" because he had a degree in journalism. Norman readily volunteered for the position when I announced the formation of the new unit designed to boost the department's sagging reputation in the community prior to my arrival.

Truthfully, Manson had worked wonders in writing positive public service announcements, small articles in the newspaper and press releases. He also deftly exploited other avenues to portray our department in a more positive light to the community. Norman conceived the idea of the two of us dressing up in Santa Claus suits during Christmas to pass out toys and other small gifts to kids in the hospital's children's wards around town. This last idea really hit home with me. As an eight year old with pneumonia, I spent one lonely Christmas in a hospital isolation ward. I knew what it was like to be young, scared and alone during the holidays. The Santa idea was a stroke of genius. Parents wrote the department and told us what a big lift we gave their kids who could not be home for Christmas. A few of the letters were heart rending, particularly when the child was afflicted with some terrible disease or dying. The letters served to remind me how brief and how fragile life could be.

Lieutenant Manson performed well in the assignment until he made the mistake of answering a reporter's question with too flippant of an answer. During a local election campaign, the reporter asked Norman if the police department considered the incumbent City Council candidates to be reliable in their promise to add a hundred new police officers over the next five years.

"Sure, we think the City Council is reliable," Manson had stated. "First they lie and then they re-lie, so they are nothing if not reliable."

The quote made the Associated Press wire service and was spread all over the country, not to mention the entire State of Kansas. In a matter of hours, both the Mayor and Mel were demanding that Manson be demoted to a Parking Control Checker or shot at sunrise. Or both. I refused to consider those Draconian measures not because Norman was innocent in thinking that the media would not quote him. He had badly misjudged the media's prime directive of "never let context or the truth stand in the way of a good story". No, shooting him was simply too difficult to cover up and out of the question. As for the other suggestion, I refused to demote Manson because first, his statement about the City Council's duplicity was probably true and second, I was not about to let Mel Michaels or anyone else start telling me who to demote inside my own department. Once I did that, I might as well stay home and let someone else be the chief. In the end, I compromised and re-assigned Norman to the Burglary Section where he supervised fifteen detectives and the most trouble he could get into there was an infected paper cut.

"Norm, how have you been lately?" I asked.

"Pretty good, Chief, I can't complain," Manson drawled.

At that exact moment, Tim David stuck his head in the door and smiled, "Is it still okay for me to sit in on this one?" I glanced at Jack Denson and he nodded his approval.

"Sure, Tim, come on in," I waved him into the last remaining empty chair in my cramped office. "Okay, guys," I decided to get right to the issue, "What have you got that is so mysterious?"

Norman looked at Deputy Chief Denson for guidance and Jack rose out of his chair and walked the short distance toward the room's entry. "Do you mind if I close the door, Chief?"

"Go ahead," I replied, knowing that everyone who walked by the outer office and saw the door closed would realize something unusual was going on inside. I did not know at the time exactly how unusual the goings on would be.

Jack eased the heavy wooden door closed and returned to his chair. He sighed heavily and said, "Chief, we're here about Detective Clarence Taylor. Are you familiar with him?"

"I know a little bit about him, I think. A quiet kind of guy that's been a detective a long time. I never see his name on any disciplinary stuff. Seems like a solid, no-problem officer. Am I wrong?"

"No. That's Clarence, for sure," Denson admitted. "At least it was until about a month ago when he started acting kinda strange at work."

"Can you define "kinda strange" for me, Jack? We all act "kinda strange" at times around this loony bin," I pointed out.

"Well, not like this I'm afraid, Chief," Jack said.

"He started seeing little green men, Chief," Tim David interjected.

Denson turned in his seat to glare across Norman's lap at Tim, who was trying to hide from the deputy chief's fiery gaze. Jack frowned at Tim as if to tell him to keep his mouth shut since this was not his story.

"He started seeing what?" I demanded.

"To be precise, Chief, they are not "little green men" that Taylor claims to be seeing," Lieutenant Manson chimed in. "He describes them as being almost translucent, to use his words."

"Wait a minute, guys. Why doesn't someone start at the beginning and let me hear the whole story from start to finish before we get to the last reel of the movie? Okay?" I requested.

"Norman, he's your troop, you give the Chief the whole story," Denson instructed.

Manson cleared his throat with such force that a two ounce lump of phlegm dislodged from his beefy throat and dribbled down his chin. He wiped a handkerchief with a massive paw across his mouth and swallowed hard.

"About a month ago," Norman explained, "Taylor began talking to some of the other detectives upstairs about his belief in U.F.O.'s. At the time, the other guys just kinda joined in with the discussions while they were passing the time of day. To be honest, a lot of people think there might be something to this UFO business that the government is not telling us."

"Just keep to the facts, Norm," Denson ordered, "and hold your editorial comments until later, okay?"

Manson took another deep breath and launched his story again. "Anyway, Taylor began to explain to some of us that he actually believes aliens are already on the Earth and they have infiltrated our society at all levels."

"Well, that would sure explain some of the stupid instructions I get from the thirteenth floor," I commented. It was obvious from Deputy Chief Denson's brief forced smile that he was not to be deterred by any of my weak humor from having his lieutenant complete the story in a serious manner.

He poked Manson in the ribs with a light elbow gesture and the lieutenant continued with his outline.

"Over a period of weeks, Clarence admitted to several of us that he belongs to this group of people who believe we are being invaded by space aliens. In fact, the club elected him as their president due to his official position with the Wichita Police Department as a respected police officer and all," Manson stated.

I closed my eyes tightly and pictured the reputation of the department being attached to a bunch of wackos with aluminum foil wrapped around their heads to deflect alien mind control beams. I was not far off in my vision.

"Taylor has been trying to recruit other detectives into his club, especially those having some special skill he thinks is needed to identify and expose the aliens. For example, he tried to induct Bob Patterson into the club because Bob has a lot of camera equipment that he uses in his off duty business, you know," Manson continued.

I knew. Bob advertised his photographic skills for parties and weddings and that sort of thing. I had even hired him for my son's marriage to his high school sweetheart when they both graduated from college. Bob cut off a lot of heads in his photographs, but his fee was cheap.

"No one else from the department has actually joined Taylor's club as far as we know, but Clarence has become more and more vocal about the strange occurrences that he says are going on all around him. You gotta remember, Chief, this activity is from a guy who is so quiet he probably didn't speak a hundred words to anyone in the month before all this started." Manson pronounced authoritatively.

"Okay, so Taylor believes in UFO's and wants to have a club to track down the proof. He gets to wear a name tag that says he's the president of the club and his own set of mouse ears, or whatever UFO club presidents are wearing these days. What's the big deal in that?" I asked.

"We've just got started into describing our situation, Chief. Just wait and listen to the whole story. Go ahead, Norm," Jack nodded again at Manson to re-start the story.

"A couple of weeks ago, Taylor began showing up for work with some strange scratches on his body," Manson detailed.

I could not resist a quick glance at Tim David and a big grin. Tim coughed lightly and stared at the floor. I could see him pressing his tongue against the inside of his cheek to keep from laughing out loud. Evidently, Tim had never considered that his "angel" from last night might be a space alien. Of course, no one else in the room could make the connection and wondered why I was grinning at the top of Tim's lowered head.

I quickly regained my composure and Manson plowed on.

"He showed a lot of the guys around the office a bunch of scratches on his arms and legs and asked the fellows if any of them noticed the marks the day before. Naturally, we didn't have a clue what the heck he was driving at. Finally, Clarence tells us when he wakes up each morning he notices new scratches that weren't there the night before."

When Manson said that, I broke out laughing thinking of the fact that Tim David had the same problem. Even Tim could not hold in the giggle that Manson's comparison had caused to bubble to the surface.

"I'm sorry, guys," I tried to apologize for my outburst of laughter when I noticed both Lieutenant Manson and Deputy Chief Denson were staring at Tim and me like we had just grown antennae from the tops of our heads. "It's just that, well, hell, anybody who's had a twenty dollar hooker down on South Broadway might have the same problem with scratches they could not explain to their old lady."

"Taylor is divorced, Chief, and he doesn't fool around with prostitutes," Manson stated seriously.

Norman, you patronizing asshole, I thought, but I hid my true feelings. "Of course not, Norm, I'm sorry. Please go on," I tried to sound apologetic and contrite at the same time.

"I finally decided to call Taylor into my office and get to the bottom of his strange behavior around the office. He confided in me that he had deduced the cuts and scratches on his body had come from space aliens who were materializing inside his apartment at night and examining him," Manson repeated with no expression in his voice or on his face.

"Well, that proves they are aliens right there. Hell, doctors don't even make house calls these days. Only a space alien would come to your house and examine you," I declared.

Manson ignored me this time. I could not blame him. I tried to restrain my comments but it was becoming harder and harder. I had made myself a little yellow stick on note that was affixed to the glass top of my desk where only I could see it. The little sign read "K.Y.B.M.S.", which meant "Keep Your Big Mouth Shut". My daughter and I had come up with the reminder when she was in trouble for talking at school. She diligently inscribed the commandment on all of her school notebooks. I thought the advice was good for me, too. I just had a difficult time adhering to the admonition.

Undeterred, Manson continued his account. "I asked Clarence if he had ever actually seen any of these aliens and he confessed that he had. He described them as being about four feet high, gray in color and with a big domed, pulsating head."

"Sounds like the City Manager," I added. I was on a roll. "Did he say anything about them having oat meal for brains, no balls and egos bigger than Chicago?"

"No," Manson answered, "but he did say these aliens can walk through walls and they have robots to carry their equipment. Taylor claims he immediately passes out after he sees these beings come into his room at night."

"I don't see anything abnormal in that. I often have people who walk through walls to see me at night. Don't you? Why just last night, Abe Lincoln showed up to ask me how I liked his speech at Gettysburg. I told him it lacked humor and he was all pissed off when he left. Well, what do you expect from a Republican?" I asked.

"Chief, please, Lieutenant Manson is trying to give you all of the facts. It gets worse," Jack Denson pleaded.

My mood snapped from being entertained to serious in less time that it took for the pupils of my eyes to widen.

"Come on, you guys, you're not serious are you?" I demanded. "Surely, this is all a joke. You're not telling me that one of my veteran detectives, who carries a gun and a badge around this city every day, is seeing little green men, er, sorry Norman, little gray men who disappear through walls after they chip away at his pudgy little body?"

"There's more, Chief," Manson admitted.

"Well, let's hear it, for heaven's sake. Get on with it," I ordered impatiently.

"Taylor says that even when the aliens do not come into his bedroom at night to examine him, strange beams of light appear and disappear at odd intervals on the ceiling. He thinks they may be controlling his mind or implanting suggestions of things for him to do during the day. Clarence broke down crying when he told me about it, Chief. He is afraid the aliens will make him do something bad and that if he doesn't do what they command, they will kill him. In my opinion, Taylor really believes what he is saying," Manson proclaimed.

I turned in my swivel chair to face the Deputy Chief. "Hell, Jack, this is not a problem. If the guy really believes this fantasy, like Norm says, then he's nuttier than a Corsicana fruitcake."

The reference to the only industry in the little south Texas farming community where I was born completely passed over Jack's head. He did not have a clue where Corsicana was or even "what" it was, much less any connection with a dry Christmas confection. I recognized all too frequently that people in Kansas did not know what I was talking about when I referenced things back in my home state. I was constantly having to explain things like armadillos and horney toads.

"Just write him up for a behavioral cause investigation and send him to the departmental shrink so we can give him a medical retirement. The sooner we get this looney tune out of the department, the better," I instructed.

I shuffled some miscellaneous papers on my desk and put them in a neat little stack to signal that our business was concluded. I was wrong.

"I did that already, Chief," Jack answered. "I thought of it myself yesterday. That's why we postponed the meeting; so I could get Taylor in to see Doctor Johnson."

Dr. Alex Johnson was our contract psychologist who we used to evaluate the psych tests for police applicants, counsel with officers and their families on a wide variety of issues and be the leader of our "Critical Incident Stress Debriefing Team". The later function was used primarily for officers involved in shooting incidents, but it could play a role in assisting officers in dealing with the job stress from any type of traumatic situation they might encounter. It was a very novel concept we had instituted in the department and the practice was being copied by many other police agencies across the country.

I liked Alex and trusted his diagnosis and advice. He once told me that he thought that the City Manager was a classic paranoid schizophrenic with delusions of grandeur in the Freudian sense. He could not be sure without a full examination, of course, but Alex explained that he thought the Manager's mental defect was probably brought on by an early sexual encounter with his mother. How could you not like a guy who could define "asshole" with such professional terminology?

"Okay, so what did the good doctor have to say about our detective?" I asked impatiently.

"Here's his report, Chief. you won't believe it," Jack said as he passed over a two page fax that was stamped "CONFIDENTIAL" in big red letters.

"Well, then it will fit in with the rest of the bull shit that I haven't believed since about six o'clock this morning." With one more shot at Tim David's equally unbelievable tale, I began scanning the psychologist's report. The whole room was as quiet as a mime's rehearsal while I read the very brief synopsis of Detective Taylor's session with the mental health expert.

I read every word of the report at least five times. When I finished, I gently laid the papers on top of my desk and looked directly into the pained expression of Jack Denson.

"Our mental health professional says that he can find no evidence of "Delusional Manifestations"? He says Taylor's mood and orientation to the present day world is appropriate? The doctor says there is no evidence of psychological illness? He claims poor Clarence is a little stressed right now over these extraterrestrial visits, but the "alien magnet" should straighten out after the holidays? My gosh, man, this is not some poor schmuck who's got a house full of in-laws devouring all of the chow in his fridge and swilling his supply of Budweiser; this man sees Martians that walk through walls!" My voice rose in intensity with each word that passed from my lips.

I seriously wondered if our psychologist had fallen over the edge of sanity with Clarence.

"We know, Chief," Jack said calmly, "That's why we're here. Something has got to be done. But there's more to the story."

"More? More? You've got to be kidding me, Jack. What "more" could there be to this fiasco? Wait, let me guess. The space aliens have cut off Taylor's balls, implanted ovaries in his abdomen, and they want him to have Elvis' baby. Am I close on this one, huh?"

"I was losing my grip again and there was nothing I could do about it.

"You're close, Chief, but not exactly," Jack admitted. "Tell him the rest, Norman."

Lieutenant Manson gave one more big, heavy sigh which contributed about twenty pounds of carbon dioxide into the room and began what I hoped would be the grand finale. "This morning, Clarence comes in to work and tells me his ten-year-old daughter and her girl friend spent the night with him last night as a part of his regular visitation rights after the divorce. Well, it seems that the space aliens visited Detective Taylor last night, according to him, and decided to examine both his daughter and her girl friend in the alien spacecraft which had landed in Riverside Park. He claims that he found alien embryo implants in the vaginas of his daughter and the other girl this morning, but he was successful in removing them."

Immediately, there was nothing funny about the situation anymore. No one said a word. It was deathly quiet in the room. I could hear my own stomach rumbling and all of a sudden the lack of sleep and this bizarre story made me feel very, very tired. I wanted to close my eyes and pretend that I had never left the safe confines of Paschal High School. My life was so much simpler when all I had to worry about was whether or not Betty Sue or Denise would show me her bra at the drive in.

I was wondering whether Betty Sue or Denise had been a space alien when Jack interrupted my flashback. "What are we going to do, Chief?"

"Do? I'll tell you what we are going to do, Jack. First, I want a written officer's report from every detective or supervisor who has had any contact with this nut case in the last month, documenting their conversations and the strange behaviors that Norm has described. Second, I want both of you to get over to Internal Affairs as soon as the reports are completed and instruct the I.A. commander to open up an immediate investigation into this latest incident with the girls. Call the state juvenile authorities up in Topeka and bring them in on this. I want these kids examined right away at the hospital for evidence of sexual abuse. Get their statements about what happened last night and on any previous similar close encounters of the weird kind. Am I making myself clear?" I asked.

"Yes sir," both Jack and Lieutenant Manson answered simultaneously.

"Third, Jack, I want you to call Detective Taylor into your office immediately and suspend him with pay, pending the Internal Affairs investigation. I want you to take his badge and police identification card and confiscate his weapon. Tell him he is relieved from duty on my orders, but he is required to be at his residence, subject to recall by Internal Affairs, during his regular duty hours. He is not to work any off duty jobs as a police officer, nor is he to be allowed to represent himself in any way as a police officer until this whole matter has been resolved. Is that clear?"

I asked again to make sure that my instructions were being recorded correctly.

"Yes sir," Jack repeated.

"Any questions on our course of action in this case?" I asked. Neither Lieutenant Manson nor Deputy Chief Denson said a word.

They seemed stunned with the rapidity of the resolution.

"Very well, then, go to it and report back to me when you've suspended him, Jack. Thank you all," I said officiously.

All but Tim David rose quickly and turned toward the doorway.

When Jack and his lieutenant had left the room, Tim said, "I told you that you wouldn't want to miss this meeting. It will be one for your memoirs, only no one will believe it."

"I'm not sure that I believe it. Between your cock in bull story about angels and our own "E.T." here, I'm not sure what to believe anymore," I said.

"I didn't say she "was" an angel, I just said she "looked" like an angel. There's a big difference," Tim said.

"Whatever. Get out of here and do some work," I ordered. "We are paying you, you know." Tim waved as he exited my office in route to his own messy desk next door.

I called Peggy and found her up and alert. After explaining some of the details of my morning, it all seemed to justify my premature departure from her bed at four o'clock in the morning. I did not mention anything about last night, particularly Jana Sims. Maybe I dreamed all of it anyway, I thought. If so, I wanted to go to sleep again as soon as possible and get back in close proximity to that exciting body.

"Victor Pasqual called again this morning," Peggy offered.

"That's twice in two days. Now what did he want?" I asked.

"Just the same thing," Peggy allowed. "Victor said he was worried about me and wanted to say a prayer for my speedy recovery. He sounded very concerned. I think he's really worried about you, too."

"Yeah, I bet. Peggy, I wouldn't be too trusting of that guy," I warned. "There's a lot of political crap happening here at work and I'm not too sure where its all leading right now. I can't tell the players without a program and I'm not sure who's on what team. Victor could be a good guy like he seems or he could turn out to be the Anti-Christ. I just don't know."

Peggy seemed to let it drop at that. I really did not want to let her in on too much of the details because I felt guilty about adding to her worries. I figured she had more than enough on her own account without trying to dip into my overflowing cup of concerns. Peggy told me she might have to return to the Mayo Clinic on short notice, but she was not sure. It seemed that a specialist in her type of cancer was due to visit the clinic from Sweden soon and her neurosurgeon wanted him to examine her personally. Peggy was expecting a call from her doctor this week. The best response I could muster was to tell her I understood and she should keep her bags packed for a quick trip, if necessary.

"I haven't unpacked them from the last trip," she said as we exchanged our good-byes.

I just hung up the phone when Suzie informed me on the intercom that Deputy Chief Denson wanted to see me again. "Well, send him in, Suzie," I instructed with a touch of annoyance in my voice.

Jack came through the door and walked directly to my desk. He looked a little relieved and I thought I could make out a faint smile, but decided that it might be just a gas pain.

"Here, Chief, Taylor wants you to have this," he said. The small cartridge clinked onto the glass top when Jack let it roll out of his hand onto my desk. I picked up the pistol round and examined it before it could tumble onto the floor. It was a standard, city issued nine millimeter bullet. The round was a one hundred and forty-seven grain, copper jacketed hollow point slug and cartridge manufactured by the Federal Corporation. The little missile was lethal and had been chosen by our departmental firearms experts because of its stopping power when launched out of our new semi-automatic handguns. We issued the hot rounds to all of the officers who were qualified to carry the new weapons and insured that the bullets were loaded in the pistols. My own Smith and Wesson, strapped on my hip, held sixteen brothers of this example loaded into the weapon's staggered clip. Thirty more rounds rested in the two extra clips on my duty belt.

"Okay, what's the story on the bullet, Jack?" I inquired.

"Well, when I suspended Taylor and asked for his city issued weapon, he pulled out his pistol kind of funny and I thought for a minute he might shoot himself or maybe me," Jack tried a little chuckle, which sounded more like a wet burp. "He dropped the clip and then racked the slide back and caught this bullet when it was ejected into the air. It was the one that was already in the barrel, under the hammer, you know."

"Sure, Jack, he unloaded his weapon just the way he was taught. What's so strange about that?" I asked with some more impatience initiated by Denson's odd attempt at a smile.

"Nothing, 'cept Taylor said that he had modified this one round so that it would be effective on space aliens. Our regular bullets don't have any effect on aliens, you know. That is, according to Taylor," Jack explained.

"Right, I knew that. It's been in all the papers," I played along. "Jack, when are you going to catch up on your reading?"

"Anyway, Taylor says he wants you to have this one bullet that he made up special, just in case the aliens come after you, Chief. Clarence said he was real concerned that they might try to invade your body and take over Wichita. He broke down and cried when he said it," Denson's voice lowered an octave or two before he finished the story's post script. "I think Taylor really believes everything he's described."

"Whew. Okay Jack, I'll keep the bullet handy in case I wake up with unknown scratches on my body some morning. I don't think I'll load it in my pistol just yet, though." I had no idea what Taylor might have done to the round. It appeared to be a regular factory manufactured bullet, but there was no way to be certain. The detective could have removed all of the gun powder and replaced it with plutonium. I was not sure what Taylor could have done to alter the round and I did not want to take any chances that the thing might melt my gun or worse yet, fail to fire if I needed it.

"Other than that, Chief, Clarence took his suspension orders quietly and left the building. I think he looked kind of relieved," Jack said. "We're getting the reports typed up like you asked and I'm heading over to I.A. now to bring them up to speed on this thing."

"Good luck. See 'ya, Jack," I called as he turned and headed out of the door.

Suzie buzzed me again on the intercom. "Chief, Renee Stark is on line one and wants to talk to you."

I briefly thought about telling Suzie to have Renee call back when my growing headache subsided below the standard necessary for morphine relief but decided against delaying the inevitable. "Okay, Suzie, I'll take it. Thank you."

I punched the blinking button on the face of the telephone and answered as if I did not know who was on the other line. "Rod Starr, may I help you?"

"Somebody called Mel about last night," Renee whined on the other end like a school girl who brought home a "D" in "Personal Hygiene" class. "Did you do it?"

"Well, good morning to you too, Renee," I answered. "No, as a matter of fact, I did not call Mr. Michaels about your cute little stage act. In fact, I haven't talked to him personally in quite a while, but what else is new."

"He called Kandi and me both into his office this morning and boy is he really pissed," Renee whispered.

"Gee, Renee, I don't know why he would be mad at you guys. Did you hum a few bars of "Baby Love" for him, or what?" I taunted.

Renee ignored my slap in the face and pressed on. "I don't know what he is going to do, but he said he wouldn't fire us. He did say that we should call everyone who was at the meeting and apologize, so that's why I'm calling you. I apologize."

In spite of my now raging headache, I could not repress a small chuckle. It was just like Mel to think he could wipe out an entire embarrassing incident by having his two sweet young favorites simply say that they were sorry. It was like a Gilda Radner skit on "Saturday Night Live". The one where she stirs up all kind of trouble and when the heat starts coming back at her, Gilda smiles and says, "Never Mind." I loved it.

"No problem, Renee. I don't think I saw anything anyway. I was in the bathroom the whole time. At least, that's my story and I'm sticking to it," I replied.

"Did you leave with Marty's wife?" Renee hit a nerve and my heart stopped. I could hear the blood pounding in my temples.

"I guess," I answered weakly. The question set me back on my heels, but there was no sense lying about it.

"Well, Marty was really mad. He was yelling and screaming about what a low down wife stealer you were and how he was your friend and you stabbed him in the back and…" Renee struggled for more vivid descriptions of Marty's tirade.

"Friend? I hardly know the clown and if I wanted to steal his wife, I could not have orchestrated that little scene last night even if I had tried," I protested.

"Marty's not a clown, he's a nice guy," Renee asserted.

"Marty's an asshole." I replied with the air of a definitive ruling.

I was really tired of people like Marty who pretended to be your friend only as long as they were around you or whenever you were in good graces with the powers that be. Just as soon as they saw a chance, guys like Marty would screw you to the wall and walk away with the screwdriver. You knew your friends in my job because they were the ones who stabbed you in the front. Marty failed to qualify on that count. No, Marty much preferred to whack you from ambush after he crawled out from whatever rock he was hiding under. Unfortunately, dealing with snakes like Marty were a big part of my job. It was a part that I hated.

Renee rang off the line by making the excuse that she had a lot of apology calls to make and I dialed the information number for Clearwater, Kansas. Surprisingly, they did have a number listed for a "J.M. Sims" and I called it. The phone rang ten times with no answer. At least there was no stupid answering machine that I would be forced to leave a message on or hang up like a school kid. It was just as well. I had no idea what I was going to say to Jana.

By the time I had handled most of the correspondence piled on my desk and returned about a dozen phone messages on everything from juvenile crime committees to complaints about the Mounted Unit's horse's droppings on the sidewalk, it was one o'clock. I had missed lunch and I was exhausted.

I picked up one last envelope and read the neatly type written contents inside. The letter was written in one long paragraph without indentations and there was no signature at the bottom of the page.

"Chief of Police—Mr. Rod Starr, Dear Chief; I'm a man in my later years; However, since the death of my first wife, I have been remarried. As I mentioned I'm not a young man anymore, but, I've taken on the mind of a man much younger than myself. I'm very much in love with my beautiful new bride. We been together for a few years, but the two of us still feel as though we're still on our honeymoon. My concern is whether we may be breaking the law. Recently we have been turning on our inside lights and our outside lights, about dusk dark. At that time we both undress and walk around the house naked, wearing nothing but our birthday suits. My main concern is that we have the drapes to our sliding glass doors open. I realize that we are in public view. Our sliding glass doors are located at the back of the house. I don't feel that our act is an unlawful one because we are in our own house and on our own property. The act is innocent; however, it stimulates me and it helps and aids my sexual performance. If you or your officers are in the vicinity, stop and be an eyewitness to the event. Park your car on Sheridan Street and walk in the direction of our backyard. You will know the house because it will be the one with the lights on. I'm too old to be a pervert. I'm just out for a good time. Hats off to Thomas Edison for inventing the light bulb. Lawrence C. Jenkins; 13161 South Hydraulic, Wichita."

The letter was the last straw in a very weird day. I dropped the envelope containing Mr. Jenkins' concerns, and his exciting offer to observe he and his wife in action, on my secretary's desk as I abandoned the office like Molly Brown leaving the Titanic.

"Suzie, since my day started at four o'clock this morning, I'm going home. Call Deputy Chief Wade and tell him he has the duty and that he's in charge. If you need me, I will have my portable radio with me, set on the command frequency," I instructed.

The command channel was a separate radio frequency that only our senior level commanders had installed in their radios. The frequency was set aside to offer ready access to each other in case of emergencies or other administrative functions where we did not want the whole world listening. The frequency was "scrambled", so our audio transmissions were unintelligible to anyone without the proper code to decipher the transmissions. The entire police radio system was a new, state-of-the-art innovation in Wichita. We persuaded the county to share the costs with us so Mel could not nix the deal. Before I arrived, the officers were using forty-year-old communications technology. Some of the ancient radio sets contained vacuum tubes that had to warm up before the relic would function. The previous antiquated system was not much better than a can and a string and the officers really loved the new equipment. The new radios were a first class system for what I hoped would become a first class police department in the future.

Peggy was not home when I arrived much earlier than my usual time. She left a note on the kitchen table that she would pick up Terri at school. They planned to go shopping and take in a movie with Peggy's friend, Carmen Hubble, the note explained. Tired and with my head still aching, I tried to take a nap but I kept waking up with every little noise in the house. Try as I might, I could not help but wonder if Taylor's spacemen would come for me. Finally, I showered, ate three Excedrin tablets and put on my best pair of semi-clean jeans. I left Peggy my own note telling her that I would be home late. I did not tell her where I was going. It was only a fifteen minute drive to Clearwater, assuming I could decipher the back roads.

Once I drove across Highway 54 going south, I found myself back in the flat farm land which I had only dimly been able to glimpse the night before. I counted the number of mobile homes along the roads and shook my head at the seeming stupidity of their proliferation in this land of the two hundred mile per hour tornado. It was apparent to me that mobile homes were constructed with some type of material which made them attract tornadoes like a magnet. The cracker boxes were forever being blown over half of the county and skewering their inhabitants on broken telephone poles. The locals called the grotesque sights, "Cyclone-Ka-Bobs". Frankly, I preferred it when the whirlwinds just dropped the unlucky victims like bags of wet cement; usually on parking lots miles away from the original homestead. It was cleaner.

In the middle of one wheat field, I watched as a farmer kicked the tires on his old Ford tractor and throw a heavy wrench at the metal monster. It clanged off the machine's red painted side and fell spent and impotent into the plowed dirt. Being a farmer was a tough life. Being a tractor was tougher, I guessed.

I could see signs that the big city life was encroaching on this part of the county. Every now and then, a huge new two story brick home would appear along the side of the road and the "Land For Sale" signs became more frequent. The farmers were selling more and more of their land to people who wanted to move to the country and become the lord and masters of their own "Little House on the Prairie".

I thought of our own little piece of the "American Dream" back in Texas. Peggy and I purchased twenty-two acres of rolling farm land about sixty miles south of Dallas. We had been paying on it for ten years and finally paid off the mortgage last year. Yep, the land was all ours.

We intended to retire on it some day and build a cozy little brick house, nestled among the pecan trees overlooking the pond. Peggy wanted to buy a couple of horses and I wanted to do nothing but roll in the hay with Peggy and teach a course or two at Navarro Junior College or perhaps even Baylor University, thirty miles away in the big city of Waco. Those vague thoughts were about as far as my retirement ambitions would allow me to go in my planning process.

Peggy wrote to several custom home building companies in answer to their magazine advertisements that she had poured over during one of her long trips to the Mayo Clinic. The companies sent us scaled down versions of various house plans Peggy thought would be perfect for our retirement cottage in the East Texas woodlands. We planned to hang a hand carved sign over the entrance gate that said, "The Hideout", in reference to our desire to finally escape the real world of assholes and politics. My only requirement for the property was a stipulation that it be surrounded by a ten foot high chain link fence, topped with the kind of razor wire you see around prison yards.

This time, the wire would be to keep people out rather than in. Peggy nixed my idea for a mine field. I compromised and announced that I would just shoot anyone who tried to climb over the fence with my trusty thirty-ought-six.

The back roads near Clearwater looked a lot different in the daytime. I considered stopping to ask directions from some of the people I saw standing in their front yards, but they reminded me too much of the movie "Deliverance". I decided to honor the genetically imprinted male aversion to ever stopping and asking directions to anywhere. Most of the older houses and mobile homes had the obligatory junk car parked in the front yard. It must be a law in both Kansas and Texas that you must have an old, rusted out junker on your country property or else the rural power company will refuse to run you an electric line. It has something to do with protection against lightning strikes, I think. I made a mental note to find a suitable hulk for our property in Texas before we retired.

I passed five kids playing on top of a 1957 Ford that had been the color of "Bondo" and baby puke yellow when Elvis was "The King". Like the kid's weary mother, who was hanging wet clothes to dry on a stretch of rope strung between two iron poles in the yard, the car had seen better days. Judging from the rotting tires and Johnson grass growing up under the hood, I guessed that the old Ford had stopped running long before Elvis fell off of his toilet seat and died of God knows what. For no reason at all, I honked my horn and waved at the kids. They waved back with such cheerful animation that it was clear strangers were an uncommon sight in these parts. The mother just turned and stared at me with dull, blank eyes.

I passed an old battered metal sign that read "Clearwater Greens Golf Course" and a big red arrow pointing to the right. I remembered seeing the sign in the darkness and recalled we had turned left just after we had passed it. I spun the steering wheel at the next turn and attempted to trace my car tracks from the night before. In my rear view mirror, I searched for anything that vaguely resembled a golf course. All I saw was a log house and a flat pasture with cows grazing contentedly in the haze. If there was a golf course concealed in the fallow wheat field, it was well camouflaged against enemy attack.

About a mile down the sandy road, I found incontrovertible proof that I was on the right track. Marty Sim's silver Lincoln Town Car was traveling down the road directly in front of me. Through the dust clouds, I could see his personalized license plate, "I-1". The plate was not hard for me to file away in my memory for future reference. "I-1" as in "I won", the observer could guess. I assumed that Marty was asserting his undeniable ability to battle back from apparent defeat following his dismissal from the police department. Marty's ultimate accumulation of wealth convinced him that he was really the winner in the game of life. Fate plays strange tricks on us all and I was in no position to argue with the result. In fact, I found myself with begrudging respect for a man with balls enough to claim "1-1" after such an experience.

When the Lincoln pulled off the dirt road into the gravel lane that I recognized as Jana's, I decided to keep driving right on by. The big white frame farm house, about fifty yards from the road, looked worn and weather beaten in the daylight. I was not exactly sure what I was doing there, anyway. But, I knew damned well that I did not want to drive into the middle of a domestic disturbance between Marty and his ex-wife.

I continued to drive down the road another mile or two and made a big U-turn at a lonely intersection dividing four different wheat fields. Each corner post displayed a coiled roll of rusted barbed wire draped around its top, like the ring toss game at the Kansas State Fair.

I stopped the car and waited a few minutes, pondering what I should do. I finally decided I should turn my car around and go home. My reasons for being out here in the middle of no where were not very clear, even in my own mind. For some inexplicable magnetic reason, I took the same road I had just come down. The one that led past Jana's house.

When I got closer, I could see that Marty's Lincoln had vanished from the driveway. Marty had obviously not stayed long and had escaped in the same direction he had come. My car turned itself into the gravel driveway without a whole lot of conscious thought on my part. Beth Miller was sitting in the rickety porch swing.

"What is this," she called when I got out of the car, "old home week?"

"Hello, Miss Miller," I called back, "It's good to see you again, too."

"Don't you guys have homes? First, it's that no good Marty and now it's the real chief. Did you guys draw straws to see who pulled in first, or what?" Beth asked.

I walked slowly through the wet grass and up on the porch with Beth. She eyed me closely. The trace of a smile crossed her lips and the swing rocked gently in the chill air.

"What was the deal just now with Marty?" I asked.

"He wanted to see Jana. I told him she wasn't here. He called me a liar and started to go in the house. That was when I sprayed him," Beth widened her smile into a grin and revealed a set of perfect white teeth.

"You did what?" I asked.

"I peppered his ass, you know, with this new tear gas spray that you got for your guys. It's great stuff." Beth held up a red and black metal canister with a red plastic top.

I recognized it immediately as the latest updated version of chemical defense spray we provided to all of our police officers.

"Where did you get that stuff, Beth? That's not a toy. You can really do some damage with pepper spray. You can't just hose down someone and let it go, you have to clean it off or it gets worse. It burns like fire and temporarily blinds you if you don't get it off right away," I lectured.

"Relax, Chief, I just sprayed a little over Marty's head and he ran out of here like a scalded ass ape. I told him that if he ever tried to come into my house again, I would douse him with enough liquid fire to light up Kansas City," Beth boasted.

"Well, I came to see Jana, but I'm not about to fight you for the privilege," I admitted. "So, before you fire a shot of that jalapeno juice in my direction, I reckon I'll be making my getaway. See ya later, Annie Oakley."

I turned on my heel to walk back down the steps and Beth said, "She's inside. I think she's been expecting you. Go on in."

"What? I thought you said Jana wasn't here," I was not sure that I had heard Beth correctly.

"No, what I said was I told Marty that Jana wasn't here. He was right. I lied. You're different. Jana was in the kitchen when I came out to meet Marty," Beth tilted her thumb toward the front door.

Mounting the porch steps with an unsteady lope, I opened the screen door and then the front wooden door without knocking. I put my head inside and called out a warning, "Police, search warrant, anybody home?"

When no shots were fired, I stepped inside the dark house. It was deliciously warm inside the front door and I could detect the smell of popcorn wafting through the living room. There were no lamps on and the only light available was filtered through dark curtains which hung over the windows. I stumbled over the couch in the dark and headed toward the back of the house, in the general direction of where I thought I remembered the kitchen being. Rubbing my sore shin from the collision with the couch in the dark, I was glad Beth and Jana had not moved all of the furniture during the night.

"Knock, knock," I called and pushed open the old style swinging kitchen door.

Jana was sitting at a wooden table covered with a red and white checkered table cloth. The microwave was whirring and the popcorn was causing the yellow and blue paper container inside the nuclear oven to expand to its maximum size.

"Hey stranger, what brings you back to my humble abode?" Jana said as she looked up with a puzzled smile.

"Are you gonna eat all of that popcorn yourself or will you share?" I asked.

"Help yourself," she offered, "There's Cokes in the ice box." Actually there were Pepsis in the refrigerator and I snatched two aluminum cans off the top shelf. The Coca-Cola company should be proud that they had done such a great job of marketing that people generically referred to all soft drinks as "Cokes", regardless of whether they were the "Real Thing" or Ramona's red strawberry juice.

Jana got up and poured the hot popcorn into a big green Tupperware bowl and sat back down at the table. I joined her with the drinks and we began to munch the butter flavored snack and sip Pepsi in silence. I could not think of anything to say that did not sound as corny as the popcorn we were eating.

Finally, Jana opened the conversation with a sigh.

"You kind of left me holding my own hand last night, Chief."

"Well, I, uh, I wasn't sure what to do. I'm sorry. I tried to call this morning and apologize," I answered lamely. I stared down at the checkered table cloth and felt even more foolish. When I looked up, Jana was smiling at me again.

"So why did you come back?" she said simply.

I was transfixed by her face. Jana was not beautiful by "Miss America" standards, but she was no Ramona either. I just wanted to stare at her and drink her in. I did not know why I came back to see her, other than it was wildly exciting just to be around her. Perhaps it was the forbidden tree syndrome. The fact that the fruit always tastes better from the tree you are not supposed to pick from. I knew damned well I was not supposed to be picking from Jana's tree.

In fact, just being in her forest was stupid and dangerous.

"Look, Jana, let me tell you the truth. I don't know why I'm here," I blurted out. "What I do know is that I am very attracted to you. It doesn't make any sense, but ever since I first talked to you, there is some kind of pull that makes me want to be near you. That sounds silly, doesn't it?"

"I'm flattered, Chief."

It was Jana's turn to stare at the red and white squares.

"Please, my name is Rod. I'm not much of a chief, anyway; and I'd appreciate it if you would call me by my first name since my feelings toward you are not exactly professional in nature."

"What exactly are your feelings toward me, Rod?" Jana asked. "I didn't notice a lot of burning emotions last night."

I kept eating the popcorn nervously. The salt and a combination of fear and anxiety made my mouth as dry as the Mayor's last speech. I sipped the cold Pepsi to regain my courage and my voice.

"I'm physically attracted to you, Jana, it's as simple as that. I don't know you well enough to call it love. All I do know, is that I desperately want to hold you and touch you and do all those things a man should do with a beautiful woman," I confessed.

"Come on Rod, I'm well over forty and the only thing beautiful about me is what you can't see from the outside," Jana stated. Her voice had raised an octave to indicate she was also nervous.

"I'm sorry, Jana. As a matter of fact, I'm sorry I keep saying that I'm sorry. It just seems like I should be apologizing for how I feel about you," I stated.

"Look, Rod, as long as we are being honest, let me tell you something," Jana began. "I have needs, too, you know. I don't understand my feelings anymore than you do. I do know that I left a husband who cared more about his businesses than he did about me. He sure spent more time with his accountants and pulling strings for political favors with Renee Stark, or whatever he does with her, than he did with me."

"Jana, I don't…," I started.

"Let me finish," Jana requested softly. "I haven't been with a man in quite a while and, well, whatever happened last night was my fault. There's nothing to apologize for. Besides, I don't think drinking chocolate in front of the fire qualifies us for "Doctor Ruth's Sexual Adventurer's Hall of Fame'.""

"Jana, it's not what didn't happen last night that I feel bad about. It's what I would like to happen right now," I confessed.

She stared long and deep into my eyes and I took the opportunity to return the gaze. I drank her in and absorbed each nuance of her features like a sponge. Hesitatingly, I broke the silence.

"Jana, I'm married."

"I know that," she answered simply.

"But what you don't know is that I am very happily married," I admitted. "I love my wife very much. We have been together since we were in high school. That's just about forever. We've been through a lot of highs and lows. When we've been on top in our life, we have shared some terrific pleasures. And when I've fallen down in my career or whatever, Peggy has reached down and helped me up. I owe my life to her. I love her without qualification and I could never do anything to hurt her. So, if you thought I was going to give you some song and dance about "my wife doesn't understand me" or "we don't communicate anymore", you're wrong. There's absolutely nothing wrong with my marriage. Nothing that is, except that I met this witty, sexy, attractive woman at a party and I can't get her out of my mind."

"Is that it?" Jana asked curtly.

"I think that about covers my life history." The tone in my voice had as much emotion as if I had concluded a report on the average fuel consumption ratio of our police helicopters.

Jana smiled and said, "Well, in that case, let's enjoy the afternoon together, what do you say?"

Before I could answer, Beth walked into the kitchen and announced her growing hunger for something besides the popcorn that we obviously had not shared with her. Beth proposed grilling steaks out on the brick barbecue in the back yard.

"Great," Jana exclaimed. "As long as I don't have to cook 'em, it sounds like a terrific idea." She looked directly at me and said, "Beth does all of the cooking around here. The last thing I tried to make, we threw out back for the wildlife to eat. The scorched mess about wiped out the whole Kansas coyote population. The local ranchers gave me an award for my poisoned meatloaf."

We all laughed at Jana's unique predator control technique. Soon, Beth had defrosted three huge T-bone steaks using the microwave and I volunteered to build a fire in the grate of the old barbecue pit out back. I was confident I could soon have a fire roaring in the bowels of the barbecue. I had a secret weapon.

As young patrolmen on the late night shift between midnight and eight a.m., we would have impromptu weenie roasts in the vast Trinity River bottoms surrounding the West Dallas housing projects. Whenever the radio calls died down after four a.m., there was plenty of time for us to socialize with each other on the shift referred to as "Deep Nights". The weenie roasts were great morale builders and even the sergeants participated in the get togethers. After all, organization was our forte in the Dallas Police Department. We were nothing if not meticulously organized in every activity we did, from surrounding a sniper to passing out condoms at community health fairs.

A couple of officers would be designated to go to the all night Safeway store at the "Dallas West Shopping Center" and buy the "Oscar Meyer Hot Dogs", mustard and "Mrs. Baird's" home made buns. The police discount was in effect, of course; meaning that we got it all for half price.

Another squad car would cruise downtown to the Farmer's Market, which was closed late at night, and "liberate" a couple of watermelons from the stacks of produce being unloaded by the hordes of illegal aliens up from the Rio Grande border. Naturally, none of the fruit vendors admitted to being able to "speak-a-the-English". It was often difficult to find one of the wetbacks to take a dollar or two from the officers for the watermelons, but we always paid somebody something. It would not have been ethical to just take the stuff. At least, that was our "Code of the West", in West Dallas.

I called my assignment, "The Law West of Stemmons", in recognition that Stemmons Freeway was the major roadway which marked the eastern most boundary of my designated patrol area. We were very territorial and took our responsibilities for protecting our areas very seriously in those days. I still held the City of Dallas record for keeping my beat free of even one crime for a whole month on my watch. Another beat officer might tie that record sometime in the future, but no one would ever find a way to surpass the accomplishment.

My job in the weenie roast plots was always to find a suitable location along the deserted river bank and get the bonfire going. The secret to the spectacular campfires was the city issued road flares that we all carried by the case in the trunk of our squad cars. The bright flares were intended to be used at the scene of major traffic accidents to warn other motorists of lane blockages and the like. We used the hot burning devices indiscriminately, sometimes laying intricate patterns with hundreds of the blazing things at the scene of a particularly bad freeway accident. In recruit school, we all learned the art to stringing the brilliant flares across the roadway so they could be seen for miles by even the drunkest driver in Big D. The flares burned like molten steel for twenty minutes, with enough sulfurous smoke to kill all the mosquitoes within twenty miles. With their extra benefit as a pesticide, the flares made great river bottom fire starters. Using his flashlight, my partner would fight the ugly mud colored water moccasins for driftwood along the river bank while I got the fire going. An occasional pistol shot in the darkness would signal that my partner had been forced to use extreme prejudice on some slimy creature who refused to give up his perch among the brush and willow trees lining the river.

By the time the other squad cars returned from their appointed rounds with the hot dogs and watermelons, the sulfurous smoke had usually dissipated and the logs were burning on their own. The flares made a roaring fire in no time flat.

I always chose a location in the bottoms near an old railroad trestle that crossed the muddy river into the suburban city of Irving. The trestle was built around the turn of the century using huge iron girders riveted together. From the base of its ancient "I" beams, you could look north and see where the Dallas Cowboys played football in a stadium with a hole in the roof. Of course, everyone in Dallas concluded that the less than completely domed stadium had been built so God could watch "His" team play every Sunday afternoon. I guess He (or She) does not have cable tv. To the south, the glittering lights of the impressive downtown Dallas skyline blazed all night long and added to the ambiance of our otherwise culturally deprived weenie roasts.

I picked the location for another reason other than the view it afforded. It was the scene of my one big failure in my young law enforcement career.

One hot July afternoon, while I was working the evening shift, I was dispatched to a call at the trestle of a man threatening suicide from atop the sizzling iron girders. The department had just issued the beat officers brand new "Matadors" to drive. Later, the officers would refer to the cars manufactured by the American Motors Company as "Mata-dogs", due to their lack of power and propensity to break down at every critical moment.

My shiny new AMC version had all of eighty one miles on the odometer when I piloted it down the side of the river levee into the dry Johnson grass near the trestle. An ambulance and a bucket-ladder equipped fire truck was already on the scene, along with a crowd of about a hundred gawkers who had somehow appeared out of the hay fields to cheer on the elderly drunk pacing back and forth on top of the trestle. I parked my brilliant white squad car, with its spiffy new ice blue reflective police markings on the side, and tried to make some sense of the chaos around the railroad bridge.

A Santa Fe locomotive was stopped on the Irving side of the river, refusing to attempt to cross until the nut was removed from the bridge. The engineer screamed at me to do something. I called for the two officers already on the scene to keep the crowd back and asked the firemen for a briefing on the situation. They reported that the man had climbed to the top of the bridge sometime earlier and had been up there, drinking from a pint of vodka, most of the day. Someone driving home on nearby Carpenter Freeway had noticed the guy on the bridge and called 911 with his cell phone.

The man had been steadily removing his clothing under the hot Texas sun and throwing the various items, piecemeal, to the jeering crowd below. The firemen had recovered his soiled pants and his drivers license in an otherwise empty billfold that identified the star of our show as "Arthur Dale Adams", age sixty two.

The potential suicide victim was stripped down to his blue checked boxer shorts when I persuaded the firemen to hoist me up to his position in the retractable bucket they had brought on their truck. I hated heights, but we were clearly making no progress trying to shout a hundred feet into the air to entice the idiot into coming down. It was hot and getting hotter by the minute as I felt the sweat trickle down the back of my dark blue uniform shirt. When the man took out his false teeth and threw them at the crowd, I reasoned we were running out of time and something dramatic was necessary. I was comforted by the fact that, without his choppers, at least the man could not bite me if I got close enough to try to grab him.

A fireman volunteered to go with me to operate the equipment and we were soon on our way to meet Mr. Arthur Dale Adams, face to face. When the fire truck's bucket was raised to the correct position, the man just blinked at us in the bright sunlight.

"Mr. Adams, I'm Officer Starr and I'm here to help you," I said in a voice more scared than helpful. Heck, even I did not believe what I had just said and neither did Mr. Adams.

"Fuck you, you little shit. Get the fuck offa' my bridge," the sweaty man ordered.

I tried all of the psycho babble that the bored instructors had glossed over with us in the police academy to talk Mr. Adams into not killing himself. It was all useless. The standard issue Kevlar ballistic vest, under my uniform shirt, was soaking up enough heat to match the glow on Mr. Adams' nose.

"Hey, have you got anymore of that to drink?" I tried another tactic, as I pointed at the print of "Absolut" vodka the drunk was holding. "I could sure use a belt," I lied. The last thing in the world I wanted right then was a mouthful of molten potato acid burning ulcers in my throat, but I was getting desperate to build up some kind of rapport with the guy.

"You want this, you snot nosed punk, huh?" the man slurred. "You're just like that worthless kid my good for nothin' wife babies all the time. Well, she did baby 'em. That was 'afore the bitch up and left me this mornin'. Always wanting something from me and never givin' anything back, right?"

I knew I had pressed the wrong note on Mr. Adams' keyboard of emotions. If he was down to just one nerve left, I had just stomped all over it.

"You want this, piss head? Huh?" The drunk screamed and waved the clear glass bottle like a hatchet. "Here take it, like you've taken everything else in my life!"

With that, the grossly overweight man who looked oddly like a semi-nude Santa Claus without the beard, threw the bottle right at my head. I instinctively ducked and crouched to draw my pistol in response to the physical attack. I stopped at the thought of the headline, "Starr Slays Suicidal Santa". However, shooting him "would" teach the bastard to try and kill himself on my watch, I thought. Only briefly did I consider expediting matters by blowing his fat heart out in front of a hundred witnesses. No, I reasoned, bad for the department's image.

My fireman partner was not as fast in his reaction time to the thrown vodka bottle. The fireman caught the nearly empty bottle squarely in the face. The stout vodka container failed to break and it careened off the fireman's head and fell intact into the crowd below. A gash was opened over the fireman's right eye and he slumped to floor of the enclosed bucket in a daze, bleeding like a harpooned whale.

At that moment, a series of shouts from the crowd caused me to turn from the nightmare I was living atop the railroad trestle and I looked down. Below, I could see my beautiful new squad car clearly. On the roof, in big blue reflective letters so the police helicopter could identify my unit in an emergency, was my radio call sign, "545".

What was not right with the picture, however; were the flames leaping up from the underside of the car.

My mind raced to find a logical reason for the fire. Arson? Not likely with the other officers nearby. What was it the lieutenant had said in roll call about these new pollution control devices? Some kind of condenser or converter or some such thing. Something about heat. For the life of me, I could not remember the safety lecture. In any case, my Matador was engulfed in flames and the firemen were torn between continuing to assist me and their cohort in the bucket or putting out my burning car. They loyally stayed with me and their team member, who was spurting blood all over my dark blue uniform pants, and ignored the conflagration nearby.

In a flash, I decided that I had endured all of Mr. Adams I wanted. "Look, you fat son of a bitch, I'm tired of your crap. That's my brand new car on fire down there because of you and I'm in deep shit now. The damn city will probably make me reimburse them out of my paycheck until the year two thousand and fifty. If you want to kill yourself, fine. Just do it and get it over with, asshole!"

I was on a roll when I concluded with, "In fact, I don't think you have a hair on your ass, unless you jump. How tough are you, fatso, huh? Let's just see whether you're a man or not. Put up or shut up. Shit or get off the pot, 'cause I'm leaving."

With that, I started pushing buttons to lower the bucket down to the ground. At the same time, I tried to revive my fireman partner by gently nudging him with my foot. Arthur looked across the six foot space of thin air separating our bucket from his perch and started to cry. "I'll come down," was all he said.

While the fireman and I were still suspended in the bucket, Adams lay head first onto one of the sloping iron girders and began slowly sliding down the forty five degree angle on his stomach. The elderly man's sweaty body lubricated his slide and the weight of his flabby stomach only increased the velocity with which he sped down the sizzling girder. Arthur tried to brake his descent with his hands, but they were too soft and wet with perspiration to offer any effective resistance. When his body reached the point where the iron girder was bolted to the concrete support pillar, Arthur's head crashed into the iron support base that jutted out parallel with the train tracks. Arthur did a double back flip off of the trestle support and fell the final ten feet to the ground, landing with a dull thud on his back. I half expected the blood thirsty crowd to hold up Olympic scoring cards. They would probably give the poor man only two or three points for his clumsy performance.

When I finally reached the ground, Arthur Dale Adams was more than dead. His neck was broken in two places. The cause of death was officially listed on his death certificate as a suicide. Since the fireman with me remembered nothing after the vodka bottle hit him in the face, I was the only one who knew that what I said prompted Arthur to make his death dive. I never truly thought he really intended to kill himself. It seemed to me that Arthur finally decided he had milked all the sympathy and attention he was going to get from the situation and just wanted to slide down to the ground and go home to his less than understanding wife. If so, he badly misjudged the physics involved in his descent.

While I was in Dallas, I kept going back to the bridge every chance I got in the vain hope Arthur's ghost would appear and inform me that my theory was correct. But the railroad trestle incident was a long time ago and in a land far, far away from Jana Sims' back yard in Kansas. Until I meet up with poor Arthur in the after life to hear his side of the story, the incident will always haunt me. I could not help but think that I had unintentionally killed the guy because I lost my temper watching my "Mata-dog" burn to the ground.

Beth walked up behind me after I ignited a sputtering road flare under a pile of wet wood chips in the brick barbecue.

"Gosh, Chief, how are we going to cook anything in that stink?" she moaned. "You know, we usually entertain ourselves out here in the country with a "Bug Zapper" and a six pack of Coors, but I think your smoke show will top anything we've seen in years."

"Very funny, Miss Pepper Spray," I retorted. "Don't worry, the smell and the smoke will fade away soon. That is, if this wet wood will catch on fire. Don't put the meat on the grille until the flare is completely gone or else we will make a one way trip to Resthaven for a face full of dirt and six feet less in elevation, okay?"

"Hey, no problem. You're the boss when it comes to fire. I can clearly see you know what you're doing," Beth said as the wind changed and completely covered us in a stinking fog of sulfur smoke.

"Where did you get those damned things, Iraqi Army surplus?" she coughed.

"No, I brought a case with me from Dallas. We carried them in our squad cars to illuminate traffic accidents at night on the freeways. If you didn't light up the scene like a Christmas tree on those high speed arteries in Dallas, the drunks would run you over like a rusty hub cap in the road," I answered. "I tried to allocate money in our budget to buy a few cases for our troops here to improve officer safety, but the City Manager overruled me. He said we had suffered "only one" incident where a police officer was run over and killed in the department's history and we couldn't afford the flares based on that kind of minimal risk history. One dead officer is an acceptable loss to Mel, I guess."

"Do you know the difference between God and Mel Michaels?" Beth asked.

"I give up," I shrugged.

"The difference is that God knows He's not Mel Michaels. Think about it," Beth delivered the punch line and a warning that I would need to give some deeper thought to her theory; me being from Texas and slow and all.

"I get it, Beth. In fact, I'd venture to say that I've had the very same thought many, many times before," I replied.

It was not long before we were devouring the steaks, along with a baked potato for each of us which Jana had somehow managed to successfully nuke in the microwave oven. Her cooking skills equaled mine, which meant that neither of us could make Jello.

After we ate and piled the dirty plates into an antiquated twenty year old dishwasher, Beth excused herself to go upstairs to her bedroom. Looking appreciative at Beth's exit, Jana suggested she and I go outside on the porch for awhile. Despite my aversion to the cold, I would have followed Jana outside even if she had said that she was going to try sword swallowing.

My host pulled a heavy knitted blanket from a cedar chest in the living room and we were soon rocking in the front porch swing. The sun had just set and there was still a pink glow in the western sky. Every movement of her body, as she spread the blanket around us, caused an invisible wave of her perfume to wash over me. I inhaled deeply and savored the scent of the forbidden tree.

"Do me a favor, will you?" she asked.

"Just about anything, except killing Marty. I'm not ready for the penitentiary yet," I answered.

"No, a real favor," she lowered her voice.

"What is it?" I asked, not sure I really wanted to hear the question.

"If you ever decide you want to make love to someone other than your wife, promise me that you'll call me first. Okay?" Jana spoke the words matter of factly.

I was caught off guard by the boldness of the not so implied offer.

"Christ, Jana, it's not an answer of "wanting" to sleep with you. You don't understand and I'm not sure I can explain. It's all I can do to keep from dragging you inside and licking your body from head to foot right now," I admitted.

She smiled at the descriptive scene and I pressed on with my point. "It's simply a matter of I "won't". Don't you understand? I "won't", for reasons which make sense only to me, I guess. I don't know another man in the whole world who could resist you, that's for sure."

Jana pressed her soft body against mine and gave me a hug that sent me into orbit. I could feel the swell of her breasts through the blanket's fabric and my own body urged me to make up lost ground from last night's retreat.

We stayed sitting close to each other for hours and talked about everything under the sun. It was dangerous and the danger made the relationship all the more exciting. I was beginning to see what Tim David had been trying to tell me about the allure of his escapades with other women. Jana was the only "other woman" with whom I had ever been tempted to sleep with in my life and right now the temptation was very strong.

"It's late, I've got to go, Jana," I finally said. "I don't want to leave you, but I have to return to my own family. This has been fun. It's been great to tempt fate and fantasize about what could be, but I need to get back to the real world."

Upstairs, Beth was playing a classic CD of Johnny Horton singing "The Mansion You Stole". The deep, country voice made me feel suddenly very sad. Another dead musician with words in his song which cut to the quick. I produced a feeble attempt to match Johnny's bass melody.

"Don't give up your day job, Chief," Jana gave me a good natured push out of the swing to signal she was releasing me to return to reality.

"I think I already gave up honest work when I became the police chief," I quipped. "Everybody's a critic. I'll have you know I have a degree from the "College of the Singing Impaired". It's a small Catholic school dedicated to reforming tone deaf Baptists."

"I love you, Rod Starr," Jana said with no preparatory dialogue whatsoever. The line took me completely by surprise as I stood there grinning like a fool at my stupid joke on the cold porch.

"Don't say that," I snapped. "You don't know a damned thing about me other than what you've read in the newspaper and some of the stuff that we've philosophized about tonight. None of that is real. Don't give your love so quickly, Jana. Some guy will rip out your heart and stomp on it before he gives it back to you."

"Not you. I know," Jana whispered.

"Come on, Jana, get real. I'm more human than you think," I admitted. "If you knew what kind of lewd thoughts that have popped into my head during the past few hours, you'd know I'm far from being a saint."

"Okay. Go back home, Saint Starr, and come see me again sometime," Jana smiled as Johnny Horton swung into the lyrics of "All For The Love Of A Girl".

"See you later, kid," I said as I slowly rose from the warmth of her embrace and walked down the concrete steps into the misty Kansas night.

FRIDAY

CHAPTER FIVE

The new day was cold, just like the last few days, but the skies were clear and the sun was shining for a change. Gone were the heavy gray clouds and the drizzle that put a damper on everything warm and right. Pulling the car out of the garage, I reached up over the visor and retrieved my "Ray Bans". They were a Christmas present from Chad during his first year at the Naval Academy. The expensive shades were bought at the campus "Mid Store" where academy midshipmen could supposedly get good prices on such things. Somehow, I managed to keep from losing or breaking the costly sun glasses. Police work is hard on sun shades, but I made an extra effort to protect the glasses. The gold and deep green glass of the Ray Bans fit the professional uniform image for both a naval officer and a police officer. I liked the shades a lot and would not trade my pair for a whole box of the new style, neon colored wrap around plastic glasses that I saw many of my officers wearing. Other than glowing in the dark, the new style shades had no advantage whatsoever over my more traditional appearing eyewear.

I wandered through the streets of my neighborhood and saw kids lining the curbs waiting for the big yellow school buses to come by and capture them for another exciting day at junior high school. I thought of last night and decided to take the longer, scenic route to work down Maple Avenue.

Peggy was there when I arrived home from Jana's the evening before and we built a fire in the den. She was bone tired, but all excited about her day with her best friend, Carmen. I sensed, rather than knew, she was pressing a little too hard to cram more than sixty minutes into each hour. Thankfully, Peggy did not ask about my day and I was definitely not ready to volunteer any of the details.

When we had the fireplace logs glowing, Peggy and Terri played a game of "Jeopardy" on the Nintendo. As usual, I was pulled into the game for both sides as the official speller.

I was always good at spelling in school. In the first grade, I brought my first spelling test home with a "C" on it. My Mom was not happy. She made me sit down and memorize every word in the entire spelling book before I went to school the next day. The only word in the book I had trouble with was "wash". I kept wanting to insert a "r" in the middle of the word, as in "warsh". That's the way my mother's deep Texas accent pronounced it. I finally mastered the contradiction and from then on, I was a regular elementary school spelling phenom.

I remembered a southern sheriff who obviously did not have the benefit of my mom to make him study his spelling words. The highway leading north from Miami to New York City ran directly through the middle of his rural Georgia county and an enormous amount of drugs flowed up the interstate pipeline. The transit route probably would not have been so bad, but all the other problems accompanying the drug trade began to appear in his county; like the dead bodies no one could identify. It was driving up the crime rate in his sparsely populated territory and Sheriff Joe Bob was facing re-election.

The sheriff knew that he had to somehow stem the flow of drugs rolling through his county, or at least make some big catches, or else some other slow talking local boy with a G.E.D. would win the election. After noticing some catchy roadside advertisements for "Bull of the Woods" chewing tobacco, the sheriff finally came up with the idea for what would become known in Georgia law enforcement lore as simply "The Billboard".

Sheriff Joe Bob went to his county commission and asked the politicians for five hundred dollars so he could rent an empty billboard on the interstate. Like all politicians, the commissioners thought Joe Bob was nuts. But then again, the commissioners all knew Joe Bob from high school and he was their sheriff. After some short but lively discussions about whether or not Joe Bob had actually thrown five or six touchdowns in the Athen's game twenty years before, the commissioners finally decided that if Joe Bob thought he needed five hundred dollars for an empty billboard then it was good enough for them. There was obviously no one on the county commission like our city manager. They trusted Joe Bob and his word was golden.

The sheriff got his brother-in-law, Hubert, to donate a gallon of purple latex paint. The can of paint had sat gathering dust in Hubert's hardware store for years due to its color and no one would buy it anyway. Hubert also threw in a new boar bristle paint brush as a campaign contribution, which he intended to write off on his taxes.

Early the next morning, Sheriff Joe Bob went down to his newly rented billboard with his borrowed step ladder and began to paint. No one bothered to tell the sheriff that billboards were not painted anymore. Large rolls of pre-printed paper are glued and pieced together to form the colorful images we see along the highways and byways of America. The subtleties of commercial advertisement protocol did not matter to

Joe Bob. The sheriff had no intention of being colorful; except for the gaudy purple paint, of course.

When the sheriff was finished hand painting his billboard, he assigned his only two deputies to the graveled turnaround fifty yards north of the sign. Joe Bob gave explicit instructions that the deputies were to stop and search each and every vehicle which made a U-turn at the turnaround. The deputies, Ed Earl and Earl Ed (they were twins), said "yes sir" without asking any questions. When Joe Bob gave an order, they jumped; or else the former quarterback would beat the tar out of them. It was southern police personnel management at its best.

In a matter of a few hours, Ed Earl and Earl Ed had stopped a sum total of six vans, trucks and cars. From these stops, the deputies arrested ten people for transporting narcotics. They recovered two and a half tons of cocaine and over one million dollars in cash during the process. The state police were called to furnish assistance in counting to numbers that high. There may have been·a minor constitutional search and seizure problem, but Sheriff Joe Bob had plenty of publicity and law enforcement officials all over the country were calling his office to learn the secret.

Joe Bob told all the best educated police professionals in America to just rent any old empty billboard along the road and paint a few words of warning on it. The sign simply read, "Narkotiks Chek Point Ahed".

It was a bluff, of course. The rural sheriff did not have the capability or the authority to set up a real check point on an interstate highway. But when anyone saw his crude sign and decided to immediately back track to avoid the imaginary check point, the sheriff had established what the lawyers would argue was sufficient probable cause for his deputies to get very suspicious. The five hundred dollar investment and the faith of the "good 'ol boys" county commission brought their jurisdiction enough seized narcotics money to buy a whole new fleet of patrol cars and hire ten new sheriff's deputies for the next five years. Imagine how successful his trap would have been if only Joe Bob had learned to spell while he was in high school, instead of passing for all of those touchdowns. Was it six or actually maybe seven in the Athen's game?

I motored down Maple Avenue, an old two lane road stretching from the western city limits to downtown, in very light traffic. The old frame houses and small businesses that lined the pitted asphalt avenue were peaceful and quiet in the early morning sunshine. I occasionally took the Maple Avenue approach to vary my route when I was not in a hurry to get to work. It took about ten minutes longer than taking the Kellogg Expressway, due to the extra stop lights and school zones.

I avoided the route like a prostitute with running sores if it was raining. When the city's master storm drainage plan was devised during the early 1900's, someone must of spilled a cup of coffee on the section that dealt with West Maple Avenue. There were simply no street level sewer drains installed anywhere along the roadway. None. When a dog pissed on the road, Maple Avenue flooded for miles all around. After a medium size rain, cars vanished into vast pools of muddy water and were lost for days. When it really rained hard, the post office needed boats to deliver the mail. But today was a beautiful dry morning and I could still remember the smell of Jana's perfume.

The office was crowded when I arrived at work. Most of my staff were milling around, drinking coffee and relaxing before the day really began. I scored a cold Pepsi for only fifty cents from the one official Wichita City Hall soft drink machine and sat down in a big brown wooden chair in front of Suzie's outer office desk. Jack Denson was sitting in the hard chair's twin a few feet away. He had a cup of coffee in a politically correct paper cup and his chin rested on his chest.

"Jack?" I said, leaning over to look to see if he was breathing.

"Ugh," he grunted. At least he was alive. People walked by us without noticing.

"Jack, are you okay?" I asked.

"Huh? Yeah, sure," he looked up with swollen eyes and a puffy face. His razor had missed a couple of places and two pieces of tissue paper blotted small blood clots where the shave had been a little too close or shaky.

"Tough night, big guy?" I inquired.

"Yeah, I think so, I'm not sure," my Investigations Bureau Deputy Chief answered. "Some of us kinda went out celebrating the Clarence Taylor deal and I don't remember too much."

"Let me guess, Jack, you let Norman Manson take you out on the town and you spent a month with him last night. Am I right?" I said.

"That's about the sum of it, I guess. God, he's got a screwed up life but boy, can he drink. Norman got to talking about his ex-wife or wives, I don't remember which, and I was in tears," Jack answered.

"Welcome to the big city, Jack. You can't run with the big dogs if you don't get off the porch," I offered poetically.

"What the hell does that mean, Chief? Is that some new Texas saying or what?" Jack looked at me quizzically with watery red eyes.

"I'm not sure, to be honest, but my dad always said it after a night out with "Old Crow"," I confessed. "Did you know that "Old Crow" was General Grant's favorite whiskey?"

"Well, I don't think we drank any "Old Crow" last night, but we tried just about every-thing else. I'm not sure how I got home. Come to think of it, I'm not sure how I got here. Where am I? I don't feel too good. I may have to go home early," Jack admitted.

"What happened to Norman?" I asked. "Did you, like, trade him to some cab driver for taxi fare? You know you can't do that, Jack. Slavery was abolished in most states over a hundred years ago. Even Texas finally accepted it about 1970."

"What's this about slavery?" Durwood Hamilton asked as he slithered through the open door. As usual, he had his "official" National Public Radio cassette recorder, with microphone ready, hanging from a leather strap around his right shoulder. The recorder was both his uniform and his badge of office as a "journalist", which was a fancy word for muckraker.

Durwood's usual tactic was to pretend he was your friend and then get you to say something stupid or controversial. Durwood was notorious for using other news agencies as the "sources" for his stories. Last year, he had been baited by a newspaper reporter into filing a story that a female county judge was under investigation for nar-cotics violations. The print reporter told Durwood the newspaper had identified two witnesses to the judge's purchase of marijuana and cocaine from a local drug house near the high school. The newspaper reporter whined that he wanted to run the story, but his editor would not allow it because the judge was a personal friend and had set-tled the editor's divorce case for him in a very satisfactory way.

The fact that he had no corroboration of the newspaper reporter's tale did not stop Durwood. He ran the story without bothering to confirm any of the informa-tion that the reporter had told him. Of course, the whole thing was bogus. That year, Durwood won two awards from the Society of Professional Journalists for his out-standing reporting. Go figure.

"Hi, Durwood. Take a hike, Durwood," I said.

"The word around City Hall is that you are in trouble with the Manager, Chief. I just thought I would come by and give you the opportunity to set the record straight," Durwood smiled.

"Buzz off," I said, being about as creative as I cared to with the snake.

"Hmmm, sounds like my story will be awfully one sided," Durwood mused.

"Since when did your stories ever be anything but one sided?" I shot back.

"Oh, now, come on, Chief," Durwood whined. "I work for a very highly regarded news organization that is famous for its fairness in reporting."

"Wrong, Mr. Hamilton. You work for yourself in that little one room outhouse at the college. I've been there, remember? Your one saving grace is that the university somehow scratches up enough money each year to buy the franchise rights for the

National Public Radio broadcasts to give you something respectable to put on your stationery. Without that, you would be reduced to airing the ever exciting City Council meetings and reporting on doughty old professors debating the spawning habits of blue whales."

"I don't think whales spawn, Chief," Jack Denson stated as he staggered to his feet. "In any case, I'm leaving." With that definitive statement, he shuffled past Durwood and out the open doorway. Jack disappeared into the hallway to catch an elevator to his sixth floor office and hopefully rest his throbbing head before our morning mini-staff meeting.

"I don't know what you've got against me, Chief," Durwood assumed his "little boy hurt" look. His rotund belly and bald head gave him the appearance of an older "Spanky", from the "Our Gang" comedy series. Just as soon as his lips stretched into a pout, I expected Darla and Alfalfa to come in the door and suggest we put on a stage show to solve all of our problems.

"Got against you? Crap, Durwood, everybody in Wichita has something against you," I stated. "You've been fired from three radio stations in five years. Doesn't that tell you anything?"

"Police chiefs get fired, too," Durwood said with an icy tone. He set his fleshy jaw and stared a hole right through me. I tried to match his gaze to see what was behind his tiny pupils, but it was like looking into a shark's eyes.

I recalled overhearing three descriptions of Durwood from the women he met around town during his daily rounds. They were "arrogant", "liar" and "bumfuck". I added my usual "asshole" to their list.

"Good bye, Durwood," I ended the conversation and retreated into my inner office. A wise old chief in Dallas had told me to never get into a word war with someone who buys ink or cassette tapes by the box car load. In other words, you can never win with the media. They have the first, middle and last say in every argument. It is impossible to win a pissing match with a skunk. Knowing the lesson did not make me like it anymore.

I sat in the chair Peggy had given me and thought of Jana. I closed my eyes and let my mind wander for a moment. I wondered how it would feel to retire. I decided my lifetime goal in retirement was to own a fireworks stand. To have no responsibilities. No worries. No three a.m. telephone calls about someone getting hurt or shooting someone. No budget battles. No Mel Michaels. No Durwoods of the world to bother you. I found myself dreaming about laying on a patch of green Bermuda grass under a huge, old pecan tree. It was warm and the sun was shining. The golden rays bounced off the blue water of the pond. I was back home on my little twenty-two acres. My mom waved from the gravel road and called me to supper.

"Huh?" I opened my eyes and sat upright in the desk chair rocker.

"I'm sorry, Chief," it was Suzie on the intercom. "The U.S. Attorney is on line one."

"Thanks, I'll get it," I said as I punched the white blinking light on my phone console.

"Hi, George, what's going on in your world this bright and shining morning," I said with way too much cheerfulness.

"Good morning, Chief," George Ghormley said tightly. "I need to see you, if you're free." He sounded tense and I knew whatever concerns he had, it would not be to ask my opinion on the plush, new decorations which had recently been installed in his office.

"Sure, George, what's the subject?" I asked.

"Well, I'd rather not discuss it over the phone, Rod. It's something we should talk about in person," George responded ominously.

Now, I "was" worried. When the United States Attorney for the Federal District of Kansas calls you by your first name and wants to see you in person because he does not trust the Ma Bell phone lines, you are usually in for quite an experience.

"Do you want to come over here, or do you want me to come by your office?" I asked.

"It would be better if you came over here, if that's all right?" he replied.

I picked up the blue, three by five index card that Suzie had left on my desk. The typewritten card listed all of my appointments for the day. I quickly scanned the day's scheduled activities and spoke into the phone. "Sure, George, today's fine with me. I've got some time this morning. How about ten o'clock?"

"Great. See you at ten." We said good bye and I waited before I hung up the telephone receiver. I wanted to see if there were any more clicks on the line which could indicate someone listening in, but there were no strange noises. Maybe we were both getting paranoid.

"Hi, Chief," Officer Karen Teaford stood in the doorway.

"Hey, Karen, come in and tell me what you are up to," I motioned to a vacant chair in my office. Karen was a stunning blonde. Slim and tall, her golden hair was pulled up into a bun to abide by departmental uniform regulations. Karen's hair was actually very long and fell down below her shoulders when she was out of uniform. Her complexion was as smooth as a baby's butt and Karen oozed sex from every pore in her body. To top it all off, Karen was unmarried. Somehow, she had fought off every attempt to capture her heart. Karen was the only woman Pete Gant openly admitted that he had struck out with. For that reason, if no other, I liked and admired her.

"Well things are kind of slow over in School Liaison right now," Karen said. "We have most of our programs running and the new guys are learning the ropes very quickly." Karen was assigned to the section in the department that taught various public school classes on everything from drug abuse prevention to citizenship responsibilities. The primary job skill for the positions required relating to kids from the age of five to eighteen since the officers taught classes from kindergarten through high school.

"I wish things were slow over here, too," I said as I returned her smile. Karen was beautiful and she made smiling easy and natural.

"Your team has a fun job being around young people all of the time. They are so enthusiastic and full of wide eyed trust. The older I get, the harder it is to keep that youthful feeling. I've got the heart of a young boy, did you know that?"

"No, I guess I didn't, Chief," she answered.

"Yeah," I said, "I keep it in a glass jar here in my desk somewhere." I began pulling open the desk drawers as if searching for the imaginary body organ.

Karen quickly caught onto the joke and began laughing.

"Okay, okay, I get the punchline. Don't bother to actually find the autopsy jar. The reason I stopped by was to see if you knew what the dress style was for the event tonight."

I did some mental gymnastics and came up blank. "I'm sorry, Karen, but I'm not sure I know what's going on tonight."

She laughed again and showed off two rows of perfect white teeth. All of the incisors and bicuspids were in their appointed places as designed by the Creator. "Chief Pasqual called and asked me to go with him to the Crime Commission Dinner tonight and represent the School Liaison Section. He said you and your wife would be going, too."

"If Chief Pasqual said I would be going, then I must be going," I gave the appropriate respect to a former chief. "I've been to these affairs before, Karen, and they are rather formal. I usually go in a suit and tie and I think the women wear a nice dress. It's on a level which ranks somewhere between tuxedos and evening gowns and blue jeans and sneakers, although you will see people there dressed up like a game show host just to show off."

"Great," Karen said, "I was just checking to make sure I didn't need to wear my formal dress uniform."

She stood and showed off a nice figure to go with the rest of her features as she turned for the door. The uniform shirt did nothing for her smallish breasts, but the tight polyester uniform pants failed to leave much to the imagination. I could faintly see the lines of her bikini panties through the fabric of her trousers.

"Hey, how did you get stuck with Chief Pasqual as your date for tonight?" I joked.

She wrinkled her nose and looked down at me. "He is a chief, you know. Even after they retire, they keep the title. When a chief asks you to do something, you do it."

I thought of at least fifty replies to that line, but everyone of them would get me into hot water. I smiled up at her and said, "Spread that attitude around, will ya', I need the support."

She laughed and waved a white, thin hand with bright red fingernail polish, "You're doing great, Chief, you don't need any help. See you tonight."

As I watched Karen's young, sculpted body disappear around the door frame, I wondered why I had no strong, burning sexual attraction to her. Sure, Karen was beautiful. Very beautiful, in fact. There was no denying I mentally undressed her like every other adult male, and most of the wide eyed lads at the schools where she taught. My mental lust was more curiosity and fashioned in a detached sort of way. Whatever it was that caused me to instantly inflate around Jana was missing with Karen and all of the other women I knew at work.

"Chief," the intercom buzzed again, "Renee Stark is on line two and wants to speak with you," Suzie said.

"Okay, it's my morning to be popular, I guess," I said as I leaned over without looking and hit the correct button on the telephone's panel of lights in only three tries.

"Good morning, Miss Stark," I greeted the other half of the "Baby Love" duo. "I see you still have a job and haven't given up our humble public service for the bright lights of Hollywood just yet."

"Excuse me, Chief, but this is a business call," she replied in her ice maiden voice.

"Aren't they all, Renee; what's up now?" I sighed wearily.

"I've received a bill from the uniform company where you ordered three shirts and three pairs of trousers and charged it to the police department's account," Renee stated flatly.

"That's right, I did. Is there a problem?" Before I asked, I knew damned well there was a problem. I had been waiting for the conflict to come to a head for weeks.

"Chief, you know the City Manager has ruled that you and your Deputy Chiefs are not eligible for a uniform allowance. Therefore, you cannot buy police uniforms with the city's money," Renee said with authority.

"Renee, I'm gonna tell you the same thing I told the City Manager. This is bull shit! And you can quote me on that!" I got furious every time I thought about this decision of the Manager.

"Chief, you may think it's bull shit, but the Manager has made the decision and Tad Roadly supports it. Mr. Roadly is the Finance Director and he's my boss," Renee countered.

"I don't care if Mother Teresa supports the decision, it's the stupidest thing in the world to expect the police chief, and his deputy chiefs, to buy their police uniforms out of their own pockets. The rookiest police officers receive an extra five hundred dollars a year to buy their uniforms, but we're supposed to go without or buy our own. Come on, Renee, does that make sense to you?" I asked.

"It doesn't have to make sense to me," Renee admitted. "A lot of things don't make sense around here. The fact is the Manager has ruled on the issue and that's that."

"That's not "that", Renee. You name one city bigger than Mayberry R.F.D, just one, where the police chief has to buy his own uniforms and I will gladly fork over the money. Wait, come to think of it, even Andy Griffith in Mayberry got his uniforms furnished. Wichita is supposed to be an "All-American City". Remember?"

I threw a low blow with the "All American City" jab. The punch hit somewhere around Renee's knee caps. I had referenced the fact that our city had been awarded the "All American" honor last year in an annual competition which was little more than a political ass kissing contest. Nonetheless, the Mayor and City Manager made a big deal of the award as recognition for our community achieving the lofty status as a first class city. Wichita was first class, all right. It was an organization where the City Manager made the police chief buy his own gun and uniforms. As instinctively planned, the comment hit a raw nerve.

"Chief, this has nothing to do with the city's award. You owe us two hundred and sixty three dollars and thirty six cents for the uniforms," Renee demanded.

"I'll tell you what, Renee, I'll pay it, okay? But before I do, you tell Roadly or the Manager or the Pope for all I care, that in order to pay the bill I'm gonna' appear on radio and television asking the citizens to send in donations to help me financially because our goofy city manager is so cheap he can't buy uniforms for his police chief. If you think Jimmy Swaggert was pitiful crying in front of his congregation, you haven't heard anything yet," I promised.

My voice was rising in volume to match my blood pressure. "You go do that right now, Renee. When I hear back from you, I'll call the television stations and that low life, Durwood Hamilton, and we'll get your two hundred and sixty three dollars and thirty six cents taken care of right away! You do that willya' and before noon the "All American" City of Wichita, God-for-saken-Kansas, can be on CNN and every major news network between Peking and Paris."

I slammed the phone down so hard the receiver bounced out of its cradle and fell onto the floor with a loud clatter that was probably heard in Oklahoma City. Disgusted, I stood up and marched out of my office, leaving the telephone handset buzzing on the carpet. I went to the rest room without making eye contact with anyone in the office and splashed cold water in my face. Looking up, I noticed how old and tired I looked in the mirror. The gray hair was more and more noticeable. I tried "Grecian Formula", but drinking it gave me diarrhea. Peggy suggested that maybe I should read the directions on the bottle before I tried another dose.

When I returned to my office, Tim David was picking up what remained of my telephone and was attempting to put it back into working order.

"What do you want?" I demanded in a voice far too loud for the question.

"Hey, Chief, lighten up," a startled Tim replied. "It's going to be a long day and we don't want a heart attack on payday, do we?" Tim soothed the situation.

"Yeah, I guess you're right, Tim" My heart rate began to lower and I felt the pounding in my temples subside a little. "I had almost forgotten that this is Friday. T,G,I,F, I guess."

"Sure. Let's not ruin the weekend by having a really crummy Friday, huh? Things can always get worse," Tim assured me.

"I'm sorry, but, damn it, sometimes the ridiculous, petty games that go on around here drive me crazy. It is all so stupid. If the taxpayers knew how much time we spent battling bureaucratic silliness in this city, instead of working on the kinds of issues they pay us for, the citizens would launch a revolt that would make the French Revolution look like a fraternity prank," I predicted.

The thought of resurrecting the guillotine to deal with corrupt and stupid politicians temporarily satisfied my constant desire to find a way to improve the system.

"Now what?" Tim asked simply.

"I just had a nasty conversation with Renee Stark up in Finance," I admitted.

"That goofy bitch?" Tim snarled. "The last time a witch like that came to Kansas, a group of midgets got together and dropped a house on her."

I knew we could not get through a week in Kansas without some sort of reference to the "Wizard of Oz" movie. Dorothy and little Toto still lived in the hearts and minds of all true Kansans.

Tim was just warming up. "In the immortal words of Senator Edward Kennedy, speaking to Supreme Court nominee Clarence Thomas, "You should have let me take her home.""

I laughed at the horrible pun, comforted only by the fact that gallows humor is a prerequisite for police work.

"Tim, I'm required to inform you that such vulgar humor constitutes sexual harassment under the city's rules. You are hereby instructed that any future violation will result in your immediate castration," I warned.

"Ouch," Tim grimaced and clutched at his groin.

"Besides," I continued, "you had your chance to take Renee home from the "Employee's Appreciation Party". Remember?"

"How do you know that I didn't take her home from the party?" Tim smiled with that sly grin of his. "Renee has a lot to offer, you know. Maybe I could cultivate her as an informant. I might be willing to sacrifice my body for the betterment of the good old W.P.D.. Rah, Rah, Rah," Tim punched his fist into the air in an imaginary cheer.

Suzie came in and saved me from trying to follow up on the notion of Tim and Renee together. The question of who would start out on top might be worth the price of admission.

"Your wife called to remind you about the Crime Commission Dinner tonight. Peggy said to tell you she would be ready at six."

"She's a little late with the reminder, but please put it on my calendar, will you Suzie?" I asked. "The way things are going today, I'm likely to forget my name before five o'clock."

Suzie handed me my paycheck and I stuffed it into my shirt pocket without looking at the totals. The entire amount was already promised to Peggy's team of anonymous doctors in Minnesota. There might be enough for a couple of Big Mac's and fries after church on Sunday.

Jack Denson and Billy Wade walked in for our morning mini-staff meeting. As usual, Pete Gant trailed them by several minutes. Pete carried a copy of the morning newspaper under his arm like a halfback cradling a football across the goal line.

"Hey, Chief, have you seen the latest Ray Kronk article?"

Pete asked with a huge grin plastered on his face. Ray Kronk had been a Wichita newspaper writer for more than two decades. He was an institution all by himself. A legend in the minds of the simple people in our fair city who read his made up stories and believed them to be the gospel. Ray wrote a satirical column in every Friday's newspaper. It was usually witty, but could be caustic. Since it was proclaimed to be satire, Ray did not bother to keep his facts straight. It was a skill that Ray learned during his first two years as a cub reporter assigned to the police beat.

A few years earlier, Ray wrote about an imaginary crime spree at the two major shopping malls in town. He concocted the ridiculous notion that gang members were hiding under parked cars and, using razor blades, slashed the ankles of unsuspecting shoppers as they walked by. The colorful and imaginary practice was a new type of gang initiation, according to Ray's twisted scenario. Of course, it was all a "Kronk of Ray Shit". After hundreds of phone calls, letters and an official inquiry from the City Council; I was ultimately forced to call a press conference to assure the entire population of Wichita, and surrounding environs, that there had never been a single, reported incident of "ankle slashing" in the entire recorded history of the city. Except in the misfiring neurons of Ray Kronk's brain, I should have said. About half of the citizens believed me. The other half believed Ray's original story to be true. After all, Ray's story was printed on the front page of the newspaper's "Local and State" section. My denial was featured on page eighteen, nestled between the obituaries and a recipe for sweet potato pie.

"No, Pete, I haven't seen the paper this morning. What's our friend, Ray, up to today?" I asked.

What would it be this time? Venereal disease found in school cafeteria milk cartons?

"Well, he refers to the City Manager as "King Mumbles The First" and calls you the "Clown Prince of Crime Control"," Pete declared triumphantly. Pete loved to dish out bad news that did not directly involve himself. "There's a picture, if you're interested."

"No thanks, I think I will wait for the movie to come out. Great. Just what I need," I buried my face in my hands and rubbed my eyes vigorously. "Pete, do you have any good news to contribute to the cause this morning? I need to cut it rather short, since I have an appointment with the U.S. Attorney at ten," I declared.

"Nothing, Chief," Pete stated, still grinning like a lip balm salesman at an ass kissing convention.

"How about you, Billy, anything going on in the Patrol Bureau this morning?" I asked.

Billy wrote something in the notebook he always brought to the meetings and looked up at my question. "Just paper work, Chief. I've got a hundred messages on my damned e-mail machine that I haven't had the time to read. Other than that, things are relatively quiet in the field," Billy stated.

"Jack, anything in Investigations?" I asked as I continued down the line of my command staff.

Denson did not respond. He just sat hunched over in his chair and stared at his brown, wingtip shoes. They were well worn. The left shoe had a large hole in the sole that was visible because his feet were resting on their respective outer sides.

"Jack?" I inquired again in a little louder voice. "Jack...Jack!"

"Huh, oh yeah," The still numb deputy chief responded. "No, er, no, Chief, there's not much going on that's of any consequence this morning. Everybody knows Taylor is gone and we're just trying to pick up the pieces and move on."

"Jesus Christ, Jack, what happened to you?" Billy asked as he blinked, owl-like, behind his perpetually broken glasses.

"You look like you tried to shave with a power sander." Tim David said as he made electrical whirring noises in the background.

"He let Norman Manson take him out drinking last night," I answered for my semi-conscious deputy chief.

"Damn, son," Pete seemed genuinely sympathetic. "That boy Manson is way out of your league in the great world of power drinkers. You better stick to some of the more amateur drinking detectives up in your bureau if you need companionship. Those professional alcoholics will kill you flyweights every time."

With that comment, I brought the brief meeting to a close and put on my coat for the short walk across the street to the Federal Courthouse. The miniature grandfather clock on my wall chimed ten times. I was late already. The clock had been a reverse graduation present from the first recruit class who went through the Police Academy in Dallas with me as their commander. The dark oak wood and burnished gold metal trim on the time piece made a very attractive wall ornament. The class members got together and bought me the clock to insure that I would remember them everyday and I did. On a brass plate affixed to the front of the clock, the newly commissioned police officers inscribed their class number and their class motto, "Starr's First". It made me proud to think of them whenever the clock chimed. I hoped each one was doing well in the city I had left behind. It often bothered me that they might think I had run out on them. I rationalized my escape from Dallas as similar to the last man out of the Alamo. I knew when I could not win the battle there and I bailed out, landing in Oz with some very strange creatures.

By the time I walked across Main Street and made my way past the metal detectors and security guards in the courthouse lobby, it was ten minutes after my scheduled meeting time. I hated to be late and seldom put myself in the predicament. I apologized to the U.S. Attorney's receptionist, safely entrenched inside a bullet proof glass vestibule, and took a seat in the small lobby. I was leafing through the latest edition of "Money Magazine" when the door behind me buzzed. The receptionist used the electric lock to open the reinforced steel door, covered in a layer of teakwood, and invited me inside the inner workings of the federal prosecutor's office.

George Ghormley met me as soon as I passed through the security door. He greeted me with a strong handshake and an arm around my shoulder.

"Thanks for coming over Chief, let's go back to my office," he offered.

The U.S. Attorney was a man of about fifty, whose thinning brown hair was having a difficult time covering what would soon be a completely bald head. His tall, athletic build exuded confidence. Despite being a political appointee, I knew George to be scrupulously honest. Furthermore, he was sensitive and understanding of the often difficult position I found myself in when dealing with my own local politicians.

When we were alone inside his office, George closed the door behind us and offered me a seat in one of the elegant old style leather chairs in front of his desk. Every piece of furniture in the room was heavy and expensive. Thinking of the decrepit plastic chairs in my own office and having to furnish my own personal chair to sit in, I envied George's position with the federal government.

"Chief, how about some coffee?" George offered.

"Thank you, sir. I don't usually drink coffee, but I think I would like something to warm me up this morning. Let me cut it with a lot of sugar and cream, if you don't mind?" Actually, I was hoping the caffeine and sugar would make me more alert for whatever bombshell George was planning to drop on me in the next few minutes.

We fixed ourselves a cup of coffee from a sterling silver serving set positioned on his ornate desk. The cups appeared to be real china. I doubted if I would know real china when I saw it. At least they were not made of plastic or paper; that much I did know. When we settled into chairs facing each other, George got right to the point.

"Rod, I need to ask you some questions that might involve matters which could be a federal crime. Is that all right?" the U.S. Attorney asked in an official tone.

I gulped and wondered if I had misplaced a decimal point on my income tax return. "Sure George, crime control is my job, remember? Didn't you read the paper this morning?"

He smiled weakly and stirred his coffee. "Rod, let's talk about the city's "Narcotics Seizure Fund"."

I puffed my cheeks with air and blew a big sigh of relief. "I'd be glad to speak with you about the narc seizure account, George," I said. "It's an unholy mess and I'm very uncomfortable with it."

Due to legislation at both the state and federal level, cities had been granted the authority to confiscate cash and property believed to be connected to the burgeoning drug trade. The laws were designed to further punish those involved in the sale and distribution of narcotics in the government's continuing "War on Drugs". As a side benefit, cities were allowed to use the seized money and the actual property, or the proceeds from the sale of the seized property, to enhance any legitimate law enforcement operations in their jurisdiction.

By federal law, cities were not allowed to supplant or replace their regular police budgets with the funds, only improve their law enforcement operations. In addition, the dollars were required to be used for law enforcement purposes only. That way, local politicians were prevented from taking the money and using the funds for things other than law enforcement. In practically every city in America, the police chief controlled the distribution of the monies and insured that it met the stringent federal guidelines in place to control the expenditures. Every city in America, that is, except Wichita, Kansas. In our town, the City Manager personally controlled the "Narcotics Seizure Fund", just like he did everything else in city government; down to the smallest detail.

Early in my tenure as police chief, I attended a special training session on the intricacies of the seizure fund regulations at the FBI National Academy in Quantico, Virginia. I was shocked to find that Mel was violating just about every major aspect of the laws which established the authority for narc seizure monies, in both spirit and principle. The U.S. Congress intended for the chief law enforcement officer in each city to oversee the legal confiscation process and decide how the funds were to be spent, within the requirements of the law. In Wichita, the City Manager put the monies in various special accounts set up by Finance Director Tad Roadly and spent the money as he saw fit. If I wanted to use a portion of the seized funds to purchase a piece of safety equipment for the police department, for example; I had to request that Mel release some of the money. Generally, my request was never answered, much less approved.

As the funds in the special accounts grew in size each year, Mel raked in the interest money and it disappeared. Where the considerable interest accruals went, no one knew. We were not talking small change. As best as I could estimate, our "Narcotics Seizure Fund" easily exceeded one million dollars. I based my estimates on adding the total of drug assets our hard working detectives had confiscated and deposited in the city's account.

In the larger cities around the country, the funds grew easily to tens of millions of dollars. As the size of the cash hoard grew, the temptation to pilfer from it rose in proportion. Even police chiefs in other cities had fallen victim to the lure of vast amounts of cash at their instant control and ran afoul of the law. The ex-chief in Detroit served time in a federal penitentiary for allegedly embezzling several million dollars from his department's "Narcotics Seizure Fund" and funneling it to his personal bank account. His civilian Finance Director allegedly fled to Tahiti, or someplace where there was no extradition treaty, with several trunk loads of large denomination greenbacks and his underwear stuffed with gold bars. For this reason, the Feds watch the cities closely to insure that everything is on the up and up.

Within the last year, Mel had become more and more bold in withdrawing large amounts from the fund. I warned him repeatedly that what he was doing appeared illegal, based on my training at Quantico. In fact, I sent the Manager a highly confidential and blunt memo informing him in no uncertain terms that if he persisted in violating the law he would find himself trying to protect his anal opening in a federal prison.

In response, Mel directed the City Attorney to draft a new city policy giving the police chief the overall "responsibility" for the "Narcotics Seizure Fund". In other words, I had the official statutory responsibility but no authority to prevent my boss, the City Manager, from looting the fund and using the money as he saw fit. It was a neat piece of political smoke and mirrors.

Since the City Manager had officially given me the responsibility via his policy, I tried to turn the tables and called the Department of Justice in Washington, D.C.. In a series of telephone calls and letters, I briefly outlined some of the problems I perceived in the administration of Wichita's seizure fund. That had been over a year ago. Nothing had changed.

Each year, an outside accounting firm was required by federal law to audit the fund. Each year, I carefully listed what I knew constituted violations of the regulations pertaining to how the monies were to be used and sent an official letter with the list of violations to the auditing firm. The letters were never acknowledged and still nothing had changed, but I had not forgotten the problem.

"Chief, before we begin, I want you to know the Department of Justice has asked me to look into what might be, how should we say, "irregularities" in the fund. In other words, this is an official investigation. Do you understand?" George advised.

"Yes, I understand, George. I guess someone finally read one of my letters in Washington. Do "you" understand that my assisting the D.O.J. will probably cost me my job?" I asked.

"Yes, I'm afraid I do, Rod. You should know that even if you do help me piece together what has been going on over at City Hall, I can't protect you in any way. In fact, Washington may ultimately determine there's not enough evidence to warrant a criminal prosecution or they may decide they do not want to pursue the matter for political reasons. I just want to make sure you understand what you are getting yourself into," George said solemnly.

"Well, George, when I took the oath of office, I swore to protect the constitution and uphold the law of the land. I know it sounds kinda corny, but I took that oath seriously. I've worn a badge since the day I turned twenty one. The job and the oath is sacred to me. I admit that when I pinned these gold stars on my collar, I did not know what went on behind the scenes here in Wichita. I guess, in retrospect, I was a little naive. Nonetheless, I intend to uphold the law until someone releases me from that oath or I die trying," I pledged.

George looked at me for a long moment, as if to assure himself that I really meant what I said. I did. A slight nod of his head told me he was able to detect my sincerity and my determination to do what was right.

"Okay, let's get started," George said with no fanfare whatsoever.

With that, we began what turned into an all day marathon session. I called my office and asked Suzie to re-schedule all of my appointments for the day. I also instructed her to unlock the confidential file drawer of my desk, since she had the only extra key, and bring me all of the brown folders inside the special drawer. The files contained every scrap of information about the "Narcotics Seizure Fund" since my first days in Wichita. She soon personally delivered the files to me in the U.S. Attorney's Office, carrying them in a large white cardboard box, and did not ask any questions.

George and I spread the contents of the box across the floor of his office. The files contained fan fold computer printouts of fund disbursements going back six years, copies of my warnings to Mel, copies of my audit reports and a myriad of other pertinent documents. I also had cassette tapes of my telephone conversations with the Department of Justice officials in Washington, which we played on a small recorder on George's desk. The facts were all there and they were disturbingly ugly, especially if you were a member of the Mel Michael's fan club.

George sent his secretary to bring us lunch as we continued to pour over the computer printouts and other incriminating documents. We worked through the noon hour, munching tuna salad sandwiches, and late into the afternoon. Occasionally, George would ask questions or make notes in a blue leather notebook, but mainly he encouraged me to tell the story from start to finish. At each important point, I supported my suspicions with a piece of documentation or correspondence. It was close to four o'clock when I finally approached the end of the files.

"Here's one of the last disbursements from the fund ordered by the City Manager. It's one of my favorites. See here on the printout where there is a forty five thousand dollar withdrawal?" I pointed to a spot on the green and white, alternately lined paper.

"I see it. How was the money used?" George asked.

"Well, here are the follow-up copies of the e-mail traffic when I instructed our police Fiscal Affairs Section clerk to determine where the money went," I replied.

"Okay, so what did she find out?" George asked with a mixture of excitement and impatience in his voice.

"He, George, He. Not all clerks are women, you know," I chided.

"Okay, "Mr. Political Correctness", you got me, so what did "he" find out?" George demanded.

I smiled and handed him a copy of the City Manager's reply to our official inquiry, which had been routed through Tad Roadly's Finance Department office.

"The Manager claimed he used the $45,000 to pay for vehicle liability insurance on our police cars," I said triumphantly.

"So? What's the big deal about that?" George asked. "Expenditures for police cars and their continuing upkeep could be a legitimate use of the funds, if there wasn't previous budgetary support for the expense."

"Don't you get it, George? Forget "previous budgetary support" on this one. That's a small potatoes violation compared to what I think happened," I declared.

The vacant look on the U.S. Attorney's face told me he still did not comprehend what I was trying to tell him.

"Listen, Wichita is like most other major cities. It is self insured," I pointed out. "The city has a catastrophic insurance policy with Lloyds of London for all of the city's routine operations. The deductible is such that the insurance only pays off if there is an earthquake or another type of horrendous disaster where the loss exceeds several million dollars.

"Like the floods in the Midwest last year," George ventured.

"Exactly," I smiled. "Catastrophic coverage is the only type of insurance the city purchases. The governing body figures that they can always raise taxes to meet any minor emergencies, so why pay the extra money for insurance premiums. The city doesn't buy liability insurance for any of their vehicles. None. When there is a minor fender bender, the city pays for the damage and settles any claims from a special budgetary line item in the overall general fund. In the long run, it's cheaper for cities to operate this way. There are no, repeat, no liability insurance policies for our police cars."

"Well, where did the money go?" George asked.

"That, my friend, I couldn't tell you," I admitted. "All I know is that the manager withdrew forty-five thousand genuine, American dollars out of the "Narcotic Seizure Fund" and where it went from there is anybody's guess."

The United States Attorney for the Federal District of Kansas slowly stood and walked across to his window. George stretched his cramped muscles as he looked over the horde of early escaping Friday afternoon office workers. He continued to stare for long minutes in complete silence while I held my breath. Shaking his head as he held both sides of the window frame in his outstretched hands, George finally spoke in a measured sigh.

"Whew. I don't know, Rod. If he's this clever, the City Manager might be able to convince a grand jury that all these shady accounting methods are just his poor interpretation of the complicated federal guidelines and regulations. Unless we can catch Michaels diverting the money into his own pocket, then all we have here is something for which he could receive an administrative wrist slap and be sent on his merry way."

"I know, I know," he held up his hand to silence my next comment. "It stinks like crap, but I have to catch him with shit under his fingernails before I can nail him."

"I know, George," I reasoned. "We don't have that kind of proof. I haven't initiated a criminal investigation on my own city manager. I may be so tough that I trim my pubic hair with a lawn mower, but I'm not stupid. Police chiefs who launch criminal investigations on their bosses, without catching them with their dick in their hand in front of fifty witnesses, usually don't last long. Know what I mean?"

"Yes, I'm afraid I do," George acknowledged. "I wish there was something I could do to protect you."

"The only thing you can do is nail the bastard if he whacks me," I offered. "And, even with all this evidence, you will have your work cut out for you. The Manager is not completely stupid. He seldom does anything himself and only directs other people to carry out his orders. He is a master at claiming someone else screwed up or didn't understand his directions clearly if there is any heat. They don't call him "Mister Teflon" for no reason. Nothing sticks to him. He is so slick he can walk through a car wash and not get wet."

"Okay, Chief," George turned to face me, the outline of his body highlighted in the sinking sun's rays pouring through the office window. "I'll call Washington and brief them on what we've got at this point. I will need the Attorney General's approval before I take any additional steps."

"What kind of steps would you do next, assuming you get the approval?" I asked.

"Well, first, the Internal Revenue boys would be brought into the picture to determine what kind of income the Manager has been reporting on his tax forms and the type of personal bank accounts he has opened. Next, we would subpoena all of the city's financial records on the "Narcotics Seizure Fund" and bring in the number crunchers from the General Accounting Office to see what they could find. From there, we…"

"Okay, George, I get the idea. In other words, the investigation would the usual federal bureaucratic mess and the media would be all over it like stink on shit. Is that right?" I asked.

"You've got it," the U.S. Attorney answered with a nod of his chin.

"Either way we go, it does not foretell a rosy outcome for my career. What city would hire a former police chief who turned in his boss to the Feds?" I asked.

"I don't know, Rod," my friend answered vaguely, although we both knew the answer to my question.

"I don't know, either, George." I stood up and began placing the scattered papers back into the cardboard box Suzie had delivered. "I guess I'd better be going now. That's about all I have to contribute to the noble cause of justice today." My facetious comment did not stop George's legal mind from continuing to churn.

"Do you want to leave these documents with me for safekeeping?" George asked.

"No offense, George, but I wouldn't trust J. Edgar Hoover with this stuff. In fact, I particularly wouldn't trust J. Edgar." We both smiled at my reference to the dead FBI Director's tarnished reputation as a cross dresser in high heels and lipstick.

"Have you heard the latest about J. Edgar?" I asked. "They finally discovered the "J" in his name really stood for "Jane"."

"Oh, really?" George answered acidly. Like most federal employees and even the political appointees, the U.S. Attorney was sensitive to any criticism of an American icon like Hoover. Most Feds half expected the iron willed former director to rise up from the grave some day and be extremely pissed off. Just in case Hoover did solve the problem of how to come back from the dead, people in government service still feared his notorious power. Some also still feared the secret files and compromising photographs he allegedly maintained on his enemies.

"It's just a joke, George, lighten up," I chided.

"I'm glad to see you haven't lost your sense of humor. Something tells me you are going to need it when all of that comes out." He waved at the mound of paper accumulating in my own personal "Pandora's Box".

When I finished my re-packing chore, George and I shook hands again and I thanked him for his interest. I meant it. It felt good to tell George about the details of what I suspected was just the tip of a very corrupt iceberg. I would feel a lot better when I turned over my box of evidence to a federal grand jury. At least someone else could lay awake at night worrying about what it all meant and where it would end. My ulcers would love the company.

By the time I reached City Hall, it was approaching five o'clock and I decided not to return to my office. I found my car in the parking lot and locked the potential evidence in my trunk. I had just enough time to drive home and get changed for the "Crime Commission Dinner". Peggy's message said she would be ready at six, but she was not home when I walked through the door twenty minutes later.

The hot shower felt good. I normally do not like hot water, but the constant cold of the week seemed to chill me right to the bone. I was ready for anything which would warm me up. Just as the shampoo started to run down into my eyes, the glass shower door opened and revealed Peggy in her birthday suit.

"Excuse me, ma'am, but this stall is taken," I spewed as I spit water and soap against the tile wall. The steam of the hot shower boiled around Peggy's pale body like an ethereal fog.

"Tough," Peggy ordered. "Move over, big boy."

"I love it when a woman knows what she wants and just takes charge," I said. "Why is it that we only seem to meet in the bath room?"

"That's simple," Peggy answered as she began soaping my chest. "I schedule my other boy friends based on the different rooms in the house. Since my surgery has kinda scrambled my memory a little, I need a system you know. The process is really very easy to remember. Let's see, there's Starr in the shower, Greg in the garage, Ken in the kitchen, Duane in the den…"

"Okay, okay, I get the picture," I moaned. "Bring this discussion a little closer and let's see if we can't get something straight between us."

* * *

The ride to the hotel was short. The Airport Hilton was within five miles of our home and it touted a spectacular ballroom for the type of formal affair mandated by the Crime Commission. It was strange to see airplanes flying so close over our heads, as the crowd of overdressed women and their escorts assembled in the parking lot before going inside. Peggy and I joined the group and slowly made our way to the entrance where a young man in a white tuxedo was checking names against the official guest list.

"I'll take a cheeseburger, an order of fries and a strawberry shake. The little lady here will have a live calf, no butter please," I told the doorman with my best straight face. He looked up from his clipboard with a frown, until he recognized my face from seeing it too damned often in the newspaper.

The change in attitude was instantaneous.

"We still have your order from last year, Chief. Hello, Mrs. Starr," he smiled and nodded to Peggy. "Please go in and enjoy the party. We have a great evening prepared."

As I walked by, I leaned over and whispered in his ear, "This guy behind me is an impostor. Make him show you his identification." I jerked my thumb over my shoulder at the Lieutenant Governor of the State of Kansas.

Inside the glittering ballroom, I caught a good look at my wife. Peggy was wearing a clingy red silk dress which fell just above her knees, a wide black belt and matching shoes. She insisted on wearing a bra, although I often tried to convince her that she should show off her prominent nipples. Peggy's hair was short, but covered most of her surgical scars. She combed her bangs downward onto her forehead to hide the most noticeable signs of the last craniotomy. Her red lipstick matched the dress and the after sex glow was resplendent on her cheeks.

"You know, you're not a bad looking old hide when you get cleaned up," I leered.

"Thanks. You have promise, too. I suggest you take more showers," Peggy replied. "Nice suit. Who picked it out for you?"

"I'll have you know that I dressed myself, except for my underwear. I think someone put my girdle on backwards," I imitated a tug at what would be my panty line.

For a brief moment, I thought I saw Jana Sims in the crowd and panic set in. The woman turned and I could see that her small chest was no match for the real Jana. I breathed a sigh of relief and relaxed. I was not ready to deal with introducing my wife to the target of my illicit lust. I was not sure exactly how to tell my wife that not only was I having repeated lewd thoughts about another woman, but I had intentionally lingered long enough to be aroused by her haunting perfume.

We gazed around the ballroom at all the pomp and circumstance present in Wichita's version of "Lifestyles of the Rich and Famous".

"Are you going to miss all of this?" I asked Peggy while we were still winding our way through the crowd.

"Why? Do you know something I don't know?" Peggy asked over her shoulder.

"No, I'm just not planning on being the police chief forever, you know. Remember, we're going home to Texas in six years to retire," I reminded her.

"Yes, I think I will miss it," Peggy stopped and turned to face me. "It's kind of overwhelming sometimes. We have definitely come a long way from Paschal High School, haven't we?"

"Yeah, that's a fact. And to think, your typing teacher didn't believe we would ever amount to much. Boy, was she wrong. We have a dozen secretaries to do all of our typing now and her technology has been practically wiped out by computers and word processors. Funny how the world changes," I reminisced.

"Hello, how are you this evening?" a tall, skinny woman with dish water gray hair greeted us. "I'm Judy Cole."

Peggy looked blank. I quickly stepped up and salvaged the situation like a shortstop fielding a carom off the pitcher's leg. "Peggy, you remember the mayor's wife. How are you this evening, Mrs. Cole? Where is "His Honor" tonight? Surely, he didn't abandon you already?"

The mayor's spouse just smiled and said, "Oh, he's off shaking hands somewhere."

The huge room was filling fast. People mingled and the conversation was light and varied. Peggy and I managed to excuse ourselves from the doughty Mrs. Cole. She reminded me of one of the underfed greyhounds at the new dog track north of town. I could almost see her ribs poking through the eight hundred dollar evening dress she was wearing.

"Hello, Peggy," the voice came from behind us, "Who's this handsome devil you brought in with you?"

Our District Attorney, Dora Davenport, was decked out like a Rose Bowl parade float. The sequin studded dress Dora was wearing glittered with every movement of her body. Dora was fighting the battle of the bulge in just about every area. She had won a few minor skirmishes, but the final end to the war was never in doubt. Luckily, Dora was good friends with the elective surgery staff at Wesley Hospital. They tucked and lipo-suctioned her on a regular basis, probably in exchange for past favors, so she could keep pace with Father Time's assault on her mortality.

"Hello, Dora, love your dress," Peggy sounded enthusiastic. I smiled and tried to peer through the glare of the flashing sequins, searching for any breast enlargement scars on Dora's partially naked chest. The plunging neckline hid just the right amount of flesh and tantalized the male curiosity. Suddenly I realized that I, and the bus boys, were probably the only men in the room that had not actually viewed all of Dora's tits in real life. On second thought, I was not completely certain about the bus boys.

We stood around for awhile and various people came by and introduced them-selves or just waved from across the room. I met an insurance salesman who was on the Crime Commission and seemed very knowledgeable about the police department. He was certainly a nice guy. Not like most insurance agents whose usual first question was "So, how much protection do you have?" I always wanted to pull two condoms out of my pocket and say, "Twice in one night is about all I'm good for these days."

The insurance guy sold only highly specialized aviation insurance from a large office near the airport. Since I hated to fly almost as much as I hated politicians, it was unlikely he would ever feel the need to promote his services to cover my Lear Jet. The salesman expressed a genuine appreciation for my efforts and was obviously interested in police work. From his questions, it was obvious he simply did not understand the personality necessary to be a police officer and that was what really fascinated him.

How could I describe what it was like for an officer to be bored one minute and frightened to death in the next? The absolute elation of making a good catch and the utter futility of seeing the guilty bastard walk out of the courtroom a free man because of some technicality? The desire to do good, when all around you was bad? The obscen-ity of the continuing radio calls for minor types of police service, while you held the hand of a dying friend wearing the same uniform that you wore.

I could not explain those kind of emotions to my new friend from the insurance business. The truth was that I could not explain them to myself.

While the insurance agent and I talked, I noticed Victor Pasqual lurking around the fringes of the room. The former chief stared at me constantly. I tried to catch a glimpse of Karen Teaford, since she said she was attending the dinner with Victor, but the stately blonde officer was untraceable in the glittering crowd. I was about to march over and offer the retired chief a color photo with my autograph, when Peggy noticed his odd behavior too.

"Have you noticed Victor Pasqual tonight?" she asked.

"Yeah, I think he wants to drag you into the shower and show you his retirement badge," I answered. "Let's go out in the foyer. We can jump on him and beat the crap outta' him if he tries to follow us. What do you say?"

"Sounds like a winner to me, let's go," my wife agreed. She was always game for a good fight.

We wound our way through the crowd, picking up a Pepsi for me and a small glass of white wine for Peggy from the beverage tray by the door. We found a couple of very comfortable chairs in the spacious hall and sat across from each other to enjoy our own company for a change. A heavy set woman walked by carrying a tall champagne glass in one hand and a wad of cheese balls squeezed into the pudgy fingers of her other hand. The woman's dress was a multicolored design of black and pink flowers.

"Someone check to see if there is a naked sofa around here," I called out to no one in particular in the almost vacant hallway. Peggy gave me one of those wicked looks of hers that would cause paint to dry faster.

"Well, it's apparent to a trained detective like me that she, no doubt, stole the material for her dress from a set of seat covers off a sixty-three Chevy Impala. We once owned an Impala, remember? I'm not sure about the seat covers, though," I declared.

"Do you love me?" Peggy asked, completely out of context with our conversation about the fat woman with the upholstery fabric for a dress.

"What? Of course not, I just keep you around for your incredible body, dear," I lied playfully.

"It's not much of a body, anymore," Peggy looked down at her stomach and legs.

"I'm no prize, either, kid. I think I'm shrinking," I countered, glancing down at my crotch. "But remember what my dad always taught me. It's not the size of the dog in the fight, it's the size of the fight in the dog."

Peggy smiled at my old joke. She had heard it at least ten thousand times in the last twenty five years. Peggy always smiled at my jokes. That, and for about a hundred other reasons, was why I really did love her. I was just never good at telling her how much I loved her. It always angered me when people professed their love so freely. For me, love comes too hard to give away frivolously and it hurts too bad when you lose someone or something that you truly love.

It was almost eight o'clock before the dinner was served. Peggy and I found our appointed table and managed to slide into place just before the emcee opened the evening's program. As we munched our prime rib and baked potato, we heard Chick Benson explain the history of the Crime Commission and its role in saving Wichita from the evil clutches of the Mafia and every other menace of society known to man.

Chick was a buffoon. He had once been a member of the police department as one of Victor Pasqual's deputy chiefs. As such, Chick kissed enough ass and knew where enough bodies were buried to weasel his way into a salaried position as the "Executive Director" of the Crime Commission when he reached the police department's mandatory retirement age. Chick was forever causing trouble and, like so many others I knew, would lie when the truth would be just as good. He was completely untrustworthy and without scruples. I avoided Chick like he was the last known carrier of small pox in the world. In fact, I could not stand the oily prick. The feeling was mutual.

The commission itself was simply a group of honest citizens. It had been formed in response to the wave of police corruption, political graft and organized crime that swept the country in the wake of prohibition during the 1920's. Midwestern cities like Chicago, St. Louis and Kansas City became notorious for the type of gangsterism that dominated the times. Since World War II, the Wichita Crime Commission rarely dealt with any significant issues. Professionally trained police chiefs took the place of political appointees and the citizen watchdog role, which was the commission's original intent, became unnecessary. To be sure, the members were powerful local businessmen and influential people, one and all. However, what we needed most was a commission to oversee the politicians, not the police department.

Chick droned on and on into the night. Chick thought he was funny and he dearly loved to hear his own voice. I spied the Mayor and his plain looking wife at a nearby table. "His Honor" was dozing off and had placed his hands under his chin, resting his elbows on the table, to inconspicuously support his sleepy head.

I leaned over to my new friend, the aviation insurance salesman, and whispered, " You know, Chick's voice has been tested by our forensic laboratory?"

"Oh, really?" he said seriously.

"Yeah, we found that it puts homosexuals to sleep," I said as I pointed to the Mayor, who chose that precise moment to let loose a subdued snore from the precarious perch on his interlocked fingers.

The evening wore on with various members of the commission patting themselves on the back for real or imagined contributions to the betterment of mankind. Mercifully, Chick finally rang down the curtain just before ten o'clock. I guessed the Mayor had worked his way through three different dreams before the finish. He obviously had a great deal of imagination. The puddle of drool under his chin was testament to what an exciting night it had been for "His Honor".

The room emptied quickly. Peggy and I were in the first wave to reach the door. Walking through the hotel lobby, I heard the familiar strains of Elvis' "Are You Lonesome Tonight." The "King" of rock and roll was questioning my carnal desires from the hotel lounge. Actually, it was just his voice on a CD. I accepted the fact that Elvis was actually dead, otherwise; why in the world would he be caught alive in Wichita?

"Let's see what's going on in there," I urged Peggy. To emphasize my desire, I steered her elbow into making a left turn toward the lounge down the hall.

"Okay, but let's not stay too long. I told Carmen we would pick up Terri around eleven," Peggy said with resignation since the decision had already been made. She was not a night owl anyway. With a half a glass of white wine, I figured that Peggy was only good for another hour of consciousness. Maybe two hours, tops.

The colorful poster on the marquee outside the hotel lounge read, "Friday's Fifties Fun". Inside, a dee jay dressed in a pink coat with black trim, white and brown saddle shoes and black plastic sun glasses was sorting through a stack of compact disks to find a requested song. There were few people inside and it was dark, except for a super nova intensity strobe light flaring like nuclear warheads exploding on the far side of the sun. The lack of formality was my kind of place and we were drawn inside.

I heard Tim David's soft Kansas drawl come from a darkened booth just inside the doorway.

"Well, howdy, Chief. You come in for some oldies and goodies?" Tim asked.

"Hey, Tim, fancy meeting you here." Tim had his wife, Sandra, with him. "Peggy, you know Sandra and Tim David, I'm sure," I offered. We had been together with the David's many times before in the last six years, but with Peggy's memory loss I could never be sure what was there and what had been wiped clean by the surgeon's scalpel and mega doses of radiation.

"Of course I do," Peggy looked at me as if I had just dropped out of the sky. "Did ya'll just sneak in from the dinner or have you been here for a while?" Peggy shifted into her West Texas accent.

"We snuck out a little early," Sandra said as she wrinkled her cute nose.

"Actually, I got tired of that damned Chick Benson," Tim admitted. "I had to listen to the fool when he was a deputy chief, but there's only so much of him I can accept as the price to eat an overcooked prime rib for free." We all laughed heartily at Tim's cost analysis of a Chick Benson meal. Peggy and I joined the David's in their booth by sliding across the imitation leather seat on the opposite side of the table from our hosts.

Soon, the bar began filling with the bored leftover attendees from the Crime Commission dinner. We enjoyed the music and I ordered two Seven-Ups for Peggy and I. She did not want any more wine and, as usual, I had no desire for alcohol. Since neither Tim nor Sandra drank, we had a non-alcoholic beverage party going on our side of the room. The lack of liquid spirits did not keep us from having fun tapping our feet to the music and arguing about rock and roll trivia.

"Are you sure about that?" Tim looked at me suspiciously.

"I'm telling you, it's a fact. The guy that wrote "Palisades Park" is the same goofy fool that hosted the old "Gong Show". He was the Chick Benson of afternoon game shows on television. His name is Chuck Barris," I argued.

"Bull. I don't believe it," Tim said. He gave me one of his patented searching looks trying to determine if I was pulling his leg. "How do you know Chuck Barris wrote "Palisades Park?"

"Because I answered a disturbance call at Connie Francis' house in North Dallas once and Chuck was there. It's the truth, Connie told me so herself. Surely you don't think Connie Francis would lie?" I challenged.

"Come on baby, I can't win arguing with a guy who has the complete collection of Bobby Vee's greatest hits. Both of them," Tim said as he turned to Sandra. "Let's see if you still remember how to move that cute tail of yours."

The dee jay was playing the Platters' big hit, "Smoke Gets In Your Eyes". Tim and Sandra were soon showing off on the dance floor. It was obvious they both had been the recipients of professional dance lessons. I did not know there could be that many moves to a slow song. Peggy and I watched them in complete amazement. Tim and Sandra appeared to be a most perfect couple. I glanced around the room and assured myself there was not a single picture of George Washington hanging on the lounge walls to remind Tim of his "angel" in the yellow rain coat and their wild night in the school library.

"How are you tonight, Chief?" the stranger asked as he walked to our table from the darkness. He had slipped up on my blind side while we were intently watching Tim and Sandra. My instincts were not what they used to be. If the man had been a Libyan terrorist or a Democrat, I would have been dead.

"Oh, hi," I stammered. He held out his hand and introduced himself.

"Will Mason, I work here at the hotel," he said.

"Mr. Mason, this is my wife, Peggy," I offered.

"Glad to meet you, ma'am. I don't mean to interrupt your evening. I just wanted to stop by and tell you what a great job we all think you're doing here in Wichita. If there's anything you need tonight, please let me know. We're glad to have you and hope you don't plan on returning to Dallas anytime soon," Will said with a serious look on his face.

I was always taken aback by the obviously sincere comments from people like our new friend. I developed a standard line which seemed to fit every occasion.

"Mr. Mason, we love the people here in Wichita. They've had four different police chiefs back in Dallas since I left. I don't have any desire to go back to Big D, unless it's to make a comeback with the Cowboys."

We all laughed and the club manager made his exit, melting back into the crowd.

"You know, Rod, the people in this town really do like you," Peggy said.

"Sure, they all like you until someone tells them otherwise," my cynical side responded. "These people don't care who their police chief is just as long as he doesn't show up on the six o'clock news too often. Besides, you see things with a biased eye, my ever loyal and "Stand By Me" wife."

"Maybe," Peggy replied," but it seems to me that people come out of the woodwork all the time just to say how much they appreciate the job you're doing."

"That's not what Mel says. He says I need to work on my relationships," I admitted.

"Screw Mel," Peggy declared.

I was taken aback by her non-typical bluntness and practically gave myself a nasal enema when her comment caught me in mid drink. I sucked the carbonated Seven-Up through my sinuses and buried my face in a table napkin to keep from drowning.

"Why, Mrs. Starr, what happened to the sweet, petite little girl from McClean, Texas? You know, the dainty little virgin I married? The one that never had a dirty thought in her life," I cooed sweetly when I regained some of my composure.

"She grew up with a policeman and was corrupted by his wicked ways and incessant ability for sex at all hours of the day and night. There's a rumor that he has been known to seduce helpless women in the shower," Peggy asserted with a smile.

Tim and Sandra returned to the booth and we continued to enjoy the great music. I invited Peggy to join me on the dance floor for the Blues Brother's version of "Shout". We jumped around like idiots and, for just a few minutes, were normal people again without the confines of professional decorum or trying to live up to someone else's expectations. It was great to just be ourselves for a brief moment in time. Peggy and I were both sweating and exhausted when we made our way back to the booth after the wild dance.

When Renee Stark and Kandi Maldonado came in the door, Tim and I looked at each other and repeated the classic line from "Animal House" in unison.

"If I was you, I think I'd be..........LEAVING!"

Renee wore a long, silver sheath dress with a matching necklace. Kandi was wearing something from Madonna's "Viking Princess" collection. All Kandi needed to complete her outrageous outfit was a hat with horns. The women were unescorted. I was certain I did not want to be around for whatever mischief the two lovers had planned for tonight.

The four of us attempted to make our way out of the bar through the back exit, without acknowledging the two newcomers. As we wound our way through the crowd, I captured the attention of the club manger who had introduced himself to us earlier. I pointed to Kandi and Renee and told him I suspected that they were hookers and he should consider asking them to leave before they started giving head jobs under the tables in his respectable establishment.

When I disappeared out the back door, the club manager was walking in the direction of Kandi and Renee's table with a determined look on his face. He pulled up his trouser belt like a cartoon character getting ready to take on Popeye. I wondered if the club manager had any idea what a wild pair of Tazmanian she-devils he was about to encounter.

Tim and Sandra said their good-byes in the chilly parking lot and Peggy and I were soon on our way to pick up Terri.

By midnight, the entire Starr family was sound asleep with hopes for a quiet weekend ahead.

SATURDAY

CHAPTER SIX

I had just cornered Sophia Loren, Bo Derek, Marilyn Monroe and Sharon Stone in my dream. All in their prime, of course. When the phone began to ring, the objects of my sleepy time lust evaporated into the ceiling. After the second ring, I decided to let the answering machine pick up the call. Let technology do some of the work, I thought.

"Hello, we're away from the phone right now. Please leave your message at the tone," I heard my own voice drone from the machine. The message was short and sweet. No catchy jingles or background music. I really wanted one of those novelty answering machine tapes they advertised at four o'clock in the morning on the "Home Shopping Channel". My favorite spoof was the tape that had Humphrey Bogart lisping, "Say sweetheart, leave your message as time goes by, 'cause, here's lookin' at you kid,". Peggy thought it to be a little ostentatious. I bought a trench coat instead.

"Chief, this is Maria at the City Manager's Office, I need to speak…"

I reached over the night stand and groped for the telephone receiver. In the process, I managed to knock over a glass of water and completely saturate my autographed copy of Oliver North's "Under Fire". I was trying to wade through the sleazy politics of Irangate by reading a few pages each night. The story always put me to sleep.

Colonel North had stopped in Wichita on his lecture tour, where he made more than twice my monthly salary for one forty-five minute speech. Naturally, as the police chief, I felt it was my civic duty to welcome the famous person to our humble city. He was gregarious and friendly. When he learned that Chad was at the Naval Academy, his old alma mater, the colonel insisted on giving me a copy of his book. On the fly sheet, he wrote, "To Chief Starr, Tough Times Never Last, Tough People Do. Ollie." The inscription was the best part of the book.

"Uh, I'm here, Maria," I coughed.

"Chief, is that you?" Maria queried.

"I think so, wait a minute, I'll check," I said. Since I always slept in the nude it was easy to look under the covers at my usual early morning readiness to deal with Sophia,

Marilyn, Bo and the rest of MGM's stable of starlets. "Yep, it's me. I've confirmed it. What's up?"

"The Manager wants to see you in his office as soon as possible," Maria directed.

Suddenly, all the drowsiness left me and I became instantly alert to danger. "Maria, what are you doing working on a Saturday? What's going on down there?"

"I work when the Manager calls me. He's the boss. All I know is that he said to tell you it was important and for you to get here as soon as you could," Maria's voice was ice.

"Okay, tell him I am code five," I announced. Instantly, I knew that neither she nor the Manager would have a clue as to the meaning of the Dallas Police radio code for "en route". Using the jargon was a difficult to break habit.

"What?" Maria answered back sounding more confused than her usual self.

"Never mind, Maria, tell him I'm coming." I looked down at the continuing bulge under the covers and changed my choice of words once more. "No, no, cancel that. Tell him I will be there in a half an hour or less. Okay?"

I hung up the phone and had picked up Ollie's soaked book when Peggy walked into the bedroom. She had been downstairs dueling with the stationary bicycle, judging from her black and purple workout tights. Peggy looked bright and cheerful, as she always did early in the morning.

One glance at my naked body cause her to leer, "What's going on up here? Dialing those one-nine-hundred sex line numbers again, big fellow?" Her eyes locked on the better part of my anatomy as I stood up.

"No, I wish that was the case. The City Manager's secretary interrupted what was promising to be the mother of all wet dreams," I admitted. I padded to the bathroom and turned on the shower to begin heating the water.

"What's the problem now?" Peggy asked earnestly.

"I don't know," I was truly perplexed. "Was there anything on the news this morning?"

"Darned if I know. I try not to watch the stupid tv news anymore. Terri is watching cartoons in the den. I'll go check and see if I can find anything on the radio news," Peggy said.

I used the speed dial function on the telephone to ring Billy Wade's house. He had the duty chief responsibilities during the month and was supposed to notify me of any critical incidents immediately, night or day. There was no answer on his phone and I left a message on his machine to call me right away.

After a quick shower, I called the 911 emergency number to see if the Communications Center had some type of major situation in the works. When the call taker came on line, I identified myself to verify the name and address information that was automatically displayed on the computer screen in front of her. Any calls to our enhanced 911 system were immediately cross referenced to the address where the call was coming from and the name of the person who paid the telephone bill at that location.

"Sure, Chief, what's up?" the clerk asked.

"Can I talk to a supervisor if you've got one handy?" I asked. I tried to sound nonchalant because I did not want to throw the entire dispatch center into a panic if I could help it.

"No problem. Hold on," she answered.

In seconds, a voice with a Texas twang came on the line. "Good mornin', Chief, what can we do for you?"

"Betty, is that you?" I asked.

"Chief, how is it you know all of our names and we don't even work for you?" Betty asked. She was right about the organizational responsibility of the 911 Communications Center. Unlike most major cities, Wichita ran a consolidated dispatch operation. Ours was actually a separate agency under the control of the Sedgwick County Commission. The people in the center dispatched police, sheriff, fire, ambulance, dog catchers and just about everybody else issued a government radio in the entire county.

"How could I forget your sweet voice, Betty?" I schmoozed. "Hey, do me a really big favor, will 'ya?"

"Sure, Chief, how do you like your eggs?" Betty asked. I smiled despite knowing Betty could not see me in my bedroom birthday suit.

"Thanks anyway, Betty," I answered. "I'm flattered you would want to cook me breakfast. Maybe some other time, okay?"

"Well, okay, if that's the way you're going to be. I always heard you were a straight arrow," her voice inflection pretended a false pouting act. In seconds, Betty's professional tone quickly replaced the friendly game we were playing. "What do you need, Chief?"

"Betty, is there anything major going on this morning?" I asked.

"I don't think so. Stand by and I will check the big board," Betty replied.

By her comments, I knew she would be reviewing the large, white vinyl rectangle mounted on the wall in the middle of the cavernous dispatch center. The board had an erasable marker surface, which was constantly being updated by the dispatch supervisors, to notify all of the people in the center of any significant activities in the county. The display was a valuable aid to insure that all of the various agencies and their communication lifelines could coordinate assignments in the often hectic environment.

Betty soon came back on the line. "Chief, there's nothing much going on; just a grass fire out by Lake Afton. We've called in an extra engine company from the county to handle it. There's not much to burn out there, anyway, I don't think. Do you want me to page the Duty Chief and find out if he knows anything?"

"No, that's okay, Betty" I replied. "I've got a call in to him now. I'll take care of it. Thanks for all of your help."

Peggy returned and announced there was nothing of any significance on the radio, just some national stuff about former Kansas Senator Bob Dole doing commercial advertisements heralding a new treatment for impotence relief. My, how quickly the mighty can fall.

I searched my brain for the last round the manager and I had played in the never ending "Wacky Wichita Game". The only one I could recall was his most recent nasty e-mail ranting and raving for three single spaced pages about how prostitution was out of control in Wichita. He had seen a portable sign in the median on his way to work that read, "For Love, Call 651-6500". It was a sure indication that the whores felt safe enough from the police to publicly advertise, the manager believed. Naturally, other than the number, the manager had not bothered to get any of his facts straight and just fired off criticism without any idea of what he was talking about. His knowledge about anything pertaining to police work was as deep as the blue water in a urinal.

When I called the number, it was a recording from the Wichita Animal Shelter advertising that they had a hundred adorable puppies for adoption who would "love you forever".

Surely the "Case of the Prostituting Puppies" was not the reason for an early morning call on my day off, I surmised. In thirty minutes, I was walking through the back door of Wichita's City Hall. The automatic sliding glass door opened and I approached the "Badge On Floor", who was quietly reading the morning newspaper.

"Good morning, Bobby, how goes the war?" I asked.

The bored officer lowered the sports section and smiled, "Hey, Chief, how are 'ya? What brings you down here on a Saturday morning?"

"That's a good question. I'm not sure. Is there anything in the newspaper about us this morning?" I asked.

"Naw, just a lot of crap about Gil Forney. He's whining about the raid on his roach room, but I don't think we're mentioned in the article," Bobby mused.

Gil Forney was a City Council member who owned a small Italian deli on West Douglas Avenue, near downtown. The specialty of the little shop was meatball sandwiches. Gil owned the old, two story brick building which housed the deli on the first floor. On the second floor, Gil rented the four rooms for a weekly rate to various low income derelicts and people down on their luck. Since Gil was a City Council member, Mel ordered the Central Inspection officials to ignore the ten thousand or so health and fire code violations that were rampant in the hundred year old building.

A week or so earlier, United States Postal Inspectors raided Gil's building while he was not there. The federal agents were looking for a nut who had mailed a letter bomb to a local K-Mart store. Fortunately, the bomb did not blow up due to a loose wiring connection, but the explosive charge was analyzed and found to be extremely potent. The bomb squad technician graded the builder of the device with diverse marks. The tech gave the bomber an "A" in chemistry and a "F" in electrical engineering. If the bomber had blown himself up, the technician would have given the lunatic a gold star for his contribution to improving the human species.

Like most federal search warrants, the postal authorities completely botched the whole affair. First, they unnecessarily kicked the unlocked back door of Gil's restaurant off its hinges. Next, the raiding party proceeded to trash the entire shop before they found the way upstairs, in search of the not-so-bright would be terrorist. Our bomber was no Einstein. He put his real return address on the bomb's mailing package.

When the Feds finally found the right room where the suspect claimed he was living, they discovered that the tiny apartment was empty except for a suspicious looking shoe box. The postal inspectors called the A.T.F.'s elite "Explosive Ordinance Disposal" unit to check the package that had been left behind. The Alcohol, Tobacco, and Firearm's E.O.D. Squad decided it would be prudent to relocate the suspicious box to the open roof of the building and detonate the package in a controlled setting.

A demolition expert, dressed in his heavily armored and hooded bomb proof suit, carefully carried the box to the top of the old building. There, the expert deftly wrapped "Det Cord", a flexible, rope like plastic explosive, around the cardboard container and connected the electrical blasting cap connections. From behind a sturdy brick fire wall, the highly trained explosives specialist set off his charge.

There was a muffled "boom" and pieces of the previous occupant's dirty underwear floated through the air and into the busy street below.

Gil was furious. For some reason, he had chosen today to take his ire public in the newspaper. According to the story Bobby handed me, the City Councilman compared the execution of the search warrant at his little shop on the scale equal to another Waco or Ruby Ridge incident. Gil demanded that the whole affair be investigated by a Congressional committee. The article was accompanied by a photo of a grinning Gil

Forney standing in front of his deli. He was holding a pair of scorched B.V.D.'s with
the crotch blown out. It was great publicity for a small time operator like Gil. I half
expected a new slogan to be painted on the sign above his door, "Try our Atomic
Meatball Sandwich, It'll Blow Your Balls Off."

"I don't think this is quite a major international incident," I mused.

"I don't know but something's going on this morning, Chief. There's been all kinds
of movers and shakers coming through the door. Not a one of the bastards has so
much as shot me the finger, let alone said "hello"," Bobby complained as he handed me
the "Sign In Log" affixed to a clipboard on the desk where he sat.

It was a policy that anyone entering City Hall, after regular hours and on the week-
ends, had to note the times of their arrival and departure. Mel called it a security
measure, as if a band of crazed terrorists would be deterred from signing the pink
sheet of paper before they went upstairs and sprayed the Municipal Court with AK-
47 fire. I decided that the log was one of Mel's methods to determine who was dedicated enough to work for free on their off-duty time to the greater glory of Wichita.
And Mel Michaels, of course.

Bobby was right. The log listed about ten or fifteen high ranking bureaucrats who
would not normally be present in the building on a weekend. It was all very strange.

"Bob, what's on the "Inner Watch" from last night?" I asked. The "Inner Watch" was
a computerized listing of the city's major crimes and incidents which occurred in the
previous twenty four hours. After a great deal of effort, we managed to integrate the
bulletin in our newly designed call-in reporting system; to keep the entire department
informed about what was happening all over the city.

"Not much there, Chief, just a helluva chase you might find interesting," Bobby
said. He handed me another clipboard and I began searching for the short synopsis of
the incident.

"Hey, Chief," Bobby yelled as if I were standing across the hall instead of directly in
front of his desk. "Did you hear the one about the "Million Man March"?"

"Huh?" I kept reading.

"You know. The "Million Man March" in Washington," Bobby chided.

"Sorry, guess I missed it," I answered.

"Of course you missed it, Chief, it was for black guys to go and walk around and
stuff to show somethin' or other, I forget exactly what," Bobby explained.

I finally looked up from the "Inner Watch" report and said, "Bobby, what the hell
are you talking about?"

"I'm trying to tell you a joke, Chief. It's a good one, I think,"
Bobby leered.

"Bobby, this better be a clean joke. I'm in no mood for one of your usuals," I admitted.

"It's clean, I promise, just listen," Bobby promised.

"Okay," I put the list of reports down and gave the desk officer my undivided attention.

"Anyways, you heard about the "Million Man March", right?"

"Vaguely, but go on with the story so I can get on with my life," I pleaded.

"Do you know what was amazing about the "Million Man March", Chief?" Bobby asked.

"No, what?" I played straight man.

"What was so amazing was that only three people had to get off work," Bobby laughed so hard his top uniform shirt button came undone. The top of a freebie tee shirt from a local topless bar peeked from underneath his tan uniform shirt.

"Not funny," I dead panned. "You need to get a life AND a different tee shirt."

I found the entry on the "Inner Watch" about the pursuit Bobby had indicated and did not see anything unusual about the incident. Just another stupid car thief trying to out run the police. It happens twenty times a day in Dallas and with enough frequency in Wichita to become routine.

"A motor officer came by this morning and told me the real scoop on the chase," the desk officer said. His grin told me there was more to the story than what was on the "Inner Watch".

I started to chide Bobby about getting his information from officers who ride motor-cycles for a living, but on second thought I decided my planned comment about iden-tifying motorcycle officers by the bugs in their teeth might be considered too critical.

"What's the deal?" I asked simply.

"Well, you know those new computers in the cars that you got for us?" Bobby asked. He was referring to the mobile data terminals being tested in a few of our patrol cars. The technology of putting computers in police cars had been around for years, but I had a hell of a time convincing Mel that the terminals would be a valuable addi-tion to our department. I finally gave up on acquiring funding for the technology in the budget and wrote a grant request to buy them with federal funds. Mel was out on sick leave with an infected tooth the week that the grant request went to the City Council for approval. I sweet talked the City Clerk into putting the request on the "Consent Agenda", which is reserved for minor items that do not need council debate. It passed with no questions asked. We were in the testing phase of installing several different types of the equipment throughout the department and checking out the various system's capabilities. The computers made the officers feel as though they were on the set of "Star Trek". We had sure come a long way from the "pencil and paper and a hundred different forms" days of only a few years before.

I nodded and Bobby continued his story. "Anyways, Joey Runnels was riding in one of the cars with the new computers in it last night. Heck, I don't know nothin' about computers myself, but Joey had a Commodore 64 back when they first come out. Anyways, Joey sees this white Ford go by him with this black guy driving it which looked sorta suspicious."

"Hold on, Bobby, if this is another racial joke, I don't want to hear it," I held up an open palm in the universal sign for "STOP".

"Naw, nothing like that," Bobby grinned. "Okay, where was I? Oh, yeah, anyways, Joey sees this black guy driving this Ford, see? Only the Ford is all clean and shiny like and has got factory rims and black wall tires that don't match the driver, if you know what I mean."

Bobby winked and I ignored his reference to the social stereotype which implied that most blacks customize their cars with chrome and whitewalls.

"Is this story going anywhere, Bobby? I'm late for a meeting," I announced.

"Hold on, Chief. Anyways, Joey cranks up this new computer in his car and checks the license number for stolen. In just a few seconds, bingo! It's hot, see. So, Joey lights off his reds and siren and the chase is on." Bobby was getting into his story and began turning an imaginary steering wheel back and forth in front of his perch at his raised desk.

"Anyways, they race all over the eastside in those back streets south of Kellogg off of Edgemoor. No, not Edgemoor, but Hillside. You know the area, Chief?" Bobby asked intently.

I nodded again. It always intrigues me when police officers tell war stories, it is important for them to get the geography, street names, and block numbers exactly right; as if they were re-writing the police report or testifying in court.

"Anyways," Bobby said for at least the sixth time, "the black dude bails out of the stolen car and starts running towards Kellogg. Joey tries to chase him, but the black guy has extra leg muscles, ya' know."

I groaned at the ridiculous bigotry, but Bobby pressed on.

"Anyways, Joey loses sight of the guy after about a block, but keeps running. Unbeknownst to Joey, the black guy runs across the parking lot of "Shotgun Sammy's". You know, that cowboy bar up on East Kellogg, about the eighteen hundred block."

I nodded and slowly blinked my eyes to signal I would stay for only one more round of the story. "The dude decides he will duck into the beer joint and chill out while the "po-leece" scour the neighborhood looking for his worthless ass. When the heat's off, he figures he will just stroll back out the door and smash the steering column of another cheap American made car and be gone with the wind," the desk officer theorized.

"Come on, Bobby, finish the story, I've really got to go," I whined.

"Wait, Chief, you are really going to love this part," Bobby promised. "Anyways, it's "Texas Toga Night" at Sammy's, see? All of these good 'ol boys are dressed in bed sheets and cowboy hats and are having a great time getting sloshed and doing the two step with their girlfriends when in runs the car thief. Not only does he run into a room that looks like the annual Kansas convention of the Ku Klux Klan, with all of the white robes and hats; but the dumb sonofabitch comes barreling through the front door and knocks over Sammy, herself. You know Sammy, doncha' Chief?"

"Not socially," I answered. I knew the owner of the bar by reputation only. She was a big, heavyset woman with artificial red hair. Sammy had been a madam and a bootlegger in the 1930's. Now she was at least eighty and ran the bar with a cigar in her mouth and a shot of Kentucky bourbon in each hand. Sammy was a veritable Wichita legend.

"Anyways, the thief knocks Sammy down and breaks her arm. When he looks up, he sees about a hundred drunk cowboys descend on him like the wrath of God. The good ol' boys wound up kicking the living shit out of the puke for breaking Sammy's arm. Naturally, a disturbance call comes in to 911 and by the time we get there, the car thief is hamburger. He's ready to confess to anything, if we will just rescue him from the "Kluxers", as he called them. Evidently, it was quite a scene. You know, Chief, every one of those cowboys was in the rest room when that poor thief got the crap beat out of him. Without any witnesses, the officers booked the bad guy for auto theft and assaulting Sammy. The thief is in a plaster body cast over at Wesley Hospital right now."

Officer Bobby "Anyways" Johnson grinned at the conclusion of his story. Every pearly white tooth was visible in his dark face. Bobby was the blackest black officer on the Wichita Police Department and he took enormous pleasure telling me the story of the unluckiest car thief in America. Unfortunately, it did not seem likely that the episode was the reason for my Saturday morning command performance at City Hall.

"Great story, Bobby. One for your grandkids," I said. He just kept grinning. "I'll be up on the thirteenth floor if anything breaks."

"Okay, Chief," Bobby waved and went back to his newspaper. I punched the "UP" button on the stainless steel control console and got an elevator immediately. The damn things only ran quickly during the weekend. Normally, you had to wait five minutes, or more, to get an elevator from the lobby. I somehow believed that the elevators were programmed to be the slowest when you needed to get upstairs the fastest.

I arrived on the City Manager's floor, accompanied by the sound of the elevator's chime announcing the floor. The hallway was deserted. I stopped and listened, like a deer sniffing the wind for an approaching hunter. It was as quiet as a tomb. Pushing open the unlocked outer door to the Manager's suite of offices revealed a similar empty scene. I walked around the corner and came upon Maria, sitting at her desk, reading a copy of "The Cat Owners Journal".

"Good morning, Maria, how are you this morning?" I asked without really caring. She looked up, absent any smile, and stared at me as if I had a green worm crawling out of my ear.

"Do you have a cat?" I cleverly asked while pointing to the front of her magazine. At least she was reading it right side up.

Maria brightened a little at my question. "Yes, I have three cats."

"Oh, I love cats, too," I bubbled. "They taste a lot like chicken, don't you think?"

Maria looked horrified. I was temporarily saved by the buzzing of her intercom line. "Is Starr here yet?" The electronic voice of the City Manager came over the speaker.

"Yes sir, he just arrived," Maria answered.

"Send him in," the Manager ordered. Maria nodded at me menacingly and I tried to dredge up a brave smile. My facial bravado came out more like the lopsided grin you feel when the dentist deadens just one side of your mouth. I checked my chin for drool and pushed the heavy wooden door open to the City Manager's inner office.

Mel was no where to be seen. He was not sitting at his desk or on the couch that lined the wall on my left as I entered.

"Over here," a disembodied voice called from my right. As I turned, I saw Mel sitting at the end of the large oval table in his adjoining conference room. The room was full of people. Every chair was taken, except one empty seat directly opposite Mel at the other end of the table. I glanced around the room and recognized most of the City Council members and various other members of the local political establishment. Mel waved at the empty chair and I tried to make eye contact with each one of the people in the room as I moved to my appointed place. Almost all of them stared at their hands or at open notebooks in front of them on the table. I immediately regretted the fact that I had not remembered to bring my hidden tape recorder. The gathering had all of the makings of being historic.

I sat down in the hard chair and narrowed my gaze to concentrate on exactly who was present. The Manager sat with Assistant City Manager, "Bullet Bob" Showalter, on his left and Mayor Ben Cole on his right. Bob was tapping his pencil on his notebook and biting his lip. Of the three, he appeared the most agitated.

The City Attorney, Jeff Needles, was on Bob's left. Jeff was a quizzical little character. He had not been able to make it in private law practice due to his unfortunate habit of being unable to control his bladder when he got excited. Jeff's incontinence made actual trial work pretty much out of the question. I am sure it was embarrassing to be arguing a case before a jury and have urine puddle around your shoes. Poor Jeff. He had found work in the city's litigation section and worked his way up for consideration as the number one attorney in city government. I liked Jeff and felt sorry for him. I had even recommended Jeff for the job he now held. Despite my favorable recommendation, Mel had appointed him "City Attorney". Judging from the atmosphere in the room, I hoped that Jeff was wearing a double set of "Huggies" diapers.

Mel began shuffling papers in front of him and finally picked up a document and began to study it intently. He tried to clear his throat several times, but Mel's mouth was too dry to speak. Finally, he managed to croak, "Rod, um, er, Rod, where were you last Monday night?"

"When?" was my less than clever reply. I did not have a clue.

"Monday night this week," Mel answered. "Where were you?" I could see his hands shaking and the document he was holding was becoming wet around the edges where his fingers touched the paper.

I did not answer. Partly because I did not remember Monday very well and partly because I was not sure what was going on. I kept looking around the table for a friendly face. None of my supporters on the City Council were present. Instead, there was Gil Forney, Ray Gondorf, and Reginald Newman. Their three votes, along with Mayor Cole's, gave them a four to three majority on any decisions.

"To be honest, I don't remember where I was on Monday night. I've slept since then and sleep usually wipes out my memory. Who wants to know, anyway?" I asked. Fleetingly, I thought about bringing Officer "Anyways" Johnson to the meeting to drive them nuts with his verbal habit.

"You don't know where you were five days ago?" Bob Showalter demanded in a voice about twenty decibels higher than the Manager's or mine. The Assistant City Manager was clearly agitated. I began to suspect that he might be self medicated.

"Would it be too much to ask just what is going on here? I came down here on my day off because the Manager called and said it was important. Well, here I am and I'd like to know what's so damned important?" I decided to attack instead of defend. 'Tis better to give than receive when the fight starts.

"It would be best if you just answer the questions," Jeff Needles said softly. The City Attorney did not look up from his gold "Cross" pen, laying on his brown notebook. I grinned at the thought of Jeff desperately trying to hold his water in the increasing tension of the room.

"I may not be Sherlock Holmes, but it would seem to me that you must know where I was Monday night or else you wouldn't be asking," I countered.

"We want to hear it from your side of the story, Rod," Mel found his placating voice. He tried to sound like Henry Kissinger, attempting to schmooze the North Vietnamese into accepting peace terms before he bombed the little rice eaters back into the Stone Age. Instead, Mel came across sounding like "Mr. Rogers" trying to get me to admit that I could not tie my shoe laces.

"Can you spell, "fucked"? I heard myself mutter under my breath in recognition of Mel's unintentional impersonation of the popular Saturday morning kid's show host.

"What? What was that?" Bob demanded. He kept tapping his pencil on the white note pad in front of him. Bob was keeping up a drum beat which Ringo Starr would have been proud to emulate during his days with the "Beatles".

I closed my eyes and tried to remember Monday night. Brief moments of my week's activities flashed incoherently across the movie screen on the back of my eyelids. There was no sound to the picture.

"Maria, please send in Chief Pasqual," Mel spoke slowly and distinctly into the intercom on the table.

Five seconds later, Victor Pasqual stepped into the room and stopped about half way up the side of the table. He slowly realized that there was no place for him to sit. Everyone turned in their chairs to look at Victor. I could smell alcohol on him from thirty feet across the room. As the former chief stood and faced the assembled group, who remained seated in their chairs, he began to weave unsteadily. Victor pulled out a pair of half size reading glasses and began reciting from a sheaf of yellow papers he was holding. I imagined hearing more blood vessels exploding in Victor's nose as he began an obviously well rehearsed litany.

"My name is Victor Pasqual. I'm a retired Chief of Police for the City of Wichita, Kansas. I do consultant work for various cities and private businesses around the country."

"Victor, we all know who you are," I said. "The only consultant work you do is for "Jack Daniels"." My reference to Victor's drinking was harsh and out of line. I immediately regretted the insult, but I was becoming angry at the obvious mysterious performances being staged for my benefit.

"Shut up," Bob Showalter demanded.

Instead of telling Bob to fuck off, I kept my mouth shut for once. I thought of Terri's little yellow sticky note on my desk, "K.Y.B.M.S.".

"A short time ago, I was hired by the City Manager to undertake a surveillance of Rod Starr, an employee of the City of Wichita. I have followed Mr. Starr from Monday until today and kept a detailed log of his activities," Victor explained.

Now it became crystal clear why Victor was calling Peggy all of the time and suddenly appearing so concerned with our well being. The bastard was an informant. Not only that, he was being paid by the city to be a snitch on a fellow police chief.

"You can comment now if you like," Bob Showalter smiled at me with the same grin you see on a pirate's flag.

"Victor couldn't keep a detailed log of his own activities, let alone mine," I offered. The City Manager flashed his own displeasure at my attempts to denigrate his hired assassin and instructed Victor to continue with his report.

As if to disprove my allegation of his inability to keep anything resembling proper field notes of an investigation, Victor began to flip through a small pocket notebook as he spoke. "I began following the suspect…"

"Hold on here, just a damned minute," I protested loudly. "Suspect in what? What exactly am I "suspected" of doing?"

Before anyone else could reply, Victor looked at me through bloodshot eyes and said, "Sorry, it's just a figure of speech. Old habit, I guess." Then the worthless bastard smiled at me as if we were the only two in the room who would understand a police officer's propensity in referring to everyone outside of law enforcement, including his own relatives, as "suspects". I wanted to tear his swollen lips off.

"In any case," Victor continued, "I followed the sus…er, the subject from Wichita to a golf course in Hesston, Kansas. I remind this group that Monday was a regular work day."

"Stop. Please. Just a moment. I suppose you didn't note that Monday was the day of the "Employee Appreciation Golf Tournament?" I asked.

"No," Victor knotted his brow and acted confused.

"I didn't think so. What a great detective you make," I spat.

"Let's get on with it," Bob demanded.

"The subject was with three other unidentified males in a city owned car in Hesston, which is outside the county limits I might add. I observed them playing golf and drinking beer during the course of the morning and afternoon," Victor announced.

"Bull shit," I exploded.

"Shut up!" Bob practically leaped to his feet. I definitely suspected some type of self-administered drug, possibly methamphetamine and maybe a mixture of steroids to handle the suspicious rash which was growing up the sides of his neck from his collar line.

"After leaving Hesston, the group returned to Wichita and attended a rowdy party, on city time, where there was more drinking and fighting throughout the night," Victor read on.

"I don't suppose you would care to list the location of this so-called "rowdy party", would you, Victor?" I asked sarcastically.

"No," Victor answered.

"I didn't think so, asshole," I was quickly forgetting Terri's note.

"Chief Starr," Jeff Needles spoke as he placed a hand on Bob Showalter's arm to keep the Assistant City Manager from jumping out of his chair again. "Chief Pasqual is just presenting the information he has gathered. Please let him continue uninterrupted. I'm sure the Manager will let you have your say in due time."

I glared at Jeff and gritted my teeth so hard I thought the enamel would flake off onto the mahogany table top. The City Attorney ignored my high intensity gaze and nodded to Victor.

The ex-chief continued with his story and highlighted the fights between Pete Gant and the various combatants at the "Employee Appreciation Party". He carefully left out any names, including Pete's. I was mildly puzzled by that lapse until I remembered that Pete Gant was one of Victor's own deputy chief appointees I had inherited.

"After a long night of partying, the subject passed out in a lawn chair at the location," Victor announced.

"What?" Showalter exclaimed indignantly. "The Police Chief of our city passed out drunk in public at some wild party. Unbelievable!"

"Well, for once, you've finally got it right, Bob. It is absolutely unbelievable, because it's not true!" I yelled across the table.

"I have pictures," Victor stated flatly.

"What? Victor, I don't know whether you're lying or just seeing pink elephants again. Let's see your fucking pictures," I demanded.

Victor looked at the City Manager who almost imperceptibly nodded his chin. The retired chief displayed two black and white photos which had obviously been taken with a cheap plastic pocket camera. He handed me one copy and began passing the other photo around the room. The photos were grainy eight by ten blow ups, but the image was unmistakable. Sure enough, there I was asleep on a lawn chair in the

Botanica's gazebo. The camera's flash caught me huddled in a fetal sleeping position with my mouth open. Someone had arranged several empty cans of Coors beer on the steps of the gazebo in the foreground of the picture. Now, I remembered being awakened by what I thought was the flash of a cruise missile launch from McConnell Air Force Base. I had to admit, all the pieces fit together and it was a beautiful frame.

"This is all a lie," I heard myself squeak. I sounded like Jack Ruby claiming he did not shoot Lee Harvey Oswald, when a hundred million viewers watched him do the evil deed on live television. With the manufactured photographic "evidence", I had a hard time believing my own version of the story and I knew the truth because I was there.

"We understand your embarrassment, Chief," Jeff Needles voice sounded distant, as if it was being broadcast from Alaska. "If you have other evidence that you would like to present in your defense, I'm sure the Manager would like to hear it."

"Other evidence?" I cried. "What other evidence? I didn't come prepared like Perry Mason to go to trial this morning. I guess telling all of you clowns that I don't drink wouldn't carry a lot of weight, would it?" I stared at the lowered heads or blank faces who definitely found it hard to believe a veteran police chief did not consume alcohol.

"I didn't think so," I concluded my defense. "Are you going to give me the gas chamber or can I request a firing squad and a blindfold?"

"This is serious, Chief. If I were you, I would concentrate on the matter before us in a sober fashion," Jeff Needles stated.

"I am sober, Jeff. I'm always sober. Which is more than I can say for some others here." I glanced around the room again and landed my gaze squarely on the ruddy face of Victor Pasqual.

Bob nodded at Victor again and he continued on with the overkill. "On Wednesday, I…"

"What happened to Tuesday, Victor? Did you take the day off to dry out?" I asked as sarcastically as I could muster.

"On Wednesday," Victor continued without notice to my insult, "I followed the subject around the city until he attended a function at the Police Academy building in the evening. I did not go inside, for fear of being discovered, but I noted the subject left the building long before the meeting was scheduled to end. The subject was in the company of an unidentified blonde woman, who was not the subject's wife. They left together in the subject's city owned car and I followed them outside the city limits to a home near Clearwater. The subject and the woman entered a farm house together and I left when it became apparent they were staying. I assume they spent the night together."

"Assume, assume? You no good son of a bitch!" I screamed. "Where the hell do you get off assuming something like that? I don't suppose you have any idea what went on inside the meeting at the Police Academy either? The one that I left so hurriedly, as you put it. You have no factual idea what actually occurred inside that farm house, do you?"

"No," Victor stated. "I returned to Wichita and conducted a search of the subject's office, pursuant to the City Manager's authorization. In his office, I found and copied medical bills in excess of $45,000 for his sick wife, who has a very grave illness." He passed out copies of Peggy's doctor's bills from the Mayo Clinic. I had brought the bills to work so I could argue with the city's insurance carrier, who refused to pay for a large portion of the costs. The insurance company called the Mayo Clinic's treatments "experimental in nature" and therefore, not covered. I was considering swallowing my pride and beg Mel to call the city's insurance carrier for me. One phone call from him would have induced the company to pay the clinic's charges. The bills had been laying on my desk when Victor burglarized my office.

The inference was complete. My wife was extremely sick. I owed a huge amount of money. Instead of tending to my sick wife, I was out getting drunk and carousing with other women while becoming a dead beat who would not pay his bills. It did not matter that Victor had his dates wrong. He had actually ransacked my office on Tuesday night, not Wednesday. I did not bother to point out the discrepancy.

"I don't suppose you thought the fifty cents you stole from my desk that night would have helped me pay my bills, huh, Victor?" I offered. He again failed to notice my comment.

I searched again for any sign of a sympathetic opening in the faces of the people around the room. I felt like Joan of Arc. The wood was being piled at my feet. It was just a matter of time before one of these assholes ignited a flame thrower to start the bonfire. My blood pressure was building. I wanted to fight but I did not know where to begin or how to counter the ridiculous fabrications and innuendo. The surreal atmosphere was like standing in a boxing ring and getting the snot beat out of you. Only this time, when the bell rang to end the round, I looked around and I was the only one inside the ring. There was no one at which to punch back.

"The next day, the subject again drove his city issued automobile out of the city and returned to the farm house in the county where he again met with the unidentified woman," Victor was beginning to sweat and sway even more. I suspected he might cut short the evidence to enable him to escape from the hot room as soon as possible. It would certainly be more merciful for both of us.

"They spent most of the evening and night together, again. I have pictures of the two embracing on the front porch of the residence," Victor said, as he began digging through the stack of papers he was trying to balance in his shaking hands.

"I don't think it will be necessary to show us more photographs," Mel interjected.

Victor looked hurt. He was clearly real proud of his camera shots from the roadside bushes of me and Jana sitting on the front porch swing.

The ex-chief concluded his notations of my week's activities with a pretty shaky version of last night's dancing at the Airport Hilton Lounge. Peggy somehow became "an unidentified woman" in Victor's recital of the evening. The logical assumption of all at the table was that it was the same "unidentified woman" I had been seen with during most of the week, or maybe a new girl friend, but certainly not my lawful spouse. Not surprisingly, Victor had no pictures of last night's outing with my wife.

"Thank you, Victor, that will be all," Bob Showalter announced and gestured toward the door. Victor looked relieved and anxious for a drink. I thought his performance rated at least twenty pieces of silver and an entire bottle of Jack Daniels. He sure earned it.

Bob turned to me when the door closed behind Victor and smiled. "Now, we would like to hear your side of the story."

"First, I'd like to say how really pleased I am to work in such a first class outfit like this. I have to buy my own uniforms and sidearm," I patted the bulge under my suit coat, "and you've got enough money to hire someone to follow me around. Great. How would you feel if I had someone follow you around, Mel, and take photographs of your activities?"

My accusers began to squirm in their chairs now realizing that I was armed. I remembered Colonel Colt's line about his "Peacemaker 45". "Fear no man, no matter what his size; call on me, and I will equalize." Unfortunately, it was not 1870 and I could not kill everyone in the room and claim it was self-defense. The solution was appealing, but not practical.

"That's the problem with you, Starr," Bob exploded. The amphetamines made him brave enough to ignore my reference to being armed. "You think we all work for you. Well, you're wrong, mister. You work for us. You are just a "dime a dozen" cop. We can hire fifty other people for your job at the snap of our fingers." He tried to make the digital popping gesture, but his hands were too sweaty.

"You're half right, Bob. That "IS" the problem around here. There are too many people forcing others to work "for" them, and not enough people working "with" each other."

"Cute. Real cute," Bob said. "Since you're so cute, let's see how you do out on your ass in the real world. How about that? You don't have a fucking contract, remember? You serve at the pleasure of the Manager and right now, the Manager is not pleased."

Jeff Needles felt his bladder give way a little and he put a moist hand onto Bob's arm. With his free hand, Jeff gestured palm down for Bob to back off. I got the distinct impression the two were about to play "good cop/bad cop" with me.

"Okay, hot shot," Bob said, "Let's hear whatever you've got to say."

"I think I will wait and do all of my talking in a court of law," I said. I was playing one of the last cards in my deck. I was half bluffing, but I remembered my conversation with the U.S. Attorney the day before.

"The only place you will get to do any talking is down at the unemployment office, smart guy. You can be "number seven", in a line of other no name has-beens," Bob shot back.

"I like the number seven. It's a lucky number and besides, it was my football number before I joined this chicken shit outfit and became a "has been"," I grinned. Actually my high school football number had been eighty-one, but I was not ready to concede that standing in line with so many other poor bastards would fatally wound what little pride I had left.

"Aw, shit," Bob exclaimed, as he threw his pencil at the notebook in front of him. If I was trying to affect an air of immaturity and arrogance, it was working with Bob.

The Manager cleared his throat and shuffled more papers in front of him. He selected one which looked vaguely familiar as I tried to read it upside down from across the long table.

"Rod, we've had numerous talks before concerning problems in the police department, haven't we?" Mel asked.

"Not really, Mel. We rarely speak in person and in six years you have been to my office exactly once," I answered. I looked directly at the Mayor, who sat quietly in his chair with this thumbs hooked under a pair of red suspenders while he stared at the dark tabletop.

"Didn't we have a talk just this week?" Mel pressed the point.

"Yes sir, you are correct about this week. You said I needed to improve my relationships," I answered. "I don't suppose you would believe I was working on my "relationships" with this "unidentified woman", as Victor calls her?"

"Not hardly what I meant," Mel hissed. "I think you are a good police officer, Rod. You do a lot of things well. You are smart, energetic, well spoken and people in the community like you. But that's not enough. You have to be loyal. You can't always be in charge. I am the boss here. You have to accept that."

"Mel," I said wearily, "why did you hire me? I mean, really, why DID you hire me? You knew what my reputation was in Dallas. You knew I was being groomed to command a much larger police department than this one and my track record indicated that I could do the job. Hell, you even had a psychological profile done on me before I took this job. You must of known that I was independent and capable of performing without constant supervision and interference in my job. Why did you hire me into this fucked up, micro-managed, Mickey Mouse system?"

"We've all been asking ourselves that same question," Bob Showalter popped off.

Mel held up his hand as if to say "enough". Bob backed off like a puppy that had been smacked with a rolled up newspaper. He was too stoked up on chemicals to whimper.

"As for loyalty, come on, Mel. I've taken a lot of spears in the chest for you along the way. When you've come down with some of your more stupid decisions, I've kept my mouth shut in front of my troops and they've gone on their merry way thinking I was the one who hosed 'em. We both know different, don't we? I've taken the heat for a hundred things you've ordered done and not once have you expressed any gratitude for my "loyalty", as you call it. Right now, I feel pretty stupid myself for ever being a part of this so called "loyal" group." I waved both arms to encompass the entire room.

"You are paid to be loyal, Rod. That's all that is required in return," Mel answered.

"That's a crock, Mel. Do you think I do this job for money? You think I became a police officer to get rich? You think I'm just another political robot like the rest of these assholes who don't care about the people they work with? They are just a bunch of numbers to you, aren't they Mel? Well, that's the difference between you and me, partner. When my guys bleed, I bleed. I happen to think police officers ARE different from clerks and lawyers and the other types of people that make up a city organization. They're different because they do the job whether you or I are there to look after them. They do the job because they want to make a difference in this sorry ass world." When I finished, I felt like I was a thousand years old.

"I realize you do not approve of my management style, Rod. That's the point. I have to consider the future. I've been giving a lot of thought to my own future, to your future and the future of this city. We simply cannot go on together. I'm willing to admit that I made a mistake when I brought you here," Mel announced placidly.

"Yes," I said in a voice not much more than a whisper, "You thought you were bringing in a young kid, naive to the ways of politics; but corruptible because he came from a big city. And we all know big cities breed corruption, right? You thought I would play along quietly in everything you did. That you could control everything because I would be so grateful for the opportunity to be the grand high "Chief of Police". In name only, of course. Well, it didn't work out quite that way, did it Mel? You discovered that I refused to let you run the police department into the ground without a fight, didn't you? And we've fought since day one. You're right about that. Not only that, but we've managed to turn a "do nothing" bunch of robots into a high tech, creative and diligent police department. I've done it in spite of your interference in a thousand different ways. We slowly culled out most of the nut cases that Victor hired. The good ones that are left and the new ones we have hired and promoted are starting to think for themselves, for a change, and that scares the shit out of you, doesn't it Mel? One of these days, someone other than me is going to start asking the wrong questions. Right, big guy?"

Mel began shaking his head from left to right as he dropped his gaze to the document in his hands. "I don't know what you are talking about," Mel lied wearily.

"I think you do," I stated with conviction. I was down to my last shot. I was exhausted from the battle and my head ached as if someone had hit me with a shovel.

Mel shuffled more papers on the table. As usual, he had a difficult time looking me in the eye. I knew from experience and training that most crooks and liars had the same problem.

"The issue is simple, really. You refuse to adjust to my style and play the game. There are members of your own staff who do not support you and I have doubts as to your loyalties. Therefore, you must be replaced. It's that simple." Mel continued to adjust the piles of papers until he had arranged them into one neat stack.

Jeff Needles opened his notebook and retrieved a sheet of blue paper. I recognized the official City of Wichita, "Flying W", letterhead. The City Attorney read the paper to himself as everyone around the table stared at him. I thought I heard the sound of running water from underneath Jeff's chair.

"The City Council met in executive session to discuss your case, Chief…" Jeff began.

"Come on, Jeff, what case? Don't I get a chance to defend myself now that I am aware of the charges? How about scheduling another executive session tomorrow so I can present some witnesses of my own to counter Victor's lies? You can meet the "unidentified woman" in person. Surely, that alone is worth the price of admission," I offered.

"This is not a court of law, Chief. The City Council has heard the evidence and the recommendation of the City Manager on the charges against you," Jeff recited.

"Excuse me, Jeff, would it be too much to ask if you could cite the specific city policy violations that I have been "charged" with, to use your words ?" I asked.

"I've told you, Chief, this is not a court. The Council reviewed all of the information provided by Chief Pasqual; which seems very conclusive, I might add. There has been neither the time, nor the need to research the specific code violations. We hope it won't come to that," Jeff stated.

There was a long pause and I wondered if Jeff's last statement offered me an opening to salvage my job. I thought of Peggy, Terri and my son, Chad. What would they say? The medical debts hanging over my head added to the panic. Where would I find a job? I had never worked in the private sector and I would not know where to begin. Bob was right. It was a cold, cruel world out there. I could not fathom how the ability to shoot a perfect score with my nine millimeter or lead troops in handling a riot would be marketable in the civilian world. I decided to make one last ditch effort to save myself.

"Look," I began humbly, "this has gone way too far. I can explain all of this so-called evidence if you will grant me a fair hearing. The truth is, I don't drink. I haven't had a beer since college. I don't like the taste, it's that simple. The golf and the party was during the officially sanctioned "Employees Appreciation Week". I admit I fell asleep on one of the lawn chairs. I wasn't drunk. I don't know who put those beer cans in front of my picture, but they weren't mine. As for the other woman, she's just a friend. I haven't slept with her and…"

"Chief, we don't want to hear the details of your sex life," Jeff Needles interrupted. His face was screwed into an agonized expression. Either he had already pissed on himself or the fight to hold his water was reaching epic proportions.

"You guys are wrong. My dad used to say "Right's right and Wrong's wrong". What you are trying to do to me is just plain wrong," I pleaded.

"We think you're the one who is wrong, big shot," It was Bob Showalter again. His medication had not worn off just yet. "The City Council has already voted. As of noon tomorrow, you are history. Do you understand? Pack your shit and get out!"

I stared at Bob's contorted smirk and counted the facial twitches in his cheek.

"There is one alternative, Chief," the City Attorney pulled another sheet of paper from his notebook and passed it down the table for me to review. I noticed that the slightest movement caused Jeff to wince at the pain from his soon-to-burst bladder.

"What's this, Jeff?" I asked.

"It's your resignation," the Mayor spoke for the first time. "We want this to be a clean break, with no hard feelings."

"No hard feelings, Mayor? You've got to be kidding me," I exclaimed. "How can I not have hard feelings over being forced out of my career by a frame up like this? I haven't done a damned thing wrong and certainly nothing like any of you have done. Damn it, if I had video tape of the women the Manager has played around with in the last six years, we would set a new box office record."

"The City Manager's conduct is not being questioned here, Chief," Jeff Needles answered with some degree of accuracy. "I believe it is fair to tell you that when the Council considered your case, there was some discussion of your family and leaving the impression, for your wife's sake, that you were in control of your decision to resign."

I closed my eyes and let the lawyer continue to speak. I heard the words, but I did not want to believe that it was all happening. I kept wishing my mom would call me and tell me that I should wake up because I was late for school.

"...and the City Manager will make this news release at noon tomorrow." Jeff picked up another piece of paper and carefully enunciated each word.

"I was informed by Rod Starr this weekend of his decision to leave the Wichita Police Department, effective immediately. Rod is a close personal friend of mine and I will miss his dedicated service to our city immensely. He has been considering a career move for quite a while and felt the time was right to meet other family obligations pertaining to the health needs of his wife. I can only say that all of us here at the City will miss Rod and wish him the very best."

Jeff laid the paper back on the desk as if it was the most fragile item on earth. Slowly, everyone at the table turned to look at me. I glanced down at the resignation letter which had been prepared for my signature then raised my eyes to gaze around the room at the assembly of hatchet men surrounding me. My guts were rolling.

"I won't quit. I won't. I refuse to sign it. I'll fight," I announced with just the bare essentials of any conviction whatsoever.

"It's over," Mel Michaels declared.

"It's not over, you son of a bitch!" I shouted. "It's not over until the fat lady sings!"

My flippant comment sounded ludicrous. The cliché seemed about as pertinent to the seriousness of the discussions as a condemned prisoner buying a lottery ticket. My head throbbed incessantly and my mouth tasted like the Russian army had marched through it.

"It's over, Rod," Mel repeated. "You have nothing to fight with."

"Oh? That's what you think. Hide and watch. We'll see whose evidence is the strongest, asshole." I thought of the federal investigation into Mel's manipulation of the "Narcotics Seizure Fund" and put all of my hopes into my last bullet. I was no longer bluffing. It had become a matter of life or death. I would to pull out all of the stops. I was committed to going public with my evidence as a last attempt to save a job which caused me nothing but pain and frustration. I had sunk that low. I was desperate. A drowning man will clutch at any straw, I guess.

Mel pressed the buzzer on the table top intercom and Maria entered the room carrying a white cardboard box. It was all so choreographed. I recognized the box immediately. It was the same box Suzie had carried when she delivered all of my evidence on the "Narcotics Seizure Fund" irregularities to me at the U.S. Attorney's Office. The box, along with my other sensitive files, was locked in the trunk of my city issued car. Or at least, it had been.

My heart sank as Mel opened the lid and revealed a stack of brown folders that had my distinctive scrawl on the side. I recognized the folders that had once contained all of my memos and documents on the "Narcotics Seizure Fund". The folders were completely empty. Every single document had no doubt been shredded or become kindling in someone's fireplace.

"Is this your evidence, Rod?" Mel asked quietly as he poured the empty folders onto the polished tabletop.

I felt sick. How could I have been so stupid? Why didn't I leave the box with George Ghormley, like he offered? The files would have been safe there. The only question remaining was who had stolen the box of incriminating materials from my trunk. Whoever it was, required access to one of our police car keys. Not an impossible chore, but I doubted anyone would have given a drunk like Victor Pasqual a key. Then I thought of Karen Teaford. What was it she had said?

"When a chief asks you to do something, you do it," was her comment. Surely, Karen would not betray me. She was one of my supporters, she said.

Whoever had provided the knife, I was fatally wounded and I knew it. I abandoned my air of defiance. In a war of dueling charges, I was out of ammunition. Finance Director Tad Roadly, who had sat quietly throughout the entire meeting, could not resist being in on the kill.

"You will also find that your electronic mail files have been eliminated and your computer records no longer exist," Tad predicted. "In fact, you no longer have access to the system. Your password will no longer work." The fat accountant smiled like he had swallowed an entire flock of Tweety birds. Imaginary yellow feathers were all over his corpulent face.

"The Wichita City Council has authorized Mr. Michaels to offer you a generous severance package in return for your resignation and in recognition of your professional and meritorious service these last six years," Jeff Needles revived his role in the last act. It suddenly dawned on me that this entire meeting had been conceived to convince me of the futility of a public fight. They clearly wanted to wash their hands of me and go on about their dirty business.

"If you resign, you will be provided with three months severance pay," Jeff continued, "and the city provided health insurance for you and your wife will continue in force for another year. In addition, the city will guarantee that your wife's medical bills at the Mayo Clinic are completely paid by our insurance carrier. We will, of course, allow you access to the money you have paid into the city's retirement system."

"Is that it?" I asked. "Three months salary, my own retirement contributions back and a phone call to the insurance company telling them to pay what they already owe? That doesn't seem like very much to me. I'm five years away from being eligible to collect my reduced retirement pension from Dallas. Please remember that I relinquished twenty percent of my benefits there to take this job. What am I supposed to do for five years? Since you're screwing me so well, should I just bend over and grab my ankles now or later?"

"May I remind you, Chief, your bargaining position does not look very strong," Jeff understated my own feelings exactly. "But, there is one other aspect the city is willing to offer you in a gesture of good will."

"Oh, yeah, what's that?" I quizzed. "Are you presenting me a key to the city, Mayor? Or maybe, proclaim "Rod Starr Appreciation Day" each year on my birthday?"

"Not quite so dramatic, I'm afraid," Jeff answered for the silent Mayor.

"The city has made arrangements with the university to offer you a teaching position on their faculty at a very generous rate of salary," Needles offered.

"How generous?" I asked half heartedly.

"Twenty four thousand dollars a year," Jeff answered.

"You've got to be kidding me, Jeff, that's about a third of what I am making now," I protested weakly. I looked at Mel and he smiled. Mel knew he had me. The son of a bitch knew and there was not a damned thing I could do to stop the train from running over me. I might as well buy the package and take my screwing like a big boy.

"Well, your position at the university will last until you are eligible for your Dallas pension," Jeff offered. "Of course, your option is to refuse this offer, which exemplifies the city's good will, and just be terminated tomorrow at noon. In which case, you will receive no additional salary and your wife's health insurance will be canceled immediately. The $45,000 you owe your wife's doctors will suddenly become due and your creditors will demand payment immediately. Without a job, any sort of job, that amount of debt would be difficult to pay off, don't you think?"

Suddenly, I was completely and totally disgusted with the entire City of Wichita. I wished I had never heard of the place. When God returned, I was going to recommend Kansas as a testing ground for the mother of all firestorms. I wanted to wash my hands of the whole matter. In a flash, I signed the resignation letter which had been prepared for my signature. The only change I made was that I scratched out "resignation" and wrote in the word "retirement". My final act of defiance was to refuse to quit. I would "retire", instead.

It sounded more definite to me, which was exactly what I intended. If every chief's job was like Wichita, then the world could kiss my ass before I lowered myself to experience another one. I was going to keep some pride, if I could.

I dropped the cheap city pen that had been provided for me to order my own demise and shoved the odious paper across the polished tabletop towards Jeff Needles. He carefully retrieved the retirement letter and finally lost control of his bladder. A mixture of horror and relief filled the city attorney's face as he proceeded to fill his specially designed underpants with urine.

"That will be acceptable," Jeff moaned. "Effective at midnight tomorrow, you will no longer be the Chief of Police. The City Manager will make the announcement of your "retirement", as you call it, at a special Sunday press conference at noon tomorrow. You have until then to clean out any personal effects that you may have in your office before the news is released. Please be certain you do not take any files not belonging to you."

"I doubt I have anything left in my office. I think you have already taken care of "cleaning out" my files," I said as I stood to leave.

"There's one other item, Mr. Starr," it was the Mayor's turn to join in on the final kill.

"What's left to steal from me, Mayor?" I glared down at the seated buffoon in the red suspenders.

"Your badge. I believe it belongs to the city. Let us have it now, if you please," the City Manager answered for the Mayor.

I remembered back to when I had been sworn in over six years previously. At the brief ceremony, the Mayor handed me the gold badge. Underneath an oval eagle, with wings outstretched, were the words "Chief" and "Wichita Police" set in gold letters on a blue enamel background. The words were scrolled around the state seal, embedded in the middle of the badge. Four small, gold stars were recessed in a final blue rectangle at the bottom of the gleaming shield. The four gold stars were a symbol of my position. A symbol of my authority. A symbol of the crowning achievement in my life.

I remembered what I had pledged during the oath of office ceremony when I was sworn in as the fortieth police chief in the history of the city. I thanked the gathered crowd and members of the media and said "I promise you I will never do anything that will tarnish this badge." Surrendering the gold orb into Mel Michael's sweating palms did not seem like a good idea. In fact, even the suggestion that I relinquish the gleaming badge was the last assault on my pride. The group could do what they wanted, but I refused to be stripped of my dignity or my honor.

"I'll tell you what, Mister Manager," I said, as I felt for the heavy badge clipped to the left front of my belt. I found the shield and moved my sports coat back to reveal it's presence. "And you too, Mayor. You gave me this badge. If you want it back, why don't you come over here and try to take it?"

I stared hard at the greasy politician. The Mayor looked directly into my eyes for the first time today and guessed correctly that I was in no mood to be further humiliated. Mel dropped his eyes into his lap again. They had finally reached the limit of my endurance.

"Never mind," was all Mayor Ben Cole said. He lowered his gaze down to the table and joined everyone in the room in avoiding looking at me as I turned to leave. I walked out the door and out of my life's ambition to make a difference in the world.

"It's over," Mel announced again.

Who cares, I asked myself? The answer coming back from deep in my soul was, "no one".

When the door closed behind me, I paused. I tried to discern the muffled voices exploding inside the conference room. It was probably merciful that I could not hear the exchange through the heavy door.

"Let me get this straight," Councilman Newman asked. "As soon as his resignation is announced..."

"Retirement," Jeff Needles corrected.

"Whatever. As soon as it's announced tomorrow, we are not obligated to follow through on any of the promises that we made today. Is that right?"

Mel nodded at the City Attorney. "Technically," Needles answered, "that is correct. There is no written contract, per se, and there are no recordings of these discussions. It will be his word against ours and a few months after he resigns, er, retires, no one will care what he has to say. His complaints will sound like sour grapes. We can refuse to pay his medical bills, insurance or whatever. He doesn't have a legal case without a written agreement. It's that simple."

"I would suggest," Councilman Gondorf spoke for the first time, "that we continue to pay his salary, as we discussed, for at least a couple of months. Those payments will insure his silence until the whole matter is completely forgotten by the public. We can stall his other claims for a similar period of time and then drop him like a hot rock. As Jeff says, there's nothing he can do about it. Absolutely nothing."

"I think it would be wise to proceed with the college teaching deal," the Mayor proposed. "After all, the university owes us a bunch of favors from the tax breaks we've given them over the years. They've always been most cooperative. Remember when they gave Victor Pasqual a bachelor's degree and he only went to class twice in four years?" The nervous laughter provided a necessary release to the tension in the room.

"It won't cost us anything," the Mayor continued, "for the school to offer Starr some piddly little job teaching freshman English or some other stupid subject. In the meantime, the job will give us continuing leverage over him in case he tries to cause trouble. One call from me to the president of the university and ex-Chief Starr will be out of that job, too. What do you think?"

"Great idea, Mayor," Mel said. "I suggest that you all be "unavailable for comment" tomorrow. I'll handle the media. It's over."

When I exited Mel's inner office, I walked around the corner and saw Billy Wade sitting in a chair in the waiting area. My deputy chief glanced up at me and then quickly lowered his head to stare at the floor. Suddenly, I recognized the culprit who delivered my files to my executioners.

"Et tu, Billy," I said. My reference to Shakespeare's "Julius Caesar" probably meant nothing to him. I stared at the bald spot on the top of his head. "I promoted you Billy. I jumped you two ranks to make you my deputy chief. Why would you do this to me? Why? I've heard a lot about loyalty in the last hour. Where was your loyalty?"

Convinced I would not receive an answer, I left Billy to receive his reward as the new "Acting Chief of Police" when the official announcement of my leaving was made on Sunday.

If Billy proved capable of "always knowing what needs to be done" then he might get the chief's job full-time. That was if the Manager felt Billy was appropriately "loyal" and Billy's wife said it was okay, of course.

I rode the elevator to the first floor without any conscious memory of the short trip. Officer Johnson waved at me as I silently walked by his post. "Have a nice day, Chief," he said. The instruction did not seem likely.

When I walked out through the sliding glass doors on the west side of the building, a vicious blast of Arctic air blew my coat open; revealing once again the gold badge of my soon to be lost position. I had long before decided that this particular location, behind Wichita's City Hall, was the coldest and windiest spot in all of North America. There was something about the design of the building or the aerodynamics of the local topography which created a veritable jet stream in that one, tiny area. I paused for a moment and swore a sacred oath that I would never come back to the spot as long as I lived.

When I reached the parking lot, Tim David was sitting on the hood of my city car with his feet dangling over the left front quarter panel.

"Hello, Chief," he said simply. He did not look at me. Tim just stared at the battered alligator cowboy boots he was wearing. The scuffed heels of his boots bounced against a steel belted radial tire. Black wall tires, of course.

I looked at Tim with a little bit of disbelief and a lot of weariness. I had no energy for whatever it was that brought Tim to my car.

"You make a pretty ugly hood ornament, Tim. But if you're going to stay there, I will have to glue your ass to the grille to keep you from blowing off," I said.

"How did it go upstairs?" Tim asked without looking up.

"The Manager finally gave me the raise that he has been forgetting to give me for the last five years and a new six year contract. He wanted me to stay longer, but I told him twelve winters in this godforsaken state was enough. I haven't been warm since the last Air Force jet tanker crashed out at McConnell," I lied.

"Really?" Tim said equally wearily. He knew I was blowing a lot of hot air. I paused for a long moment and looked at his craggy face.

"You knew, didn't you, partner?" I asked.

"Yeah, I guess I did, Chief," Tim answered simply.

"How, Tim? How did you know? Why didn't you warn me? Answer me that, huh? I thought you were my friend," I whined woefully.

It all sounded so trite. I could not believe I was reacting this way. Big tough police chief. Hot shot, my ass. My eyes watered. "Did you set me up for Pasqual at the gazebo. Did you, of all the people in this worthless state, set me up? The one guy that I trusted on my staff. How about it, old buddy?" My bitterness welled up inside me. The muddy taste in my mouth was awful.

Tim looked up from his downward cast and we made eye contact. I could not see his face very well through the moisture swelling in my eyes. The emotions of the last hour were pouring out. Chiefs do cry sometimes. This time, I was crying for myself and I was ashamed of the fact.

"No, Chief, I didn't set you up. But if I were you, I wouldn't believe me," Tim sighed. "I just wanted to tell you to hold your head up. You've done a great job here. I'm proud to have worked for you. It's not much, but it's all I've got to give."

With that, Tim David slid off the polished hood of my car and walked across the parking lot toward Main Street. I watched him until he disappeared from sight. It was getting colder. I looked skyward and found no solace in Tim's suggestion to hold my head up.

* * *

The remainder of Saturday was a blur. Somehow, I managed to drive home. Each routine radio call that the police dispatcher sent over the air waves seemed to mock me. Vainly, I found myself listening through the jumble of calls and coded signals for a bank robbery or a hostage situation. Any kind of major incident where I could reaffirm my worth as a police officer and as a human being in a final act as a member of the department I had built. There was nothing. Nothing except the same old Saturday morning and afternoon "found bicycle" calls and shoplifters captured at the mall. I wandered the streets aimlessly for awhile and considered not going home until I figured out what I was going to do, but I really had no other place to go. It was useless to put off the inevitable. I knew Peggy would be worried.

When I pushed the electronic button to activate the garage door opener, Peggy was waiting for me on the steps inside the garage leading into the house. One look told me she had guessed that I was not bringing home good news. I tried to put up a weak false front. It was the only semi-brave thing I could find to do.

"Hey, you know that cruise to the Bahamas I have always promised you?" I called out as soon as I turned off the ignition and stepped out of the car. "Well, guess what? It just so happens I now have a little time on my hands and I might be able to work you into my busy schedule?"

Peggy walked across the garage and put her arms around my waist. She buried her face in my chest and I felt her hot tears moistening my shirt.

"Hey, baby, don't cry," I said as I became misty again. "We were looking for a job when we found this one, remember?"

Peggy did not respond. She only hugged me tighter. I was always amazed at how Peggy and I could read each other's thoughts. After twenty-five years of marriage, she instinctively knew I was in trouble long before I arrived home. We stayed locked in the hug for several long minutes.

"We knew this would happen," Peggy finally said. "Remember, you said when you took this job that police chiefs seldom last more than three years in one city. Look at us. We made it over six years. I'm so proud of you."

That was it. I could not hold back my tears any longer. We went inside and I told Peggy the whole story, or at least all of the story that I knew for sure. I did not leave anything out. It hurt to tell Peggy about Jana. It hurt her and it hurt me to admit my attraction to another woman. After being the Police Chief for so long, it was deeply painful admitting I was fallible. I did not want anything that might be released publicly, in the aftermath of my leaving, to be a surprise to her.

Breaking the news to my daughter was even tougher. Terri looked at me with her big blue eyes and said, "Daddy, does this mean you won't be the Chief anymore?"

"Yes, Terri, that's exactly what it means," I sighed. The child who had never known me in any capacity other than "Chief Dad" gave me a big hug and said, "It's okay, I still love you."

Peggy and I talked long into the night. We discussed our finances and estimated how long our meager savings would last until I would be forced to take another job. Surprisingly, Peggy and I decided we might be able to make it until my official retirement age delivered the guaranteed pension from Dallas. It would be tight, but Peggy and I could make it if we tried. I gained confidence from being with her. Peggy was my rock. She was my reason for living.

Neither of us could sleep, despite our emotional state of exhaustion. Four amitriptyline tablets, from Peggy's ample supply of prescribed medications, soon wiped me out. Peggy seldom took any of the wide variety of mood altering pills or capsules that the doctors were constantly sending home with her after her visits to the Mayo Clinic. She had an entire bathroom medicine cabinet full of the prescriptions. All shapes. All sizes. All colors. The bottle of little green anti-depressants had never been opened. Peggy and I decided this was about as depressing a day as we were likely to experience any time soon. Since the only chemicals my body was accustomed to have flowing through my veins were aspirin and vitamin c; the four twenty-five milligram tablets hit me like a baseball bat between the eyes. I vaguely remembered that it was almost midnight when Peggy swallowed her dose of the potent drug and crawled into bed beside me. We fell into a deep sleep, wrapped in each other's arms. I dreamed of nothing.

SUNDAY

CHAPTER SEVEN

Bart Francis sat by himself at the bar. Business was slow on a Sunday night. He had been there since seven o'clock and it was nearing ten. Bart was having no success. He called to the bartender for one more Miller Lite. Bart was trying to pace himself to avoid getting drunk while he was waiting. He could not afford to get bombed before he dealt with the reason that brought him to "Bad Leroy Brown's Downtown Bar".

Despite the name, the beer joint was owned by a guy named Ralph something or other. A child of the sixties, Ralph chose the "Leroy Brown" tag because he liked the old Jim Croce song. The owner catered to the upwardly mobile set and his place projected just the right touch of sleaze to attract those fascinated by that sort of thing. The waitresses wore mini skirts and exposed lots of tits. If the girls hooked a little on the side, that was okay with Ralph as long as they did it discreetly. Ralph also looked the other way while some of the big boys in the local coke trade did business at his tables. He did not care what people did inside his bar, as long as it did not attract the attention of the police. Just keep things cool and don't get rowdy, that was Ralph's motto.

The "Leroy Brown" rarely attracted police calls. In fact, there had been just one 911 call to the location in the last year. The police were called when one of his stupid bartenders overdosed in the bathroom on a "thunderball" of heroin and cocaine. The dumb shit still had the needle in his arm when the police kicked in the door on the toilet stall. Since then, Ralph had been more careful about his bartenders. He did not need any more attention from the police. His clientele certainly would not stand for the scrutiny. They were the type who did not want any notoriety.

Ralph's latest bartender was a slight, almost gaunt young man named Robert, with no last name. Robert seemed like a good hand. He was quiet and smoked a little weed every now and then, but he swore he did not mess with the hard stuff. Robert proved to be a good listener for the combination of yuppies and power drinkers that frequented "Leroy Brown's". The customers tipped him heavily. Robert was cool and minded his own business. Unknown to anyone except Bart, Robert was a paid informant for the Wichita Police Department.

"How much longer do you think?" Bart asked.

"I don't know, man. He's usually here by now," the bartender answered, keeping his voice low as usual. The expression on his bland face did not change as he retrieved a pair of one dollar bills for the beer from the bar's wet surface.

"Are you sure he's the guy with the power?" Bart asked for the tenth time.

"I told you, man. This guy has been in here every night for a week, bragging that he has this kinda gun and that kinda gun. Last night, he said he was gonna haft' to unload some of them, since his old lady ran out on him. It was a sad story. I almost cried," Robert murmured, with a faint touch of a smile.

"Okay, dickhead, but if you're jerking my chain, I'm gonna have your ass. Know what I mean?" Bart stared intently at the smaller man's face.

Sure, Robert thought. He knew just what the prick meant. Robert was on parole for a string of pharmacy burglaries from a couple of years back. His specialty was cutting the alarm wires and then chopping a hole in the roof. The damned police helicopter nailed him one night just as he had crawled out of his best score. It was pure bad luck. After having his asshole stretched in prison for six months, Robert knew damned well that he did not want to go back to the joint. He aimed to keep the long haired detective happy.

Bart Francis was a narc. He had been in the undercover section for less than a year. Before that, Bart had been assigned to the Traffic Division as a motorcycle officer. Riding a motor was not bad duty, but there was too much pressure to write more nit picking tickets. When the opportunity came to take the detective's test, Bart jumped at it. He studied hard and placed high on the exam. Bart did not worry about his lack of connections with the higher ups on the department. Chief Starr's policy was that if you scored high on the examination, and there was a vacancy when your name ranked at the top of the list, you got promoted. It was as simple as that. For once, the system was fair and being fair was all you could really ask for in a boss.

Before heading for "Leroy's", Bart watched the six o'clock news which replayed the noon press conference announcing the Chief's "retirement". The City Manager was vague and it was very confusing. All of the City Council members were mysteriously "out of town and unavailable for comment". The rumors around the squad room in the Narcotics Section were flying hot and heavy. He was not quite sure what to make of all the conflicting reasons given for the Chief's leaving, but he was sad to see him go. Bart liked the Chief. Not because Chief Starr had promoted him, but because he appreciated the new changes the Chief had brought. It was no secret the Chief and the City Manager did not get along. They had fought for years over just about everything. There were rumors the Chief was going to leave for another job, or get fired, just about every other month. Take your pick. Bart wondered how he would repay his boss for all he had done for him and the department now that the Chief really was gone.

Bart thought about his last month on motorcycles. He had been involved in two accidents in the last month. Sure, they were his fault. Bart was tired and he had not been paying attention. He had been staying up late at night studying for the promotional exam and taking care of a sick baby he and his wife had just brought home from the hospital. Times were tough and they were barely scraping by on his less than adequate patrolman's salary, but the city's policy was clear. If you were found at fault on a second motor vehicle accident within a year, the penalty was a mandatory one day suspension without pay.

Bart requested a hearing and appealed to the Chief, but nothing could be done to override the city's policy. When the meeting was over, the Chief asked Bart to wait in the hall. Chief Starr soon exited and handed him an envelope with the official suspension letter. Also inside were five crisp new twenty dollar bills. Nothing was said, but the Chief winked at him and walked away.

It made Bart angry to see the City Manager sitting in a booth at "Leroy Brown's" having such a grand time celebrating the Chief's demise. But the undercover officer was not there to worry about the Chief or the City Manager. Bart had a job to do and his job did not involve either of the two public figures tonight.

"Tell me again what the guy said about the heaters?" Bart whispered to Robert.

Robert pulled a greasy white cloth from his back pocket and began to wipe the spilled beer and moisture from the bar in front of him. "I told you, man, all he said was that he had a couple of Thompsons he needed to unload. He said if I heard of anyone wanting to buy 'em to bring 'em by the bar. That's all, man, just that."

Bart passed the time by staring at the wide screen television in the corner near the city manager's booth. The Kansas City Chiefs and the Dallas Cowboys were playing in football's version of "David and Goliath". Bart swore that the Chiefs had to be the most inept football team in American history. For the past twenty years, they had always folded when the pressure was on. Now, the boys from "Big D" were showing the Chiefs how to wear their jock straps. The score was 42 to absolutely nothing in favor of the guys with blue stars on their helmets..

Bart noticed that Mel Michaels was not watching the football game. The Manager was wrapped around a woman with red hair who looked vaguely familiar. It was dark in the bar and Bart could not be sure, but the woman resembled a high dollar prostitute he had busted at the Marriott Hotel last month. In Wichita, the undercover officers worked every type of crime where the special ability to mingle unobtrusively was necessary. The assignments included drugs, whores, guns and whatever came up.

Bart decided he would count the number of drinks being delivered to the City Manager's table, just to give him something to do, when the target of his investigation walked in the bar's front door. The guy was huge. Holy shit, Bart thought, this character must weigh three hundred and fifty pounds. Robert told him to expect a big man, but not this big. If he had known the asshole was going to be a giant, Bart would have enlisted some back up. The First Armored Division would have been appropriate, if they were not off kicking the living shit out of some third world country this week.

Bart glanced at his informant for confirmation. The wimpy bartender gave one slight nod of his fuzzy head to indicate that the behemoth standing in the doorway was the guy. Bart kept his seat and concentrated on his beer, while Robert moved to serve the big man.

"What'll it be tonight, sir," Robert asked. The giant sat on two bar stools at the same time.

"Gimme' a draw and a whiskey chaser. I don't care what kind, just make it quick. I've had a really shity day," the potential gun dealer announced loudly. No one seemed to notice nor care.

Robert brought the drinks and began the casual, low key type of conversation which made him such a great informant. After ten minutes of intermittent talk, during which Robert left several times to serve other customers, the informant nodded towards the other end of the bar where Bart sat quietly sipping at his Miller Lite. Bart pretended not to notice and kept staring at the giant television where Kansas City continued to fumble and stumble as usual. The game had become a rout and few people in the bar were paying any attention to the action on the wide screen.

Soon, Bart was forced to acknowledge the presence of his target. The big man rose from his "seats" and walked over to Bart's stool. He stood in front of the undercover officer, blocking the view of the tv. If the two were outside in the daytime, the giant would have blotted out the sun.

The stranger's bulging muscles indicated he could hire out to small Islamic countries to pull the arms off of convicted thieves.

"Hey, buddy, move your fat ass. I'm watching the game," Bart complained, just like a typical character in a beer joint would say who was either too stupid or too drunk to take notice of his potential adversary's size.

"No shit. Well, I didn't think anybody watched those pussies play with themselves anymore," the guy answered. He sat down next to Bart and Robert brought the man's drinks from the other end of the bar.

"I understand you are lookin' to buy something special for Christmas," the big man said in a quiet but distinct voice.

"Oh, and you're the one with some quality merchandise to unload?" Bart asked calmly, trying not to move too quickly in soliciting the incriminating statement he needed to make a case.

"I might be. It depends. Whatcha' lookin' for?" the man answered.

"Well, the bartender told me you have some serious heat. You might say that I'm a collector of heat," Bart said. The undercover officer attempted to look around the big man to see the tv, as a sign he was interested in the guns, but not too eager. Actually, any chance of seeing the screen was hopeless. Bart would need eyeballs on his thumbs to look around this guy.

"Well, mister serious collector, do you have the cash to back up your wants?" the stranger asked sarcastically.

"What do you have and how much do you want for 'em?" Bart replied quickly.

Right away, Bart knew he had made a mistake in being so abrupt. That was not the way it was done, damn it. He was still learning the ropes. In his new assignment as an undercover officer, Bart had not made a gun case yet, concentrating on dope and women; but he knew in his gut that he was about to blow this one.

The mountain masquerading as a man eyed Bart with a puzzled look and finally hissed, "Shhheeeeeeettttt". The long drawn out profanity was accompanied by a spray of saliva that dribbled down the big man's full beard. Bart figured the next sentence would be a challenge that he was a cop, but the dreaded accusation did not come.

"I like a man who gets right to the point!" To punctuate his enthusiasm, the giant slapped Bart on the back with a meaty paw the size of Rhode Island.

"Let's go outside and do some bizness'" the man ordered.

"Hey, you, bartender! Watch our drinks. We'll be back."

Ordinarily, Bart would have made some excuse to stall the suspect and used the phone in the Men's Room to call headquarters for back up, but he was relieved he had not blown the deal by moving too quickly. Bart allowed his sense of relief to overcome his caution and he followed the man through the scattered tables to the front door.

It was a rookie mistake of the first order.

Outside, the man motioned to a parking lot on the other side of the street from the bar. Curiously, Bart's own undercover Toyota was parked there as well. He wondered why the guy had not parked in the bar's lot adjacent to the lounge, but then decided the guy had chosen the lot of the closed appliance store across the street for the same reason that he had. It was safer not to park your car too close to a dive like "Leroy's" if you were on the wrong side of the law; or pretending to be on the wrong side.

As they walked, the seller laid out his terms. "Look, I've got two Thompsons, .45 caliber, with fifty round drum magazines for each. They're cherry. Not a spot of rust on 'em. I've shot 'em both and they're sweet. I need fifteen hundred each or you can have 'em both for twenty five hundred. What d'ya say?"

The guy sounded as if he was selling the one and only "Magik Ginzu" knives, which cut through tin cans on late night tv infomercials and have handles that melt in the dishwasher.

"I say I want to see these beauties before I lay out any dough. But, if they're as good as you say, I'll take both of 'em off your hands," Bart answered.

They reached the back of a battered blue Oldsmobile and the big man fumbled for a massive set of keys dangling from a chain hooked to his belt. "I've got 'em both in here. Have you got the money with you?" the stranger asked.

"Yeah," Bart lied. After he confirmed the guy had the illegal automatic weapons, Bart hoped to stall the goliath long enough to make a call and get the cavalry down here to complete the arrest safely.

"Dynamite," the man said.

Bart was wondering what "dynamite" had to do with anything when two unseen men threw open the sliding door and jumped out of a van parked next to the Olds. Each wielded a big automatic pistol and pointed them directly at the third button on Bart's shirt. The narc's heart skipped a beat and the vital organ almost blew itself out of his chest and onto the pavement.

"Oh, fuck," Bart said. He was going to die and he knew it. How could he have been so stupid? First, these characters were going to drag his ass out into the country and rob him. When they discovered that Bart did not have the money like he said he did, they would put a bullet in his brain, or where a brain would have been if Bart had one. His first big mistake would be his last. A major boner that spelled the end to a promising career as an undercover agent. While his mind read the bleak future, Bart played the only remaining card left in his hand.

"Police officer, you're all under arrest!" Bart announced in the loudest voice he could muster. The tone had a squeak to it, but it was the best he could do under the circumstances.

The three robbers froze as if by magic. They did not lower their pistols, but they did not blow his stupid head off either. Bart sensed somehow that progress had been made.

"Bull shit, asshole! Up against the car and spread 'em," the giant gun peddler ordered.

"That's my line!" Bart shouted.

With that, all three slammed the undercover officer onto the trunk of the Olds and began frisking him, police style.

"Hey, what's going on here?" Bart demanded.

"If you're a cop, where's your badge?" one of the gunmen asked.

Bart thought about the old movie line from "Treasure of the Sierra Madre", "Badges? Badges? We don't need no stinking badges…", but quickly decided to save it for a better audience.

"I don't have it on me," Bart admitted truthfully.

The big man made the decision. "He's full of shit, let's book him."

"Book me? Wait! Are you police officers?" Bart cried out in a mixture of confusion and relief.

The three hundred pound Federal ATF Agent, who had been pretending to be a machine gun dealer, showed Bart a small gold badge and a green identification card inside a wallet size black leather folder. "Grimes, ATF, you're under arrest for solicitation to purchase an illegal weapon. We'll read you your rights inside the van. Let's go."

When Bart saw the badge, he rose from his draped position over the Oldsmobile trunk. Before one of the other agents could knock him down again, Bart replied with new found confidence," I don't think so guys. I'm Detective Francis, Wichita Police. My badge and ID are in the Toyota right there. The keys are here in my pant's pocket."

While Agent Grimes continued to guard their prisoner, the other two federal officers used Bart's keys to open his undercover car. They soon found his city issued nine millimeter Smith and Wesson, portable radio and Bart's wallet with his silver detective's badge and beige Wichita P.D. identification card. When all three officers had examined the credentials to their satisfaction, Agent Grimes handed the equipment and wallet to Bart and said, "Sheeeeeeeettttttt". In unison, all four burst out laughing. In a jumble of raw emotions heightened by healthy doses of adrenaline, each one of the participants in the drama tried to out do the other in telling his side of the story.

"Man, when you offered to buy the heaters so quickly I thought you were the easiest mark we've had in years," Grimes laughed.

"Yeah, and when Tommy here gave us the code word that you had the money and the deal was complete, I about busted a gut getting out of the van. Shit, I think I broke a rib or something," the other agent laughed. The ear plug from the recording unit monitoring Grimes' hidden body microphone was still dangling from his right ear.

"Let me guess," Bart asked in tears, "the code word was "dynamite", right? I couldn't figure out what the heck "dynamite" had to do with machine guns?"

"You got it," they all announced. "It's a good thing you weren't carrying your gun when you put us all under arrest." The image of unarmed Bart boldly arresting all three of his assailants brought forth new howls of laughter.

"Yeah," one said, "we might have shot your ass off by mistake." The hoots of more laughter bounced around the deserted parking lot.

"Say," Grimes was beginning to come down from the hilarity high, "Why didn't you have your badge and gun? Surely, the P.D. trusts you to carry them or do you have to go back to your car if you need 'em in a hurry?"

"Hey, we're not like you guys. We don't just work one kind of undercover case. We work whatever we run into. Whores, dope, whatever. It's kind of embarrassing to have a hooker you're trying to make a case on, reach over to grope your ass and find your badge or squeeze your balls and discover you're carrying your rod with your other rod. Know what I mean?" Bart lectured.

The agents all nodded thoughtfully, although not a one of them had a clue as to what it took to make a misdemeanor prostitution case. As with most federal agents, the actual number of arrests they made in a year was minuscule compared to the average big city police detective.

"So, we usually leave our stuff in the car and try not to get into anything without backup. I just fouled up tonight," Bart admitted. "But it probably saved my ass."

They were still chuckling, and swapping other war stories, when the city manager and his date barged noisily through the front door of "Leroy Brown's" and onto the sidewalk. A blare of juke box music and laughter of their own making accompanied their less than discreet exit.

Bart jerked a finger over his shoulder and said, "There's our fearless leader now."

"You mean your chief? I thought he got the boot today. That guy doesn't look too sad," Grimes noted.

"Naw, that's not Chief Starr. He wouldn't be caught dead in a place like Leroy's. No, that's our asshole city manager. He thinks he's the real chief," Bart answered.

"Hey, get a load of the red head," one of the agents instructed.

From across the street, the officers could see that the woman was draped all over the diminutive city manager like a bad suit. The woman kept grabbing at the City Manager's crotch while she firmly tongued his ear as they weaved their way through the bar's adjacent parking lot.

"Is that his wife?" Grimes asked.

"Are you shitin' me? What the fuck is the matter with you guys?" Bart responded sarcastically. "Surely you Feds have seen a twenty dollar hooker before."

"Hey," one agent spoke for the second time in a minute, "try the view with these babies." He passed Bart a pair of "Starlight" binoculars to use. The "Starlight" scope was a sophisticated night viewing device which gathered whatever light was available and magnified it a thousand fold. It even enhanced vision on totally dark nights by using the dim light emitted from the moon or stars; hence the "Starlight" name. Most police departments could not afford the expensive technology, but the Feds had access to all of the stealth gadgets left over from the various minor wars in the Middle East and Balkans.

Bart watched through the bulky scope as the City Manager and the woman finally made it to manager's city owned car hidden in the bar parking lot. The gray Ford Taurus was backed into its stall so the special white Kansas license plates, identifying the vehicle as being owned by a city government, would not be visible. Bart glanced around and noted that all three of the agents had produced their own individual "Starlight" scopes and were enjoying the show.

"We should send out for popcorn or maybe a pizza," Grimes suggested.

"I don't think we're gonna have time," Bart correctly predicted.

When they reached the Manager's car, the woman leaned her back against the driver's door and pulled Mel Michaels close to her body. The two then put a lip lock on each other with enough suction to shame an octopus. All the while, Mel was groping the woman's breasts and thrusting his hips at her body. The repeated bangs of the little man's humpings was beginning to gently rock the Taurus from side to side. The pre-fornication ritual went on for several minutes while the undercover officers watched in shocked silence from the darkness across the street.

"Boy, you guys in Wichita sure put on some kind of show for us visiting federal dignitaries," Grimes announced. He had to admit that he was becoming aroused. The experience was similar to watching a dirty movie or window peeping, except the scene in front of them was occurring in a public parking lot. The "Starlight" scopes gave the actors in this X rated live performance a greenish tint, but it was clear there was about to be a serious finale in the making.

"Yeah, it's our version of catching Willie Clinton and the maid humping in the Oval Office," Bart admitted. In a way, Bart was embarrassed that the person who governed his city was being viewed in the act of dipping his wick in public. It was especially embarrassing that the scene was being savored by a bunch of law enforcement officers from outside his own department.

Some things should stay in the family, he thought.

"Geez, don't you guys have a law against this kind of thing here?" The agent who first produced the "Starlight" scope asked.

"They do have an ordinance, but I don't think it applies to the head man," Grimes replied.

"The hell it doesn't," Bart mumbled. Despite his embarrassment he could not take his eyes off the erotic actions of the two people in the other parking lot.

Suddenly, the woman hiked herself up onto the side of the Taurus, placing her butt level with the driver's side window. She braced both feet against the side of the parked car in the next stall, effectively capturing Mel in the vee of her elevated crotch. With one deft move, the woman pulled her coat and skirt above her waist, revealing nothing underneath but the anatomy with which she had entered the world. The two stayed locked in a lingering mouth to mouth war dance between two tongues.

Like a teenager on his first hot date, Mel fumbled with his trousers. He finally managed to free his equipment and make the correct connection. The woman broke the kiss, if you could call the human vacuum cleaner method a kiss, and threw her head backwards in pleasure. Her guttural moan was clearly audible in the parking lot across the street. Bart thought that she seemed to be enjoying her work more than most prostitutes usually admitted. Mel kept thrusting for all he was worth. He was too short to take full advantage of the situation, but tried to compensate for his lack of height and lack of length by standing on his tip toes. They were both frantically rushing for a climatic finish that would be an all time show stopper when the car alarm went off, as if on cue.

It was not Mel's city car that was blaring. The ear piercing wail came from the car the woman was using to brace her heels against each charge of Mel's light brigade. The rocking motion had finally set off the less than sensitive vibration sensor in the car's burglar alarm system.

In moments, the four law enforcement officers were observing chaos. Mel was desperately trying to ignore the alarm and finish his business. The woman was frantically attempting to push Mel away before the cops came and busted her again. She began screaming at him to stop. Lights were popping on inside the apartments behind the bar's parking lot. A man came charging out of the bar to see what was going on, probably the owner of the car with the screaming alarm. Inside "Leroy Brown's", someone yelled, "Call the police!" If it could be captured on film in full Technicolor and surround sound, the spectacle had Oscar winning potential.

The City Manager, with his pants and boxer shorts down around his ankles, came to his senses and panic set in. He pulled the woman away from his car and, in a frenzy, tried to find his keys in his trouser pockets that were jumbled together on the ground. The woman was irate with her unappreciative customer and began calling him all sorts of non-Christian names.

The alarm continued to wail, and had shifted into an obnoxious "yelp" mode, when the hapless Manager finally found his keys and dove into the safety of his car.

"Damn, what's next, Wichita?" Grimes called Bart by the name of his city. "Do we get to see Miss Kansas give the Mayor a head job or maybe the Governor will masturbate an elephant right here in a parade down the middle of the street. Perhaps we could bring in some spotlights to add to the effect, what do you think? Huh?"

"I think this is about all of this shit I'm gonna stand for," Bart answered with determined resolve. Bart tossed the "Starlight" scope to the guy with the dangling ear plug and jumped into his battered undercover Toyota. The federal agents stood and watched in amazement.

By the time Bart started the car and backed out of his parking spot, the Manager was roaring out of the bar's parking lot across the street at a speed exceeding Ford's design limits. The Manager threw a spray of gravel on the woman, as she called him a "cocksucker" one last time, and floored the Taurus' accelerator.

"615 to dispatch," Bart spoke his designated call number into his portable radio as he tried to maneuver the puny Toyota into the street and follow the half naked City Manager.

"Go ahead, 615" the Eastside Patrol dispatcher answered. The female dispatcher was a little perplexed. Normally, the vice guys, with the six hundred series call numbers, did not broadcast on the patrol channels. They usually stayed on their own special frequencies, where their radio transmissions were electronically scrambled to prevent anyone other than authorized personnel from monitoring their activities.

"615, send a unit to Leroy Brown's on East Douglas, please. There's been some type of disturbance and I am attempting to catch up with a subject leaving the scene at a high rate of speed," Bart radioed.

"Ten four, 615. 242 and 245, take the disturbance call at Leroy Brown's Bar, unknown numbers on East Douglas. 615 is in pursuit of an individual fleeing the scene," the dispatcher made the initial call and entered the information into the preformatted computer screen in front of her. Both patrol units acknowledged the call and she keyed the microphone on her command console to obtain an update from the narc unit.

"615, are you in a plain car? Will you need assistance in stopping the vehicle?" the dispatcher asked calmly.

There was no answer from 615. Bart was watching in awe as the Manager was weaving from one side of the road to another. He must surely be drunk, Bart thought. Any second now he will crash into another car and kill himself. Bart kept his hand away from the radio transmit button on his walkie talkie, thinking that his next transmission would be to call for an ambulance.

Actually, Mel was trying to pull his pants up and drive at the same time. It was a more difficult chore than it looked. The damned boxer shorts had wadded up around his knees and were complicating matters in the narrow confines of the smallish Ford's driver's seat. It did not help that Mel was perpetually forced to drive with the car's seat pulled as close as possible to the dash so he could reach the steering wheel and the pedals. Such is the life of the vertically challenged.

"615 to dispatch, we're still Eastbound on Douglas. I will need assistance in stopping the vehicle. It's a gray Ford Taurus. I'm not close enough to make out the license plate yet. He's all over the road at a high rate of speed, possible DUI," Bart reported.

"244 to dispatch, I'm at Douglas and Hydraulic now. I can intercept," the nearest beat's patrol unit volunteered.

"Ten four, 244, where are you now 615?" the dispatcher called. She had not yet declared it an official pursuit, since she knew the narc unit had no emergency equipment such as flashing lights or siren, to stop the fleeing car.

"615, I'm gaining a little on him, I think. We should be coming up on Hydraulic soon," Bart replied.

"Ten four. 244's at the location and ready to take over the pursuit," the dispatcher relayed.

"615, also advise the units responding to Leroy Brown's that there are three federal law enforcement officers across the street in plain clothes. They may or may not have intervened in the disturbance, I'm not sure," Bart advised the dispatcher. He did not want any patrol officers to see the guns of the Feds and start shooting before they asked any questions.

"242 and 245, did you copy 615's transmission?" the dispatcher asked.

Both patrol units responding to "Leroy Brown's" radioed their acknowledgment of the undercover officer's warning concerning the federal officers. The other patrol officer assigned to intercept the fleeing Taurus keyed his radio's microphone to ask for a repeat of the suspect vehicle's information and a description of the narc officer's car, for verification that he had the correct target vehicle in sight. It was doubtful the patrolman would need the extra information to determine the culprit in the light traffic.

"615 to 244, the car is approaching Hydraulic on Douglas now. I'm about two hundred yards behind him in a red Toyota." Bart was not admitting over the radio that he knew exactly who was driving the Taurus. The detective was not sure how he was going to deal with that situation just yet.

Officer Don Steele was riding Beat 244's patrol unit tonight. A six year veteran, the patrolman had been in the first recruit class of officers Chief Starr hired after coming to Wichita. Like everyone else in the department, he had heard about the City Manager's noontime announcement that the Chief was stepping down. Shortly before going on duty at three o'clock, Officer Steele tried to call the Chief's house to wish him luck. There was no answer. Don owed his job to the guy, not to mention how much his mom was touched when the Chief attended his dad's funeral last year. It surprised everyone in Don's family for the police chief be present at the service. As far as Don could tell, the Chief met his dad only once, at his class graduation ceremony. The time the Chief spent talking to his mom at the church meant so much to her and the family. The officer was confused about the announcement of the Chief's retirement, but he had his own police business to take care of right now.

The Taurus ran the red light and took a sharp, squealing left turn onto Hydraulic Avenue. A chrome plated hub cap popped off the right front wheel, due to the strain of the closed angle turn, and clattered down the street like a spinning top.

"244, I'm on him. He's northbound on Hydraulic at high speed," Don radioed.

Despite a standing start from the gas station parking lot, where he waited to make the intercept, Officer Steele rapidly closed the distance. The new Chevys in the police fleet could really accelerate and go, not like those old, worthless piece of shit Dodge's he was force to drive his first year on the force. Don punched the red plastic rocker arm switch on the mid-seat console at his right elbow and the night lit up with a blaze of red, white and blue lights from the complex array on his high tech roof mounted light bar.

Inside the Taurus, Mel still had not managed to get his pants above his knees when the intersection suddenly appeared. Mel knew he was running the red light because he could not find the brake pedal in time. It was all he could do to make the turn without jumping the curb and wrecking into the houses that lined the narrow street. Mel hazarded a glance into his rear view mirror and felt sick. There was a damned police car behind him. For the second time tonight, panic gripped him by the throat. Mel knew he could not be captured with his pants and underwear down around his ankles, that was certain. What to do? The only answer that came to him was "run". Mel Michaels, the most powerful man in city government, was afraid. Terrified, in fact.

Instead of slowing and pulling over to the right side of the roadway, as the law required, the Taurus accelerated. Officer Steele noticed the change in speed immediately and reacted by increasing his own pressure on the accelerator.

"244, he's running. I'm in pursuit," Don called over the radio. He could no longer hide the excitement in his voice.

"Ten four, 244. 240, we have 244 in pursuit of a suspect, northbound on Hydraulic from Douglas," the dispatcher assigned a supervisor to monitor and control the chase, according to established policy.

"240 to dispatch, what's he wanted for?" the patrol sergeant asked.

"240, all I know is that 615 called in a report of a disturbance at Leroy Brown's and 244 is attempting to stop one party fleeing from the scene. We don't really know what was going on back there yet. We are receiving citizen calls from the location now. 244, what do you have on the suspect?" the dispatcher asked.

Steele could barely be heard over the wail of his siren that he had activated when the driver of the Taurus refused to stop. "244, the suspect is wanted for traffic violations only at this time, but he's weaving all over the road; possible DUI."

The more serious potential drunk driving charge and the uncertainty of the events back at the bar caused the Sergeant to allow the chase to continue. The Chief had given strict instructions that pursuits were to be held to an absolute minimum to prevent needless injuries to officers and citizens. Even if Starr was not police chief anymore, the Sergeant knew the chase policy was a good one and he was determined to follow the Chief's rules.

"240 traffic dispatch, have 615 drop out and assign another unit to assist 244," the sergeant ordered. He knew the undercover unit was not equipped to be involved in a pursuit. The policy also required any unmarked units to discontinue their involvement when a fully marked squad car, with flashing lights and siren capabilities, intercepted the chase.

"Ten four, 240. 251, can you back 244? He's attempting to stop a gray Ford Taurus, northbound on Hydraulic from Douglas," the dispatcher inquired.

There was actually no need to formally assign 251 to the task. Every police car on the east side of Wichita was steadily drifting towards the general area of the pursuit. Although the policy limited the number of chase cars involved to three, the other units floated around the periphery of the pursuit like vultures; waiting to swoop down for the capture whenever the suspect crashed or bailed out.

251 acknowledged his assignment and 615 was ordered by the dispatcher to drop out. Bart ignored the instruction and pushed the old Toyota to go faster. He had to be in on the finish, if for no other reason than to explain to the uniformed troops what he had seen at the bar. The dumb shit City Manager was doing exactly what he should not do. By running, he was admitting his guilt. Surely, the Manager did not think he could elude the entire Wichita Police Department.

In Mel's tormented mind, befuddled with hysteria, that was exactly what he thought. Mel's only desire was to run until he could get his pants up. Once that happened, he could think of some semi-plausible story to cover it all up. Try as he might, Mel was having no success untangling the knot of fabric that were once his trousers. They remained jammed around his knees and the balled up boxer shorts, wet from perspiration and bladder leaks, prevented the pants from being pulled any higher in the car's tight confines. "Shit, shit, shit," he swore.

Mel took his eyes off the road for a second to quickly determine a better way to pull his pants up. With one hand on the steering wheel, Mel barely missed the bright yellow "Fill N Flush Plumbing" truck that pulled into his path from the right side of the intersection with Central Avenue. He jerked the wheel once again into a hard left turn and skidded through another red light. Mel finally regained control of the Ford when he was a half a block away from the intersection. He peered into the mirror and saw that the police car had not made the turn behind him. It was just the break he needed, Mel thought.

"244, I've lost the suspect. He's turned westbound on Central from Hydraulic. I'm caught in traffic," Officer Steele groaned. As he skidded into a panic stop, he damned his luck. Don was not about to give up just because some stupid yellow toilet fixing truck blocked the intersection. Don jerked the Chevy's heavy duty transmission into reverse and the smoke boiled from his radial tires as he backed up and then passed the stalled truck. The plumber waved at him as the officer wheeled the big Chevy across the median strip and back on the trail of the Ford. Don was not sure whether the plumber was yelling "go get him" or "you sonofabitch". It really didn't matter. The officer was a mile behind the Taurus and could barely see the Ford's tail lights by the time he re-entered the chase.

"240 traffic dispatch, do we have the chopper in the air?" the Sergeant asked.

Before the dispatcher could answer, the helicopter pilot answered for her. "Air One, we are airborne from the helipad. Our ETA is about two minutes to the pursuit's last known location."

The helicopter pilot was Lieutenant Al Orr, a twenty year veteran of the Wichita Police Department. Lieutenant Orr, referred to in the police vernacular as just "Lieu" by his troops, was nearing retirement, but he still loved to fly. His baby was the Hughes, Model 300-C, light observation helicopter that was the mainstay of the puny W.P.D. air fleet. The department had three helicopters. Only two could fly, however. Al and his mechanic used the third bird for spare parts to keep the other two flying. Every year the City Manager cut their budget at the Air Section more and more. Pretty soon, Al thought, he and his other two trained pilots would be reduced to towing the helicopters around on a flat bed trailer.

Al and one of his pilots, Officer Renny Burleson, were sitting around the hangar talking about the latest news on the Chief's departure when they picked up the transmissions describing the pursuit on their police radio. Al was telling his partner about the time he had scored number four on the captain's test and there were only three vacancies that year. The day before the promotional list expired, Chief Starr called him into his office and apologized for not being able to promote him. Al really wanted those silver captain's bars and he knew the Chief had the authority to skip over one of the others on the list to promote him. But that was not the way Chief Starr operated. You either earned it or you didn't. It was that simple. Al respected the principle more than he ever told the Chief. When Chief Starr called his parents that night, back home in Nebraska, to tell them what a good son they had and that Al would get his promotion some day, the Lieutenant was doubly impressed. But the story would have to wait until they caught the guy 244 was chasing. One glance at each other and Al and Renny ran outside to warm up their bird, sitting cold and isolated on the concrete pad in front of the hangar.

Renny and Al had a surprise in store for the patrol troops on the ground and they were dying to try it out.

* * *

Mel breathed a sigh of relief at being a free man. Now, he could continue down Central Avenue to City Hall, a few blocks away, and pull into the parking lot and report that someone had stolen his car. Yeah, that was it, he thought. Mel would report his car stolen and it would take the dumb cops hours before they found it parked in the city lot. Maybe days. The City Manager would blame the whole affair on the inefficiency of the police department and claim he would see that the new chief turned things around. All of this, of course, would be after he had pulled up these damned pants. Mel cursed the small interior of the Taurus and blamed the designers in Detroit for causing him all of this trouble tonight. It was a classic Mel Michaels' habit of projecting the blame onto someone else.

Mel did not know about 251. Officer Ray Rhodes lay in wait at Broadway and Central Avenue for the approaching Taurus. When the car went by, the officer activated his overhead lights and siren and slid in close behind the suspect vehicle.

"251 traffic dispatch, I've picked up 244's fleeing vehicle," Ray announced. Officer Rhodes had been on the department for only two years and his youthful voice sounded more excited over the radio than the veteran in 244's car.

"251, the vehicle is westbound on Central, passing Broadway. I'm closing in for the license plate, stand by," Ray advised.

Mel heard 251's siren and did not want to look in the mirror. The Manager slowed the Taurus by letting up on the accelerator, but he did not stop as they approached Main Street and the City Hall complex.

"251 traffic dispatch, the license is Kansas…," the young officer released the red microphone button and stopped transmitting.

After several long seconds elapsed, the dispatcher became worried. "251. 251.251, are you okay?"

There was no immediate answer to the dispatcher's inquiry. Just silence on the deathly quiet police radio frequency where only moments before there had been excited, but professional, transmissions by Officer Ray Rhodes.

Officer Rhodes completely forgot the proper radio procedures he learned in recruit school and in the field training program that Chief Starr had designed. When he finally found his voice again, Ray shouted into the microphone, "Hey, you guys, the suspect 244 was chasing is in a city car! It's got city license tags. I think he's going to pull into to the lot here at City Hall."

Ray was wrong. Mel saw the flashing red and blue lights and cursed his luck. He could not stop now. Mel had the same problem that he had before 251 found him. All the Manager could do was to continue running and loose this cop like he had lost the last one. Mel punched the accelerator on the tired Ford and roared past the city building, continuing west on Central Avenue. He tossed a sorrowful glance towards City Hall as his "stolen car in the parking lot scheme" evaporated from useful consideration.

Lieutenant Orr and Officer Burleson were flying over the Arkansas River at an altitude of five hundred feet. They had flown the river's course, after leaving the helipad on the near south side of the city, in a roughly plotted interception course for the chase heading west towards downtown. Their timing and their plot was right on the money. After thousands of flight hours in the little two seater Hughes, Al and Renny were pros at this game.

"Air One traffic dispatch, we're on top of 251 and the suspect vehicle now," Al keyed the foot pedal activating his radio and announced their presence into the boom microphone fitted to his flight helmet. The helicopter's arrival was exactly what the Sergeant controlling the chase in Unit 240 was waiting to hear.

"240, traffic dispatch, tell 251 and all other units to disregard the pursuit, repeat, drop back and let Air One take over," the Sergeant ordered. The dispatcher activated the special electronic warning tone that preceded important information or high priority calls and repeated the instructions so everyone could hear the Sergeant's orders.

Officer Rhodes, in 251, immediately slowed down and came to a halt in the middle of the street. He shut off his flashing lights and siren and simply waited for 244 to catch up from behind or for Air One to give him further instructions.

The engine of the overheated Chevy ticked audibly and seemed to chafe at being denied the opportunity to continue the pursuit. Like a bloodhound with the scent in its nose, every part of the officer's essence wanted to be in on the finish.

Overhead, Al and Renny grinned at each other in the glow of the instrument panel. They loved this part of the chief's policy on pursuits more than the "ground pounders", as they called the street patrol officers who were not free to fly through the air like hawks on a hunt. The policy was clever, really, but it took discipline and training to work correctly. Discipline was imperative primarily by the officers on the ground to do something that was counter to their adrenaline induced urge to continue the chase. The pursuing patrol units were instructed to drop back and let the fleeing suspect think he had escaped. The training came into play by the helicopter pilot and his airborne observer whose job was to hover overhead, out of sight and sound, and direct the patrol units to the best capture location when the suspect finally stopped and got out of the car.

The basic premise was simple. Ninety-nine percent of all suspects who ran from the police were waiting for a little breathing room to dump the car and make their escape on foot, where they could more easily hide. The chief's policy gave the suspects the illusion they had achieved their goal of acquiring time to bail out of the car and "beat feet". From their view overhead, the helicopter's observer's role was to vector the officers in on the suspect when he was out of the car and much safer to capture. It was a hell of a lot more efficient, and less risky, than chasing the high speed guided missile that a fleeing automobile became in the hands of a frightened suspect. As long as the helicopter was up and flying, the good guys always won. Especially tonight. Al and Renny had their secret weapon ready.

"Warm it up, Renny," Al ordered over the helicopter's intercom which could not be heard by anyone except his observer.

"I'm way ahead of you, Lieu, we're up and running. Hot, straight, and normal," Renny used the old navy slang for a torpedo that was operating as designed. But the chopper duo was not using torpedoes. They had F.L.I.R.

"Forward Looking Infrared Radar", or FLIR, was another futuristic piece of military hardware which had been adapted to law enforcement use. The equipment allowed the user to visualize objects emitting heat. Unlike the "Starlight" scopes, which magnified whatever light sources already available, the FLIR displayed heat patterns on a small, thirteen-inch color television screen mounted in front of the observer's seat on the helicopter. Body heat was more than sufficient to be displayed on the screen and the images were not hidden by things which would normally obstruct vision, like trees or bushes.

Al and the Chief had been working on getting a FLIR for the Air Section for over four years. They finally convinced one of the local electronics manufacturers, whose military contracts were essential to the local economy, to donate a unit on a sort of "Lend Lease" agreement. A promise to write several articles in the standard law enforcement magazines, touting their equipment to other police departments, had been the deal clincher that Al and Chief Starr used with the company. It had taken a month to get the new equipment installed and everyone trained. Tonight would be the first operational use of the FLIR. To say that Al and Renny were excited would be an understatement. From their tests, they knew what a fantastic piece of equipment the FLIR could be. Al only regretted that he had not been able to finally prove the equipment's value before the Chief quit. The FLIR had been as much the Chief's baby as it was his.

Mel had no idea the police helicopter was above him. At five hundred feet, little noise from the craft's small piston engine reached the ground. Mel checked his rear view mirror again and noticed that the second police car had vanished from sight. Mel was not certain how he had escaped, but naturally assumed he was just far smarter than the police. No wonder the stupid bastards were such an easy mark for his budget cutting knife. They could not catch a cold, much less keep up to speed with his wily ways, he reasoned.

Mel had another trick up his sleeve, just in case that there might be another dumb cop lurking in the area.

"Air One traffic dispatch, be advised that the suspect vehicle has killed his lights and is turning north on Mims Drive, from Central," Lieutenant Orr spoke into his radio microphone. The fact the suspect had doused his lights might make him more difficult to locate from the ground, but it made no difference to the view from above. On the FLIR's futuristic display screen, the hot engine on the Taurus glowed a bright red.

Mel formulated a new plan now that he believed he had escaped once again. Mel turned north into Riverside Park. Without his headlights, the Manager slowed and navigated by the dim street lights until he came to a darkened parking lot near the deserted tennis courts. There was no one in the park at this time of night, not even the usual homosexuals or street fairies that lurked in the bathrooms and cavorted on the picnic tables during warmer weather. The secluded setting was perfect for Mel's new plan.

"Air One traffic dispatch, the suspect has pulled into Riverside Park. It looks like he is stopping," Renny observed over his radio link.

"Ten four, Air One. All units in the area, Air One has 244's suspect in the vicinity of Riverside Park. Begin converging on the location, but do not move in until Air One gives us the go ahead," the dispatcher ordered. No less than ten police cars, occupied by officers that had been carefully monitoring the pursuit on their radios, began quietly moving into the neighborhoods surrounding Riverside Park. The officers tensed and began to tingle with the anticipation of what would occur next. It was the thrill of the chase's end. The capture. The atmosphere was exhilarating, even for veteran officers who never lost their taste for chasing and catching bad guys.

Mel hatched a fool proof plan. He would simply park the car, get out, pull up his damned pants, and calmly walk to his little hideaway at the "Fox Run Apartments" across the footbridge from the park. Once there, Mel would lay low, take a shower, get cleaned up and get a good night's sleep. Hopefully, that stupid twit of a secretary, Maria, had stocked the refrigerator with some decent food for a midnight snack. In the morning, Mel would call a taxi to take him home and report his car stolen from the street in front of his house. It was almost too easy, Mel thought.

"Air One traffic dispatch, the suspect has exited the vehicle and appears to be standing in the parking lot. Have the units stand by to move in. We'll advise just as soon as the suspect gets away from the car," Al radioed. He then changed the switch on the control bar to activate the private intercom to his observer, "Renny, what's he doing?"

"Hell, Lieu, damned if I know. It looks like he's just standing there by the car. It's hard to tell from the image on the screen, but I think he's squatting to take a dump," Renny guessed.

In the FLIR, the suspect glowed as a bright, electric blue figure. His body shape was indistinct and radiated like some type of nuclear ghost. The vision was an eerie sight and one that required a great deal of experience before a trained operator of the system could distinguish specific hand and arm movements.

In fact, Mel was not dumping a load of crap on the dark tennis courts. His anal opening was far too tight for that. No, the Manager was simply squatting to get his boxer shorts untangled and his pants pulled up. Mel felt like a new man when he finally had his trousers arranged correctly and his "Gucci" belt firmly buckled around his skinny waist. With a confident air, Mel walked away from the Taurus and headed for a hot shower and the soft bed of his secret apartment. "It's over," Mel spoke out loud as a smirk crossed his sweaty face.

"Cancel that thought, Lieu," Renny called over the intercom. "He's walking away from his car now and he didn't leave any little glowing globs behind. If he tried to take a shit, he didn't accomplish his mission." The FLIR was so sensitive that a warm turd would have been clearly visible on the cold parking lot below.

At that moment, the two patrol units which had been dispatched to the disturbance at "Leroy Brown's" decided it was the perfect time to transmit the information they had learned at the scene.

"242 traffic dispatch," one of the officers at the bar called on his portable radio.

"Stand by, 242. We have emergency traffic," the dispatcher ordered, meaning all routine radio transmissions should be curtailed until the suspect was captured or the situation otherwise resolved.

"242, we're aware of the emergency traffic but we have information for the units attempting to stop the suspect," the patrolman countered.

"Go ahead, 242," the dispatcher relented.

"242, we haven't ascertained the reason for the disturbance here but witnesses at the scene advise that the suspect 244 is chasing is a white male, age fifty to sixty, five feet two, a hundred and twenty-five pounds, wearing a dark suit and white shirt. He is identified as a Melvin Michaels." The officer read the description as if he had no idea who Melvin Michaels was. In reality, it was all he and his partner in 245 could do to keep from shouting the revelation into the radio. The federal officers had been most helpful.

"Ten four, 242," was all the dispatcher said. As soon as the dispatcher unkeyed her microphone, there was a stunned silence and then cheers went up from everyone in the Communications Center who was monitoring the frequency. Immediately, all outgoing telephone lines were jammed as everyone tried to spread the news simultaneously. Melvin Michaels, Wichita City Manager, the most hated man in the entire city organization, and possibly the free world, was being hunted like a rabbit on opening day of the season. It was too good to be true.

All over the city, officers reacted to the news with the same disbelief at first. Their second reaction was the same as the dispatchers. In seconds, the ten units surrounding the park had grown to twenty. Eighteen other units were en route to the scene to help capture the asshole who, rumors said, was responsible for the resignation of their chief. Other that 242 and 245, who were assigned to the call at "Leroy Brown's", there were only two units left on duty in the entire city and they were tied up with an injury accident call on West Kellogg. Hearing the news over the police radio, the two traffic units working the accident threw the injured drivers into their squad cars and raced toward Riverside Park. The wrecked cars were abandoned in the middle of the street.

The officers ignored the stunned motorists bleeding in the back seats of the traffic cars. No one wearing a Wichita Police Department uniform was going to miss this.

Circling high above the park, Lieutenant Orr and his partner were also stunned by 242's information. They heard the earlier broadcast identifying the suspect vehicle as a city car but they had no idea of who, or what, the driver might be. All of a sudden, the helicopter crew was thrust into a totally new ball game.

"Renny," Al spoke into intercom which could not be heard by anyone except the two in the helicopter's cockpit, "If you lose this bastard, I'll shoot you and toss you out of this bird over that nasty river, so help me."

"Lieutenant," Renny replied formally, "if I lose the sonofabitch on the scope I'll shoot myself and jump out over the river. You won't have to push me." Renny bent lower, straining against his shoulder harness, toward the screen between his legs. He adjusted the FLIR's controls to keep Michael's perfectly centered in the camera's cross hairs.

"Air One traffic dispatch, the suspect is on foot, southbound from the park, crossing the bridge towards the apartment complex," Al reported. "Have the ground units move in."

The dispatcher did not have to repeat the instructions.

In a flash, dozens of police cars accelerated and screamed into the area from all directions. They bounced over curbs and through yards. One squad car narrowly avoided diving headlong into the apartment complex swimming pool as the officer attempted to drive directly through the middle of the buildings to cut off the Manager's assumed escape route.

In the middle of the bridge, Mel heard the throaty roar of the big V-8 engines and the squealing tires all around him. He did not know how the cops knew he was in the area but the police were everywhere. Mel could see the flashing lights begin to bounce off buildings and trees. Panic set in once again. The perspiring Manager hurried his pace as fast as he could. Mel was in no condition to run on foot, even if he had wanted. The most exercise Mel's body experienced lately was in screwing the whore tonight. And the effort drained him of all physical strength.

Mel could see the apartment in the distance. All he had to do was to get inside and he would be free of this madness. The stupid cops could not prove a thing. His plan would still work if Mel could only make it to his corner apartment on the second floor. Calling upon his final reserves of strength, Mel quickened his pace.

"Lieu, he's picking up speed. I think he's trying to make it to those apartments," Renny called on the intercom.

"Air One traffic all units, the suspect is running southbound across the footbridge into the apartment complex," Lieutenant Orr bypassed the dispatcher with the hot information. If the son of a bitch ever made it inside one of those apartments, he was home free and Al knew it.

"Okay, Chief, this is where I pay you back," Al spoke to himself. He did not bother to key the radio's microphone or the intercom. In the rotor noise of the helicopter, his words were washed quickly out into the night air. With a soft touch on the control stick and the rudders, Al dove the little chopper directly at the spot where the suspect was last seen, according to the image on Renny's FLIR screen.

At two hundred feet of altitude, Al stabbed at the button on the instrument panel to turn on the high intensity "Nightsun" spotlight, mounted under the nose of the aircraft. The "Nightsun" burned with millions of candle power and its beam was the brightest thing on earth after dark. One could light up a football field with the thing, but the heat it generated interfered with the FLIR. The choice had to be made. Stay hidden above with the FLIR or light this asshole up like the Fourth of July and maybe stun him long enough for the ground officers to close in. It was a gamble either way.

Al, as was his nature, chose the direct intervention route. A devout Christian, Al said a quick prayer and hoped he did not clip an electric power line in the dark sky on his way down. If that happened, he and Renny would become crispy critters in a flash; roasted in high octane aviation gasoline in the middle of the apartment complex below.

"What the hell are we doing?" Renny screamed into his intercom. The observer, believing his lieutenant had gone stark, raving mad, gave up on trying to monitor the FLIR and grabbed the shoulder straps which held him tightly in his seat.

"Hold on, partner, we're gonna set this sonofabitch on fire," Al ordered. Either way, he would be right.

Mel crossed the narrow parking lot and was gasping for breath as he reached the corner of the apartment building when the helicopter's dazzling bright light hit him. It was like the second coming. Mel saw the world blaze up around him before he heard the noise from the helicopter's engine. The Manager was confused and made the mistake of looking up over his shoulder at the blinding light. Instantly, both pupils of Mel's eyes slammed shut in reaction to the brilliant light and he was temporarily without sight. Mel stood transfixed at the edge of the building, next to the small patio area of the first floor apartment. Safety was only a few feet above, in his second story hideaway, but the haven seemed a million miles away.

* * *

Clarence Taylor had not slept since Thursday. In the days after he had been suspended by Deputy Chief Denson, Taylor had neither eaten nor left his small apartment. Taylor had no idea what was going on in the outside world. He had pulled the telephone and cable tv lines out of the wall to keep the aliens from traveling through the wires. Clarence wore the steel helmet from his Vietnam days as protection from the aliens reading his thoughts or attempting to send him telepathic messages. Taylor knew that just as soon as he fell asleep, the little blue men would come for him. They would enter through the walls, like before, and carve him up or carry him to their spaceship in the park. Taylor decided that he would not go without a fight. He was ready.

Taylor's paranoia had reached epic proportions by the time he heard the whirling and thumping noises outside his patio door. It was time. He knew it. They were coming for him. Taylor's eyes burned red with lack of sleep and fatigue as he checked his equipment one more time. The single shot, twelve gauge shotgun lay across his lap. Taylor's grandfather had given him the gun when he was a kid, long ago. The room began to glow despite the fact that Taylor had no lights turned on. It was time. He knew it.

The ex-detective could clearly read the shotgun's brand name, "Newport" on the side of the blue steel barrel. Taylor moved the lever with his thumb and broke open the action one final time to check the load. Under the hammer, a single round rested in the lone chamber. A rifled slug. Taylor stood in the now bright glow and quickly moved to the glass patio door. It was time. He knew it. Taylor decided he would not wait for the aliens to come and get him. He would go get them. In Taylor's mind he was still a police officer, by God, and he was tired of being afraid. Clarence Taylor was past fear.

Clarence jerked the curtain back and pulled the sliding glass door open. He did not feel the blast of cold air swirling across the narrow concrete pad that served as a patio in happier times. Taylor did not look up at the source of the bright light. It was time. He knew it. Taylor focused on the small alien standing ten feet away. The little creature was surrounded by light and glowed brightly.

In a matter of seconds, former Detective Clarence Taylor walked directly up to the alien and raised the old shotgun. Sensing, rather than hearing, the officer's movements, the alien turned around to face his assailant just as Taylor cocked the weapon's single hammer and pulled the trigger in one swift motion.

* * *

The deep boom of the shotgun rolled across the parking lot and reverberated through the numerous identical buildings comprising the cookie cutter apartment complex. Mel, blind from the dazzling light of the "Nightsun", never saw the instrument of his destruction nor his executioner. The heavy lead slug, designed for deer hunters who are able to get close to their prey, weighed a full ounce and was propelled by a massive charge of gun powder to push the missile at sub-sonic velocities. The round was awesomely lethal at close range and Taylor made sure the muzzle of the old weapon, with its tiny brass ball as the shotgun's front sight, practically touched his extra-terrestrial target.

The blunt end of the soft metal projectile struck the City Manager squarely on the bridge of his nose and immediately began to mushroom. Accompanied by the hot gases generated by the burning powder escaping from the shotgun's muzzle, the huge slug caved in Mel's face and sinus cavities as it blasted an ever expanding hole into his cranial vault. Both eye balls exploded from their sockets and dangled down Mel's cheeks, tethered uselessly by the optic nerve connections and attendant soft tissues. By the time the now massively deformed piece of lead expended its remaining energy in creating an enormous exit hole in the back of Mel's head, the City Manager was already dead. He fell backwards in a heap and spurted blood from a crushed face and shattered skull, until there was no more sticky red liquid for his evil heart to pump.

"Jesus Christ! Did you see that?" Officer Renny Burleson screamed over the intercom.

"Air One, Air One, we have an emergency," Al shouted into his flight helmet's microphone. He was fighting to control the helicopter while Renny was jumping around in his seat, dangerously altering the delicate weight balance of the light craft.

"Be still, Goddamn it!" The lieutenant shouted. In the confusion, he had transmitted on the radio frequency and not the copter's private intercom. The entire police department heard Lieutenant Al Orr use the Lord's name in vain for the first time in his life and they knew something was seriously wrong.

"Dispatch traffic Air One, repeat your transmission. It was garbled," the frightened dispatcher tried to keep her tone calm.

"Air One, Air One, we have shots fired, the suspect is down…repeat, shots fired, one suspect down and another suspect on the scene. He appears to be armed with a rifle, stand by!" Al groped with his free foot for the radio transmit pedal and yelled into the microphone.

Before Air One could continue his radio broadcast, at least ten officers charged Clarence Taylor from three different directions. The former detective stood over the lifeless body of the late Mel Michaels only briefly before he was quickly wrestled him to the ground by his former colleagues. While the officers struggled to remove their handcuffs from their belts and managed to do more physical harm accidentally to each other than they did to the suspect, Taylor did not say a word.

* * *

It was two o'clock on Sunday afternoon before Peggy and I awoke from our drug induced sleep. Terri complained that the telephone had been ringing off the wall since noon. She had taken all the receivers off the hook and buried them under pillows from the sofa. Smart girl.

Peggy and I were both groggy all day. We swore that if feeling this bad was the price we had to pay for curing our depression, then we would just as soon deal with the gloom and doom attitude without the prescription drugs, thank you.

By 6:00 p.m., Peggy and I felt almost human enough to eat. Terri made the decision for the three of us and ordered pizza. When the delivery boy arrived, he refused to take my money.

"It's on us. My boss said to tell you that Pizza Hut appreciated the job you did. Good luck, Chief," the young man called as he retreated back down the sidewalk to the street. The free pizza was a small gesture from the Wichita based company, but it made Peggy and I feel a little better. Obviously, the word was out.

Sometime around eleven o'clock, we decided it was safe to put the phones back on the hook. No sooner had we replaced all of the receivers back into their cradles, than the damned things started ringing again.

"Take 'em off the hook, Rod, we don't want to talk to anybody tonight, do we?" Peggy asked.

"I might as well face the music and get it over with, baby. Besides, we've slept enough today to hold us through the night," I answered. On the twelfth ring, I picked up the red plastic wall phone in the kitchen and said, "Hello". It sounded like an incredibly stupid thing to say.

"Chief, is that you?" The voice sounded familiar but my head was still shrouded in a fog and my tongue felt like a fuzzy pink house shoe. The anti-depressant drug had left a horrible taste in my mouth that even pizza could not mask.

"Yeah," was all the response I could muster. I was not exactly sure if it was after midnight and, consequently, did not know if I was still the chief or not. Did the title go with you after you officially "retired", I wondered?

"Chief, this is Betty down at dispatch. We've been trying to reach you. I've got two cars en route to your home now. Hold on." I could hear her yell to someone in the background, "Hey, Annie, cancel 125 and 126, I've got the chief on the line now!"

"Betty, what are you doing working nights? I thought you worked days," I asked. My mind was slowly beginning to function. Peggy handed me a can of cold Pepsi from the refrigerator to wash away the nasty taste in my mouth. The fuzzy bedroom slipper continued to function as my tongue and my speech was mildly slurred.

"Baby, we're all working tonight," Betty declared in a long, Texas drawl. I tried diligently to understand why the dispatch supervisor was calling me "Baby". I came up with a blank. In fact, try as I might, I could not picture Betty's face even though I had seen her practically every day for more than six years. No more drugs, I vowed.

"Chief, I know you're officially retired and all, but we need you bad right now. We have an emergency situation and we can't locate the Duty Chief or any of the other Deputy Chiefs. You've got to come quick," Betty ordered.

"I don't think so Betty. You're on your own now," I sounded as sad as I felt.

"Chief," Betty lowered her voice in a stern monotone, "Trust me, we need you right now. Don't let us down."

"Is someone hurt?" I asked.

"Yes," Betty said simply.

From years of experience, that was the one piece of information Betty knew would get me to respond.

"Okay, I'll be en route. Where do you need me?" I sighed.

Betty gave me the address to the Fox Run Apartments and I was in the car in five minutes. For the last time, I wedged my Smith and Wesson in my belt, pulled on an old tweed sports jacket and clipped the gold badge to the belt on my Levis. The drive to the scene was a blur. I tried to decipher what was going on by listening to the police radio traffic, but none of the transmissions made any sense to my woolly brain. I decided my mind was just too doped to interpret either the words or the codes in the radio traffic. There was something about an ambulance and then the coroner, but the theme was all muddled and unclear. I was confused. Somehow, I cautiously managed to steer the Chevy in one last late night foray onto the deserted streets of Wichita.

Once I arrived at the apartment complex, a group of officers met me at the entrance and I parked the car in the middle of the street. Television cameras and lights were everywhere. Vaguely, I could not believe that Pete Gant would miss an opportunity to be the center piece in the media frenzy scene greeting me.

"What's going on, Bryce?" I asked the first patrol officer I encountered upon exiting my car.

"Jesus Christ, Chief, you won't believe it," he answered.

The officer was perspiring profusely and sweat was running down his forehead from underneath his brown uniform cap. I could not make the temperature outside and Bryce's heated appearance compute. The air felt as though it was about forty degrees and I was freezing, as usual in Kansas.

"Come on back, the Captain is waiting for you," the officer said as he placed his hand gently on my left elbow to guide me. His frosted breath hung in the air momentarily before dissipating into the chilly night.

I followed the officer to the rear of the apartment complex like a zombie. One strange residual effect of the anti-depressant drug was that I did not seem to be curious about anything. The entire scene was so very surreal. Nothing had any meaning. It was as if I was watching the events flow before me on a television screen, without really being a part of the activities.

"Hey, Chief, boy are we glad you're here," Captain Beavers called out when he spotted me moving through the crowd of officers.

Cy Beavers was a good man and I had chosen him to serve as the patrol Watch Commander during the more hectic evening shift hours. He was loyal and a hell of a natural leader. Cy was young and enthusiastic, but inexperienced. I had promoted him twice in six years and marked the youthful captain for an up and comer that only needed some seasoning to really bloom. He reminded me of myself just a few years ago in Dallas.

"Cy, what's going on?" I asked simply, without much emotion or inflection in my voice.

The Captain proceeded to give me a briefing on the incident, starting with the undercover detective's call on the radio from "Leroy Brown's" and ending with the fatal shotgun blast. I noticed that all of the officers he mentioned by name were standing around us in a group. They all nodded at me when I made eye contact as the Watch Commander went through the story. I could see Al Orr's shiny white and blue helicopter in the park, across the small footbridge in the distance. Both he and Renny Burleson stared at me with apprehension. Their flight helmets looked awkward and out of place. From the looks on everyone's faces, I could not tell if they were sad or wanted to shout for glee. It was all very strange.

"Come over here, Chief, and take a look at this," the captain requested.

Cy had one nervous habit. He just could not stand still. Even when the Captain was telling me the story, he bounced up and down on the balls of his feet; constantly shifting his weight from one leg to the other. Without feeling much interest, I followed Cy across the crime scene barrier line; marked with yellow plastic tape that read "Police— Do Not Cross" in black letters. On the edge of a roped off square by the corner apartment's patio, Clarence Taylor sat in a cheap vinyl lawn chair. Taylor was handcuffed behind his back and his head was buried in his lap. He was crying and his shoulders shook with his sobs.

"Hello, Clarence," I said softly. The tormented officer looked up at me and tried to clear his throat. Mucus poured down his chin from a runny nose and the watery tears were real. Taylor sniffed hard enough to suck some snot back into his nose and tried to straighten himself up to project a professional bearing in my presence.

"I guess everyone will believe me now, Chief," he sobbed. The snot poured back out both nostrils.

"I guess so, Clarence." I put my hand on his shoulder.

Despite the cold air, his fevered flesh burned under my hand. "I believe you," I said softly. The shattered ex-detective lowered his head and began to weep again.

The shotgun was still laying on the ground near the feet of the victim when Captain Beavers pulled back the yellow plastic casualty blanket covering Mel Michaels' body. There were few remnants of Mel's face and head. Everything above the neck was an oozing pile of mangled pulp and bone fragments. The maroon colored coagulated blood seemed to be all that was holding what remained of Mel's head together. I doubted if any of his family would recognize the corpse, even after the coroner cleaned him up.

"Are you sure it's the Manager?" I asked.

"Well it's hard to be sure of anything, Chief. He's torn up so much. Clarence really worked a number on his sorry ass with that big twelve gauge. We can't be sure without fingerprints, but we found the City Manager's wallet and driver license in his pant's pocket. The bastard also had a thousand dollars cash in his suit coat. Can you believe that? It's more than I've got in my life savings," Cy answered.

"Do you know a next of kin to notify, Chief?" Beavers' question brought me back to earth. I had been staring at what was left of the City Manager's bloody face.

"Not really. His mom died when he was a baby. His family is back in Missouri, I think. He's got a wife locally, but I doubt she cares. You might send a car by the address on his driver's license to see if anyone is at home," I offered.

After a few more minutes of staring down at the body, I looked up at the crowd of officers surrounding me.

"What time is it?" I asked quietly.

Bart Francis, the undercover detective, was the first to answer. "It's almost midnight, Chief."

I slowly unclipped the badge holder from my belt and unpinned the heavy shield from its leather backing. I hefted the three ounce symbol of my office a couple of times in my open palm. The glittering gold metal and blue enamel oval sparkled in the headlights and portable crime scene lights that illuminated the area. The four gold stars on the badge seemed to burn like fire.

"I think you wanted this," I spoke down to the City Manager's crumpled body. Suddenly, I felt duty bound to comply with my boss's last demand of me.

I let the heavy badge fall directly in the pool of gore that was once Mel Michaels' face. The shield landed with a sickening splat and soon sank into the ooze. No one moved around me. I continued to stare at what was left of the Manager's head until the glittering gold badge, and its shimmering stars, disappeared from view.

"Now, Mel. Now. This time you'd be right to say that it's over," I said in a level voice.

I looked up and turned to Captain Beavers. "Make sure you report to the coroner that I disturbed the crime scene in the course of my official duties," I ordered.

In someone's apartment on the other side of the parking lot, I distinctly heard the classic rendition of the "Star Spangled Banner" sung by Kate Smith. It was being played on Howlin' Hank's radio station. The national anthem was the patriotic trademark Hank used on all of his radio stations to symbolize the traditional close of the broadcast day, as it had been done in the early days of radio and television.

It was midnight. The fat lady had sung.

EPILOGUE

Exactly twelve hours later, the sun was shining as we pulled into the short term parking lot at Wichita's "Mid-Continent Airport". All of our luggage was piled into the back seat of my unmarked city owned car. Terri rode in the front seat with Peggy and me in a somewhat tight fit. I turned the police radio off and tuned in the noon-time "Howlin' Hank Show" on the country and western station.

It did not take us long to park in the practically deserted lot and get our bags unloaded. I left the car's engine running and the radio on as we finished the task of removing our luggage from the back seat. Popping the trunk latch open with the elec-tric release button on the dash, I quickly re-filled the car's back seat with every piece of police equipment the City of Wichita had issued me during my tenure on the department. Every item except one. As requested, Mel had my badge.

And the coroner had Mel.

I had left my pistol at home. The Smith and Wesson was my own personal prop-erty because, like my uniforms, Mel refused to purchase a sidearm for those of us who did not have an employment contract. I locked the weapon in the small wall safe under the stairs. For the first time in twenty-three years, I was unarmed. I felt no difference.

My final touch was to drape my uniform shirt over the head rest of the car's front seat. The award bars and decorations above the shirt's right pocket gleamed in the sunlight. The single gold stars on each collar were polished to a brilliant shine.

As if on cue, Hank's hillbilly accented voice came over the car's radio.

"Now, here's a little number for a special guy to this city. He had a heckuva day yes-terday and we want him to know we're gonna miss him. Good bye, Chief, and good luck," Hank broadcast.

Patsy Cline began singing, "Have You Got Leaving On Your Mind". It was a favorite of mine.

I punched the red plastic rocker arm switch on the car's dashboard and activated the flashing red and blue lights under the Chevy's grille. With a touch of sadness, I said, "Yeah, I do, Hank. I've got leavin' on my mind."

I closed the driver's side door, intentionally locking the car with the keys in the ignition and the motor running.

Peggy smiled as I took her hand. We carried our bags over our shoulders as we walked toward the airport terminal.

Terri said, "Hey, Dad, what about your car?"

"I'm sure someone will find it sooner or later," I replied. We both grinned at each other.

Inside the almost vacant terminal building, we checked the first airline monitor we saw for flights to Fort Lauderdale and connections to the Bahamas. Peggy gave the young ticket attendant a credit card and asked for three one way fares. Peggy and I decided we would make plans for the rest of our life after we had a chance to warm up on the beach for a few days.

The airline ticket agent looked up from her counter and gazed at me in recognition with wide brown eyes. A copy of the morning's newspaper, with my picture on the front page, rested on the desk in front of her.

"Excuse me, sir. Aren't you Rod Starr?" She asked the question as if it meant anything anymore.

"I used to be," I smiled.

Special Offer Direct
from the Author!

"The publisher, distributors, retailers and I all hope you have enjoyed Behind the Gold Star. If there were a few laughs and surprises along the way to hearing the fat lady sing; we are very happy. Please, no hate mail from heavy women, its just a cliché.

Over the years, I have purchased many copies of my favorite books to send to friends and relatives, often wishing that their editions could be made extra special by a personalized inscription and autograph by the author. Well, here's your chance to design just the right message for someone you know.

Just copy or remove this page and fill in the blanks below. Attach your payment and mail today. A special edition will be sent immediately to the person you indicate, complete with its own customized dedication and autograph. Shipping is FREE!"

Chief Rick Stone

Dedication you wish to be written inside the book's cover

TO   _____,

_____

_____

_____

           Ship book to:
           NAME   _____
           STREET   _____
           CITY   _____
           ZIP   _____

Enclose $19.95 for each special edition ordered and mail your payment to: DETEX CO., BOX 221353, HOLLYWOOD, FL 33022-1353

A portion of the proceeds from each special edition will be donated to law enforcement sponsored charities designated by the author.

9 780595 091669